NEMESIS

Rory Clements was born on the edge of England in Dover. After a career in national newspapers, he now writes full time in a quiet corner of Norfolk, where he lives with his wife, the artist Naomi Clements-Wright, and their family. He won the CWA Ellis Peters Historical Award in 2010 for his second novel, *Revenger,* and the CWA Historical Dagger in 2018 for *Nucleus.* Three of his other novels – *Martyr*, *Prince* and *The Heretics* – have been shortlisted for awards. *Nemesis* is the third of his thriller series featuring Professor Tom Wilde. The first two, *Corpus* and *Nucleus*, are available in paperback from Zaffre.

To receive exclusive news about Rory's writing, join his Readers' Club at www.bit.ly/RoryClementsClub and to find out more go to www.roryclements.co.uk.

RORY
CLEMENTS

NEMESIS

ZAFFRE

First published in Great Britain in 2019 by
ZAFFRE
80–81 Wimpole St, London W1G 9RE

A CIP catalogue record for this book is available from the British Library.

B format ISBN: 978–1–78576–750–0
Export ISBN: 978–1–78576–909–2

Also available as an ebook

1 3 5 7 9 10 8 6 4 2

Typeset by IDSUK (Data Connection) Ltd
Printed and bound in Great Britain by Clays Ltd, Elcograf S.p.A.

MIX
Paper from responsible sources
FSC® C018072

Zaffre is an imprint of Bonnier Books UK
www.bonnierbooks.co.uk

For Emma,
with love

JUNE 1931

CHAPTER 1

This was the best day of his life, watching his beloved boy, here in this ancient chamber of light.

Above him, his gaze drifted to the high, soaring fan vaults and armorial badges that made the great chapel celebrated throughout the world. On every side, he sensed the enclosing history of the mellow limestone walls, held tall and perpendicular by massive buttresses. And within these frames, he was dazzled by the coloured glass that filtered and split the heavenly rays, and told the story of his faith.

Candles flickered in glass sconces along the choir stalls. The choristers and choral scholars were ranged on both sides of the aisle in white surplices and red cassocks. In a few moments, their voices would well up and soar into the vast echoing space and dance off the tracery and the carvings.

Colonel Ronald Marfield knew now that even in the dark nights of war, God had never deserted him. This was His promise made good.

At his side sat his elder son, Ptolemy, slumped awkwardly in the pew, and his wife, Margaret, erect and dignified.

But it was the thirteen-year-old boy at the front of the choir who held his eye and his heart. The head chorister, his beautiful younger son, Marcus. Marcus with the perfect voice, the pale golden skin, the blue eyes and the tousled sandy halo of hair. Every father's ideal son; truly a gift from heaven.

King's College chapel was packed, but the congregation made not a sound. And then the organ broke the hush and the first haunting notes of Charles Stanford's *Magnificat* in G crept forth, sempre staccato.

Marcus opened his lips and his voice emerged. '*My soul doth magnify the Lord . . .*'

Every boy, every man in this fine choir sang wonderfully. But only one stood out. Marcus's treble notes were not just flawless, it seemed as if they rose on angel wings. Those watching and listening barely breathed.

Colonel Marfield's eyes were wet. How could he not weep at such perfection? At the divine sound of his own son?

He reached for his wife's hand, but they were clasped in front of her. Through eyes blurred with tears he looked at her, beseeching. She stared straight ahead, refusing to meet his gaze. Her eyes were dry.

AUGUST 1939

CHAPTER 2

For a man of fifty, the American was in reasonable shape: good teeth, breath sweet in a whisky way, a decent head of hair, though it was receding from his brow. And his round tortoiseshell spectacles lent him an intellectual air. Elina had made love to men half his age who had less going for them.

'Take care of me, Elina,' he said. 'Take care of me and I'll take care of you.'

'It will be my pleasure, sir.' She was undoing the buttons of his shirt, slowly, from the collar down.

With the last button popped, she drew open the shirt front and eased it off his shoulders so that he stood before her, naked from the waist up. A sportsman, no doubt about it; rode a lot, very little spread around the girth and muscle tone in the arms. A few curls of hair snuck up above his trouser line. Below, he was stirring. But she wasn't going to touch him there. Not yet.

'Now you,' he said. 'Let's see what you've got.'

Elina Kossoff, known in this place as Elina Ulyanova, was no more than five feet four, with fair wavy hair. She stood on her toes and placed her full lips on his, then stood back, smiling. Teasing, tantalising, she removed her blouse slowly, and at last turned around so he could unhook her ivory-coloured bra. As it fell to the floor, she turned back to face him, still smiling. She let him feast his eyes on her breasts, full, with small pink nipples. 'Well, sir?'

'God damn it.' He reached out and took them in the palms of his hands. 'God damn it, and the Lord forgive my blasphemy.'

They made love on the single bed, in a small room tucked beneath the eaves – a servant's room, assigned to Elina when she arrived at this great Palladian mansion two days earlier with the invented title of 'general assistant' in the estate office. It was common knowledge that whenever this particular guest was entertained at weekend house parties he would take one of the servants into his bed. And if they pleased him, he would be generous, might even arrange to see them again. Elina would make sure he did just that.

When the sex was over, she was surprised that it had been good. The old man knew what he was doing.

'So, Elina, where are you from?' He lay back on the pillows, the fingers of his right hand idly playing between her legs.

'My parents brought me over here from Moscow as a child. They escaped the Bolsheviks.'

'Like so many others. Those Reds have made a mess of a fine country . . .' He turned to face her. 'Elina – I want you on my staff. Full time, starting today. I'll pay your notice. I take it you've got Pitman's?'

She laughed out loud. 'No, I don't do shorthand. A little two-fingered typing, that's all.'

'Two fingers is plenty good enough for most everything in life. Anyway, who cares? You're coming with me wherever I go. I'll buy you a car. What car do you want?'

She kissed Joe Kennedy's cheek and pressed her sex into his delving hand, demanding more. So far, so good.

CHAPTER 3

It was Lydia who noticed the man in the street outside the villa. He was bedraggled and foot-weary, but that didn't mean much these days when half of France seemed to be on the move. Refugees travelling in all directions, seeking safety without being at all sure where that might be; soldiers on the roads eastwards to the frontiers of Italy and Germany. The *paniquards* and the reluctant squaddies. None of them wanted a war, not when there was a harvest to be brought in.

'He's probably a beggar,' said Wilde. 'I imagine he saw our car outside, reckoned we must have money.'

'He's been hanging around all day. I've seen him several times from the bedroom window. He was still there when I went upstairs just now. Won't you go and see what he wants?'

Wilde, who was enjoying the wine and the warmth of the evening, reluctantly put down his glass. He turned out his pockets. 'I don't suppose you have some change to send him on his way?'

'There are a few francs in my purse – in the kitchen, on the table.'

They were on the courtyard terrace, soaking up the last of the sun. The air was hot and dry, but it was beginning to lose its intensity after the fierce heat of the day, and there was still time to sit outdoors with a bottle or two of chilled wine.

Wilde turned to their host. 'See the way she orders me about, Jacques?'

'This is only the start, Tom. It's all downhill from here.' Professor Talbot, tall and languid, fished in his pocket and brought out a handful of coins. 'Do you wish me to deal with the fellow?"

'No thanks, Jacques. I'm under orders.'

'Here then, give him these. That should be enough for bread and wine.'

Wilde nodded, took the money and sauntered out to the front of the house. It was on the outskirts of the small village of Aignay, to the east of Toulouse in the south-western corner of France. A weathered old manor with small windows, it was cool in summer, warm enough in winter. It gave nothing away from the exterior, but was large and airy inside, leading on to a lush courtyard at the back, with a central fountain and fruit trees: lemons, olives, oranges, just waiting to be picked. And behind them, a vineyard stretching across endless acres of France.

The road at the front, by contrast, was dusty and dry. Across the way, two women in black peasant dresses, their faces lined like old parchment, trudged along, slowly and silently. There wasn't much here in Aignay – a boulangerie, a bar for the *paysans* and another for those with a little money and education – doctor, lawyer, landlord, owners of the vineyards – and that was it.

A man was sitting on the ground at the base of a fig tree. As Wilde approached, he stood up. He had no cap and his greying hair was razored almost down to the scalp. His beard was grey stubble, yet his heavily tanned, dirt-streaked face suggested he was no more than thirty. Of average height, in working man's blue shirt and threadbare trousers, his boots were wrapped with rags in place of soles. The dead butt of a hand-rolled cigarette clung to his lips. One of those nomadic types who travelled the land at this time of year to earn a crust harvesting grapes.

Wilde held out the coins. '*Pour vous*,' he said in his excruciating accent. He had hated French at school and hadn't bothered to put things right in the intervening years; his German had been rather more passable.

'Monsieur Wilde?' The man did not remove the cigarette from his mouth.

'How do you know who I am?' Taken aback, Wilde reverted to his native tongue.

'I have been looking for you.' The man spoke accurate but strongly accented English. This was no peasant. 'I was led to believe you had come to this village. I guessed this must be the house. The fine car . . .'

'Who are you?'

'I am Honoré.'

'Just Honoré?'

'It's enough. This is not about me, but someone you know. He needs your help. Please.'

'*Who* needs my help?'

'*El Cantante.* He is sick . . . he may die. He *will* die if you do not help him before the war comes.'

'I have no idea what you're talking about. Don't you think you should explain?'

'*El Cantante* – that is his nom-de-guerre. We were comrades in the Spanish struggle, but now he is beyond my help. He has spoken of you, monsieur. He needs to get back to England or he will waste away and die. The French government – Daladier and Reynaud, Bonnet and Laval and the rest of the fascist swine' – he spat on the ground – 'they do not care. We are all dirt to them.'

Realisation struck. Wilde had little enough Spanish, but even he could work out that *El Cantante* meant 'the singer'. 'Are you by any chance talking about Marcus Marfield?'

'*Oui*, monsieur, I believe that is right. He told me your name and spoke of Cambridge. You were his teacher – his *professeur* – yes?'

Wilde had indeed been Marfield's supervisor at Cambridge. And Marfield had been a noted choral scholar. But when, like several of his contemporaries, he had disappeared in March 1937 – almost two and a half years ago – to join the International Brigades in the Spanish Civil War, Wilde had never expected to see him again. He would not have been the first undergraduate to lose his life in that bitter conflict.

'I still don't understand how you found me here.'

The Frenchman shrugged. 'I have friends in England.'

That didn't really explain it, but Wilde let it pass for the moment. 'Where is he?'

'He is in the internment camp at Le Vernet, south of Toulouse. I would say he is in a bad way. A very bad way.'

Wilde hadn't heard of Le Vernet. But he had been desperately sorry when Marfield, one of his best history students, left Cambridge. Marcus Marfield, the beautiful youth with the voice of an angel and the world at his feet. At times he had served as crucifer – cross-bearer in the chapel choir. It was said that in his treble days as a King's chorister his Stanford in G could make the hairs at the nape of your neck stand on end and bring a tear to the hardest of eyes. His voice since breaking had developed into a most remarkable tenor. His disappearance had seemed a tragic waste. If Marcus was alive . . . well, that would indeed be wonderful news.

'How long to drive there?'

'Two hours, perhaps three.'

Wilde looked at the sky. The sun was low, he had been drinking and the roads in this part of France were treacherous at the best of times. 'You say he's in some sort of camp – I assume he'll still be there in the morning, yes?'

'He will not get out without your help, Monsieur Wilde.'

Wilde moved back towards the door, but the man did not follow him. 'Please, come in . . .'

'No, I must go.'

'I'm sure we could find you some food and a glass of wine. You can tell us everything you know.'

'I have told you everything you need to know. You will find Le Vernet on the map, on the way to Pamiers. Follow the stench.'

'Why not come with me? Take me there.'

The Frenchman shrugged his broad shoulders. 'And be put back inside? No thank you, monsieur. Give *El Cantante* my fraternal greetings, if you would. He is in Hut 32.'

As Wilde watched, he turned and shuffled away, without a backward glance.

CHAPTER 4

Talleyrand Bois was drenched in sweat but his right hand, clutching the revolver beneath his jacket, was steady. He wiped his left sleeve across his brow, then took the scrap of newspaper once more from his pocket and studied it. The cutting was from a newspaper from the previous year with a photograph of Sigmund Freud on the platform at Paris's Saint-Lazare station as he made his escape from Vienna to England by way of France. At his side was an aristocratic woman who meant nothing to Bois and, more importantly, a man in a pale hat, wearing a buttonhole and holding a cigarette. That was the man Bois stared at; a man wearing a suit so expensive it would have kept a poor family in food for a year.

Bois held the picture close, trying to imprint the image of the man in the pale hat on his brain. Then he looked out across the dark green beneath the trees, to the far side of the grand chateau where the early morning sun threw long shadows across the vast lawns. This was unfamiliar territory. Chantilly, with its racecourses and palaces, built on the blood of the working man for the parasites of the ruling class, was everything he despised about his country. *Merde*, how he hated the bourgeoisie.

The man he had come to find was over there, walking alone. Bois shaded his eyes and stared at him and then looked back at the picture. The face was right, but he had looked leaner in the photograph. In the black-and-white picture and wearing a hat, it was impossible to discern the colour of the man's hair; this man, bare-headed, had short fair hair with a sharp parting on the right. But the face *was* the same, he was sure of that. William Bullitt, America's ambassador to France. Bois, hardened by a lifetime of physical work, began to move towards him.

Bill Bullitt was taking the early morning air. He loved it out here in the countryside of Chantilly, to the north of Paris. He'd have to nip into the city later, to the embassy at the corner of the Place de la Concorde, where it would be as hectic as always, but doubly so with the crisis. He needed his hours here every day, riding out, swimming a few lengths in the pool, playing tennis – or just walking alone, minding his own business, as he was doing this fine, sunny August morning.

Bullitt had saved this place from ruin, and it had been worth every goddamned cent. Paris wasn't always easy, but it was a glory of the world compared to Moscow, his last posting, and the murderous bunch of criminals who ran the place. Now the Red swine had shown their true colours: forging an alliance of shame with that other lethal crew, the Nazis. He stopped by the trees, took a deep breath of the beautiful air, then lit a Virginia cigarette. Yes, this was better than Moscow or Berlin, war or no war.

Bois was only a hundred yards away. He could almost shoot the man from here. But the instructions had been clear. He must be within a metre of his target: one bullet to the chest then, as he goes down, the other five in his head.

'*Oui*, of course.' Bois knew how to fire a gun well enough. Spain had taught him that, though he had used a rifle, not a pistol, until now. But what was the difference? They both had triggers, they both pumped pieces of metal into men.

The man, almost within touching distance now, nodded to him and smiled. '*Bonjour, monsieur.*'

Talleyrand Bois pulled out the gun and shot his target in the heart. The man did not go down, but looked with astonishment at Bois and then clutched his chest. Bois fired again and the man's knees began to buckle. Four more bullets flew; each one went into the man's head. As blood spewed from the dying man, Bois threw down the gun.

Walk away slowly and steadily, don't look back, don't panic. That's what he had been told.

But no one had told him what to do if a gendarme appeared.

Bois panicked. He should have saved bullets: four to kill the man, two to defend himself. He began to run south towards the road. The first shot caught his shoulder and Bois spun, and then tumbled forward to his knees. A second shot hit him in the lower back and he fell flat, chin crunching into the earth. I survived Spain, he thought, but this is where I die. At least I have done my duty. At least I have rid the world of an American bourgeois dog.

A few hundred yards away, in the shadow of his beloved Chateau de St Firmin, Bill Bullitt heard six shots. They came from somewhere to the west, in the area of the palatial and much larger Chateau de Chantilly. In his head he had been composing a cable to FDR. The President needed to know that the French were still deluding themselves; still convinced that America would ride to their rescue against Hitler. But the shots put all thoughts of the cable out of his head. At first he imagined someone must be out there shooting partridge, but then he shrugged. No, that wasn't a shotgun.

He considered going to investigate, but thought better of it. It was French business and none of his. And there were more important things to think about: the cable, and what he was going to say to the French prime minister when he saw him later today. He had to find some way to disabuse Daladier and the rest of the French government that there was any hope of salvation from across the pond. He took a last draw of fine American smoke from his cigarette, then tossed the butt into the grass.

As he strode back towards his grand house, he heard two more shots.

Wilde had been up since dawn, closely followed by Lydia and their hosts, Professor Talbot, his wife, Françoise, and their young son and daughter.

'So then,' Wilde said as he sipped his coffee. 'Who's up for a drive down to this holding camp?'

'Well, I could come . . .' Lydia said without enthusiasm.

'Jacques? Françoise?'

'Of course,' Professor Talbot said. 'You'll need me to show you the way, otherwise you will get horribly lost.'

Wilde and Lydia had been in France for three and a half weeks, sometimes staying with friends, other times at hotels. It was the last day of August now and they would be wending their way home in a couple of days' time.

They had travelled slowly down the east of the country on their planned honeymoon, stopping only one night in Paris, then on to Burgundy for three days, calling in at vineyards, feasting on the local food. Next came the Haute Savoie – Geneva, Chamonix, Mont Blanc, Lake Annecy. A lot of mountain walking; it was the region Wilde liked best.

They had soon become used to the constant army manoeuvres, the march of uniformed men, the trundling of armoured vehicles ever eastward along roads both small and large, sometimes blocking their way. At first there had been few refugees on the roads, but every day brought a different story. One day war was imminent, the next day peace was assured. The people who lived on the frontier with Italy didn't know whether to stay at home or make their way west. Wilde and Lydia had carried on south regardless.

The Riviera was gorgeous, and they had spent ten days there at a spectacular villa on Cap Ferrat with ten acres of coastline and first-rate company. It was the home of a feted English author, an old friend of Lydia's family, and they were among a diverse group of his acquaintances: various beautiful young men, including an Italian they took to be the author's lover. The author said that the Nazis could come, but he wasn't going. Anyway, he rather admired their uniforms, he added with a mischievous twinkle.

A female American writer with an acerbic column in a New York rag did her best to monopolise the dinner table conversation, and a jazz musician who had been playing his way along the coast played for them. Oh, and there was a former beauty who gave her profession as 'gold-digger', but whose gold-digging days must have been waning before the Great War had even begun.

It had been idyllic. The sound of the waves, the continuous inrush and retreat of the sea against the shore, the movement of their bodies in the heat of the afternoon, him inside her, sighing and moaning, breathing in the heady scents of salt water and wild herbs. The window was open and their sweat-slicked bodies moved with the sea.

And from there, the drive to this ancient stone house in this village of dust and wine near Toulouse. The first leg of their trek back to the northern coast and the ferry home. Jacques Talbot held a history chair at the University of Toulouse. He and Wilde had met when he visited Cambridge on a lecture tour the previous summer. His favoured subject, the House of Guise, dovetailed neatly with Wilde's own interest in the late-Tudor era and they had quickly become firm friends.

'Well,' Françoise said in halting but correct English. 'I will stay here with the children, otherwise we will have to take two cars.' She was a woman of warmth and rare beauty; plump and well-rounded with a smile that shone with almost every word she uttered.

As they stood around Wilde's rented blue Citroën – a fine touring car – Lydia shook her head. 'Tom, even if I go into the back and Jacques takes the front passenger seat, we're going to be pushed to get Marfield in here. Assuming he's even there, of course. I'll stay with Françoise. You two go.'

The drive was easier than Wilde had feared. To the west, they saw the dark green foothills of the Pyrenees. 'The fighters' route to freedom,' Jacques Talbot said with an edge of bitterness. 'Some freedom, huh?'

'From the Spanish war?'

'When the Republicans lost back in the spring, they streamed across the mountains. Our government was woefully ill-prepared for their arrival. Hence the internment camps. It was always obvious to me that this would be the outcome. Why were we not ready to help?'

On the way, Talbot had told Wilde what he knew about the place. 'It was originally an army barracks, but in recent months they have been putting the refugees here and in similar camps all over this corner of France, right down to the beaches in the south. Some say almost a million men, women and children have fled the Falangists and their fascist allies. I suppose they had to put them somewhere and feed them. But I don't like it. We are French, not Nazis; this is not how democracies should treat people.'

'They had to do something with them, surely?'

Talbot wouldn't have it. 'They call the places "assembly centres", but that is a euphemism. They are concentration camps by another name – and they are a stain on our country, just as Dachau is on Germany. Le Vernet and the other camps are France's dirty little secret.'

They made good time and arrived on the outskirts of Le Vernet before eleven. Wilde stopped the car, his heart sinking. The day was burning hot and the place was nothing but a remote railway siding with barracks attached, all enclosed in barbed wire, a wasteland of dust and rock. Jacques was right – this was not a refugee camp, but a prison. And the smell was overpowering.

At the entrance, two armed members of the *Garde Mobile* stood in front of a small guardhouse built of stone. A wooden gantry over the roadway bore the words *Camp du Vernet*. Beyond this, an endless vista of basic barrack blocks. This place could hold tens of thousands of men.

Wilde sniffed the air and grimaced. A stinking miasma spoke of disease.

'This is horrible,' Talbot said.

One of the sentries walked casually towards them. In one hand he held a rifle, with the other hand he curled his fingers slowly but insistently, tilting his unshaven chin towards the sky, signalling to them to get out of the car.

'Let's do as the man says, Jacques.'

As they got out, around twenty men approached the gateway from the central area of the camp, heads shaven, bare against the scorching sun. Their bodies were hung with rags and their feet wrapped in scraps, as Honoré's had been. They carried spades at their shoulders in the way that marching soldiers carried rifles. A couple of bored-looking *Garde Mobile* officers, carrying riding crops, accompanied them: 'Left-right, one-two, one-two . . .'

'Good God.' Wilde looked at the men with dismay. He watched the work party pass along the road at the edge of the rail track.

Talbot turned to the sentry.

'What crime have those men committed?'

The guard wiped sweat from his brow and shrugged. 'Their crime? They lost a war.'

It was not a conversation worth pursuing. 'We wish to speak with your commanding officer.'

'You think he has nothing better to do than take tea with tourists? Who are you, monsieur, that the CO should speak with you?'

'I am someone who can make your life very difficult if you seek to impede me.' Greying and handsome, Professor Talbot had the unmistakable air of authority.

The guard suddenly looked less confident. 'Name?'

'Talbot. Professor Jacques Talbot.'

'What organisation do you represent?'

'It is a private matter concerning one of the internees. I will discuss it with the camp commandant, no one else. But you can tell him that I am a very good friend of Maurice Sarrault.'

The guard shrugged. The name meant nothing. He nodded towards Wilde. 'And who is he?'

'His name is Wilde. Professor Thomas Wilde. He is an American citizen.'

'Wait here.'

CHAPTER 5

Within five minutes they were inside the camp commandant's office. To Wilde, the CO looked like the caricature of a nineteenth-century French military man: extravagant moustache, proud chin, a belly that told of a great love of food.

He introduced himself as Major Cornet and grudgingly offered them seats.

Talbot did the talking. 'We believe there is an Englishman here among the refugees from the Spanish war. He is an undergraduate at the Cambridge college of Professor Wilde, my companion here. We would very much like to see him and find out if there is anything that can be done to repatriate him.'

'An Englishman? There are no Englishmen here.'

'Well, we believe he is and we intend to find him.'

'Monsieur, there are nine thousand men in the camp, I cannot know them all. What is this man's name?'

'Marcus Marfield. He is in Hut 32.' Wilde spoke in halting French.

'Hut 32? They are mostly German communists. International Brigaders. What makes you think he is here?'

'We were told this.'

'By whom?'

'I cannot say, but that is not the issue.'

Cornet tutted. 'One moment.' He pulled back his shoulders and left the office, his boots clicking on the stone floor. Wilde and Talbot could hear him addressing a subordinate. A minute later he returned. He looked less sure of himself. 'My adjutant tells me it is possible there is an Englishman in the camp. He doesn't speak and won't give his name, so we don't know who he is – but others say he is English.'

'May we see him, Major?' Talbot asked.

'These are dangerous men, messieurs. They are all communists and anarchists. Whatever your student was before, he will not be the same person now. I can promise you that.'

'Still, we would like to see him.'

'You told the sentry you know Monsieur Sarrault, the editor and proprietor of *La Dépêche de Toulouse*?'

'Indeed.'

The major blinked, weighing the matter up. One should not cross people such as the Sarraults; they wielded great influence.

Talbot continued. 'Maurice Sarrault is a close family friend. And I am sure you know, too, that he is the elder brother of Albert Sarrault, minister of the interior.'

The officer began to sweat. 'Perhaps a glass of wine, gentlemen? I will have the Englishman brought in short order. But you know it will not be possible for him to leave Camp du Vernet? Not without the proper permissions.'

'First things first, major,' said Talbot. 'Let us meet the fellow.'

'It may take a little while to locate him.' Major Cornet sounded uneasy. 'I am told he has suffered an injury and is in the camp sanatorium.'

Talbot stiffened. 'Injury? What kind of injury.'

'He was shot, monsieur.'

Even shaven-headed, in rags, limping and bruised, his left arm in a filthy bloodstained sling, Marcus Marfield was immediately recognisable.

Slender, fair-haired with sea-blue eyes and golden skin, he lit up the room the same way he had at Cambridge. He had an aura that defied description but which none could ignore: in chapel, in lectures, in Hall and in supervision, but most of all singing, with a voice as pure as bells. To Wilde, he had always had a little of the look and ethereal romanticism of a young T. E. Lawrence. And yet, as with Lawrence, there was, too, a steely determination.

And yet now he was so weak, the guard was holding him upright. Wilde leapt out of his seat and took the boy's uninjured arm, which, like the rest of his body, was shaking as though he had a fever. Marfield stumbled forward, and then his eyes met Wilde's and flickered in recognition.

Marfield sat down and slumped forward, breathing heavily, his left hand flopping on his thigh, quivering. His face had retained its luminescence, but his hands were those of a farmhand, swollen, red and calloused.

Wilde turned to Talbot. 'Jacques, this is appalling. Marfield needs medical attention. He has a fever.'

The major tried to explain the bullet wound. 'Someone took a potshot through the wire. By chance this man was hit – but it could have been anyone.'

'Who shot him?' Wilde demanded.

'Most certainly, a local man.' The major shrugged. 'The villagers are angry about this camp. They do not like all these fighters held so close to them and their women.'

'I don't believe him,' Wilde said to Talbot in English.

The French professor turned to the major and spoke quickly and angrily. 'One of your guards has done this.'

The commandant threw up his arms. 'No, no, monsieur, that is not so! We cannot patrol every centimetre of our fence. Nor are we nursemaids. We have a pittance from the government to feed nine thousand exhausted fighting men. There are bound to be . . . incidents.'

'I want to use your telephone,' Talbot said. 'Get me a line. Call *La Dépêche*. The operator will provide the number.'

The real reason Lydia had opted out of the journey was that she couldn't face the drive. She didn't feel at all well and wanted nothing more than to lie in the cool of her room – but not wishing to appear rude to her hostess, she compromised by stretching out on a reclining chair in the courtyard. She had offered, half-heartedly, to help with the chores, but Françoise had refused all offers of assistance. And so Lydia read poetry and dozed in the shade while her hostess busied herself around the house.

Of all the people they had met these past weeks, Françoise and Jacques were her favourites. Françoise was in her mid-thirties – a little older than Lydia and about ten years younger than her husband. She not only ran a busy home but also had a career – she was that rarity in French hospitals, a female doctor. While she worked, the children had a nanny. But now Françoise was on holiday, and so was the nanny, who had returned to her family in Nantes for a few days.

Lydia was asleep when she felt a touch on her shoulder. She woke with a start.

'Would you care for a little lunch, Lydia? I have some fresh sardines and tomatoes from the market. Perhaps with some bread? And I thought you might like a lemon cordial to cool off?' She spoke in her own tongue, because Lydia's French was good. They only reverted to English when Wilde was about.

'Yes to the drink, Françoise, but I'm not awfully hungry yet.'

Françoise smiled. 'How long is it?'

Lydia frowned, not sure how to reply.

'I'm sorry. Perhaps I am intruding but I think that you are suffering from *le mal de matinée*. It is much the same expression in English – morning sickness – is it not?'

'How did you guess?'

Françoise laughed, enveloping Lydia in her comfortable bosom. 'I am a mother and an obstetrician. How could I not know?'

'Please, don't tell Tom. I haven't said anything yet. It is only a few weeks. Maybe ten or eleven.'

'He will need to know quite soon. Especially if you are suffering with the sickness.'

'He lost his first wife in childbirth. The baby, too.'

'Ah, I see. You are worried because you do not know how he will take the news. But, Lydia, your husband is a good man. Nothing mends a heart better than the arrival of a child – especially when it is your own.'

Lydia knew all this, and yet there was more, wasn't there? What about the coming war? Why would anyone bring a baby into such a world? So much for bloody Dutch caps and Volpar gels.

There was another reason she didn't want to tell Tom yet: she still hadn't ruled out abortion. There was that society abortionist in London who did the debs, the one whose number was in all the Girton girls' address books. Was he still practising? Easy enough to find out.

'Don't worry, *cherie*,' Françoise soothed. 'I will say nothing. It is your place to break the good news.' She patted Lydia's hand. 'Tell me,' she said briskly. 'Do you have this sickness every day? You must find these long car journeys a great trial.'

'Oh, it hasn't been so bad. I'm quite strong.'

'Yes, I see that. But, Lydia, you can confide in me while you are here. Now, as your hostess I will fetch you that lemon cordial. And as a doctor, might I suggest a little less wine in the evening?'

'Am I being lectured?'

'Professional advice, nothing more.' Francoise laughed. 'I smoked and drank through my own pregnancies, so what can I say?' She turned to go, but Lydia put out her hand.

'Can I ask you something, Françoise?' she said. 'I'm interested in training to be a doctor, but I'm almost thirty, so am I too old? Would it be possible if I have a baby to care for? I am particularly interested in psychiatry.'

'*Cherie*, if this war comes, there will be a great need of doctors of all kinds.' Francoise smiled. 'I don't know the situation in England, but if any woman can make it happen, I'm sure you are the one.'

The wire arrived from the office of the Ministry of the Interior in the late afternoon:

> *Release authorised from Camp du Vernet of internee Marfield, Marcus, into the charge of Professor Talbot of University of Toulouse, conditional on the internee's removal from France by September 3.*
>
> *A. Sarrault, minister.*

'So, *messieurs*, he is yours,' the major said.

In the hours of telephoning back and forth, first to Maurice Sarrault in Toulouse and then to the ministry in Paris, Wilde had requested some sort of mattress be brought for Marcus. When Cornet saw the way things were going, he ordered a straw palliasse. As an afterthought, he called out to the lieutenant: 'Make sure it is clean!'

The stench was everywhere. Wilde did not want to imagine what conditions must be like inside the barrack blocks, nor the quality of the food. His former undergraduate, stretched out, shivering, was evidence enough.

Wilde helped Marfield to his feet and, with Talbot's assistance, walked him slowly towards the front gate. All around them men wandered aimlessly, their work details finished. As they got closer to the fence, a man in his fifties approached them and said something in German, before switching to broken French. Talbot stopped and spoke to him, then turned to Wilde.

'This is Wilfrid Zucker. I have heard of this man, Tom; he is a composer. His work has been performed in Paris and Salzburg.'

'Why is he here?'

'Because he is a refugee. These are not all Brigaders or fighting men.'

The composer was holding out his left hand and shadow-writing on it with his right. Talbot fished inside his jacket for a scrap of paper and a pencil. With a trembling hand the man wrote down his name, and another name – Gerhard Sankte – with a London address. Talbot took it. 'He says this man Sankte in London will vouch for him and asks that we contact him.'

'I'll take it,' Wilde nodded. He had enough German to understand what Zucker had said.

Other men were now clustering around, grabbing at their coats. Some tore pieces of cigarette packs and playing cards, fighting for the pencil to write down their names and the names of contacts. They spoke in myriad languages and stank of overflowing latrines. More than anything, thought Wilde, they stank of neglect and desperation. He took all their pieces of paper.

Major Cornet bustled up, shooing the inmates away, as he escorted the visitors and Marcus Marfield to the main gate. The men looked on like beaten dogs, a sad, defeated bunch.

With some difficulty, Wilde and Talbot helped Marfield into the Citroën and made him as comfortable as they could on the rear bench seat. Cornet ordered a guard to go to Hut 32 to see if there was any property to accompany the released man. Marfield himself had not yet spoken a word.

A woman walked past at a leisurely stroll. She was small and wore a long dark skirt and a billowing white cotton shirt, with a cotton neckerchief knotted about her throat. Her hair was long and dark, her skin bronzed by the Mediterranean sun. She stopped and looked at them through black eyes, then spat at Wilde's feet and moved on.

'Good God, Jacques, what was that about?'

Talbot shrugged. 'As the major suggested, I don't think the locals like having these camps on their doorstep.'

The guard returned five minutes later with a small, tattered book in a red leather cover. Wilde took it and flicked through the pages. It was a well-thumbed copy of the Book of Common Prayer, a school prize for poetry awarded to Marcus Marfield in 1931. So the communist revolutionary hadn't quite given up on religion. Wilde smiled for the first time that day.

In the distance, in the lee of an overhang, the small dark woman squatted on her haunches, watching the scene unfold through binoculars. A rifle lay by her side.

She felt a grim satisfaction. She had a good idea where they would be going, and she would be there, waiting.

CHAPTER 6

The drive home was slower. Wilde and Talbot didn't want to shake up the sick man any more than necessary. Every few minutes Talbot turned around to check on him.

'We could drive him straight to a hospital,' suggested Wilde. 'What do you think, Jacques? How urgent is it?'

'Let Françoise look at him first. If you go straight to the hospital, you will just get tied up in red tape. They are bureaucratic places, typically French, and you will never get home by Sunday.'

At the villa, Marfield was helped up to a small attic room with a single bed and a cross on the wall. Wilde and Talbot undressed him gently and put him in a pair of Talbot's pyjamas, before helping him to lie down.

Françoise checked his temperature, looked in his mouth, noted the regularity of his heartbeat and breathing, then removed the dressing from his left arm and examined the wound, before cleaning it and applying a new bandage.

'Well,' she said at last when she came downstairs. 'He has undoubtedly suffered beatings, but I cannot find any broken bones. There are cuts and bruises and many bites from fleas and bedbugs, also sores on his feet and a fungal infection on his private parts from lack of cleanliness.'

'And the bullet wound?'

'The bullet went straight through flesh – muscle. The bone is undamaged. Of course, it will take some time to heal, but at the moment there is no evidence of infection. The camp doctor did at least clean it properly, which is a blessing. I'll make him a new sling.'

'Nothing life-threatening?' Wilde asked.

'He needs nourishment and rest, that's all.'

'Permanent damage to the arm?'

She shrugged. 'I am no expert, but I think not.'

'Bastards,' Talbot said.

'He was shaking as though he had a fever,' Wilde said.

'It is not fever, some sort of tic or spasm – I think it may be neurasthenia, the effects of the war perhaps. It comes in many forms. Some men are paralysed, some cannot speak, others shake uncontrollably or are rendered immobile through lassitude. This is something that must be investigated when you get home.'

'How soon can we take him?'

'If there are no other underlying problems, and if he eats, he should be strong enough in two days.'

'We don't have two days.'

Françoise shrugged. 'That is up to you, Tom. Just keep the wound clean and bandaged, then get him to a specialist as soon as you can when you're back in England. Two specialists, perhaps – one for the bullet wound, another for his soul.'

She had made some thin broth and fed it to Marfield with a spoon like a small child. He did not resist, eating slowly. But before the bowl was empty, he shook his head to indicate that he didn't want any more. It was the first communication any of them had received from him. Françoise told him she would clean him properly in the morning, but suggested that now he go to sleep. Marfield obediently closed his eyes like a child, and she left him.

In the evening, after the Talbot children had gone to bed, the four friends ate dinner on the terrace to the background chatter of cicadas and discussed how they should proceed.

'To be sure of getting home before Sunday, we really do have to leave tomorrow,' said Wilde.

'I tell you what,' Françoise said. 'I will give you the name of an old friend of mine from medical school who practices near Orléans. It is on your route and if you need help, I am sure he will oblige. I will telephone him in the morning so that he is prepared.'

For the first time in the four days they had been there, the conversation turned to the prospect of war. They all agreed that conflict was certain, but its imminence was where they parted company.

'Spring 1941,' Françoise said.

'No, earlier than that,' said Talbot. 'Autumn next year – perhaps September. Certainly not before and not much later.'

Wilde and Lydia glanced at each other. They both thought that the war would arrive within days or weeks. 'We believe it has been planned for months,' Wilde said. 'I have even had a rather tasteless bet with an old friend that we will be at war before November.'

Lydia threw him a disapproving look.

'With Horace, darling, dutifully recorded in the Combination Room betting book. A bottle of best claret to the winner.' What was in doubt was whether Horace Dill, a fellow don, would live to see the result. Lung cancer was killing him. Wilde returned to the present. 'Hitler will attack Poland within days. The pact with the Soviets ensures it. Next stop Warsaw.'

Talbot was pouring more wine. 'You sound as though you have inside information.'

'Oh, nothing that's not in the papers. Just putting two and two together.'

'Papers! Rags – have you seen *Le Matin* and *Le Journal*? Antisemitic rags – some in France seem to be longing for Hitler to walk in.' Talbot sighed. 'Oh, I hope you are wrong, Tom. But if you are right, then all will depend on your people.'

'*My* people?'

'The Americans. The British and French are not strong enough alone against the Nazi war machine.'

'Come on, Jacques. You've got the Maginot Line. You have the world's greatest land army. What can those goose-stepping blackshirts do against such defences?'

'You wait and see.' The Frenchman shrugged. 'But, of course, the US cavalry will ride to our rescue again.'

'Don't count on it,' said Wilde. 'Won't happen if diplomats like Joe Kennedy and the other isolationists have their way. I was over in America back in the spring and the non-intervention lobby is very, very strong.'

Talbot suddenly became agitated. 'But non-intervention – that is the old enemy, my friend! If the British or the French or the Americans had done the right thing and backed the Republican government in Spain, Franco's rebels could have been beaten and Hitler given a bloody nose. That would have given him pause for thought before he set off attacking Czechoslovakia and threatening Poland. It would have done the world a lot of good if we had demonstrated that the Nazis could be stopped in their tracks. Now there will be war and we will suffer a thousand-fold.'

'Well,' Françoise said. 'I thank God that my children will be too young to fight.' She caught Lydia's eye, and Lydia looked down towards her belly. No one wanted to think of the high explosives that would be dropped from the air on military and civilians alike in this coming war. Babies would be on the front line with their mothers.

There was a noise from inside the house. The diners turned, expecting to see one of the children demanding a glass of water, but it was Marfield. The pyjamas he wore were far too big and served to emphasise his emaciation. His left arm was held in a clean sling and his feet were bare. He shuffled towards the table and stopped beside Wilde.

'Marfield? Don't you think you'd be better off in bed?'

Marfield smiled wanly. A shade of the old smile that had charmed and won the hearts of dons and undergraduates alike. 'You shouldn't have bothered, you know, Professor. I don't deserve it.' His voice was hoarse and he spoke hesitantly.

Wilde was on his feet. 'You did your best, fighting for a cause you believed in. There's no shame in that.'

Marfield stood there swaying. He was still shaking, but less so.

'You will be home soon,' Lydia reassured him.

'Will I?' He blinked. 'Where's home?'

'England. Cambridge.' Wilde spoke firmly.

'Of course, I remember England.' He tried to laugh, but it was strained and it was unclear whether he was jesting. 'Cricket and Evensong.'

'And your family. And everyone at college. We've missed your singing.'

'Who won the cricket?'

The others at the table looked at Marfield mouths agape, then at each other – and all began to laugh.

Marfield's smile broadened but his eyes seemed a little bemused as he looked at each in turn. 'Have I said something funny?'

'You just sounded like the archetypal Englishman asking about cricket in the middle of a foreign country. Anyway, what cricket?'

'The West Indies tour. It must be finished by now.'

'Ah,' Wilde said. 'I suppose I should know. No, hang on, I *do* recall hearing something. Last match drawn so England win the series. Does that sound right? Century for Hutton.'

'Then all is well with the world – and so I shall forsake arms and come with you.'

CHAPTER 7

The drive north was gruelling for all three of them. Until now, Lydia and Wilde had been in no hurry and could enjoy the countryside in its summer finery. But with Marfield in such a bad way, they left at dawn, keenly aware that they would need to cover 500 miles before nightfall.

Wilde had wanted Lydia to share the driving, but she declined. Irritated and tired after a bad night's sleep, he was reluctant to stop when she asked. Only when her nausea became unbearable did he stop for ten minutes. He gave her one of those meaningful looks that couples give each other: *This is not like you, Lydia. Not at all like you.*

Before leaving, Talbot had taken Wilde into his study and closed the door. 'Don't expect too much from Marfield, Tom,' he said. 'Françoise believes he is shell-shocked. I was at the front in the war, at Verdun, and the best of men suffer. You see things no man should see, and you cannot talk about them with those who were not there. I imagine your undergraduate has witnessed things that will leave deep scars. Don't expect him to talk about such things – I have never told a soul the truth of my own wartime experiences.'

Françoise Talbot had given Lydia a bag full of bandages and some torn sheets to turn into slings, with instructions on dressing Marfield's arm. 'If he is in pain, give him some aspirin.'

Lydia was in fact already well versed in basic medical aid; her own father had been a doctor.

'I am so sorry you are leaving,' Françoise had added, giving her a farewell hug. 'Such an abrupt end to your honeymoon. We would have loved the pleasure of your company a few more days.'

Marfield was silent for most of the trip. At the dinner table the night before, the conversation had not gone much further than the introductions and cricket. He had sipped a glass of red wine and smoked a couple of cigarettes, then nodded, said 'good night' to no one in particular, and taken himself to bed.

Today he wore a spare pair of Wilde's trousers that hung around his fleshless waist as if he was a scarecrow. He also wore Wilde's second pair of brogues, which were a size too big, and a casual white linen shirt. Lydia had insisted on helping him to wash and on shaving his stubble; he had sat on the edge of the bath as she warmed his face with hot, damp towels and soaped his face with Tom's brush. Finally, she had held up the cut-throat razor. His eyes opened wide in alarm, but then he smiled and she laughed. 'You'll soon be your old handsome self.'

The first thing Marfield said on the drive north came a couple of hours into the journey. 'How did you find me?'

'A friend of yours came to us,' Wilde said. 'Honoré.'

There was silence for a minute, then. 'I don't know anyone called Honoré.'

'He may have used a false name. From his rags and shaved head I assumed he had been in the camp with you.' Wilde described him in detail, but Marfield didn't offer even a flicker of recognition.

In the long silences, Wilde recalled all he could of Marcus Marfield and his time at Cambridge. The boy had been well read and had shown a keen interest in the fifteenth and sixteenth centuries, though he was sometimes slow in joining discussions, only making a point when sure of his ground.

What Wilde remembered most about Marfield was his presence. When he entered the room, eyes turned his way and people went silent, as though he were some Hollywood actor. If Marcus noticed the effect he had, he made nothing of it. The only time Wilde recalled being surprised by him was when discussing Henry VIII. Most students seized on Henry's cruelty to his wives and courtiers when they fell from favour; Marcus had taken an opposing view; Henry, he maintained, was exactly the monarch England needed at the start of the sixteenth century. Through calculated ruthlessness he restored stability and let the rest of Europe know that his England was a country to be reckoned with.

They stopped for lunch at an auberge. Marfield ordered an omelette and bread in monosyllables and said *yes*, *no* and *thank you* when required, but ventured no further information. Over their meal, Lydia read aloud from a rushed-out edition of a French evening newspaper: Germany had invaded Poland. What would France and Britain do? The headline posed the question: *C'est la Guerre?* Outside, a radio was blaring and people crowded around it.

They kept moving. In mid-afternoon, when they had made another stop – for fuel and another newspaper – Marfield spoke again.

'You must know that I am a marked man, Professor. They will come for me and kill me.' The words came out without emotion.

Wilde and Lydia looked at each other with dismay.

'Who will do this, Marcus?' Lydia said very quietly.

'Enemies. In Spain I gathered many enemies . . .'

'That's all in the past now.' Wilde tried to cheer him up. 'You'll be safely back in England soon.'

'They shot me once – do you not think they will try again?'

Wilde drove on without stopping at the doctor near Orléans. His plan was to push hard, get to the ferry and get home. They wouldn't make it tonight, but maybe Amiens or even St Omer would be a fair target.

By the time they were cutting through the centre of Paris, Lydia had had enough.

'Let's find a hotel for the night,' she suggested.

Although reluctant to call a halt, there was a nagging anxiety at the back of Wilde's mind about Marfield's lack of a passport. He headed for the Place de la Concorde, parked the car in a side street and asked Lydia to stay with Marfield.

'The Bristol can't be far from here,' she said. 'Shall I see if they have a couple of rooms?'

Wilde raised a doubtful eyebrow: this holiday had not been cheap. He looked away, out of the driver's window. On the wall was a poster showing a gipsy woman smoking a Gitanes; next to it a defaced poster with the skull and crossed swords of the banned *Croix-de-Feu*, France's very own fascist outfit.

Far more prevalent, though, were the large signs they had seen in every town and village along the route from Toulouse to Paris: *Mobilisation Générale*. The call to arms.

'I'll pay,' she said.

He turned back and shook his head. 'No, it'll be wasted. We'll come and do the Bristol another time when there's no pressure. Somewhere cheap and cheerful a little further north will be fine tonight.' He indicated a cafe across the road. 'Have a coffee in there and I'll be back in half an hour or so.'

'You like to be mysterious, don't you, Professor Wilde?'

'Do I, Miss Morris?'

She laughed. 'We'll see you soon.'

The US Embassy stood close to the north-west corner of the Place de la Concorde. It was crowded with Americans seeking passage home before the onset of war, but Wilde managed to get the attention of a middle-aged clerk on the main desk.

'I need to place a call to James Vanderberg, second secretary at the US Embassy in Grosvenor Square, London,' he said, giving her his best smile.

Within five minutes he had been shown into a small ground-floor office and was through to London.

'What's going on, Tom? When am I going to see you?'

'Tomorrow, all being well. But I need a little help, Jim.' Wilde explained about Marfield's lack of a passport.

'Don't know what I can do to help, buddy. Everyone and his mother wants a US passport now, and I doubt your man qualifies.'

'No, no, that's not what I'm asking for. What I need is a good contact in the British Embassy here in Paris. This boy has to be out of France by Sunday, and from what the papers say it looks like a war's going to be under way by then. We can't hang around. Any old friends who might pull a rabbit out of a hat for me, Jim?'

Wilde could hear an uncertain sigh at the other end of the line.

'The trouble is hell's breaking loose here and all leave is cancelled. Several thousand of our countrymen want a boat home. It'll be the same at the British embassy in Paris with Brits trying to get back. No one's going to spend time finding a visa for some commie ex-student of yours. But for you, Tom? Wait there. I'll talk to someone and get back to you soonest.'

'OK. Thanks, Jim. I appreciate it. Look forward to seeing you and Juliet and the kids.'

'Just me, Tom. I'll explain all when you arrive.' Vanderberg paused. 'Are you certain about this guy, Marfield? Not everyone coming out of a war zone has clean hands, if you take my drift, and you have to vouch for him.'

Could he? In the circumstances, what option did he have?

'I'll vouch for him,' Wilde said.

As Wilde waited, he looked out of the window at the bustle of humanity – Americans wanting to get out of Europe. He knew that the story was the same or worse elsewhere in Europe. God alone knew what Berlin and Warsaw must be like right now.

Half an hour later the phone still hadn't rung. Wilde trusted Vanderberg implicitly. If Jim said he'd get back to him, he would. The only worry was the approaching end to the working day. Could anything get done in this city after 6 p.m.?

He picked up the phone on the first ring. It was five forty.

'Tom, get your ass over to the British Embassy with your student. Ask for Burton Goff. He'll write out and stamp a temporary passport there and then.'

'I owe you one.'

'You sure do, buddy. A bottle of France's finest. Good luck, and I'll see you tomorrow.'

Wilde fetched Marfield and hurried to the British Embassy, a short walk from the US Embassy. Outside, dozens of Britons were queuing for gas masks or help with travel home. Mr Burton Goff, an assistant in the passport office, was overwhelmed by the welter of work, and looked in need of a drink and sleep.

Although clearly frustrated that he had to waste time dealing with Wilde and Marfield, he organised the papers in twenty minutes flat. Only at the last moment did he manage a handshake for Wilde and – his eyes on the incapacitated left arm – a brisk nod of acknowledgement for Marfield.

'You're Cambridge men, I understand?'

'Yes.'

'Oxford myself. You know Chamberlain should be rising in the Commons about now? Word is, he's going to give Hitler an ultimatum, although it won't be called an ultimatum. And then war.'

It was after nine o'clock before they found a small hotel a little way north of Montparnasse. The restaurant was closed, but the concierge agreed to bring them some cheese and bread in the bar if they wished. 'And a bottle of red,' Wilde said.

'A cup of tea for me,' Lydia said.

Wilde pulled a face.

'Don't look at me like that as if I'm some sort of dipsomaniac. It's what I want, Tom!'

After eating, mostly in silence, they went upstairs. Lydia changed Marfield's dressing; there was no excess heat in the wound, no sign of sepsis.

'When did it happen?' she asked.

'About ten days ago.' Marfield seemed more inclined to talk. 'Just minding my own business, eating the dishwater they called soup, then – *splat*. It had to be a sniper. There's cover two or three hundred yards beyond the perimeter fence. Definitely aiming at me. Bloody fascists.'

They left Marfield sitting on the edge of his bed, staring blankly at the wall, smoking a cigarette. As he closed the door,

Wilde wondered whether he would still be there in the morning. Marfield's disappearance over two years earlier had been sudden and unexpected; it was difficult to have confidence in the same person again.

While Lydia washed and brushed her teeth in the bathroom down the hall, Wilde took a look around their room: it was at least clean. He took a couple of swigs from the half-empty bottle of wine he had carried up from the bar and then set it aside. Better to keep a clear head.

In the night, perhaps three or four o'clock, Wilde was woken by a prolonged scream from the next-door room, then silence. Lydia, at his side, had not woken. Silently, he slipped from the bed, padded down the hall and knocked gently on Marfield's door. There was no response, so he turned the handle. A little moonlight from the uncurtained window showed that the bed was empty. Marfield was lying flat out on the hard, wooden floor, straight as a soldier, with a single blanket covering him.

The scream had sounded like someone in mortal terror. But as Wilde approached Marfield there was nothing but steady breathing, and the small movements of someone fast asleep. However, Marfield's eyes were open and when Wilde whispered his name there was no response; the eyes were unseeing. Marfield looked at peace with the world, a beautiful child. Except that his face was coated in a film of sweat. Had Wilde imagined the scream? He turned away. There was much unsaid and more unknown.

In the morning, they ate a good breakfast of coffee and croissants, and then paid the bill. As an afterthought, Wilde asked for the best bottle of wine from the cellar. The concierge disappeared for five minutes and reappeared with a bottle from which he blew a cloud of dust. Wilde looked at the label – it was a 1930 Gevrey-Chambertin premier cru. Wilde had no idea whether or not that was a good year, but he certainly knew the domain name, and was reassured by the extortionate price. He bought it and packed it away amid his clothes.

As they left Paris, Wilde's heart sank at the thought of what might happen to this beautiful city if France went to war with Germany. Notre-Dame, the Eiffel Tower, the Louvre, the Arc de Triomphe and the Elysée Palace, all would be reduced to twisted metal, rubble and ashes.

It was a difficult drive because the *Mobilisation Générale* was in full swing, with troops massing eastwards in ever-increasing numbers. At railway crossings, soldiers waved from train windows, while on the roads, endless trucks and armoured vehicles trundled towards the border. When they needed fuel, they had to join a long queue and were limited to ten gallons. It would be enough to get them to the coast.

They reached Calais at three in the afternoon and handed the Citroën back to the hire company. It was a warm, still day and the sea looked calm, but it was certainly not empty; French and British warships were making their presence felt close to harbour and out on the horizon. These were their waters to patrol, but who could know what terrors lay submerged; had the Kriegsmarine already dispatched U-boats to this vital strait?

Whatever the risks, there was a long line of would-be travellers, and it was not until 10 p.m. that Wilde, Lydia and Marcus Marfield embarked on the ferry.

As he watched the lights along the coastline of France fade into the distance, one question still nagged at Wilde. How had the man who called himself Honoré found him in that remote village near Toulouse? Wilde had left a rough itinerary with the college, but he had not been specific about where they would be on which dates. So who had told Honoré their whereabouts – and why?

CHAPTER 8

In the early hours a storm broke, but at dawn the day was calm and hazy. By mid-morning they were on a crowded train back to London. They looked out over the peaceful glory of southern England in late summer – orchards heavy with apples, hop fields crowded with harvest workers; a working holiday full of sweat and laughter, cider and beer. Only the occasional roar of a squadron of planes in the skies above suggested anything might be amiss.

At Victoria Station the news was on everyone's lips. Eleven o'clock – the time of Chamberlain's deadline to the Germans to retreat from Poland – had passed without response. At 11.15 a.m. the Prime Minister had announced that Britain was at war with Germany. Foreboding hung in the air.

A car was waiting for them at the station, and they were whisked through the sandbagged streets to the Chelsea square where Jim and Juliet Vanderberg lived.

Mrs Harley, the housekeeper, let them in. 'Mr Vanderberg is at the embassy, sir. He insisted I make you comfortable and make sure you have everything you need. Would you all like lunch?'

'Thank you,' Wilde said. 'And where are Mrs Vanderberg and the boys?'

'They've caught the ship home to America, sir. It was all very last minute. Mrs Vanderberg couldn't bear William and Henry to be evacuated and she was worried about them remaining in London.'

Wilde understood. His own mother had feared for his safety in the Great War as he neared the age when he might be tempted to join up. She had taken him out of Harrow and back to America for the last of his schooling. When he read of former classmates killed or missing in action, he had found it hard to come to terms with what she had done on his behalf. How can you rejoice in your own safety when your friends are dying?

'You'll have missed the broadcast,' Mrs Harley said as she showed them round the house. 'Mr Chamberlain told us we were fighting evil, sir, and he said we would prevail.' She looked a bit uncertain.

'I'm sure he's right,' said Wilde. But at what cost, he thought – and how long would it take?

The Vanderbergs' house had been equipped with all the necessities of life as enjoyed by American families – icebox, proper shower and bathing facilities, even a television set, which stood blank-eyed in the corner of the sitting room. The housekeeper also pointed out the Anderson shelter which had been constructed in the back garden in case of air raids. 'Mr Vanderberg is not at all sure about it, sir. He thinks it looks rather Heath Robinson and has suggested we might be safer in the tube station.'

After their tour, Lydia said she would like to lie down for an hour or two. Wilde eyed her a little askance; she normally had more energy than this. These past few days seemed to have knocked the stuffing out of her.

'What?' she demanded irritably. 'I hardly slept in that crummy guest house last night. This hasn't been the smoothest of ends to our vacation, you know – and I'm bloody exhausted.'

Wilde sighed and shrugged his shoulders helplessly. Yes, the Buckland guest house in Dover had been pretty damned poor, but just finding a couple of unbooked rooms that late at night had been a miracle. They had both lain awake, wondering at the smell of the place and how long it might have been since the sheets were laundered. When they finally dropped off, they had been woken by Marcus's moans and occasional screams in the next room.

'Have your nap,' Wilde told Lydia. 'We'll wait for you for lunch.'

Just then, at precisely 11.27 a.m., the first air-raid siren of the war went off and Marcus Marfield's legs gave way.

Marfield slithered to the floorboards and appeared to vomit, although little emerged from his mouth. He bunched his knees into his chest and curled his right arm tightly around them. He was shaking and dry-retching. His breathing was shallow and fast. Lydia rushed to kneel beside him, putting her arm around his shoulder. 'What do we do, Tom?' she mouthed over his head. 'Shouldn't we be getting to the shelter?'

Wilde crouched down next to her. 'We can't move him, not in this state.'

Outside, the siren continued to blast out its deafening warning. In the street a constable's whistle shrieked. They could hear shouting as residents were marshaled into shelters.

Mrs Harley hurried in holding out gas masks. 'We really should get to the shelter,' she said. 'Or at least into the space beneath the stairs. They say that's the safest place inside the house.' And then, just as she spoke, the air-raid siren was replaced with the soothing moan of the all-clear. She allowed herself a smile. 'False alarm,' she said.

'Well, that's something.' Wilde handed back his gas mask, its rubbery stink hanging in the air.

The housekeeper nodded towards the spittle on the floor; all that had emerged from Marfield's retching. 'I'll get a rag and some water.'

Lydia held Marfield until his breathing slowly subsided, and the shaking diminished. When he was calm, she and Wilde helped him to his feet.

'It must have been terrible out there in Spain,' she said gently.

Marfield took a deep breath and shook his head. Wilde had a sudden vision of war machines and black-clad warriors with guns, decorated with the cross and swastika of the new Germany. Was this the future for Britain? To have its spirit destroyed by these nightmarish men and their iron devices?

The housekeeper broke the spell. 'Would you all like some coffee?' she inquired brightly.

Her cheery voice made Wilde smile. If the rest of Britain had something of this woman's backbone, things might not be so bad after all.

Wilde sat in a window seat in the sitting room and read the English newspapers while Lydia slept upstairs. Occasionally, he looked out on the beautiful, late-eighteenth century Chelsea square, still in full summer leaf. High above, however, he spotted the evidence of what was to come – barrage balloons, shaped like fat cigars, had been launched at the sound of the siren as a deterrent to low-flying enemy aircraft. He pulled his handkerchief from his trouser pocket and several scraps of paper fluttered to the floor.

Of course – he had promised various internees of the Camp du Vernet that he would call their friends and families. Reaching for the telephone, he began to work his way through the numbers. This would take up the afternoon.

Across the room, Marfield sat at the grand piano, the fingers of his right hand poised like talons above the keys. Wilde watched him from the corner of his eye. Finally he nodded in his direction. 'You know, I'm sure Jim wouldn't mind if you want to play it.'

'I don't think I can.'

'Well, why not try? If it doesn't work, no harm done.'

The silence stretched between them.

'No, I think not,' Marfield said at last. He lowered his fingers, closed the lid and rose from the piano. 'Excuse me.' He wandered off into the depths of the house. Wilde let him go. This wasn't going to be easy.

As darkness fell, the housekeeper put up the blackouts and Jim Vanderberg arrived home. He was not alone.

Wilde shook his old friend's hand and then gave him a bear hug. They were of similar height; but Wilde appeared half an inch taller because he held himself erect, shoulders back like the boxer he was.

'Tom, it's grand to see you. Sorry I'm so late, but as I'm sure you can imagine things are getting a bit hectic at Grosvenor Square. The wires are red hot and the ambassador's in a blind funk. The siren almost paralysed the bastard.'

'Don't worry, your housekeeper has been looking after us a treat.'

'Mrs Harley's a treasure.' Vanderberg shook his head. 'God, Tom, the streets out there are a madhouse! No streetlights, no headlights. I heard two crashes and lots of screeching of tyres on the way home. The blackout's going to kill more people than Adolf's bombs.'

Jim Vanderberg had been Wilde's closest friend since they roomed together at college in Chicago. The divergence of their career paths had done nothing to lessen their bond; they shared a world view which included a certain disdain for the despots of right and left, and their appeasers. Wilde's eyes drifted towards his host's companion, who stood awkwardly by the door.

Vanderberg turned. 'Tom, this is Lincoln Tripp, my young colleague from the embassy. Harvard-educated, fresh out of his first posting to Moscow. And no doubt very glad to be back in civilisation.'

'Pleased to meet you, Tripp.'

'And you, sir,' the young man said. 'I greatly admire your Tudor biographies.'

'That's very kind of you.' Wilde cast an appraising eye over the young man. He was a bit of a dandy – good three-piece suit on a day that didn't really warrant a waistcoat, silk kerchief falling from his breast pocket and bespoke shoes that had been polished to a mirror shine. His hair was clean and a lick fell carelessly across his brow. Wilde wondered how long he had spent in front of the bathroom mirror to achieve the effect. Maybe young Tripp fancied himself as a poet. He also wondered what the Soviets had made of him.

'So,' Jim said, 'where are my other guests? Where, pray, is the gorgeous bolting bride?'

'Oh, she's just popped up to our room to put on a dash of lipstick in your honour.'

'*Our* room? Why, you're not even married yet, you dirty dog!'

Wilde laughed. 'Let's just say I feel married in spirit.'

Vanderberg lowered his voice. 'I wouldn't mention to Mrs Harley that you didn't actually manage to get darling Lydia to the altar. Awfully proper, my housekeeper. And where is the mysterious young man you rescued from the French?'

'His name is Marcus Marfield and he's parked himself in your library. He's rather fragile. What they used to call shell shock or battle fatigue . . .'

As he spoke, Marfield appeared in the doorway. He surveyed the newcomers without expression. Wilde beckoned him into the room. 'Marfield, come and meet our host, Jim Vanderberg, and Mr Lincoln Tripp.'

At supper, they ate roast lamb. Jim Vanderberg cracked open the Gevrey-Chambertin that Wilde had brought from France and proclaimed it superb; then Tripp regaled them all with tales of Moscow. Wilde noted how Tripp could not keep his eyes off the exquisite face of Marcus Marfield.

'What really got me about Moscow,' Tripp was saying, in full flow now, 'was the smell. No one washes. No one cleans their homes. I don't think they have soap. Sweat, vodka, cabbage and cooking fat. Not a good mixture.'

'I take it you're not a great admirer of Bolshevism then, Mr Tripp,' Wilde said.

'Oh, I wasn't talking about politics. Their idea of politics is a thing called dialectical materialism. Have you heard of that?'

'Of course.'

'It's hogwash. Dialectical materialism is a quasi-intellectual excuse for murder and theft.' Tripp directed a glance towards Marfield. 'But the shambles they're in, I really think that's just the Soviet culture. They've got a hungry peasant society that they're trying to shoehorn into an industrial class. And, well, bread and trains come way ahead of soap on the list of priorities.'

'I suppose', Lydia said, 'that if no one washes or cleans they all end up smelling the same and no one notices. Sounds a sensible idea to me.'

'The other thing's their teeth,' Tripp said. 'Even worse than the English.' He laughed aloud.

Vanderberg was unimpressed. 'First lesson of diplomacy, Mr Tripp – don't insult the host nation.'

Tripp's face fell. 'Gee, I'm sorry, Mr Vanderberg. That was really out of order.' He nodded towards Lydia and Marfield. 'Please accept my apology.'

Lydia smiled thinly. 'Nothing to apologise for, Mr Tripp. Your observation was perfectly accurate.'

After supper, Lydia said she would have an early night, so Vanderberg and Wilde retired to his study, leaving Marfield and Tripp smoking cigarettes in the sitting room.

'What's going to happen, Jim?' asked Wilde, as he settled into a comfortable chair. 'Are we Americans going to join this war like we did the last?'

'What do you think?'

'I think Roosevelt sees the danger of the despots, but he's hamstrung by the American people. They don't want to join a European war.'

Vanderberg snorted. 'FDR doesn't like the Germans. To tell the truth, there's a lot about the British that he doesn't care for either – particularly their Empire. But his negative feelings about the Germans go a lot deeper. I don't think he enjoyed his time as a schoolboy at Bad Neuheim back in the nineties. His problem is the non-intervention lobby.'

'Can he overcome them?'

'The British and French are counting on him. Bill Bullitt, our man in Paris, is harried constantly by the French. They are convinced we'll save them. Bullitt sent a cable to Roosevelt saying that every day he is obliged to explain to the French in no uncertain terms that America *will* remain neutral, but to no avail. The Frenchies tell him – and these are pretty much Bullitt's words – "Yes, we know all that, monsieur, but the Germans will make it impossible for you to remain detached, and you *will* be drawn in."'

'Maybe they're right.'

'Maybe.' Vanderberg leant over and filled Wilde's glass from the whisky decanter.

Wilde held up the glass. 'Your health, Jim, and safe passage for Juliet and the boys.'

'Cheerio.'

They sipped in companionable silence, then Wilde asked about young Lincoln Tripp.

'He needs guidance,' said Vanderberg. 'A little too brash for his own good. Well, you saw that with the teeth. Bit of a blunder.'

'Oh, he's OK. You'll smooth those rough edges.'

'You're right. He'll learn.' Vanderberg laughed. 'You know, I didn't want to embarrass him, but the truth is he begged me to be allowed to come along and meet you. Seems he's a big fan of yours. Particularly mentioned your work on Walsingham.'

'I'm flattered. Is he a history graduate?'

'Indeed. Anyway, he was keen to meet you – and I was happy to oblige him. It's good for a young diplomat to make influential friends. Meeting people is three quarters of the job.'

'Tripp will be fine. He has the look of privilege.'

'Oh yes, he's very well-connected, but he's not without merits of his own, so I don't want you thinking Daddy got him the job.' Vanderberg paused and looked his old friend in the eye. 'Look, I make light of it, but I was really sorry you and Lydia didn't tie the knot. I had my speech written, and there were some good jokes and reminiscences in there. Juliet was very sad for you. She thinks you're the perfect couple.'

Wilde nursed his whisky. 'So do I, of course. That's why I wanted to marry her. I'll try again one day, but I'm not going to hold my breath. This has been going on almost three years now. Will she, won't she? Maybe, maybe not.'

'Is she OK? She seems very tired – not her usual dynamic self.'

'These last few days have knocked her.'

They sat in companionable silence, both aware of the gaps in each other's lives.

'And you?' Wilde said eventually. 'You must be missing Juliet and the boys.'

'I'll miss them like crazy, but at least I'll know they're safe,' said Vanderberg. 'I had the devil's own job securing them berths – almost every Yank in Britain was looking for a way home. They'll be somewhere in the Atlantic by now, cruising steadily on a westerly course.'

Wilde couldn't argue with the decision. God alone knew what this city would be like when the bombs rained down. In the meantime, here in this room, with his best friend close by in an armchair, and both of them with good whisky warming in their hands, he felt at peace with the world.

And then, from far off in the house, he heard a sound that checked his breathing and made the hairs on his neck stand on end.

Marfield was singing.

CHAPTER 9

Philip Eaton had still not mastered the problems associated with dressing and undressing with only one arm and a badly damaged left leg. Tonight was doubly difficult. Having spent ten minutes getting from his day clothes into his pyjamas, the telephone had rung and he had to set about reversing the operation.

At last he was dressed. Almost. He couldn't put on a necktie or cufflinks without assistance and he still had trouble with his shoelaces, so he left them loose and sat down on the sofa to wait. Five minutes later the bell rang and he called out that the door was bloody open.

Guy Rowlands came in, cigarette between his fine fingers, a benevolent smile on his charming, well-bred face. 'Oh dear, Philip, let me help you.'

'Damn it, Guy, this is the bit I hate. Pain is simply something to be endured, but the humiliation of not being able to dress properly is intolerable.'

'I know, truly I do. Let's get that tie on you and be on our way. The first lord awaits us.'

'I'm an adult for pity's sake, not a bloody infant.'

It was clear to Eaton that Winston Churchill was a changed man. Even at this late hour, you could sense his energy. And why not? He was back in charge of the Admiralty as First Lord and had been asked by Chamberlain to join the War Cabinet. He had accepted, of course, and had wasted no time in heading off up Whitehall to the Admiralty, a place he knew well and loved from his time there in the Great War, to meet the Sea Lords, chiefs of staff, civil servants and section heads. It was said he had closeted himself with these men from 6 p.m. until late, acquiring detailed information on fleet deployments and their needs. This was the first day of a conflict that he believed would be a second great war, and there was no time to lose.

Now it was half an hour past midnight and Churchill was back at his apartment in Morpeth Mansions across the road from Westminster Cathedral. But he had no intention of retiring to bed just yet, for important men were arriving from their homes, summoned secretly by telephone.

At last they were all assembled in his sitting room. It had the intimacy of a college common room, with men lounging wherever they could on sofas, armchairs, hardback chairs, even the floor. Every man was equipped with a brandy glass and their smoking implements of choice, be it cigarettes, cigars or pipes. A single, low-wattage bulb barely lit the room, and the lack of light and the pall of tobacco smoke simply added to the atmosphere of mystery and conspiracy in this blacked-out space. Eaton knew it was no accident but design – for drama had suited Winston Churchill all his life. He had always been something of an actor, and he liked to have the leading role.

He got right to the heart of the matter.

'We all know what has to be done, gentlemen. We have to impress our cause upon the American public and political opinion. With the minimum of delay.'

Churchill's growl was commanding. He clutched a long Havana cigar between his puffy fingers. A wisp of blue smoke spiralled lazily from the burning tip to join the cloud that hung around the ceiling.

Eaton, like every other man in the room, felt the weight of the moment.

Churchill had clearly taken a risk in calling this meeting, for its purpose could not be discussed outside this room; even the prime minister had not been told, and nor would he be. But this was a time for such risks; wars were not won by faint hearts.

'And we must bear in mind,' Churchill continued, 'that the Hun will do all in his power to deter our American friends from intervening or supplying us with arms. You may think that this will be a war of many tons of steel and iron. You may think that it will cost countless lives and much misery. And you would be correct. But it will also be a war of words, of propaganda, and that, in the first instance, is a battle we must win.'

Philip Eaton watched him and listened with admiration. And yet he wondered why he had been summoned here when he had only been out of the plaster cast on his leg two weeks, and had still not mastered life without a left arm. He was beginning to understand.

Since the hit-and-run incident, he had been away from his MI6 desk, convalescing. Oh, he had received reports from Terence Carstairs on a regular basis, so he knew what was going on, but that wasn't the same as being there, taking vital decisions, analysing reports from abroad, dispatching agents into the field or travelling overseas to the stations under his control.

Churchill growled on. 'We need aircraft and we need ships, and America is our best hope of acquiring them in short order. The Nazis and their allies in the States will work to thwart us at every turn. Nor should we underestimate our foe, for Dr Goebbels is a master of the dark propaganda arts. He will tell the Yanks that Britain should be left to rot and that Europe should be left to Germany – and many will listen to him.'

While Eaton had been away, his work at MI6 had been covered by Guy Rowlands. Now that he was back in harness, Rowlands was literally a shoulder to support him. Not only had he done his tie and shoes, but he had driven him here from his Chelsea home in his silver BMW 328, a two-seater sports roadster that seemed rather out of place in the smoky, almost empty London streets.

'I think I'm going to have to swap this little beauty for something a bit more British,' Rowlands had said with evident regret.

'You always were a flashy bugger, Guy.'

'What do you think I should go for – Bristol? Aston Martin?'

At Churchill's flat, Rowlands had helped Eaton up the stairs then made him comfortable on a rather fine sofa.

Eaton tried to ignore the pain. His leg was worst. The fractures had healed, but he would never walk without a limp. The loss of an arm was another matter; the difficulty there was more to his sense of self than the physical handicap. If he had been a religious man, he might have thought the injuries just reward for his sins. His many sins. But there was no God.

He gazed around the room at the others present. He recognised them all and knew most of them. What they shared was either loyalty to Churchill or a role in the dissemination of information, or both. The press baron Beaverbrook was there of course, as was Sir Frederick Ogilvie, director-general of the BBC. Who else? Duff Cooper, still on the back benches; the ever-present Brendan Bracken, one of Churchill's best friends; Desmond Morton, who had provided Churchill with so many secrets regarding German rearmament; the scientist Frederick Lindemann.

And then there were the secrets boys: Eaton and Rowlands sharing the sofa while their boss Sir Hugh Sinclair, chief of

MI6, occupied a wing chair. Sir Hugh – known to one and all as Quex – had nodded in acknowledgement at Eaton on entering the room. Eaton had afforded him a smile in return and tried to conceal his shock; Quex was gaunt, his flamboyance gone. 'God,' Eaton whispered to Rowlands. 'He looks worse than me. Is he ill or simply under pressure?'

'Both, perhaps.'

Across the room, Maxwell Knight and Guy Liddell from MI5 sat in the shade nearest the door, watching, evaluating. Like cats.

Liddell had passed a few words with Eaton before taking his seat. 'Good timing, Eaton. Don't want to miss the war.'

'Are you sure?'

'Come, come, don't be like that. Anyway, we'll need you boys. Five's really up against it. We have upwards of sixty thousand German nationals resident in Britain, and they've all got to be checked out. That's without the other aliens and undesirables we need to vet. My complement of staff doesn't quite make a couple of rugby teams.'

Eaton smiled at Liddell but made no promises. His gaze now was focused on Churchill's pug-like features, as he tried to spur on the impish Beaverbrook.

'Max, your papers sell more than any in the land; you will be at the forefront of this battle for America's hearts.' He stabbed his cigar towards Ogilvie. 'The BBC, too, of course. Goebbels most certainly understands the power of the wireless – we must do even better.'

He began to address the men from the Secret Intelligence Service. 'Your role will be obvious to you. Your agents in Germany and the occupied territories must report anything that shines a light on the filthy behaviour of Hitler's thugs. We know there will be atrocities and great cruelty, for we have seen such things from them already. These degradations must be publicised so that the decent men and women of the free world cannot turn away and say "This has nothing to do with us." In our own operations we must ensure that civilian casualties are kept to a minimum. And at home, it is the task of the MI5 to prevent anything being done by fifth columnists to harm our country's reputation in the wider—'

He stopped in mid-sentence because there was a knock at the door. It opened and Churchill's wife Clemmie stood there, attired in dressing gown as though she had just risen from her bed. She nodded briskly to the assembled men, then approached her husband and spoke a few words in his ear. He instantly rose from his seat and followed her from the room.

The men sat silently save the occasional cough. Churchill returned five minutes later, his face grave. Eaton knew the old boy was an emotional man and, watching his fallen face, he wondered for a moment whether he might cry.

'Gentlemen, a report has come through. We have had the first casualty at sea in this war. An unarmed British passenger liner has been torpedoed by a German U-boat in the Atlantic off Northern Ireland. There were fourteen hundred aboard, crew and civilians, including Americans, British and other nationalities. It is certain that many have perished. The ship is the *Athenia*, out of Glasgow and Liverpool, bound for America. She is still afloat two hundred miles north-west of Malin Head, but mortally wounded.' He paused, his voice choking. 'Now perhaps the world will see why we have chosen this fight.'

Something woke Wilde. He leant over and checked his watch: three o'clock in the morning. He listened. No siren, no moans from Marcus's room, no screaming. But something was wrong.

Creeping from the double bed so as not to wake Lydia, he moved stealthily across the room. He stubbed his bare toe on the corner of the bed and just managed to suppress a yelp of pain. At the window, he inched back the blackout and looked out on the rear garden: nothing.

Feeling his way back across the room, he found the door and turned the handle. The door creaked as he opened it and he stopped momentarily, before stepping into an impenetrable darkness. All the windows in the house were curtained in blackout material so dense there was not even a chink of light. With hands outstretched he manouevred his way by touch to the top of the stairs. He was about to switch on the light when he noticed the front door was open. He took the steps down slowly, clutching the banister. At the front door, a quarter moon brought some visibility to the street.

Why was the door open?

He stood on the front doorstep, as his eyes adjusted to the gloom. Across the road, beside the fenced-off garden at the centre of the square, he thought he saw shadowy movement. At first he dismissed it, but then, he heard voices too.

'Marfield?' He called in an urgent whisper. 'Marfield – is that you?'

They had gone to bed at eleven o'clock, soon after Lincoln Tripp had left. Wilde had joined Lydia in bed without waking her and had lain there on his back waiting for sleep to come, the sound of Marfield's voice in his head. He had sung a Brahms lied, 'An Die Nachtigall'. Wilde was no expert on music, but he knew perfection when he heard it. Whatever Marfield had been through, whatever the dust and smoke of the Spanish war had thrown at his vocal cords, his voice remained intact.

'Marfield,' he called again, this time a little louder, but not so much that it would wake neighbours or those already asleep in this house.

Now Wilde could make out a figure about fifty yards away. *Two* figures. Wearing nothing but his pyjama bottoms, Wilde padded silently along the front path and out of the gate. A cloud passed and the fragment of moon brought the faint outlines into sharper relief: Marfield and someone else, someone smaller.

As Wilde stepped out into the road, he saw that the two figures were tussling. Wilde moved faster. At that moment one of the figures broke away and stalked into the road. It was Marfield. As he passed, Wilde reached out to clutch his right shoulder, but Marfield didn't seem to register that he was there. He strode, instead, to the front door.

Wilde's instinct was to follow him, but instead he took two steps towards the other, smaller figure. At first he thought it was a woman, but then, no, it was a slender young man. And then he changed his mind again: it *was* a young woman. As she started to hurry away, he followed and caught her easily. 'Stop, I want a word.'

She turned abruptly and pushed the muzzle of a pistol into his bare chest, the cold metal pressing on his sternum. He had a clearer view of her face now. Dark, small, olive-skinned, with raven hair. A face he had seen before, fleetingly, outside the main gate at Le Vernet. Then she had spat at his feet; now she pressed the gun barrel hard into his chest so that he momentarily backed off. He wasn't afraid. She had already had her chance to use the weapon, either on Marfield or on him.

'Why are you here? What do you want with Marcus?'

She said nothing, pushed him again with the gun, and then turned and vanished.

Wilde lost her within a few strides. For a couple of moments he stood looking into the darkness after her, then returned to the house. He found his way to Marfield's room. As he opened the door, there was a glow. Marfield was sitting on his bed, smoking.

'What in God's name was that all about? Who was she? She had a pistol!'

'I told you, Professor. I have enemies.'

'That woman was outside the camp in France. She's followed you here, for pity's sake! I've helped you this far – but if your enemies have weapons and the means to follow you to England, you're going to need a great deal more professional protection than I can offer. And you're going to have to tell me what's going on.'

Marfield pulled deeply at the cigarette so that the tip burned bright orange, then exhaled a long stream of smoke. 'You shouldn't have bothered with me. You should have left me to rot at Le Vernet. Don't put yourself in the line of fire, Professor Wilde.'

CHAPTER 10

In the morning, Wilde was up before either Lydia or Marfield and went downstairs hoping to talk to Jim about the events in the night. There was no sign of him. Wilde cornered the housekeeper in the kitchen. She seemed agitated.

'Mr Vanderberg was called away to the embassy early, Professor,' she said. 'He left a note to say there was urgent business and that he would call you later. He wished you a safe journey back to Cambridge. An embassy car will collect you at eleven to take you to Liverpool Street.'

'Thank you, Mrs Harley.' Wilde paused. Her face was drawn and pale. 'Is everything all right?' he asked.

The housekeeper took a series of shallow breaths, as though gulping for air. 'There *was* something else, sir. On the wireless this morning, the newsreader announced that the Germans have torpedoed a British liner off the coast of Ireland.'

'Oh, my God.' Wilde understood at once.

'I'm worried it might have been the ship Mrs Vanderberg and the boys were on. I think that might be why Mr Vanderberg rushed away so early . . .' She burst into tears. 'I'm so scared, sir!'

They arrived in Cambridge in the early evening, all three of them exhausted. The train's departure had been delayed as hundreds of evacuee children, some alone but most with mothers, crowded into the carriages and companionways on their way to new lodgings in the country. The journey was long and arduous, standing room only, with no refreshments available, and the train kept stopping en route without explanation. Apart from the evacuees, there were many soldiers and airmen in uniform.

Cambridge felt alien and grey. It was full of removal trucks, and of workmen digging with pneumatic drills, picks and shovels in places that should have been oases of calm. Walls of sandbags were going up everywhere, disfiguring college facades and all other buildings deemed important.

Wilde felt sad and angry – and helpless. He now felt almost certain that Juliet Vanderberg and the boys, William and Henry, *had* been on the *Athenia*. He had tried calling Jim at the embassy but could not get through, and there was nothing else he could do. The headline in the *Evening Standard* he had bought at Liverpool Street Station said that hundreds had been saved, but it was clear, too, that there had been many deaths. The thought of children jumping for their lives in to the bitterly cold waters of the Atlantic was too much to bear. He and Lydia scarcely spoke on the gruelling journey to Cambridge. Their companion, too, had gazed out of the window in listless silence.

'Well, Marfield,' Wilde said as the cab drew up outside his house. 'I suggest you stay here with me tonight and then I'll go to college in the morning to discover the lie of the land. Perhaps they can find accommodation for you.'

Marfield shrugged. 'Whatever you think best.'

'And I feel I should contact your parents.'

'Please don't do that, Professor. My father won't have me across the threshold.'

Doris, Wilde's housekeeper, was there to greet them. 'I was expecting you a lot earlier, Professor. I've left out some cold meats and pickles with fresh bread. I could rustle up something more substantial if you'd like.'

'What do you think, Lydia?'

'Don't worry about me. I'll open a tin of soup,' Lydia said. She smiled at Marfield. 'As for you, young man, I'm taking you to Addenbrooke's first thing tomorrow. College can wait. I want that arm to have some proper attention. Nine o'clock sharp.' What she didn't mention was that she had also suggested to Wilde that there might be a way to get Marfield some professional help for his psychological problems, and Wilde had asked her to see if she could sort something out.

Marfield nodded, as compliant as a lamb. How different from the young man involved in that strange confrontation on a dark London street a few hours earlier, thought Wilde. There had been real anger, even aggression, on both sides.

Lydia kissed Wilde and walked the short distance to her own, larger property, *Cornflowers* – a splendid eighteenth-century house inherited from her parents. Doris, meanwhile, was upstairs making a bed for Marfield in one of Wilde's spare rooms.

The phone rang. Wilde picked up and immediately recognised the voice.

'Jim?'

'Hello, Tom.'

Just two words, but Wilde read distance and despondency into them. He knew Vanderberg too well. 'Any news?' No time for small talk.

'You know about the *Athenia*?'

'I put two and two together. Please tell me they're all OK.'

'I wish I could, Tom. Henry's been rescued, but there's no word on Juliet and William.'

'Jesus, Jim, I'm sorry. Have you spoken to Henry?'

'No, but I know he's aboard a destroyer bound for Greenock.'

'Where are you? Can I do anything?'

'I'm on a train straight up to Glasgow. We've stopped at this goddamned station in the middle of nowhere, and I found this phone. Tripp's driving up so we'll have a car at our disposal and Jack Kennedy, the Ambassador's son, will be joining us with one or two others. Tom – I just can't think straight.'

'Why Glasgow? I thought she embarked at Liverpool.'

'They're taking survivors to Glasgow and Ireland. Joe's sent a couple of Naval attachés to Galway to find out what's happening. We'll be looking after any Americans brought in to Scotland . . . there were a lot on board – over three hundred – and hundreds of Canadians too.'

Wilde wanted to say: *She'll be OK, Jim*. But that was worse than a bromide. 'What do we know? I saw the piece in the *Standard*, but that was pretty threadbare.'

'All I'm sure of is that two, perhaps three ships went to the rescue. Apparently there are survivors and I know there are deaths. I'm hoping things will be clearer by the time I get north of the border. I'll call you, Tom, I promise. Jesus, how could a goddamned U-boat captain think an unarmed ocean-going liner is a fit and proper target? Is that the way this war is going to be fought?'

As Wilde put the phone down, he saw that Marfield was watching him. Wilde shook his head. 'I suppose this is nothing new to you. Death and destruction.' He had an edge of bitterness in his voice, anger at everyone whose profession was war.

'I saw some bad stuff.'

'Do you want to talk about it? The offer stands.'

'I can't.'

'I understand, I suppose. But I know one thing that might help both of us. I've got whisky. Do want to get tight? You might sleep better.'

'Thank you. I'll drink your whisky, Professor, but it won't help me sleep. I've tried it too many times before.'

'No harm in trying again.' Wilde found the bottle and poured two tumblers. They clinked glasses. 'Good to have you home.'

Wilde and Lydia owned separate houses next door to each other. They had been neighbours before they became lovers. When Wilde went next door to check on Lydia, he found her sitting at the kitchen table, head in hands. 'There's something wrong, isn't there?' He put an arm around her.

'I'll be all right. It's just everything: the bloody war, the end of summer. All I need is a couple of good nights' sleep.'

He wasn't convinced but knew better than to press the issue. 'Can I use your phone?'

'Something wrong with your own?'

'I don't want Marfield to hear.'

He called the porters' lodge at college. The phone was answered by an unfamiliar voice.

'Is Scobie there?' Wilde asked. Scobie was the head porter.

'Just a moment, sir.'

A few seconds delay. 'Yes?'

'Scobie, it's Professor Wilde. Have I caught you at a bad time?'

'Just knocking off, sir.'

'I'll make it quick. Do you have a home number for Marcus Marfield?'

'The choral scholar who ran away to the Spanish war?'

'That's the one. He's home and I want to call his people.'

'Well glory be. Now then . . .'

Wilde heard the rustle of paper.

'Ah, here he is. Yes, got it. Ipswich number.'

Wilde thanked Scobie and hung up, then called the Marfields' home. It rang for almost a minute and he was about to give up when it was finally answered.

'Hello, Marfield residence.'

'Is that Mrs Marfield?'

'Yes, who's speaking please?'

'It's Professor Wilde, from Cambridge University.'

'Ah, yes, I remember. You supervised Marcus's history studies.' She sounded polite but wary.

'That's right. Look, Mrs Marfield, I have some news. I hope you and your husband will think it excellent news.'

'My husband is dead, Professor Wilde. Is this something to do with Marcus?'

Her voice was very flat, he thought. Why would a mother not leap upon the possibility of some good news – any news – about her vanished son? 'I am very sorry to hear about your husband's death, Mrs Marfield.' He paused and when there was no response, ploughed on. 'But I am pleased to tell you that I have brought your son back to England. He is presently staying with me here in Cambridge. He didn't want me to call you, but I have taken it on myself to do so. I thought you should know.'

'I see.' No emotion. No joy, no sadness. 'My husband shot himself this morning, Professor. It was Marcus's fault, of course. Ronald couldn't bear the loss of his son. He loved him more than anything else in the world, you know.'

Wilde was deeply shocked. He didn't know what to say. He thought back to his conversation with Colonel Marfield when Marcus first disappeared. He had called him up to ask if they knew where he had gone, and it had been stilted and awkward. The Marfields hadn't come to college to meet him, and nor had he been invited down to their Suffolk home. Now it began to make sense; whatever damage had been caused to Marfield's relationship with his parents had occurred some time before he went off to join the International Brigades.

'What would you like me to do, Mrs Marfield? I don't know if I can persuade Marcus to come down to Ipswich with me. Would you like to come up here?'

'No. No thank you, Professor. My son is dead to me – and I would be grateful if you say nothing to him about this call. I will not expect to hear from you again. I thank you for your good intentions, but that is my decision. Good evening to you.'

The line went dead. Wilde stood for a few moments looking at the handset in astonishment. What could Marcus Marfield have done to drive such a wedge between him and his parents? And what had driven his father to shoot himself on the very day of his return to Cambridge?

CHAPTER 11

Wilde went to bed alone. It was a strange, cold feeling, but Lydia had made it clear she wished to have time to herself, and Wilde wanted to be in his own home while Marfield was there.

He wondered whether he should try once more to get through to Marfield, to persuade him to talk either about his time in Spain and Le Vernet, or about the rift with his parents. He needed, too, to find the right moment to tell him that his father was dead, but he was worried that the boy seemed too fragile. The change in him was a great deal more profound than a shaven head and a bullet through the arm.

Once more his sleep was broken.

He woke at four in the morning to the distant sound of breaking glass. Rising from bed, he flicked the switch, but the lights didn't come on: a fuse was gone or the power supply had failed. He fished for the torch that he kept in his bedside table drawer and hurried on silent feet towards the spare bedroom. Marfield wasn't there and the bedclothes were hardly ruffled.

Wilde went downstairs to find him standing by the kitchen door to the garden, gazing into nothingness. He didn't appear to notice Wilde or the flickering flashlight.

'Marcus?' Wilde spoke gently.

No response. Wilde swept his torch beam round the room. A sugar bowl had fallen to the floor and smashed into pieces; sugar was scattered across the boards. It was this that had awoken him.

'Marfield, what is it?' he said, more urgently.

'Junkers 87s. Don't you hear them?'

'There are no planes, Marcus.'

'We are in the ravine. There is no shelter from the sun. Two hundred of us. A bird dives, but it is not a bird. It is a Stuka, screaming and defecating, fouling the earth with its 500lb load and a roar of death. And then there is silence and smoke amid the rocks until the wails and cries fill the void.' He intoned the words as though reading them from an essay or novel.

'Is this something that happened?'

Marfield closed his eyes, his breathing deep and heavy.

'Marcus, talk to me.'

'It's my watch. I'll stay here. You go to bed.'

'No, you're in England now. Home in Cambridge. You're not on watch.'

'Cambridge . . .' Marcus suddenly shuddered. He took three sharp breaths, and then opened his eyes.

Wilde put an arm to his shoulder. 'Do you want to sit down? Coffee perhaps?'

Marfield was catching his breath. 'I'm sorry. I think I'm off balance. I'll be all right in the morning.' He managed a smile.

'How about that coffee?'

'No, I need sleep.'

He had passed from a dream state to lucidity in a matter of moments. Was this the time to get him talking? Wilde plunged in. 'That woman in London – the one with the pistol. If you're in danger, then I need to know – and you need protection.'

'That was Rosa. I knew her in Spain. We were comrades.'

'What did she want of you in London?'

For a few moments Wilde thought he might get a straight answer, but it wasn't to be.

'I'm going to bed now,' Marcus said. 'In the morning I intend to watch some cricket.'

No, thought Wilde, in the morning we have other plans for you.

Lydia came around for coffee at about eight. Wilde arrived downstairs a little later, bleary-eyed, and then Marfield appeared.

'I am going to the college to see if I can find you a set of rooms,' Wilde said as the young man came into the kitchen. 'Lydia, meanwhile, will take you to Addenbrooke's for a thorough check-up.' It was a firm statement, not a suggestion.

'There's nothing wrong with me. The wound is healing.'

'No,' Wilde said. 'You will do this thing – not for us, but for yourself. You need to be fit and healthy. I'm sure it hasn't escaped your notice that there is now another war on. There is every possibility you will be asked to join many thousands of other young men to fight once more against the fascist thugs. You will need to be sound in body for that.'

'You know what I need most?' Marfield sounded sulky. 'I need to sit and watch a cricket match.'

'If there's any cricket to be had, it will most likely start this afternoon.' Wilde hid his impatience as best he could. 'By then you'll have had a thorough check-up, and, with any luck, you'll have rooms of your own at college – and you'll be on your own. We'll make no more demands of you. Before then, however, you can give us one little morning. Yes?'

Marfield forced a weak smile, then shrugged. 'I seem to be outnumbered.'

The college, usually a haven of tranquillity, was in turmoil. Lorries were parked outside the main entrance and teams of men were carting boxes of books from the ancient library to be loaded up into them. Wilde collared Scobie.

'Where are the books going?'

The head porter tipped his black bowler. 'State secret, Professor. Somewhere safe where Jerry won't be able to get at them. Perhaps they'll store them down a coal mine, who knows?'

The books were irreplaceable. From medieval manuscripts to rare works through every century. 'I suppose it makes sense.'

'I believe they have been talking about the stained glass in the chapel, too. They started removing it all from King's back in June. Very far-sighted. The question now is whether we should be doing the same? Will it do more harm than good, that's the question. Need delicate hands and superb craftsmen to get all that out without breaking it. Anyway, no decision has been made as yet, I believe.'

'The old place is being torn apart.' Wilde looked about him.

'They're digging trenches in the courts. The bike sheds are being turned into shelters, so Lord knows where the bikes will go. And you'll spot a bleeding great water tank parked slap bang in front of your rooms. That's there for fighting fires. As are the piles of sand. And if you're staying around, they'll doubtless want you to sign up as a fire warden.'

'I'll give it some thought.'

Scobie chuckled. 'Utter mayhem, sir. The bedders have been making blackouts and the staircase windows are being painted blue. That Hitler chap is a bad lot.'

'I'm not going to argue with you about that.'

'Anyway, good to have you back, as always. You may or may not be pleased to know that your gyp Bobby is still here, despite his attempt to join up. The recruiting office sent him away with a flea in his ear; said they wanted men, not creatures.'

'On the plus side, he wouldn't have made a very big target.' Wilde smiled as he thought of his college servant. Bobby had been a jockey, but a bad fall had ended his career and left him with a twisted spine.

'Indeed not, sir. And by the way, let me offer my congratulations to you on finding young Mr Marfield and bringing him home. We all thought he'd gone and got himself killed in that Spanish affair.'

'He's alive and kicking.'

'Well, thank the Lord for that! I'd give anything to hear the voice again . . .'

'There was one other matter, Scobie. You know I left a scribbled itinerary of our journey through France?'

'Of course, sir.'

'Did you have occasion to show it to anyone – or did anyone ask you or any of the other porters about my movements over there?'

'No, sir. I can say with certainty that no one has been looking for you.'

Lydia and Marfield arrived at Addenbrooke's Hospital mid-morning. As they walked through the Cambridge streets, her hand went to her belly, wondering whether it was her imagination that it seemed to be swelling. She thought back to Friday August 4th when she had woken in a cold sweat and realised that she couldn't go through with the next day's wedding.

It wasn't that she didn't love Tom – she felt more for Wilde than any man she had ever known – it was the thought that she wouldn't be being true to herself if she went through with it.

Mrs Wilde? It didn't sound right. Marriage to any man, promising to obey him, would be a betrayal of everything she had always believed in. Telling Tom had been the hardest part, of course.

In the event, he had shaken his head with a weighty sigh and had then broken out laughing. 'Lydia,' he had said, 'I would expect nothing less from you.'

'You're not angry?'

'No, I'm just surprised it took you so long to come to this decision. We set this date six weeks ago, we sent out two dozen invitations and organised a party and honeymoon, and you have to wait until the last minute to cancel it all?'

'Not *all*, Tom. We can still have the party, can't we?'

'Of course we can. But no speeches.'

'And the honeymoon?'

'And the honeymoon.'

Of course she had known that underneath it all he was angry. But surely some small part of him must agree with her that marriage was a hateful institution, devised by men to turn women into property? But what now? Her brain was fuzzy. With a baby, what would Tom want? If the world was unforgiving to women who, like her, 'lived in sin' then it was a thousand times more intolerant towards their illegitimate offspring. The very word they used – *bastard* – tainted a child for life. Whole tracts of 'good' society would be fenced off before the poor child was even born. Who had ever heard of an illegitimate Cabinet minister? Who among the great and the good would allow their son or daughter to marry a 'bastard'?

She wondered what she would have done if she had known she was pregnant. Gone through with the wedding ceremony, she supposed. Done the decent thing. Promised to obey him. Become the man's property, bundled up with his chattels.

Well, these decisions about marriage and babies would have to be put off until they couldn't be put off any longer. For the moment she had to apply herself to Marcus Marfield.

'How long have you and the professor been married?' he asked suddenly.

Lydia stopped, surprised. They had been walking along in silence for about ten minutes. To her left was the alley known as Petty Cury. Sandbags were piled outside the office where gas masks were distributed, next door to the post office. She was carrying her box and had lent one to Marfield. 'Did we say we were married?'

'Well, I sort of assumed. You know, given your sleeping arrangements.'

'Dangerous things, assumptions.' Lydia laughed lightly – and was pleased to see him grinning.

A little later, just before they reached Addenbrooke's, he continued the thread. 'Of course if you're not married . . .'

'Yes?'

'Well, it means there's still a chance for others.'

She laughed again, somewhat embarrassed. 'Let's just concentrate on fixing your left arm, shall we?'

After a short discussion at the main reception desk, Lydia deposited him with a doctor who had long experience of dressing bullet wounds in the last war, while she sought out Dr Eric Charlecote. She had met the psychiatrist at a dinner party the previous year and he had caught her imagination by telling her about his work with victims of shell shock.

*

The Master of the College, Sir Archibald Spencer, KC, poured Wilde a sherry. Wilde took it without demur and pretended to sip it.

'Your very good health, Wilde.'

'And yours, Sir Archibald.'

They were in the Master's vast study with windows to the west overlooking the old court and to the north overlooking the rather smaller master's court with its aged and very beautiful mulberry tree stranded in the middle of a small lawn. There was no doubt that Sir Archibald had the finest lodge and views in all Cambridge. But not today, disfigured by workmen digging trenches and shovelling sand into bags, then building them up as protective walls. It was the enormous water tank that looked most out of place, but one had to be prepared: fire was the worst of the threats.

'We're burying all the plate,' Sir Archibald said. 'Still not sure about the chapel glass. It's so fragile, we rather fear the workmen, however expert they are, will break it. As a Fellow, you have a say, of course, Wilde. What do you think?'

Whatever he said could be wrong. Damned if we remove the glass, damned if we don't. He went with his gut instinct. 'I don't think they're going to bomb Cambridge, Sir Archibald. Not the most industrial of English towns, is it? Apart from anything else we've got Duxford nearby with its Spitfires to protect us.'

The Master was a man of distinction and achievement. A rugby blue from his days as an undergraduate at Magdalene, he had carved out a fine career at the Bar, handling some of the highest profile cases in the early twentieth century with acuity and elegance. The Great War had brought a hiatus and he served at sea without seeing much action. After the war, he returned to the law and money. He eschewed the bench despite facing pressure to sit as a judge and, on hanging up his wig in his early fifties with a nice pile in his bank account, he was elected to parliament for a Hampshire seat, and served as a junior foreign office minister in the first year of Baldwin's government. The death of his wife had broken him and he resigned. It was said Baldwin wanted him to have a peerage, but he turned it down. A year later he was offered this mastership. Thus far he had proved immensely popular with the Fellows. 'So leave it in situ? If that's what you're saying, I think I agree with you.'

Wilde placed his sherry glass on the table and hoped his failure to drink it would not be noted.

'Anyway, Wilde, you'll be expected to do your bit. All the Fellows have been chipping in, boxing up books and so forth. And everyone will have to do their air-raid duty if they're to stay here for the duration. That'll include you.'

'Of course, Sir Archibald.'

The Master poured himself more sherry, ignoring Wilde's glass. He must have been a formidable prop in his rugby days and, later on, an imposing presence in the law courts. 'I thought we'd done with war for good. Not at all sure how many undergraduates will turn up for Michaelmas, but we're not counting on more than half of them. We've also lost six of the Fellows to uniform and I have it on authority that the science men will all be called off to various hush-hush installations. So my question to you is pretty obvious – what are *your* plans?'

What indeed? The question hadn't been far from his own mind these past few days. He wasn't British, but surely he could still join up and do his bit to fight the fascist crew? 'I'm still debating the matter, Master.'

'As I see it you have three choices. Scoot off to America, enlist in one of the forces here, or stay and teach – which I would consider war work. Education cannot be brought to a halt on the say-so of Herr Hitler.'

'Of course not.'

The older man threw back his second sherry. 'Anyway, this could all be neither here nor there. It's no great secret that various ministries are thinking of moving into the colleges. We could well be one of them. Trinity was turned into a hospital during the last big show, so who knows what will happen this time?'

'Do you need to know my plans today?'

'Good Lord, no, Wilde. Take as long as you like. This thing has hit us all for six. I don't want any of my men – or my boys for that matter – rushing into things. As for myself, it looks like quite a lot of my time will be taken up with Civil Defence for East Anglia.'

It seemed an opportune moment to bring up Marcus Marfield's return.

The Master's eyes widened. 'Well, now, that is good news. Very good news. He left just before my arrival but I believe he had a remarkable voice.'

'He's still got it, Master.'

'Has he indeed? Then he will be welcomed back with open arms. I assume he's given up on all that Bolshevik nonsense.'

Wilde wasn't at all sure he had, so he left the question hanging. 'I was hoping rooms might be found for him.'

'Of course. Easier than ever with numbers depleted. We'll arrange it today. Have you brought him with you?'

'He's having a once-over at Addenbrooke's. He didn't come out of Spain totally unscathed.'

'But he's alive. That's the important thing.' The Master's eyes strayed to Wilde's untouched sherry. 'Now then, Wilde, drink up. Have you been to see Horace Dill yet?'

'I was about to ask you how he was.'

'Go and see for yourself. He'll be thrilled to have a visitor.'

So the old don was still alive. When Wilde and Lydia had taken their leave before heading off to France, they had both thought that they would not see him again. It would be a pleasure to drop in on him. But first he had a couple of calls to make – one to see if Jim Vanderberg had heard any news and one to an acquaintance named Philip Eaton. There was a question to which only a member of MI6 might know the answer.

'I use hypnosis, Miss Morris. I don't like electric-shock treatment – and no one has time for psychoanalysis unless they are very rich. But hypnosis is the thing. Gets right to the heart of the problem very quickly. And I'm very good at it.'

Dr Eric Charlecote was not lacking in confidence and self-belief. A slight man with a rather aggressive moustache and a brusque manner, his movement was strange and awkward for such an energetic man. He had walked stiffly and slowly as he moved the few steps from his desk to greet his visitor, peering at her like a specimen through half-moon spectacles.

'So you will help?' Lydia asked.

'I will see what I can do. I'm sure my services will be called on a great deal in the near future, so it will be useful to me to brush up on the work. I like to think of it as healing men's souls. The War Office will see it as getting men back in the trenches.'

Charlecote had an office on the ground floor of Addenbrooke's, out of the way at the back of the building. Compared with the wards and clinical rooms, it was homely with a Persian carpet and a couch for his patients and a pleasing smell of rich pipe tobacco.

'As it happens, Miss Morris, I've got nothing on this morning. Where is the young man?'

'He's having a bullet wound looked at, here in the hospital.'

'Well, if you can guarantee he's not a neurotic, bring him along directly. Can't abide neurotics – particularly women of a certain age.'

Lydia didn't quite understand what he meant by that, but she didn't think Marcus Marfield was 'neurotic'. She thanked Charlecote, and was about to take her leave when she had another thought. 'There was one other thing, Dr Charlecote. I have been thinking for some time that I would like to train as a doctor, specifically a psychiatrist. Do you think that would be possible for someone my age – twenty-nine? Haven't left it too late, have I?'

The doctor ran a finger across the bristles above his top lip and raised a dubious eyebrow. 'Have you thought of nursing? There will be a great need for nurses in the war. Pretty faces and kind hearts – that's what our wounded boys will need. Along with clean wards, properly laundered sheets and square meals, of course.'

Lydia hoped she managed to keep her irritation concealed. 'I don't want to be a nurse – I want to be a doctor. I have great admiration for the psychiatric profession, Dr Charlecote.'

His expression fluttered between exasperation at her temerity and pleasure at her flattering words. 'Well, if you're sure, I would suggest the Maudsley is probably the place. Or you could of course study medicine here in Cambridge. Bit late for the coming year though. You know, Miss Morris, there aren't many women in our profession. The only name that springs to mind is Melanie Klein. Have you heard of her? I could call her and ask if she would talk to you, if you liked.'

Lydia smiled. 'That would be wonderful, Dr Charlecote. Thank you, so much.' She really wanted to ask a further question, but she knew what the answer would be. *Could I have a baby and train at the same time?* He would snort with derision and tell her not to be so damned ridiculous.

Charlecote clicked his fingers. 'Just like that, Miss Morris. I could hypnotise you just like that. No one better at it. Bring the boy along and I'll see what's to be done.'

Eaton's assistant Terence Carstairs answered the telephone.

'Mr Carstairs,' said Wilde, 'it's Thomas Wilde here, from Cambridge. I have been trying to call Mr Eaton at his home in Chelsea, but he doesn't reply. Could you get a message to him?'

'Ah, good day, Professor Wilde. One moment please.'

There was a click on the phone and silence. Half a minute later Carstairs came back on. 'Mr Eaton is here and will be happy to speak to you, sir.'

Another series of clicks and suddenly Eaton's voice was on the line.

'Wilde, it's good to hear your voice, old boy. How are you and the delightful Miss Morris?'

'We're well, thank you, Eaton. I take it you're back in harness.'

'Only just. Relying heavily on a stick and the supporting arm of Guy Rowlands, whom I sure you remember from around the time of my accident.'

Accident? They both knew that the hit-and-run that had resulted in Eaton's terrible injuries had been a deliberate attempt on his life; but nothing had ever been proved.

'Yes, of course I remember Rowlands.'

'He's a good man, had to deputise for me when I was convalescing, which doubled the poor chap's workload. Now he's got an invalid on his hands as well. Anyway, enough about me, how can I help you?'

'I wanted to ask you a question. Lydia and I have spent the past month in France, travelling around, staying with people. The thing is: someone found me – a stranger, who knew my name and quite a lot about me. What I wanted to know, Eaton, is how the devil he found me in a dusty, out-of-the-way village to the east of Toulouse?'

There were a few moments of silence at the other end of the line.

'Eaton? Are you there? I'm only asking because it seems the sort of thing you might know about.'

'Yes, I'm still here. Can you tell me a little more, Wilde?'

'He came to me with a remarkable tale. He said he knew the whereabouts of one of my students – a young man who took himself off to fight with the International Brigades in Spain – who was being held at one of the French internment camps, Le Vernet. I got him out, and I've brought him home. All well and good, you might think. But it's *my* involvement that worries me. How in God's name could anyone have known where Lydia and I were? I left a vague itinerary at the porters' lodge in case of emergencies, but other than that . . .'

'What is the young man's name, may I ask?'

'Marfield. Marcus Marfield. One of my history undergraduates and a choral scholar of some renown.'

'Ah . . .'

'Does the name mean something to you, Eaton?'

'Tell me a little more, Wilde. What condition is he in?'

'No, hang on, Eaton. I called *you* for information. If you've heard of Marfield, then I'd like to know what's going on.'

A pause. 'Look Wilde, I'm going to take you in to my confidence. I'm only doing this because I trust you. Marcus Marfield is one of mine. He was passing information to us from the front line in Spain.'

'You mean he was a spy?'

'Call it that if you wish. Unfortunately we lost contact with him over a year ago. We thought he was dead.'

CHAPTER 12

To Lydia's astonishment Marfield agreed to see Dr Charlecote. 'I thought I was going to have to drag you there.'

'No, I think it's a good idea. I don't like these sleepless nights. I don't like my dreams,' he said, 'but I do have one condition. You let me take you for a drink afterwards.'

'I thought you wanted to find some cricket to watch. And besides, I don't think you have any money.'

He grinned. 'Oh, you know, plenty of time for cricket. To be honest I'd rather look at you than a gang of sweaty men in whites.'

Lydia raised an eyebrow. This felt uncomfortable. 'If I wasn't old enough to be, well, your older sister, I could almost imagine you were making a pass at me, young man.'

'Would that be so bad?'

'It's bad form to make a pass at the lady friend of a man who has gone out of his way on your behalf.'

'Just a drink or two . . .'

A quick drink couldn't do any harm. Perhaps he might even loosen up and talk about his experiences in Spain. 'Very well, you spend two hours with Dr Charlecote and I'll spend half an hour in the pub with you. Will that do?'

'Half an hour it is.'

He was no longer wearing a sling, so clearly the doctors thought his wound was healing well. She pushed him along the corridor. 'Come on, you're turning into a seaside postcard.'

Wilde called in at his rooms. At the top of the stairway, he received a warm welcome home from Bobby. 'I trust you had a fine holiday, Professor. Sad you had to come back to all this.'

'Indeed, Bobby.'

'Coffee, strong and black, sir?'

'You read me like a book.'

Wilde had been unable to contact Jim Vanderberg: the US embassy couldn't or wouldn't offer a number for him in Glasgow and nor did Mrs Harley have his contact details.

There was news in the papers of the *Athenia*. Of the 1,418 passengers and crew listed, it was possible two hundred or more had died with many more injured. No definite figures as yet. Four ships were known to have helped rescue survivors: the destroyer HMS *Escort*, a Norwegian tanker the *Knute Nelson*, a Swedish yacht named *Southern Cross* and an American cargo ship *City of Flint*. Possibly other Royal Navy ships, too.

The big problem was that passengers had been taken on at three ports and many of them were last-minute bookings, so the Donaldson line was having trouble matching the different passenger lists with the names of those who were known to have died and survived. Most were still unaccounted for, so there was still hope for Jim's family.

Wilde sipped his coffee and sifted through his mail. To hell with it, he'd deal with all that later. First he would call in on his colleague and friend Horace Dill.

Trudging up the stairs to Dill's rooms, Wilde sniffed the air. It was strangely different. He knocked on the door and then pushed his way in. Horace was sitting there in his wing chair, reading a book.

'Good Lord, Horace, you're up!'

'Tom Wilde. Heaven be praised.' His voice was little more than a wheeze and as quiet as a whisper.

'Heaven? Has the Molotov–Ribbentrop pact driven you to religion?'

Dill tried to laugh but instead began coughing. He gripped his chest. 'Damn it, I can't bear this.'

Wilde sniffed again, then realised what was missing – the stench of Horace's cigars. 'You haven't been smoking.'

'Can't abide the taste or smell any more.' The words came out slowly and painfully. 'Perhaps I'll buy myself a few more days or hours, but God damn it, Tom, it feels strange not to be smoking. I'll never understand how an otherwise intelligent man like you has survived without tobacco all these years. Most odd.'

'We could argue about which one of us is the odder, Horace. But anyway, you've already beaten the bookies. They must have had you down for dead months ago.'

Dill managed a smile this time. 'Won't you sit down, Tom, spend half an hour with me? You mention the German–Soviet pact – well, I have to tell you I have done something I never thought I would do: torn up my CPGB card.'

Wilde cleared a mountain of books from Horace's sofa and perched in the corner. There would be other members of the Communist Party of Great Britain who would resign their membership, too. The Hitler–Stalin devil's pact was too much to stomach even for those who had remained loyal through the Soviet purges and show trials.

'Now tell me all about France. I can't talk much, but I like to listen.'

Wilde took a deep breath. There was a lot to talk about, including the war. But he went straight for the matter that interested him most: Marcus Marfield.

Horace Dill's rheumy eyes widened in surprise.

'Was he one of yours, Horace? I always rather assumed he must be, but I never felt very certain. Despite being his supervisor I'm not sure I knew the young man very well. Outwardly charming, but he certainly never struck me as political.'

'No,' Dill said. 'He wasn't mine. I know you were angry with me when he went, but I swear to you I had nothing to do with it. I was as surprised as you were.'

It had always been rumoured that Dill had sponsored students to go off and fight for the Republican side in the Spanish Civil War. 'So if not you, Horace – then who?'

'Just off his own bat, I suppose. I never saw him as political either. The lad had the romance of John Cornford, but I didn't see the idealism.'

Dill's voice was now so laboured it was almost inaudible. He started choking again.

'Whisky?'

Dill shook his head, which only made things worse.

'Water then?' This time Dill nodded, so Wilde poured him a glass from a jug.

'Have you spoken to Laker?' Dill said at last, when the coughing subsided.

'Not yet,' said Wilde. Timothy Laker was the Director of Music. He had probably known Marfield as well as anyone.

There was a discreet knock at the door. Wilde opened it to reveal a porter, not one he had seen before. There would be quite a few changes around the college as servants and undergraduates raced off to the recruiting offices. The porter tipped his hat respectfully.

'Professor Wilde, I was told you might be here. There's a visitor for you at the lodge. Lady named Mrs Marfield, sir.'

Well, well, so Marcus's mother had had a change of heart. That had to be progress, didn't it? Now, at last, they might get to the heart of the young man's problems. 'Bring her to my rooms if you would. I'll be there in a couple of minutes.'

Lydia waited patiently outside Dr Charlecote's office. Marfield had been booked in for a two-hour session. She wanted to see if it had been any help – and to find out whether more sessions were a possibility.

During her wait, she tried to chat with the rather severe secretary, Miss Hollick, but she made it clear she had work to do, and did not have time to engage in small talk. To make her point abundantly clear, she stood from her desk and handed Lydia a bundle of torn and dog-eared magazines, then returned to her chair without a word.

Finally the door opened and Marfield stepped out. The light behind him seemed to give his stubbly fair hair a sort of glow, almost like an aureole. He strode past Lydia and along the corridor without acknowledging her presence. She rose to her feet and found herself face to face with the psychiatrist. He was gripping the door handle, his knuckles white.

'Thank you so much, Dr Charlecote.'

He looked at her like a rabbit in the beam of a torch. 'Indeed.' He rubbed his moustache with brisk, tense strokes of his thumb and forefinger.

'Did it all go well? Might I have a quick word?'

Charlecote pulled back his narrow shoulders as though startled, then quickly held up his wrist and glanced at his watch. 'I've rather overrun. Call me in the morning about Dr Klein if you wish.'

'I was thinking more about Marcus Marfield,' she said. 'Can he be helped . . . his nightmares?'

'I can't say. Good day, Miss Morris.' Charlecote nodded brusquely, and was about to take a step back.'

'Wait, Dr Charlecote – what happened?'

She saw a flash of anger in his eyes. He seemed to be controlling himself with difficulty. 'Your young man has been playing with me, Miss Morris. I don't like to be played with.' He turned abruptly and slammed the door shut in her face.

There was a knock. 'Come in,' Wilde called.

The door opened and the new young porter entered, touching his hat. 'Mrs Marfield, professor.' He ushered his guest in and left her standing in the doorway, facing Wilde.

He had expected a woman of middle years; certainly in her forties, perhaps fifties. But this woman, attractive but not ostentatious, was in her early twenties. Her hair was dark and long and curled around her shoulders and she wore glasses, which gave her a slightly bluestocking air. He wasn't quite sure what to say. This *couldn't* be Marfield's mother.

'Professor Wilde?' she said at last, still not stepping inside.

'Yes. I'm so sorry. I was expecting someone else. Crossed wires, I imagine.'

'I'm Claire Marfield, Marcus's wife.'

'Marcus's *wife*?' His voice betrayed his incredulity.

'Don't be so shocked, Professor. People do have wives, you know.'

'I'm sorry. I just had no idea, that's all. Please,' he said, 'Do come in, Miss . . . Mrs Marfield.'

'Thank you.'

'Would you like some tea or coffee?'

She shook her head. She might have lacked confidence, but she didn't appear to be timid.

'I'm sorry,' he continued. 'I was expecting Marcus's mother. He never mentioned that he had a wife.'

'We married a week before he went to Spain, Professor Wilde.' She paused as if to summon courage. 'Is he really back home?'

'He is. We brought him from France at the weekend. But I'm afraid he's not here in college just at the moment. He should be along a little later, though, all being well.'

'Can I ask – where did you find him?'

'In an internment camp. It's all a little bit mysterious, to be honest . . .' The rest of the story could wait, Wilde decided. First he had a couple of questions of his own. 'What do you know of his time in Spain?'

'I haven't heard a word from him since he went.'

Wilde led her to the sofa. When he had settled her, he went to the door and called for his gyp. 'A pot of tea if you would, Bobby.'

'Tea for two? Coming up, Professor.'

Claire Marfield was sitting bolt upright, her hands knotted. He pulled up his desk chair and sat opposite her. 'Now, Mrs Marfield, you'd better tell me everything – then I'll fill you in on what I know.'

The woman looked down at her twisting hands. 'The thing is, I still love him, Professor Wilde.'

'Did he tell you he was going away?'

She nodded slowly. 'He said he had to. He was sorry, he said, but it was something he had to do. He wanted to marry me before he went, but then he said I should forget about him, because he probably wouldn't be coming back. When I heard nothing from him, I thought he must be dead.'

'Why do you think he wanted to marry if he intended to leave straight away?'

'Who knows with Marcus? He doesn't think like others.'

'But it was a cause he had to fight for, yes?'

'We never spoke politics. I didn't know he felt so strongly until he went.'

'How did you hear he had returned?'

Her glasses had slipped on her nose, and she pushed them up. 'One of the college servants called me. I had asked him to ring me if he ever heard any news. This was the first time he called.'

As his supervisor, Wilde had always found Marcus Marfield easy to teach and receptive to both advice and encouragement. But while everyone harboured secrets, even the most open of men and women, it was beginning to look as though Marcus Marfield had more secrets than most. He had become a married man at the age of what, nineteen or twenty? And within days of his wedding, he had gone off to join a left-wing army to fight against the fascist rebels in Spain. Not only that, but according to Philip Eaton, he had agreed to pass on information, which made him a spy.

'What matters is that you're here now. But I do have a bit of bad news for you. Marcus was wounded by a bullet in the arm. Nothing life-threatening, but he is presently at the hospital to see that it is healing properly, which is why he isn't here in college. The idea was to find him rooms here – but that was before we knew he was married . . .' Wilde tailed off. How should he prepare this young woman for the change in her husband? 'I think I should also tell you,' he began carefully, 'that he appears to have been rather disturbed by his experiences of war, which is no surprise, of course. Many men suffer nightmares and are haunted by their memories.'

Claire Marfield bent her head in acknowledgment. 'I understand that, Professor. But I'm not sure he will want to see me. He said he loved me and I believed him, but I have to accept that he loved the cause more.'

'Does he have your address?'

She nodded again. 'I haven't moved. I wanted to be there still if he returned.'

'If I may ask, Mrs Marfield, how have you been supporting yourself? Do you have work of some kind?'

'No, I don't have work. I was at Newnham, studying history until two years ago. In fact, I met Marcus at one of your lectures in November 1936. I had to leave college though. Fortunately I have a generous trust fund set up by my mother's father.'

'I see. Do you want to wait here for Marcus – or shall I ask him to come and visit you?'

She took a sudden sharp breath and for a moment Wilde wondered whether she might cry, but she didn't really seem the type. She was thinking, weighing something up.

There was a knock on the door and Bobby appeared with a pot of tea and two cups on a tray.

He placed them on the low table in front of the sofa. After Bobby had taken his leave, Wilde began to pour. 'I know you said you didn't want tea, but I certainly do. Can I persuade you to change your mind?'

'Yes, thank you, Professor.'

Wilde handed her a cup. 'This must be very difficult for you, and dreadful when he went away. No one deserves to be left in the lurch like that. At the very least he owes you the courtesy of an explanation. Look – I'll make sure he comes to see you, all right?'

'Thank you, Professor.' Claire Marfield put the cup down and turned to him. 'Please don't tell anyone else in the college about our marriage. He always told me how he trusted you, but he wouldn't want anyone else to know.'

'I can't promise that,' Wilde said. 'But the important thing is he's home – and I will certainly urge him to visit you.'

'He might not want to talk to me. But that's neither here nor there. What matters is that he meets his son.'

CHAPTER 13

Lydia searched the corridors of the hospital for Marcus Marfield but there was no sign of him. Nor could she see him outside on Trumpington Street. All she could think was that Charlecote's talking therapies or hypnosis had proved too intense and the young man had fled.

What had Charlecote meant when he said Marfield had been 'playing with him'? Had he not taken the session seriously? Charlecote had been absolutely furious – and she, too, felt angry. No one liked to be used or taken for a fool. Well – let Marfield do what he damn well pleased. She had better things to occupy her time than chase after him.

A wind whipped along the street and she wrapped her cardigan around herself as she walked northwards. There was a life growing inside her and she really didn't know how she felt about it. Motherhood had always seemed some distant possibility, but now – with the outbreak of war? Dear God: men, women and children – people they knew – had been thrown to their deaths in the icy waters of the Atlantic. And that was just the first day of the conflict. How much worse was to come?

In Bene't Street, she fished her keys from her bag and unlocked the door that led up to her first-floor office, the place where she compiled, edited and published books of poetry.

The room was cold. Unsold copies of books lined the shelves. A half-consumed bottle of beer – over a month old – stood on her desk. She slumped down in her chair. Everything seemed pretty hopeless now. And Tom would know soon enough, too. He wasn't stupid. He must have seen it all before when his wife Charlotte became pregnant; he would know the signs. She felt her options closing in.

Wilde had rather hoped Lydia would turn up at the college with Marfield: it would have been interesting to see his face when confronted with his secret wife. Before leaving, Claire had told him a little of the circumstances of their romance and marriage. At the time she thought he loved her, but in retrospect it now seemed that it had been her pregnancy that made him ask for her hand. 'But he didn't seem at all reluctant, Professor. I didn't force him into it.'

'What of his parents and yours?'

'I have never had a chance to get to know his parents properly. He said his father was angry with him. I imagine he told Marcus he was a fool, that it was all his own doing and that he could suffer the consequences. There would be no more money forthcoming. If he wanted to stay at Cambridge, he could live by his own means. That's the way these things usually go, isn't it?'

'But *you* had money?'

'Yes, and it would have been enough to keep him on at college and to bring up our son.'

Wilde had sipped his tea. 'What is the boy's name?'

'Walter Marcus.'

Things were beginning to come together. Perhaps it was the pregnancy and shotgun marriage that had caused the rift between Marcus and his parents. Had the shame been too much for them? For a father who worshipped his son such an episode might have seemed disappointing to say the least, but was it really enough to drive a man to suicide? Still, thought Wilde, who could ever tell the ways of the human heart?

The question that puzzled him was the timing: why wait until the day his son returned to England to kill himself? Had he somehow discovered that his son was back? There had to be some sort of connection between the events.

But there was something that didn't quite add up: why would any parent, however traditional, be ashamed of a respectable daughter-in-law like Claire Marfield? Even if the marriage was rushed and there was a child on the way?

After tea, and with no sign of either Marfield or Lydia, Claire had taken her leave of Wilde. She lived a little to the north of Cambridge, at Histon, and she gave him her address and telephone number. He promised he would talk to her young husband and gauge his reaction. One way or another, he would contact her.

At the main gate, he watched as she walked up Trumpington Street towards her bus, then turned and ambled back into the new court. As he did so, he saw the stick-thin figure of the choirmaster Timothy Laker walking towards the chapel, and followed him.

He caught up with him just as he was entering the ancient building and hailed him. 'Laker, a quick word if you will.'

Laker turned and smiled warmly. 'Oh hello, Wilde, good to see you back from your travels. We were all a bit concerned you might get caught behind enemy lines.'

Wilde laughed. 'We had to fight our way past Nazi tanks, all the while being strafed by dive bombers. It was hellish.'

'Worse than the hall dinners you steadfastly refuse to attend?'

'Well, no, not that bad. Why, Laker, have *you* started eating them?'

'You know me.'

Laker chain-smoked, but never appeared to eat. He couldn't weigh more than nine stone and would have made a whippet look fat. Horace had once whispered in Wilde's ear that Laker considered food a sin. 'More food for you then, Horace,' Wilde had retorted.

Laker removed the last half-inch of a cigarette from his mouth and ground it into the paving stone beneath his foot. 'How can I help?'

'Marcus Marfield.'

'Ah yes, I heard he was back with us. Marvellous news.'

'Is it?'

Laker looked slightly startled. 'You sound as though you have doubts, Wilde.'

'No, of course it's good news. But things seem to be getting rather complicated, that's all. Would you mind having a little chat with me about him? I think you must have known him better than any of us.'

'Always a pleasure to talk to you, Wilde. Here in the chapel suit you?'

He followed Laker into the splendid building. They walked towards the vestry where the cassocks and surplices hung, all bright red and white. Laker pulled out a small trestle table and a couple of heavy oak chairs with hard, straight backs.

'Your tipple's Scotch, isn't it, Wilde? All I can offer you is a sip of communion wine, I'm afraid. Pretty revolting stuff.'

'I'll happily pass on that.'

'Me too. God, this bloody war – you see all these beautiful surplices? I've been told they are to be intermitted for the duration – too bright apparently. Might attract enemy aircraft. I'm sure the Hun have nothing better to do than strafe choral scholars as they progress across the courts. Mind you, the way things are going, I fear we might not even get a choir together when Michaelmas term begins.'

'Oh you'll manage somehow. The boy choristers will be at school – and Marcus Marfield is back.'

'Yes, that *is* a bonus. He's got perfect pitch, you know. You say C, he'll sing it. You play C – or any other note – and he'll tell you what it is. Remarkable.'

'I think the voice is still there. He sang a little Brahms while we were staying in London on our return home.'

'Thank heavens for that.' Laker brightened. 'Now, what do you want from me?'

'His background. Everything.'

'Why do you want to know?'

'Curiosity. He seems somewhat troubled and I'd like to help him.'

'Well, he entered the King's School as a boy chorister when he was about eight or nine and ended up as head chorister, before going off to –' Laker paused ' – Uppingham or Oundle, I think. Then of course he came here as a choral scholar. That's about it to date, apart from his venture to Spain, of course.'

'Why didn't he go back to King's?'

'Are you suggesting we're somehow inferior to King's?'

Wilde laughed. 'Good Lord no! Now, I saw him as just another extremely bright undergraduate. Always produced his essays on time. Always attended lectures as far as I knew. But beyond that,

I knew nothing. Who did he consort with? What girlfriends did he have? Did he belong to any political societies? It occurred to me that he might have confided in you sometimes.'

Laker pulled out a packet of cigarettes. Wilde shook his head and Laker took one, lit it and drew deep. 'This is just between you and me, Wilde?'

'Of course.'

Laker hesitated, then shook his head. 'No, I really don't want to tell you this.'

'Come on, Laker. You know you can trust me.'

'Can I? Oh, very well. In fact he didn't confide in me, but another young man did. He – let's call him Smith – came to me in great distress because Marcus Marfield had been making approaches to him of a distinctly sexual nature, and the poor lad didn't know how to deal with it. He was utterly distraught because, despite his protestations that this wasn't welcome, Marfield wouldn't let it lie.'

Wilde wasn't surprised. Seeing him together in London with Mr Lincoln Tripp, the junior diplomat from the US embassy, he had wondered on which side of the bed Marfield took his pleasures. The appearance of a secret wife had not changed his thoughts on the subject. 'What happened?'

'Smith awoke one night to find Marfield climbing into bed with him. Smith tried to push him out, but Marfield was determined and there was a tussle. Smith just about managed to maintain his chastity, but he was deeply shocked by the events and confided in me.'

'You must have said something to Marfield?'

'I did, but Marfield brushed it all aside. He was a little drunk, he said, it was all a bit of a lark, no harm done. I'm afraid

I believed Smith's version, but I didn't take it any further. It seemed to me Smith needed to toughen up. If he goes into the forces, as they all probably will, he's going to come across plenty of uncomfortable situations, so he'll need to be able to look after himself.'

'And besides, Laker, you didn't want to lose your finest tenor?' Wilde couldn't resist the dig.

Laker blew out a ragged cloud of smoke and shrugged. 'There are always Smiths; a voice like Marfield's comes along only once in a lifetime.'

CHAPTER 14

Elina Kossoff drove her new red sports car at high speed along the road south, then turned off down a secluded farm track to the isolated farmhouse.

She parked the car and hammered at the door. There was no reply, but then she hadn't expected there to be anyone here. The door was unlocked and she pushed it open and stepped into the large kitchen. It needed some care, this place. It could be quite nice if anyone took a paintbrush to it, added some utensils and furniture that wasn't quite so basic. But that wasn't the point of the house, was it?

Climbing the stairs, she found what she was looking for in a small back bedroom, concealed beneath floorboards behind a plain old coffer. There was a kitbag of Great War vintage and a soft cloth wrapped into a weighty bundle and tied with string.

Her plan had been to leave them here a few more days, until they were absolutely necessary. Better that way, of course, but things had moved on; she needed them now.

She didn't open them, because she knew what was inside. Lifting the contents out carefully, she replaced the boards and slid the coffer back into place. With the bag and bundle safely deposited in her car, she drove back towards Cambridge, a great deal slower this time. She didn't want to be stopped for speeding. It wouldn't do for the police to examine the contents of these particular bags.

Lincoln Tripp was waiting for Jim Vanderberg at Glasgow Central Station. He immediately offered to carry his bags and escorted him through the concourse.

Preoccupied with thoughts of his family, of torpedoes exploding, steel ripping through steel, and the bottomless depths of the cold Atlantic, Vanderberg made desultory conversation. 'I was sure I'd beat you up here, Tripp. These British roads are not good.'

'It seems the railroad has its problems, too, sir.'

'It's usually a whole lot better than this. Any word from Jack Kennedy?'

'He'll be up in short order. We're staying just across the road at the Central Hotel. Not the best rooms, but all I could get. It was either that or accept an offer from the consul general for his spare room. I didn't think it sounded an appetising option.'

Vanderberg met Tripp's eye. 'What about—'

'No word yet, Mr Vanderberg. I'm sorry. But your boy Henry is here, among the first to arrive, and being well looked after. He's in hospital. Not sure he needs to be there any more, but it seemed like the best place in the circumstances.'

'I suppose he'll be asleep now?'

Tripp nodded. 'They don't encourage late visits. You know, sir, I hate to break it to you, but some of the news isn't at all good. Looks like more than twenty-five, perhaps thirty, Americans have lost their lives.'

'Along with many others.'

'Yes, sir.'

'OK, well let's get some food and whisky and make an early start in the morning. Do what we can for the survivors.'

Henry Vanderberg was eleven, the elder of Jim and Juliet's two sons. He was sitting up in bed reading a comic book when his father and Lincoln Tripp arrived in the ward at the Victoria Infirmary in the south-east of the city.

A young nurse in crisply starched uniform was at the bedside and she smiled a welcome as the visitors entered. 'Mr Vanderberg?' she said. 'Your son is doing very well. He is a brave boy.'

'Is he hurt?'

'A bang on the head leaving the lifeboat, nothing more. He was brought here to keep an eye on him, but everything seems fine.'

Vanberberg took his son in his arms. He couldn't hide the tears in his eyes. 'You look swell, Henry.'

'I'm OK, Pa.' The boy clung to his father as if he'd never let him go.

'There's no word on Ma and William yet. But the chances look good . . .' Jim detached himself and gazed at the boy. 'What's the damage?'

'Bumps, that's all.'

'Are you going to tell me exactly what happened, son?'

Henry had sandy hair, cut short, but his usual ready open smile wasn't there today. He was tall for his age, and strong. One of his teachers back in the States had said he had the eye and hands of a quarterback. Jim Vanderberg, who had never been sporty, had seized on this. What father wouldn't want their son to be a sports star?

'I don't know,' Henry said, twisting the sheet in his hands. He looked up at his father. 'It was kind of confusing. We were in our cabin below decks. It was, you know, crowded, and we had to share with this old lady, Mrs Ballantyne, and her maid, Emmy. I asked Ma if I could go up on deck for a while to watch the sun go down before dinner, and she said I could. I saw this line of bubbles in the sea, Pa, like soda water. Just bubbling through the water like a white streak, coming directly at us. I didn't know what it was. I thought it might be a whale. But then it hit us with an almighty great bang and I was thrown from my feet. I guess it was a torpedo.'

Jim put his hand on the boy's shoulder. 'Can you remember what happened then?' he asked gently.

'When I got up, I saw black smoke at the back of the ship, and in the last of the sunlight I thought I saw a submarine break the surface not far away, maybe a couple of hundred yards. I wanted to get back down to the cabin to Ma and Willie, but all the lights had gone inside the ship and I got lost. Then the lights came back on, but I still didn't know where I was. A sailor grabbed me and told me to get out on deck, to the lifeboats. I told him I needed to find my mother and brother, but he said they'd be all right. Everyone was going to get off. I struggled with him, but he put me under his arm and hauled me out on deck to the lifeboat. Pa, there were people there who had fallen down. I didn't know whether they were dead or alive. I couldn't do anything. I couldn't help Ma and Willie.'

The boy was fighting back tears. Vanderberg put his arm around him again, and the boy buried his head in his father's neck, overcome with hot angry sobs.

'I know, son. I know you would have walked through fire to help your ma and brother. I know that, son.'

At last the boy won the battle against his tears and furiously wiped them from his face with his pyjama sleeve. 'Someone put a lifejacket on me and tied it tight, then a lady put a fur coat around my shoulders. After that, I don't remember. Next thing I know we were at sea in a boat, all crowded in together, looking back at the ship. At first it didn't seem to be sinking, but it began slowly going down at the rear.' He shuddered.

'How long were you in the lifeboat, Henry?'

He shrugged. 'All night. It was really cold and I couldn't sleep and it seemed like forever. I gave the fur coat to an old man who looked like he was about to die, then he passed it on to someone else.'

'You must have seen people in other boats.'

'I kept looking for Ma and Willie, and calling for them, but I didn't see them, nor hear them. There were a lot of lifeboats out there and it soon got dark. The sea roughened up and the wind was blowing up too. I thought we'd get turned over. The sun was just rising when the warship came and picked us up. She was called the *Electra*. HMS *Electra* – that stands for His Majesty's Ship, Pa – did you know that? They put me in one of the sailors' hammocks and I fell asleep. That's all I know. Here I am. It's Scotland, right, Pa?'

Vanderberg secured Henry's discharge and, together with Tripp, they toured the hospitals and the hotels seeking out American survivors to see how they could be helped. He had spoken to the ambassador and had been reassured that all survivors would be offered alternative transport home and that they would be cared for.

None of the surviving passengers Vanderberg spoke to knew anything of Juliet and William. No one even recalled seeing anyone of their description. They all expressed their gratitude to the crews of the *Athenia* and the rescue ships, but there was deep anger and resentment towards the Germans for attacking a civilian liner. And they were fearful of being put on another ship home unless it had a sizeable escort of American warships.

Many passengers had still not arrived in Glasgow, but Vanderberg was beginning to lose hope. He couldn't let Henry know that. His mind stretched back across the years to the day he met Juliet at a dinner party in Chicago. It was apparent to both of them that they had been fixed up by their friends, and as it turned out, their friends had been excellent matchmakers. Juliet came from a well-to-do middle-class family. Her father was an attorney-at-law and her mother the daughter of a judge.

Juliet had had every advantage. Private school, tennis lessons, a pony and holidays in Europe. The one thing she lacked was a pretty face. But she had a great smile and a dirty laugh. Anyway, Jim Vanderberg knew he wasn't much in the looks department.

Some might call them a quirky twosome, and to be honest they probably were. Even before the boys were born, she didn't have a movie star figure, but in his eyes she was gorgeous and he longed to get her into bed. That had had to wait until the wedding night, however; nothing modern about Miss Juliet Bader. Not that she was prim – her humour was too rough-edged for anyone to think that of her – but she had made a promise to her mother and to herself that she would wait. And if a man wanted her enough, he would have to wait, too. Well, Jim Vanderberg thought, she had been well worth the waiting. And they had a lifetime of loving ahead of them.

Please, God.

By mid-morning it was clear Henry was flagging, so Vanderberg took him back to the hotel for bacon and eggs in the lounge. While the boy was feasting himself, Vanderberg and Tripp ordered coffee.

'It doesn't make sense, boss, you know that.'

'Torpedoing innocent civilians? It sure doesn't make sense.'

'I mean it doesn't make sense the Germans doing it. Why would they attack a ship with Americans aboard? The Nazis might take a hard line, but are they really that dumb? Goddammit, sir, the sinking of the *Lusitania* in the last war didn't help the German cause any.'

'What are you trying to say, Tripp?'

'I'm saying, sir, that maybe it wasn't a German U-boat that sank the *Athenia*. Maybe someone put a bomb on board. Or a mine – maybe it hit a British mine. That's what the Germans are saying.'

'Why would the British place a mine two hundred miles out in the Atlantic? Anyway, Tripp, you heard Henry. He saw the torpedo – and he saw the sub.'

'OK then, not a bomb or mine, a torpedo. But maybe the sub that fired it wasn't German. Who stands to gain from sinking the *Athenia*, sir? That's what we should be asking ourselves.'

Lydia called Addenbrooke's. She needed to know what had happened to Marfield during his session with Dr Charlecote. The main switchboard put her through to the psychiatrist's secretary.

'Can I speak to the doctor, please?'

A slight pause on the other end of the line, then Miss Hollick's crisp voice. 'Are you one of his patients, madam?'

'I'm a friend.'

Another pause. 'It's Miss Morris, isn't it? The lady who brought that young man in yesterday.'

'Yes. I want to talk to the doctor,' Lydia said, failing to contain her irritability.

'Does that mean you haven't heard, madam?'

'Heard what?'

'Dr Charlecote's body was found early this morning up on the Gogs.' Miss Hollick sounded close to tears. 'The police say he shot himself.'

Wilde removed the tarpaulin cover from the Rudge Special, checked the oil and gave the chrome a quick polish with his sleeve, before riding her to college. It was a 500cc racer that could do a hundred miles per hour if pushed, but this was one of his more sedate trips.

He parked at the gate and wandered into the porters' lodge and sought out Scobie.

'Did Marfield arrive yesterday evening?'

'Indeed he did, sir, and I showed him to his new rooms myself. He's on your staircase for the time being – Dr Birbach's old set.'

'Ah.' Wilde wasn't sure what difference it made, but he somehow felt uncomfortable at the thought of Marfield being quite so close to him. And poor Birbach's rooms? He doubted Marfield was superstitious. If he was haunted, it would be by what he had seen in Spain, not by the ghost of a deceased German scientist.

'The young gentleman went out not more than five minutes ago. You might have passed him.'

'Do you know which way he was headed?'

'Northwards, towards the Senate House.'

'You know, I think I might go after him.' Neither he nor Lydia had seen Marfield after the appointment at Addenbrooke's yesterday. 'Look out for my motorbike, would you.'

'Of course, sir.'

Earlier, he had told Lydia about Claire Marfield. She was as surprised as Wilde to discover Marcus was married. She had been less surprised to hear what Timothy Laker, the Director of Music, had revealed about him.

What most interested them both now was what had gone on in the psychiatrist's room. 'The rules of privacy relate to the couch, just as much as the confessional,' Wilde had said. 'We have no right to pester him. Whatever mess he has made of his life is his own responsibility.' But that didn't mean they weren't curious – particularly in Marfield's marriage and the birth of his child. He must have realised the child had been born – it was odd that he never seemed to have shown the slightest interest in his offspring.

Hurrying along Trumpington Street, Wilde was sure he spotted Marfield a couple of hundred yards ahead, turning right into Saint Mary's Passage towards the market place. He followed, keeping his distance, interested to discover where he was going.

Ahead of him, Marfield stopped outside the Samovar tea shop on the far side of the square, to the right of the Guildhall close to the corner of Petty Cury. It looked warm and inviting with bicycles parked outside. Marfield looked around, then ducked in through the low doorway.

Wilde waited a couple of minutes, then approached on the far side of the road, casually glancing in through the front window. There were a dozen tables, half of them occupied. Marfield was sitting with a fair-haired woman and they were talking. She had her back to him, but Wilde recognised her. He walked on, and waited, then walked back past the window. Marfield and the woman had disappeared.

Lydia put the phone down, desperate to find Wilde. What on earth had happened to make Dr Eric Charlecote commit suicide? Surely it could have had nothing to do with his hypnosis session with Marcus Marfield? She shook herself: *Get a grip on yourself, woman.*

She and Tom had slept together last night in her bed in her house. At last, it felt like home again. His lovemaking was beautiful and tender. Had he guessed? Surely not. Not yet.

She walked into town. A constable on his beat stopped her. 'Where's your gas mask, miss?'

'I'm just off to the distribution centre to collect a new one,' she lied.

'What happened to the other one?'

'We've just been to France on holiday, and of course we took them. Somehow mine got mislaid in the rush to get home.'

He looked at her with a disbelieving eye. 'Well, all right then. But go straight there. I don't want to see you without one again.'

She thanked him and carried on her way to the college. Wilde wasn't there, but she left a message for him in the porters' lodge. '*Something awful has happened, Tom. Dr Charlecote has died. I'm going to my office. Join me there. Please. We need to talk.*'

After fifteen minutes, Marfield appeared at the Samovar door. He looked both ways again and Wilde shrank back into a shoe shop doorway to avoid being seen. He watched as Marfield disappeared across the market square back in the general direction of Great St Mary's. When he was no longer in sight, Wilde entered the tea shop. He glanced around as though looking for a seat, then plumped himself down opposite the young fair-haired woman. 'Mind if I sit here? Is it taken.'

The woman was sipping her coffee. She looked up and smiled in recognition. 'Professor Wilde!'

'Hello, Miss Kossoff.' He had been right: it was her.

'Miss Kossoff? What is this? Am I no longer Elina to you?'

'How are you?'

'I am well, but business is not so good. Who wants to sit reading the paper with tea or coffee when there is a war to be fought?'

'Oh, I'm sure you'll be as busy as ever. Of course you will – you have the best coffee in Cambridge.'

'It won't be easy to come by if British ships continue to be sunk.'

Wilde had ventured to this cafe and tea shop almost every week since he arrived in Cambridge. With other places, you never knew what you were getting. But here you had a fine choice of superb coffees from around the world – Kenya, Java, Jamaica and several others. They had a remarkable selection of teas, too, not that it was usually Wilde's first choice of beverage. The Samovar was run by Elina and her parents, but it was Elina whose company he enjoyed most. It wasn't flirting exactly but there was certainly a spark of warmth between them.

Elina clicked her fingers and the waitress approached. 'Fetch Mr Wilde whatever he wants – on the house.'

'No, no, I'll pay.'

'Nonsense. But tell me, how was France?'

'Very pleasant – and I couldn't help noticing that you have been consorting with the souvenir we brought back.'

'You mean Marcus?'

'I didn't know you were friends.'

Her eyes creased into a smile full of mischief. 'Well, Professor, there are many things you don't know about me, and I think I shall keep it that way.'

'I'm serious. I'm worried about him, Elina. You know he's been off to that bloody war in Spain? Well, I think he's brought back a bad case of shell shock, or whatever they call it these days.'

'So you are not here by chance? You are spying on him!' She laughed. 'Well, if you want to know what he talked about with me, it was the war. This war, not the Spanish one. He said he was planning to join up and do his bit for King and country. I think he wanted to show off and hopefully get a bit of, you know, sympathy. No chance though, Mr Wilde, even for one as pretty as Marcus. I'm not that kind of girl.'

Really? Wilde had always surmised that she was exactly that sort of girl.

The waitress arrived with his coffee and Elina Kossoff rose from her seat. She leant over and kissed Wilde's cheek. 'Enjoy your coffee, professor. I'm afraid I have to dash.' And she was out the door and gone.

CHAPTER 15

Wilde found Lydia in her office. She almost ran to the door to greet him and he took her in his arms. This wasn't like her. One moment she was tired out, the next minute emotional. What was going on? Before he could tell her about Elina Kossoff, she was blurting out what she knew about Dr Charlecote.

'Wait,' Wilde said. 'Slow down.'

'He's shot himself.'

'My God! Who told you this?'

'His secretary at Addenbrooke's. She's in an awful state. I had called to speak to him . . . oh, Tom, this is dreadful. Everything's disintegrating.'

'Did you talk to her?'

She shook her head. 'I don't think she knew much. But there was one other thing – she said he did it up on the Gogs and that's where they found the body. Can you imagine that, Tom?'

Wilde brushed the tears from her cheek. He had never met Eric Charlecote, but he knew of his reputation and couldn't imagine what might have driven such a distinguished man to such a desperate act.

Was there something more to it? He thought of Colonel Marfield. Two men had shot themselves in the space of two days. No connection between them, save that they both knew Marcus Marfield. Coincidence, surely.

'I'm sorry, Lydia. Perhaps it's the war. A lot of people can't cope. Perhaps memories of the last one flooded back.'

'I hate it, Tom. I hate war. I hate what it's done to Marcus Marfield and what it will do to thousands of other young men.'

'Dr Charlecote might have had just those thoughts.'

'But he was a psychiatrist! He specialised in trauma! Why did he do it? Someone must know. We have friends at Addenbrooke's.'

Wilde, too, would like to know what had happened. 'I'll talk to Rupert Weir. I think suicides require a post-mortem so he'll have been notified by now. Meanwhile, why don't you visit Charlecote's secretary – see if she knows any more?'

Wilde called Adenbrooke's and was told Dr Weir was on the new golf course at Girton. He wasn't expected in today but he was on call via the clubhouse.

Collecting the Rudge from college, Wilde rode out there and found Weir on the eighteenth hole, just about to take his tee shot. Wilde hung back, out of sight, until Weir and his two partners had made their shots, then approached them. The doctor's broad face broke into a smile of pleasure on seeing Wilde.

'Tom, you're home!'

'Glad to be back.' Wilde shook his hand and then apologised to the other two men for interrupting their game. They didn't seem perturbed.

Weir, as always, stood out. He was wearing tweeds with waistcoat and a knitted tie and he dwarfed his two companions, both in height and girth. 'Walk with us, Tom,' he said. 'Good to see you – how are you finding unmarried life?'

'Much the same as before.'

Weir turned to his companions. 'This man was supposed to be getting married a month ago, but he was stood up by the girl – and then he went on honeymoon with her anyway. Some old farts might think it scandalous and purse their lips disapprovingly, but I call that style.'

'You are so understanding, Rupert.'

'Well, of course, I know the girl, don't I? You were quite right not to let her get away so easily. And your failure to marry, well I suppose that is in the revolutionary tradition of Engels and Mary Burns. Bit of a bohemian and a socialist, your beautiful girl . . .'

'You have her summed up perfectly, but I don't see myself as an Engels.'

'No, nor me. Anyway, Tom, why are you here? Not taking up golf, are you?'

'Not old enough yet. You have to be eighty, I believe. No, there's something I want to talk to you about. Play this hole and I'll buy you a drink.'

In the bar, they ordered coffee with whisky chasers and sat at a distance from Weir's golfing friends. Weir did not seem his usual ebullient self. 'I have to say, Tom, this day did not begin well. A friend of mine died this morning.'

'You're not by any chance talking about Dr Charlecote are you, Rupert?'

'You've heard, eh? Ah, God, what an awful bloody waste. I got a call at home from the police a couple of hours ago. It shocked me to the core, Tom.'

'I'm sorry.'

'To tell the truth, I still don't believe it. Never thought of Eric as the sort of man to top himself. Still don't.'

Weir was both a GP and police surgeon, the man called on by the constabulary for any number of reasons, from judging the intoxication of a drunk driver to examining corpses in the case of sudden or unexplained deaths.

'Will you be performing a post-mortem?'

'No, not me. I can't do it with friends. Played too many rounds with Eric, had too many fine drinks and dinners with him. When I look at a corpse on the slab, it's a cold, inanimate object, a matter of pure science. Someone else will have to do it. Anyway, Tom, what's your interest? I take it he was a friend of yours, too.'

'Lydia knew him vaguely, but I never met the fellow. I am interested in the manner and timing of his death, however. There is something strange about it all.'

'Something you have taken it upon yourself to investigate? Have you ever thought of quitting academia and joining the CID?'

Wilde told him of Lydia's visit to Charlecote and of Marcus Marfield and his nightmares. 'Lydia said the doctor had changed when she saw him after the session. Probably means nothing, but I hate coincidence or anything left unexplained. Anyway, that's why I'm here. All slightly tenuous, I realise.'

'Perhaps not, Tom.'

'What do you mean?'

'Well, actually, I have my own doubts about the death of poor Eric. You know he was found up on Little Trees Hill?'

'Yes, I heard it was the Gogs. I didn't know which hill precisely.'

'Wonderful place, beautiful views over Cambridge. Perfect for walking dogs.'

'And birdwatching.' Wilde had seen a meadow pipit up there earlier in the summer before their trip to France.

'I've spoken to the desk sergeant from St Andrew's Street,' Weir continued. 'He told me a service revolver was found at Eric's side, one bullet fired into the temple. Burn marks suggest close range. The sergeant assured me that it's quite commonplace to see a rise in the number of suicides at a time of great crisis in national affairs, but I already knew that. So everything would naturally point to a self-inflicted death.' He shrugged. 'Case closed, eh?'

'But you don't think so?'

'No, I don't. He had been through a lot, but everything I know about him tells me he wouldn't have done it. Not Eric. And there was something else . . .'

'Tell me.'

'It's a matter of practicalities. How did Eric get there? He lived at Great Shelford. And that's a couple of miles from Little Trees.'

Wilde knew Great Shelford. 'That's no distance, Rupert. Surely no more than half an hour's walk. Perhaps he was building up his courage as he strode alone late at night. Perhaps the hill had some significance for him.'

'Maybe it did. And yes, Great Shelford to Little Trees Hill would be a short walk for you and me. But not for Eric. He had severe arthritis in his hips. He couldn't play golf any more and had to drive everywhere. To get there by foot would have taken hours and every step would have been sheer bloody agony.'

'But you say he could drive still?'

'Yes. But he didn't on this occasion. I asked the sergeant and he said there was no sign of a car at the hill, and Eric's own car was still at home. So how in God's name did he get there, Tom?'

Miss Hollick had been crying. Her cheeks were streaked and her eye make-up had run. She no longer looked like a ferocious gatekeeper, merely a distraught human being. Lydia put an arm around her and tried to comfort her.

'Don't you think you should go home, Miss Hollick? No one would expect you to work after this.'

'I have to call all his patients,' she said. 'Someone has to be here to sort everything out.'

'Of course, but I'm sure someone else could take over. The switchboard, perhaps? Look, why don't I see if I can fetch you a cup of tea?'

'That's very kind of you, but I won't. Oh dear, I'm not coping well.'

'I met Dr Charlecote once before, at a party. He seemed a very charming man.' Far more charming than he had appeared yesterday, she mused.

'He was.'

'But I suppose he must have been very unhappy.'

'Well, his wife died last year, but I really don't think that was it. And he had suffered a lot of pain with his arthritis, but he never gave me the impression of being a man who would give up on life. The thing is, we never know what's in another person's heart, do we?'

'That's very true.'

'You know, Miss Morris, the young man you brought yesterday morning was the last patient he ever saw. People came to him with a multitude of problems, many of them extremely distressing, and I always knew when one had affected him deeply. There was a woman in the summer who couldn't get over the death of her twins in a car crash. Dr Charlecote was terribly upset by her story.'

'Could something like that have driven him to despair this time?'

'That's what I'm wondering. I had certainly never seen him the way he was after meeting your Mr Marfield. What was strange was that Eric – Dr Charlecote – wasn't so much upset, as angry. I couldn't understand it. He could be tetchy, particularly with people he considered time-wasters and hypochondriacs, but I had never seen him in such a blinding rage before. He barely spoke to me before he went home.'

'What time was that?'

'About two o'clock. He locked himself in his consulting room after the visit from your friend, then left abruptly.'

'Would he have taken notes during his last session?'

'He always took notes. He was meticulous. But they are private. I couldn't allow anyone to see them.'

'Do you think in this case we might make an exception?'

Miss Hollick's mouth stiffened. 'No, Miss Morris, I do not. Dr Charlecote would have been appalled at the very idea.'

Wilde arrived back at college, crossed the disfigured courts, and climbed the staircase to his rooms. Halfway up he was accosted by Bobby.

'You have a visitor, Professor. Young Mr Marfield.'

'Really?'

'He just barged straight past me. I'm sorry, sir, I didn't know what to do.'

'That's all right, Bobby, I wanted to talk to him.' But, of course, it wasn't all right. There were one or two friends, among them Lydia and his old chum Geoff Lancing, who had the run of his set, but certainly not Marcus Marfield.

He pushed open the door and stepped inside. Marfield was standing looking at the one picture to grace the walls. A painting by Winslow Homer of a boy looking out across a prairie.

'What do you think?'

'It's wonderful, Professor. Superb.'

'My father left it to me. Whenever I look at it, it makes me want to go home.'

'My father wouldn't leave me anything.'

It was the moment Wilde had been putting off. 'Look – I have some bad news. Your father's dead, I'm afraid.'

Marfield turned around, as though bitten. His hands were in his pockets, his injured left arm minus sling and clearly functional again. 'What?'

'I'm sorry.'

'No, that's nonsense. It can't be true.'

'I spoke to your mother on the telephone. I hate to be the person to break it to you.' Wilde moved forward and took Marfield gently by his right arm. 'Come on, sit down. We really need to talk about a few things.'

'I'd rather stand, I think.'

'And I'd rather we didn't, and as these are my rooms, I think you should accede to my wishes. Yes?'

Marfield shrugged. 'If you insist.'

Wilde took the desk chair while Marfield removed his hands from his pockets and placed himself rather stiffly on the sofa. He sat there with rigid shoulders like a tailor's dummy, his back hardly touching the cushions.

'My father . . .'

There was no point in dissembling. 'It seems he took his own life.'

'My God, I had no idea. I thought the bastard would live forever.'

'Well, you've been away a long time.' Wilde studied the young man closely. He had definitely been shocked to hear of his father's demise; now he was feigning indifference. 'Were you close?'

'Oh, once upon a time, but then . . . well, things went awry.' He let out a deep sigh. 'What of my mother?'

'She is deeply affected. I'm afraid she seems to hold you accountable in some way and she's not in a very forgiving mood. This is only supposition on my part,' he added hastily.

Marfield looked askance at Wilde. 'So she doesn't want to talk to me?' he said eventually.

'No, but I think Claire does.'

'Claire?'

'Your wife.'

'Ah, so you know about her, do you? How did that come about?' Marfield spoke as casually as if he were asking about the cricket score.

'She came here yesterday. She thought you might like to meet your son. His name is Walter Marcus.'

Marfield looked away, towards the Winslow Homer painting.

'She's not expecting anything of you.'

He turned back and his eyes met Wilde's. 'You are a sentimental man, Professor. You want to get lovers together, put the world to rights and give everyone a happy ending, just like the flicks.'

'And you aren't sentimental?' Wilde demanded, suddenly angry. 'You go off to fight for a foreign cause like some latter-day Byron and you say there's no romance in your soul? That doesn't add up.'

Marfield laughed, but Wilde didn't.

'Misplaced romance, I'd suggest,' Wilde continued. 'Forgive me for being judgmental, but I really think you should have stayed with your wife while she brought your son into the world.'

'I hadn't thought you quite so bourgeois, Professor.'

'God damn it, Marfield, don't spout your bloody agitprop slogans at me! As it happens, she isn't expecting anything of you, but that doesn't mean you don't owe her anything.'

'Oh, you're right, of course. The rational college Fellow speaks. But I can't go to her, you see. It would be too dangerous. And she should never have come here. But she always was a damned idiot.'

'What are you talking about?'

'I mean that if they knew about her and my child, they would get to me through them. Isn't that obvious? I'm trying to keep her and the boy safe, for pity's sake. That's why I'm not making contact.'

'*They?* Who exactly are you talking about?'

'My enemies. I think we've been through this already, but you don't take me seriously. It still hasn't occurred to you that you and Miss Morris are in danger merely for being associated with me. You don't know these people.'

'Do you have secrets?'

'I *know* secrets. And if you need proof that I am in danger, remember the sniper's bullet at Le Vernet. Remember the woman with the pistol in Chelsea? I know when I'm being followed, Professor. War sharpens the senses. I knew I was being followed today, all the way to the cafe. Did you think you weren't seen?'

Wilde had thought just that, of course. He clearly wasn't as skilful as he had imagined. 'I wanted to chat with you, that's all. Nothing sinister. But when I saw you with the girl in the tea shop I didn't want to intrude.'

'Very thoughtful of you, Professor.'

'She's a pretty girl, Elina.'

'Is she? I hadn't noticed.'

'Not sure I believe that.'

'If you must know, she's an old girlfriend from times gone by. Even before Claire. No, that's not true, they coincided.'

'She's a few years older than you isn't she?'

'Is there a problem with that? Look, the truth is that when Claire got pregnant, I had to end it with Elina. When I saw her this morning I just ducked in to say hello, hoping there were no hard feelings.'

It was a plausible enough explanation. But more answers were needed. Wilde went straight in. 'Yesterday you spent two hours with Dr Eric Charlecote. How did that go?'

'The bloody hypnotist? What of him?'

'I was wondering whether he helped you at all. Perhaps you managed to sleep better last night. No nightmares . . .'

'Oh they're still there. Damned quack.' Marfield made a dismissive gesture.

'He thought you were playing him along.'

Marfield shrugged.

Wilde waited, his eyes on his guest's averted face. At last he spoke, softly, little more than a whisper. 'What did you do last night, Marfield? Where were you?'

The young man's eyebrow creased as though bewildered by the question. 'I had some supper from the Buttery, I read, I went to bed. Why? Is this an interrogation?'

'I feel responsible for you – you disappeared on my watch.'

'Well I'm a big boy now, battle hardened, so you don't need to worry about me any more. Anyway, I'm not worth it. I'm bad news.'

'It's not that simple though. You see, I know things about you.' Wilde was about to tell him that they had an acquaintance in common, Philip Eaton, but at the last moment he held back. Not now, not yet.

'Really? What do you think you know?'

'I think you may not be as charming as you seem.'

'Who is, for God's sake?'

'And I wanted to tell you something. A little item of news you probably haven't heard. Dr Charlecote is dead.'

Marfield nodded. 'I know. That's why I came up here to see you.'

Wilde decided it was time to get the whisky bottle. He poured them both a healthy shot, then sat down again.

'You'd better explain.'

'They must have killed him. He was a hypnotist – should have been on the bloody stage doing tricks. But they must have thought I told him things in a trance.'

'Is that what you thought? Is that why you were angry?'

'I didn't want to be bloody hypnotised! I was inveigled into going to the man against my better judgement. But I couldn't have told him anything, because there was nothing to tell. That's probably what made *him* so angry. He probably wanted gory details. All the blood and guts and severed limbs I had seen, all the stuff that shatters men's nerves. I wasn't at Guernica, but I was at plenty of other places where the bombs tore people apart. Not sure exactly what I told him, but it clearly wasn't enough for his morbid tastes.'

This didn't make sense. 'Look – whatever you did or did not tell Dr Charlecote, how on earth could your "enemies" have even known about your session?'

'They know everything.' Marfield spoke sullenly.

'That's it? That's your answer?' This really was beginning to sound like full-blown paranoia. Except there had been a woman with a pistol in London, and Dr Charlecote was dead, in circumstances his friend Rupert Weir considered suspicious.

Marfield shrugged again.

'And you still haven't explained how you found out Dr Charlecote was dead.'

'I called Addenbrooke's first thing this morning. I wanted to say sorry, you see. It wasn't Charlecote's fault he was so useless, and so I thought he deserved an apology. The man on the switchboard told me what had happened. He intimated it was suicide, but I didn't believe that for a second. That's why I'm so scared, Professor. Cambridge isn't safe.'

CHAPTER 16

Wilde stood up. 'I'm taking you to the police. If you're in danger, they'll protect you.'

'No,' Marfield said. 'Not the police.'

Wilde had had enough. 'Then look after yourself! You seem to have managed that quite adequately during two years of one the bloodiest wars known to mankind. As you say, you're battle hardened. So the choice is yours. But I will be talking to the Master and Fellows about your marriage and we will be discussing whether you are a suitable person to be continuing your studies. Sir Archibald will certainly have second thoughts about allowing you the use of rooms in college, and I don't think I'll be disagreeing with him. Now if you'll excuse me, I have things to get on with.'

Wilde was a strong man, an amateur boxer, and he hustled Marfield from the room without difficulty. Closing the door after him, he sank into his sofa and put his feet up for a few moments. But then he had a sudden thought; another word with Timothy Laker might be in order.

Laker was listening to Debussy on the gramophone. A coal fire was burning in the hearth, despite the warmth of late summer. It was a well-presented room, with an expensive baby-grand piano and some very modern paintings on the walls. As always, the choirmaster was welcoming. He leapt to his feet and turned down the volume.

'Cold, Laker?'

'A fire cheers the soul, Wilde.' Laker ushered him in. 'If you've come in search of whisky, you're out of luck. All I can offer is tea.'

'No, I've come in search of a name. Actually, I've come to suggest a name. The lad who complained about Marcus Marfield – would I be correct in thinking that was Gus Percheron? I think he read modern languages.'

Laker laughed. 'The detective at work! What makes you think it was Percheron?'

'Because they were on the same stairs and they had been to the same school. I suspect this is a complaint that had a bit of history to it.'

'Wilde, you know the complaint was made in confidence. I can't possibly confirm your suggestion . . .'

'But you're not going to deny it either, are you?'

Laker shrugged. 'Just don't implicate me, all right?'

Wilde went up to his own rooms and called through to the porters' lodge. A couple of minutes later, they came up with a telephone number and London address for the Percherons. Wilde immediately called, but the only person at home was a maid, who told him that Captain Percheron had been called up as a reservist.

'What of his son, Gus . . . Angus?' Percheron had been a shy, rather diffident young man on arrival at college, perhaps because he was on the small side, but he had grown in confidence these past two or three years and Wilde knew he was held in high regard as a linguist.

'He has travelled to the west country with his mother and sister. They are staying with friends for a few days. I believe they will be home by Sunday. Would you like me to ask them to call you?'

'Thank you. It's Gus I want to speak with.' Any clues to the truth about Marcus Marfield would be welcome. Despite giving him the brush-off, the fact was Wilde couldn't get the man out of his mind.

Wilde found Lydia in her sitting room, dozing. When she was awake they discussed their days. Lydia had had more than enough of Marfield.

'I just want to get on with my own life. There are things I have to do.'

'Me too, Lydia. I used to think he was a fine young man. The more I learn, the more I dislike him. I'm sick of the sight of him.'

But neither of them could quite bear to let the subject drop.

'You know that Dr Charlecote kept meticulous notes?' said Lydia. 'I imagine he would have done so after his session with Marcus, but I couldn't get anything out of Miss Hollick. Do you think Rupert Weir might be able to help?'

Wilde called the physician who listened intently. 'A good thought, Tom. Eric was a stickler for notes. I think we should take a look at them.'

'Could you get access to his office?'

'Well, they might just drop in to my hands. Strange what can happen in a public hospital, people wandering around as though they own the place . . . Will you be in college tomorrow? I'll call in on you.'

Wilde woke early. The telephone was ringing downstairs. He was in bed with Lydia, but she was still asleep. Cursing silently, he dragged himself downstairs and picked up the handset.

'Hello?'

'Tom, it's Jim. I'm still in Glasgow. Still living in hope. The passenger lists are chaotic, but there's a good chance Juliet and William are on the *City of Flint*, headed west, for Halifax, Nova Scotia.'

'Did someone tell you that?'

'No, but the good news – if there is such a thing in this God-awful atrocity – is that their bodies have not been found.' For a moment, Jim's voice faded, but then he recovered. 'It seems the rescuers had plenty of time to get survivors off the ship and into lifeboats. They even went back hours later for a woman lying unconscious in the sick bay.'

'But there were a lot of casualties, yes?' Wilde spoke cautiously.

'Over a hundred certain deaths. One lot chewed up in the prop of a rescue ship. Too awful to contemplate. A few dozen injured in hospitals here and in Galway. I'm running out of good resolutions to this, so I'm pinning my hopes on the *Flint*. For all our sakes – particularly Henry – I have to stay positive.'

'How is Henry?'

'Tough, square-jawed, tears have dried – but I can see through that. He's a big strong boy, as you know, but he's miserable, poor lad . . .'

'Jim?' Wilde could hear that his friend was choking back tears.

'What a boy. God, Tom, I hope you have kids one day. I'm sorry, I'm trying to hold it together.'

Wilde didn't know what to say. He'd have liked children, too. He thought of the baby he had lost with his wife Charlotte in childbirth, and he thought of his failure to marry Lydia; the chances of fatherhood were looking increasingly slim. He changed the subject. 'How are you spending your time up there?'

'Organising, buddy. Making myself available to the survivors and their families. Keeping London and Washington in the loop.

Listening to a lot of complaints and demands, if truth be told. They are very happy with their treatment by the Scottish people and their hospitals, but they all say the same thing – why in God's name didn't the *Athenia* have a US Navy escort? And they don't want to go on another ship unless it's in a convoy and has the American flag painted large on the side of the vessel.'

'I can see their point.'

'Me, too. But there's even more ugly talk. Look – I know he was just playing devil's advocate, but young Lincoln Tripp suggested that the Brits might have sunk their own ship so they could blame the Nazis and turn US opinion against the Germans. Crazy, huh? But he won't be the last American to suggest this sort of thing – most of the folks back home want nothing to do with this war.'

'Tripp's talking nonsense, you know that, Jim. We all know that.'

'I know, I know. He knows it too, just doing the diplomat's job of trying to work out what the other guy's thinking. This is a propaganda war, you see – and who will they believe in the Midwest? I just hope our glorious ambassador doesn't swallow the German line entirely. Anyway, that's not why I called. I'm sending Lincoln Tripp back to London. We've got thousands of Yanks camped at the embassy trying to get away from the war. He asked if he could stop off in Cambridge briefly, as it's on the way. He'll only be there a few hours, but could you give him a bite to eat, maybe show him around? He'll leave here later today.'

'My pleasure, Jim. And you – how long will you stay up there?'

'Until I know what happened to my beautiful wife and son. This is the home berth for the Donaldson Atlantic Line, so this is where the news is coming. I'm staying put, buddy.'

Wilde left Lydia a note on the kitchen table, then slipped out of her house and went next door to pick up his jacket and goggles.

As he fired up the Rudge, he felt a chill in the morning air, a portent of summer ending.

In the early light, the motorbike purred southwards through the almost empty streets of Cambridge. He had a choice of routes and opted to go through the quiet village of Trumpington and on into Great Shelford. Rupert Weir had given him directions to Eric Charlecote's address and he pulled up outside a thatched house in a large tree-lined garden not far from the parish church. The gate carried the legend *The Foragers*. The house looked empty and bleak. In the driveway a soft-top black Riley Nine stood sentry. Twisting the throttle on the Rudge, Wilde rode on, turning south-east into Stapleford and then gradually turning further east, and a little north.

He killed the engine on the silent, traffic-free road at the base of Little Trees Hill, then dismounted and looked up the easy slope towards the summit and the thicket of trees that crested its brow. To anyone in hill country, this place would seem as nothing, but in the flatlands of the east, it was a marvel, and the views were spectacular.

With a glance back at the Rudge, he began the ascent. It was effortless – hardly more than 200 feet high – but to one with a disability such as Charlecote's it would be almost impossible.

A flock of goldfinches caught the light and dazzled his eyes. These hills, the Gog-Magogs, had always had a special place in his heart – and in the hearts of Cambridge students. In high summer, there was no better site for a picnic and a bottle of wine, all carried in the baskets of their bicycles. From the top they could gaze to the north and try to make out their college. The only certain landmark that was clearly identifiable without a pair of binoculars was the soaring contour of King's College Chapel.

On the way up the hill, Wilde noted faint tyre tracks; they could mean something or nothing. In the copse, still dense with summer leaf and tangled with briars, he tried to work out where Dr Charlecote's body had been found. He walked through the middle of the little woodland, closely examining the dry ground with every step. Not far from the northern edge of the spinney, he found the place.

Here dried blood clogged the dusty earth, marking the spot. He knelt down. There was not a great deal of blood, but enough to make it certain that this was the location of death.

He found footprints in the dust, and more than one set. But why wouldn't there be? People came here every day with their dogs or their lovers. He looked around for an empty shell case, but there was no sign of it. Of course, the police would have taken it away.

A large dog appeared at his side, wagging its tail, sniffing the ground. It looked friendly enough, so he stroked its neck. He looked up to see a man in his sixties standing there.

'Beautiful dog,' Wilde said as he rose to his feet.

'Retriever,' the man said. He was dressed in country clothes, and he carried a rough walking stick. 'I suppose you know what happened here?'

'Yes,' Wilde said.

'Sad affair. I found the body. More precisely, it was Scout. My name's Parker – I farm round here.'

Wilde introduced himself and shook hands. 'Did you know the dead man?'

'I didn't. Never seen him up here before. What's your interest, Mr Wilde?'

'He was a friend of a friend. There are some doubts that the deceased would have taken his own life.'

Parker looked thoughtful. 'Well, my first impression was suicide. The body was splayed out on its back, the pistol inches from the outstretched right hand.'

'What sort of gun?'

'Smith and Wesson revolver. US army issue from the last war. Recognised it at once.'

'I wonder where he would he have come across an American pistol?'

'Brought it back from France, I should think. We all brought weapons home – French, American, German. Guns, bayonets, helmets. Nice souvenirs.'

'Did you find the spent cartridge?'

'No, but you wouldn't with a Smith and Wesson. His spectacles were a couple of feet away. Half-moon things – the sort doctors like to peer at you over.'

'Nothing suspicious?'

'Not as such.' Parker hesitated.

'But something's bothering you?'

'Can't put my finger on it really. It was just – well, something didn't feel right. But how could it? I walk Scout here every day, morning and night, hot weather and cold, and I haven't found a body before, so of course it felt out of place. You don't expect your dog to sniff out a corpse in rural England, Mr Wilde.'

CHAPTER 17

Wilde parked outside *The Foragers* in Great Shelford again, but this time he left the bike on its stand and approached the house. There was no doorbell or knocker so he tapped with his gauntleted hand. No reply.

Glancing about to make sure no one was watching, he slipped around to the back of the house. He was about to check the doors and windows when he spotted an old man hoeing a garden bed. Wilde hailed him. 'Excuse me, do you live here?'

The man turned around without haste or obvious concern. 'Do I look like I live here? I'm Jobson, the gardener.'

'I expect you've heard the news about Dr Charlecote?'

'Aye, I have. Don't stop the weeds growing though, do it? And who are *you*?'

For the second time that morning, Wilde explained who he was and his interest in Dr Charlecote.

'Fair enough,' the gardener said at last. 'What do you want from me?'

'You must have known the doctor quite well.'

'Aye.' He jutted his chin across the road to a small terraced house. 'That's where I live. Been neighbour as well as gardener to him these past fifteen years.'

'Did he seem like the sort of man who might kill himself?'

'He was hit awful hard when Enid died last year. Cancer of the blood. Shocking thing – wasted away . . . but I thought by last spring he'd picked himself up. Couldn't get about easily, what with his hips, but he seemed a great deal more cheery.'

'I gather he had bad arthritis. Made me wonder, how could he have got up Little Trees Hill?'

'I hadn't thought of that.' The gardener scratched his head. 'It was hard enough work for him just to get from the car to the front door.'

'And he couldn't have walked there from here?'

'No, no, that's certain. And, of course, his Riley's still here. Hadn't put two and two together at all on that. Now this is a rum business, isn't it?'

'It is indeed.' Wilde paused. 'Do you know his next of kin, Mr Jobson?'

'Two daughters, he's got. Both migrated to America about ten, twelve years back. One after the other. Vicky and Marge. Missed 'em awful, he did. They never came to visit him, he never went over there. Never even saw his grandchildren. Crying shame.'

'You must have seen his comings and goings. Did you see him come home after work the night before last?'

'Aye. I wanted to talk about the vegetable patch because it'll all need to change now there's a war on. But he put me off, said perhaps we'd talk at the weekend.'

'Did he seem in a strange mood?'

'Well – he could get a bit testy if he'd had a trying day. I thought nothing of it.'

'And I don't suppose you heard him go out in the night?'

The gardener frowned. 'Now you mention it . . . about eleven, my wife said she thought she'd heard a car so I pulled back the blackout a little, and looked out. There was just enough moonlight to see the Riley was there and there was nothing showing at the front of the doctor's house, so I thought no more of it.'

'But someone could have picked him up?'

'There's no denying it, is there?'

It was time to move the weapons. They had been here, quite safe, since she recovered them from the floorboards at the secluded farmhouse, but her instinct told her it would not be a good idea for them to remain any longer; not since Wilde had followed Marcus here.

The two pistols and the ammunition had been packed haphazardly in soft cloth, and tumbled out onto the carpet as she endeavoured to sort them out. At least in the other soldier's kitbag all the constituent parts of the sub-machine gun were self-contained.

Carefully, she re-wrapped everything, then packed them all into a single valise – the sort of bag a woman would carry; an item that would not arouse suspicion.

She carried the bag down to the car, which was parked outside the Samovar, and placed it in the passenger footwell. Climbing into the driver's seat, she switched the ignition.

As Wilde arrived at the college gate, he heard a car horn, turned and saw a nice little open-topped sports car being driven by a young woman. She raised her goggles and he saw that it was Elina Kossoff. He waved a greeting.

She held up her right hand with her index finger extended like the barrel of a pistol. But the motion switched seamlessly to a gentle touch of the fingertip to her generous pink lips and she blew him a kiss. She replaced her goggles over her eyes, put her foot down – and the car roared off down Trumpington Street, heading south.

Wilde watched her go, slightly bemused. In his mind, he was trying to place Marcus and Elina together in a relationship, and was struggling. Difficult to imagine what they might have in common, except for the obvious – they were both good-looking and young.

At the porters' lodge, he discovered that he had two visitors. 'Mr Eaton and Mr Rowlands, sir,' Scobie said. 'Been here an hour.'

'Where are they?'

'With Dr Dill, sir. I know that Mr Eaton is an old friend of his so I took the liberty of escorting them to his rooms. It perked him up no end, Professor Wilde. Would you like me to let them know you're here?'

'No, no. I'll drop in on them.'

Crossing the new court, Wilde saw that the door to the chapel was open. From inside he heard the strains of an unmistakable singing voice. He stopped and went in.

Marfield was standing at the side of the choir stalls, sheet music in hand, singing Schubert's *Ave Maria* without accompaniment under the keen gaze and critical ear of Timothy Laker. Taking a seat in the pews, Wilde closed his eyes and listened to the pure tenor voice as it filled the ancient space. His spine shivered at the sheer passion of this paean to the virgin, and he found himself wondering yet again about the contrast between Marfield's extraordinary physical beauty and the perfection of his singing, and the worrying complexity of the rest of his life. What had drawn him to Spain? What had happened there to give him such nightmares? Who were his enemies – and what was he hiding?

As the song finished, Wilde stood up from the pew. Laker looked over with a beaming, exultant smile. His star singer was back and the voice was unscathed.

Marfield had his head down, studying the sheet music. If he had seen Wilde, he didn't acknowledge him.

'Bravo, Marcus.'

The young man looked up and smiled. 'Perhaps a little Catholic for such a Protestant place of worship.'

'Oh, this chapel was Catholic once – as was I.'

'I had no idea, Professor.'

'Well, my mother is Irish and I was brought up as a Catholic, but I think you would probably say I'm lapsed now. What about you?'

'Church of England. Anglo-Catholic.'

'The prayer book you took to war?'

'I confess there were times when I turned to it. Do you think it pathetic?'

'Not at all. My only wonder was how it fitted in with your attachment to international socialism.'

'Now, Professor Wilde, that doesn't sound at all like you. You always told me to think for myself, that there were a great many more shades than plain black and white.'

Wilde laughed. So he *had* got through to Marfield on some level at least. He turned to the choirmaster. 'Are you finished with him yet, Laker?'

'Not quite. Another ten minutes.'

'Then I'll come back shortly. I want a word, Marfield.' Best not to mention the presence of Philip Eaton, perhaps.

*

Wilde was shocked by what he found in Horace Dill's rooms. When he first met Philip Eaton back at the end of 1936, he had been as sleek and smooth as a cat. Now he was much diminished, his face gaunt, his body shrunken. The hit-and-run crash had taken his left arm, given his left leg a permanent limp and dimmed the light in his eye. He was a shadow of his former, elegant self.

The MI6 man and his fellow officer Guy Rowlands sat either side of Horace Dill's bed, where the old history professor lay propped up on a bank of pillows. He had not bothered to take down his blackout but had his bedside lamp on. The whole scene reminded Wilde of a tableau by Joseph Wright of Derby.

Eaton rose with difficulty from the chair, aided by a stick. Rowlands, who was smoking a cigarette, made a move to assist him but Eaton put up his hand. 'Don't nursemaid me, Guy. You're doing too much, but thank you anyway.' He turned to Wilde. 'What a pleasure to see you again.'

'You, too, Eaton.' They shook hands.

'You remember Guy Rowlands, don't you?'

'Of course.' Another handshake. 'Outside the Cavendish back in June.'

'He's my spare part, if that doesn't sound rude,' Eaton continued. 'Poor chap has spent these past three months looking after my work and now I'm back in harness he's helping me get about. But I've got to learn to do it myself, you see.'

Rowlands grinned. Hair thinning, grey at the temples, he wore an expensive pin-striped suit and some sort of club tie. Wilde imagined that Englishmen of a certain class would immediately know which club. The last time they had met, he had worn a regimental tie, and Wilde had been equally at a loss to know which regiment it might have been, except that the cannon motif suggested a gunnery outfit. As before, he had a yellow silk kerchief flopping from his breast pocket and a pair of small-bore bullets adapted as cufflinks. He removed his cigarette from his mouth and blew out a long trail of smoke. 'Good to see you again, Wilde. I would like to be able to say in less dire circumstances than last time, but with a war on, that's probably not quite right.'

'Well, gentlemen, I am rather pleased to see you both,' Wilde said.

Horace Dill banged his hand on his bedside table. 'Excuse me, if I might interrupt, there's a fourth fucking person here. To wit, me.' The effort of his outburst was too much and he collapsed into a series of wheezing coughs.

'Ah, Horace,' Wilde said. 'I hadn't noticed you there.'

'Bugger you, Wilde.' He brushed aside the glass of water Wilde offered him.

'Well,' Wilde said, 'enough of this.' He turned to Eaton. 'I take it this isn't just some social visit? You've come to see Marcus Marfield, yes?'

'Indeed.'

'He's just finishing off some singing practice in the chapel. If you go to my rooms, I'll fetch him.'

'Thank you,' said Eaton. 'You have done us a great service in bringing him home. We thought we'd lost him.'

'And when you're done with him, Eaton, I'd rather like a quick chat with you, if you can spare me a few minutes.'

Tim Laker was still in the chapel, but there was no sign of Marfield.

'Where's he gone?' demanded Wilde.

'Went off to relieve himself. He said he'd meet you in his rooms.'

Wilde headed off to his rooms, but Marfield wasn't there either. He waited a few minutes, then cursed and went to the porters' lodge, where he grabbed Scobie. 'Has Marfield been through here?'

'You missed him by about ten minutes, professor. Headed off towards the river.'

'Damn and double damn.'

'He asked if you were in college, sir, and I told him you were with Mr Eaton and another guest.'

So Marfield had got wind of Eaton's presence. Clearly he was avoiding him.

'Shall I ask him to seek you out on his return, sir?'

'No, leave it, Scobie.'

CHAPTER 18

'Good God, the bastard's gone rogue.' Rowlands spoke quietly. He shook his head in disbelief.

Wilde tried to lighten the tone. 'Well, he certainly seems to be avoiding you both, but is that really what you'd call going rogue? He's been behaving oddly, I agree, but he's still recovering. He was in a terrible state when we found him.'

'This goes back a long way. Why hasn't he made contact in the past year?'

'Perhaps he wasn't able to.'

'No,' Rowlands said. 'That's not it. I think we know him rather better than you do, Wilde . . .' Rowlands had been lounging in Wilde's armchair, his Homburg occupying pride of place on the desk. Eaton was lost in the corner of the sofa, nursing a glass of whisky. One of them – he had assumed Rowlands – had found the bottle and poured them both hefty measures. The air smelt smoky and as Eaton didn't use cigarettes, Wilde assumed Rowlands was the culprit.

'So where is he?' Rowlands asked.

'I don't know,' was all Wilde could say. 'I think he got wind of your presence.'

Rowlands lit a cigarette, drew deeply and flicked the tip of ash on the floor.

'Don't do that,' Wilde said.

'What's that, old man?'

'Your cigarette. Put it out.'

'God, I'm so sorry – should have asked.'

Wilde handed him his only ashtray and Rowlands obliged by stubbing out the offending article. 'Now look,' Wilde said. 'I may not know Marfield the spy, but I certainly know the young student – and I can see that he has been deeply affected by his recent experiences. It's possible he is concealing something, but that's not really my concern. What troubles me is his state of mind. I have no idea what happened to him over in Spain, but I do know he has waking nightmares: he talks about a ravine and some sort of aerial bombardment.'

'That doesn't explain why he's avoiding us.' Rowlands began pacing the room.

Wilde sighed. 'Eaton, what's going on here? What on earth do you think Marfield might be up to? You're worried about something, yes?'

Eaton had said nothing until now. He turned to Rowlands. 'I think we probably owe Professor Wilde some background, don't you?'

'What I think is that we need to trawl the streets of Cambridge, find Marfield, pull him in, close confine him in a small, windowless room with a single electric bulb, and feed him short commons for a few days. Then start the hard questions.' Rowlands spoke with uncharacteristic vehemence.

'No,' said Eaton, shaking his head. 'That won't do.' He winced, and shifted his position on the chair. 'Look, Wilde, you know I don't make a habit of offering information but you've put yourself to a great deal of trouble and we need some help on this.'

This was not like the Eaton of old. First he revealed Marfield was acting as a British agent in Spain, now he was offering more.

Had the accident that cost him his left arm changed him? Wilde wondered. Or perhaps he had another motive. 'Fire away.'

'Guy has known Marfield for many years.' Eaton curled his fingers, inviting his colleague to take over.

Rowlands looked askance at his colleague.

'Carry on,' Eaton said in a firm tone. 'The professor is aware that we work for the intelligence service, and he knows Marfield was working for us. The story I want to tell him is not a state secret.'

Rowlands began to play with his bullet cufflinks. 'Your call. You're the senior officer.'

'Then I'll start you off,' Eaton said flatly. 'Rowlands here was a lieutenant in the same regiment as Marfield's father at the end of the war.'

Rowlands fished out his cigarette case, saw Wilde's critical glare and pushed it back into his pocket. 'Ronald Marfield was my colonel and he took me under his wing. I became a family friend, and I had the privilege of watching Marcus and his brother growing up.'

'I didn't know he had a brother,' Wilde said.

'Ptolemy Marfield – about twenty months older than Marcus. Very different: dark, brooding, heavily built rugby player. Damned clever, too. Read Greats at Oxford. The brothers never really got on, perhaps because their father favoured Marcus so obviously. But Toll – that's what everyone calls him – is not relevant to this.'

It might not be relevant to Marcus's actions in Spain, but it certainly seemed relevant to the father's devastation when his favourite son threatened the family name by getting a girl pregnant and then went off to fight for the Communists in Spain. The fact that all the family's love had been lavished on a boy who – in their eyes – turned out bad was entirely germane.

'A couple of years ago,' Rowlands continued, 'Ronald called me. He was pretty distraught, said Marcus was heading off to Spain and could I do anything to stop him, take his passport away or something like that? Well, of course, the horse had already bolted by then, but I wasn't without influence.'

Eaton put up his hand to interject. 'I should explain that Guy had recently taken over the Iberian desk from me.'

'I was working from London most of the time, but through contacts I got word that Marcus had signed up for the International Brigades in Paris and was training with them in the rather unromantic town of Albacete. A curious bunch, full of zeal, quite disciplined, but problems with communication. All sorts of non-Spaniards kicking their heels and waiting to be sent somewhere to shoot Falangists. As it happened, I had to go out to meet some people in Barcelona, and so I thought I'd travel a little further south and pay him a visit. I had to be discreet, because the militias wouldn't have taken kindly to one of their men conversing with a British agent.'

'A bullet in the head?'

'There was plenty of that on both sides. Anyway, I found him in the old Civil Guards HQ in the Calle de la Libertad and managed to make contact with the boy. Later he came to me at my hotel, the Mirador. All rather furtive. But curiosity had got the better of him. I greeted him guardedly, then we retreated to my room, where I ordered us both a decent meal and asked him what he bloody well thought he was doing. Didn't he know the effect on his poor parents? I told him he was a damned fool and was almost certain to die for someone else's pointless cause.'

Wilde was aware that men had gone to join the fight in Spain for many reasons. Some went to fight fascism and to help found a socialist utopia; others to escape the grinding poverty of unemployment in their home countries. There were those who were trying to avoid a prison term or merely have an adventure. And, yes, it was possible some men went simply to get away from marriage and fatherhood. Into which category did Marcus Marfield fit?

'Obviously I tried hard to persuade him to come home with me. I failed. No fool like a young man in search of danger. And so I suggested that if he insisted on sacrificing himself for the Spanish Republic, the least he could do was to perform a few tasks for me on the side.'

'How did he take that?'

'He didn't take a lot of persuading. Young men love all that spy stuff: the tap on the shoulder and the whisper in the ear. He was intrigued and a little flattered. He had been there for some weeks and I know from my own army days that there is nothing quite like the parade ground to knock the idealism out of young recruits. He was sick to death of being shouted at and starved, and so I went out of my way to make him feel useful.'

'What did you say you wanted from him?'

'Very little. Nothing to betray his cause, of course. He knows that my own political leanings aren't a million miles from his. I think he already suspected that I was working for the Secret Intelligence Service. I told him I would be interested in details from the front when he got there – relative strengths of the lines, manoeuvres, the usual military stuff. And in return I would feed him information he could use to assist his own brigade and perhaps to win favour with his commanders.'

'And he went for it?'

'I persuaded him that if we could paint a picture of the Republicans fighting for decency and honour, we might yet persuade the British to intervene on the side of the elected government. Not a cat in hell's chance, of course – but it was a message Marcus liked. And so, yes, he went for it.'

'He worked for you?'

'Oh yes – and it soon became clear that he was a natural intelligence officer. More than that, he was a good soldier and rose through the ranks of the International Brigades. Kept me informed for months so that I gained a very clear picture of the areas in which he operated. Certainly a much clearer idea of what was going on than the world ever got from official briefings. But then in April last year, it all stopped. Complete silence. I tried to find out where he was – whether he was dead or captured – but not a dicky bird. It was as though he had vanished from the face of the earth. I feared the worst. Bullet in the head or killed in battle, and then dumped in a mass grave. So when we heard you had found him and that he was alive, well, it meant a great deal to us, Mr Wilde.'

Wilde's gaze shifted from Rowlands to Eaton. 'And you know Marfield, too?'

'I met him in Madrid, a few weeks after he was recruited by Guy.'

'When you were there reporting for *The Times*, I suppose?'

'As you say.'

'You know, of course, about his father?' Wilde asked.

'A great tragedy,' Rowlands said. 'When Marcus disappeared, Ronald thought – like we did – that he was dead. He fell apart.'

'But he shot himself within hours of his son's return. Very strange timing, don't you think?'

'Well, I agree it's odd, but it must be a coincidence. Ronald couldn't have known Marcus had come back. You didn't tell him, Wilde, and I certainly didn't – I didn't know.'

Wilde nodded. There was still one thing that bothered him. Neither Eaton nor Rowlands had mentioned the rift with Marcus's mother, or the fact that he had a wife and child. Did they know – or were they holding the information back? Wilde decided to keep quiet for the time being. Let the information come from them, if they had it.

'So what now?' he asked.

'We're going to find the boy,' Rowlands said. 'I want to know what he's been up to and, more to the point, what his plans are. He might have gone to Spain an innocent, but no one has come back from that war undamaged.'

Wilde understood. For all their urbane maners, Eaton and Rowlands were hard men. Marfield might once have been a darling of the British secret services, but if he had turned against them, there would be no hiding place.

At the end of the day, Dr Rupert Weir strode purposefully through the corridors of Addenbrooke's Hospital until he arrived at Dr Eric Charlecote's office. Miss Hollick had gone home and the door to the office was locked, but Weir found the key in the top drawer of her desk.

He wasn't concerned about being stopped or questioned: everyone knew how close he had been to Eric. He had spent many a half hour drinking coffee in this office when things were quiet. Walking in now felt horrible. Everything was as his old friend had left it: the couch with its single embroidered pillow for patients, the beechwood desk with its ink pot, its neat row of six fountain pens, its closed notebook, and the overflowing bookshelves.

Weir sat down in the swivel chair and thought about Eric Charlecote. He could be a bit of an acquired taste, but once you got to know him he was a warm and loyal friend. Steady, too. If he had killed himself – and neither the post-mortem nor the police report on the weapon suggested otherwise – then he must have had reason: the physical pain in his hips, perhaps? And Enid's death had been a blow.

Well, Eric might have had his reasons, but Rupert Weir was bloody certain he didn't walk to the Gogs and climb up Little Trees Hill unaided. What a shame the officers at St Andrew's Street hadn't shared his doubts.

Weir flicked open the notebook. For a man who kept such a tidy desk, Charlecote's writing was a nasty surprise. It was a scrawl, pure and simple. Not only that, but from the words that Weir *could* unravel, it seemed that he largely ignored vowels. He flipped through to find the entry for Marcus Marfield, which, as Eric's last patient, should be the last one. He found Marfield's name at the top of the penultimate page clearly enough, but the words after that were a manic mangle of black ink and blotches. Weir tried to take it one scribble at a time, but he couldn't manage more than half a dozen words, and none of them in isolation meant a thing.

He'd have to get help on this one. Examining bodies and determining the cause of death was easy compared to reading Eric Charlecote's handwriting. He picked up the notebook, left the office, locked the door and returned the key to Miss Hollick's desk drawer.

The car, a red Morgan 4-4 two-seater, made a healthy growl as Elina Kossoff sped south along the empty roads. She should have been enjoying the car, but something was bothering her. She hadn't liked the appearance of Professor Wilde at the Samovar. Marcus said the man had followed him, but he hadn't seemed concerned: 'What can he do? He is a history don, nothing more.' But it was *her* job to be concerned and this was no time for little complications to start emerging. Wilde had brought Marcus home from France; unwittingly, he had already played his part.

Elina looked over at the tan valise on the seat beside her. The weapons it held were more than enough for her purpose. Her thoughts turned to her middle-aged lover and to Marcus Marfield. Lambs to the slaughter, both of them.

CHAPTER 19

Wilde took his leave of Eaton and Rowlands at the porters' lodge. They were staying the night at the Bull and would contact him in the morning to see if he had found Marcus Marfield. Wilde promised nothing, merely wished them a good evening, and set off home. Instead of turning right at Jesus Lane, however, he carried on along Bridge Street, up past Magdalene College onto Castle Street and then veered right on to the Histon road.

He found Claire Marfield's house on the edge of the village, backing on to a plum orchard. A gatepost sign said *Chivers and Sons*. The trees, all in tidy rows, were heavy with fruit, which was already being picked by a team of harvest workers. The air was heady with sweetness.

Claire's house was large and imposing, an early Victorian merchant's property which stood a little way apart from the orchard, surrounded by a ragged privet hedge. A small fair-haired child was playing in the front garden. The child looked at him with interest, then ran giggling around the side of the house. So that was Marfield's son, Walter.

Wilde knocked at the front door. Claire appeared within seconds, drying her hands on a floral apron.

'Professor Wilde.'

'I hope you don't mind me calling on you, Mrs Marfield, but I wondered if you had had any word from Marcus?'

'I haven't, I'm afraid. But do come in – I've got the kettle on.'

Wilde took a seat at the kitchen table while Claire Marfield spooned leaves into a china teapot and poured in boiling water, then replaced the top and left it to brew.

'I think I just met Walter – but he ran away before I could say hello.'

'Ah, he'll come in soon enough, then you can meet him properly. Do you think he looks like Marcus?'

'He certainly has his colouring . . .' Wilde paused. 'Can I ask you something else – who knows about your marriage? Your parents? His parents? Anyone else?'

'The vicar and a couple of people we dragged off the street as witnesses. The idea was we were supposed to keep it a secret, you see, because Marcus was an undergraduate. He said the college wouldn't allow it, that he would be rusticated.'

Wilde had to concede that might indeed have happened, given the circumstances. 'But once he had gone to Spain, there was no motive for secrecy then?'

'Who should I have told? It was no one's business. I get enough looks and whispered comments about my status as it is, Mr Wilde, but I'm damned if I can be bothered to tell anyone the truth. Anyway, Marcus wanted it kept quiet, so that was good enough for me. I kept hoping he'd get bored by the war and return home within a couple of weeks. That was two and a half years ago.'

When she visited Wilde in college he had thought her spectacles made her look rather serious. Now, in her workaday clothes, dark hair awry, with a kettle in hand, she looked like a young housewife. She was certainly a great deal more relaxed and warm than she had been at their first meeting.

'Your feelings are understandable.'

'But why do you ask, Mr Wilde?'

Just then the child ran in, saw Wilde and began giggling again. He jumped on his mother's lap and she stroked his hair fondly.

'Apart from his fair complexion, I actually think he looks more like you,' said Wilde. 'Look, can I ask you something else: what do you know about your husband's family. I take it you've met them all?'

'Well, I liked his brother, Toll, but I couldn't abide either of his parents. I found his mother particularly unfriendly.' She shrugged and gave a weak smile.

On the basis of his short phone call with her, Wilde could imagine that the elder Mrs Marfield could be a hard woman to warm to.

'You know his father's dead?'

'I saw the death notice in *The Times* this morning. It didn't give a cause of death. Did the witch poison him?'

'He shot himself.'

'Oh my God, I'm sorry to hear that. Truly, no one deserves that.'

'I suppose he was very disappointed by the turn of events with Marcus. Was he very upset by your pregnancy?'

Claire hesitated before answering. 'Certainly the pregnancy had a big impact on the harpy. Marcus told me that gin and knitting needles was one of her less extreme suggestions, a nunnery another, even a one-way ticket to Canada.'

'And Colonel Marfield?'

'You know, I'm not sure how concerned he was about the baby. Of course, he supported his wife, but I got the feeling there was something else between him and Marcus.'

'Marcus's plans to go to Spain?'

'I suppose that had something to do with it. They are not a very forthcoming family, so it's difficult to know. I wasn't on speaking terms after Marcus left. There was nothing said and no attempt to make contact. But I can imagine Colonel Marfield was beside himself. Do you think that had something to do with his suicide?'

'It has to be a possibility. What about his brother? Did you have no contact with him?'

'Toll? I met him only the once. He came over just before the wedding. I liked him. Very different to Marcus, of course. Nowhere near as good looking and didn't have the voice, but there was something quite sweet about him.'

'But he and Marcus didn't get on?'

'No, Marcus was stand-offish, made it quite clear he didn't want him in his life – and I think Toll felt the same. He only came over to meet me because he thought it his duty as a brother.'

'Where's Toll now?'

'I'm afraid I have no idea. He must have graduated and left Balliol.'

'One more thing, did you ever meet an old friend of his family named Guy Rowlands?'

'No, should I have?'

'So there would be no reason for him to know of your existence?'

'God no, they wouldn't have told any of their friends about me or Walter – or the marriage for that matter. The harpy wouldn't have breathed a word. How would they have explained their son's frightful behaviour at the Mother's Union and the golf club? Why are you asking these things?'

Why indeed? But there was something about Marcus Marfield that didn't add up – and hadn't ever since the mysterious Honoré had run Wilde to earth in rural France.

'Just curiosity,' he said lamely. 'Now – how about that tea before it gets stewed?'

It was twilight – just after seven thirty – when he left Claire Marfield's house. As he kicked the motorbike into life, a van across the street caught his eye. It was an ordinary dark-green delivery van, without markings of any kind, except that the driver's side wing mirror was hanging loose.

He had seen an identical green delivery van outside the college before he came here. That, too, had its wing mirror almost detached. Why would a vehicle parked near his college in the centre of Cambridge now be here in a side street at Histon an hour or so later? Coincidence? Wilde switched off the engine, dismounted and started to cross the street towards the van. Now he could see that there was a figure in the driver's seat.

He was three yards from the vehicle when it pulled out sharply and sped away. But he had already seen enough.

The driver was a woman. The woman he had seen first at Le Vernet and then, later, in the early hours of the morning outside Jim Vanderberg's house in Chelsea. She had had a pistol in her hand and had been engaged in a confrontation with Marcus Marfield. Rosa, that was her name. Someone he had known in Spain, he said.

For a few moments, Wilde watched the van as it disappeared down the road, going south. By the time he decided to follow it, he had lost precious time and, for once, the Rudge let him down.

In his haste to fire her up again, he flooded the engine and had to wait a minute before trying once more.

When he finally got going, the van was long gone. He rode at speed back into town, hoping to find it, but in vain, and so he headed for home. He wanted to see Lydia.

She was in her kitchen and the aroma suggested she had something in the oven. Rupert Weir was there, too, warming a glass of brandy in his hands.

'Food,' Wilde said. 'And drink. Now that's the kind of welcome I like.'

'Fish pie,' she said.

'You know the way to a man's heart, Miss Morris. Anyone would think we had something to celebrate. I hope you're staying to dine with us, Rupert?'

'No, no, Tom. I just dropped in to show you this.' Dr Weir patted the notebook on the table in front of him. 'These are Eric Charlecote's notes. I was hoping one of you two might make head or tail of it, because I'm damned if I can.'

Wilde examined the scrawl and shook his head. 'Bloody doctors and their handwriting! I suspect there are only two people who can unravel this and unfortunately one of those is dead.'

'The other being Miss Hollick, his secretary,' put in Lydia.

'Of course,' said Weir. 'But how can I ask her to deciper it when she'll know I stole it from his office?'

'Borrowed, not stole,' Lydia said. 'And she might be happy to help if she can be persuaded that this might throw some light on the death of a man she cared about.'

'Will you take it to her then, Lydia? I know it sounds cowardly, but I really don't want to jeopardise my professional reputation. Confessing to light burglary of a colleague's office might not go down too well at Addenbrooke's.'

'Yes, I'll do it.'

'Good, then I'll leave it here and wish you two lovebirds goodnight.' Weir grinned and held up an admonishing finger in Lydia's direction, then downed his brandy with a flourish.

'Before you go, Rupert, I wanted a favour,' said Wilde. 'Can you get hold of some coroner's records? Marcus Marfield's father shot himself on Monday morning. Colonel Ronald Marfield. Down in Ipswich.'

'Of course. I'm not sure if the inquest will have been held yet, but the coroner should already know just about everything there is to know. I'll give him a call in the morning. And you, Lydia, go easy on the wine!' He gave her an ostentatious wink.

'What was that about?' Wilde demanded after Weir had departed. 'Since when did Rupert Weir ever suggest self-denial or restraint in anything!'

'Oh, just being proprietorial, I suppose, the way GPs tell one not to smoke too much as they're lighting their own cigarettes.' Even as she spoke, she realised this must be the moment. She smiled at him cautiously. 'Actually, there was more to it than that, Tom . . . What would you say to the prospect of a child?'

The question threw him. 'I'm sorry?' he said.

'A child. You heard me.'

His brow knitted. 'You mean take in one of the evacuees? Why not? Good idea. We could give one or two of them a good home between us.'

'Yes, that's a good idea. But it wasn't quite what I was thinking.' She took his hands. 'Haven't you noticed anything different about me recently?'

His creased face betrayed his puzzlement, and then his eyes widened as it dawned on him. 'Oh my God, Lydia, are you saying—'

She nodded.

For a few seconds, he held back, stunned, and then he took her in his arms. His heart was thumping and he clutched her tightly to his chest. 'Is this true? Are you sure?'

'Yes, I'm sure.'

'How long? When?'

'Eleven or twelve weeks. It must be due around the end of March. Easter probably – perhaps just after. Tom, are you pleased? I've been so worried about telling you.'

'Pleased?' He hugged her even tighter and kissed her mouth. 'I've wanted this for longer than you could imagine.'

'I've been trying to tell you for days.'

'How did I not notice?'

'Indeed. Rupert Weir suspected, so did Françoise Talbot when we were in France.'

'Well, they're doctors, aren't they! But I should have realised, too – the tiredness, the sickness on the journey home, the abstinence.'

'There's something else I haven't told you. I don't want to publish poetry any more. I'm considering retraining to be a doctor. The country needs doctors more than ever – but how can I do that and look after a baby?'

'You're throwing questions at me and I haven't even had a chance to adjust to prospective fatherhood yet!' Wilde was terrified, and hoping desperately that it didn't show. The loss of Charlotte and their baby all those years ago . . . his son would have been thirteen by now. Sometimes it felt like a lifetime away, sometimes it was only yesterday and the pain cut him to the heart.

Lydia saw the fear in his eyes. There was little in life that scared Tom Wilde. Certainly not physical pain; you couldn't be a boxer if you feared getting hurt. But any threat to those he loved, that was something else.

CHAPTER 20

They woke both rested and confused, and wondering the same thing: what next? Should they get married after all?

As Lydia made coffee and cooked eggs for breakfast, she could see that something wasn't right. She had never felt the need to compete with Charlotte's ghost and nor would she start now, but this was difficult. She couldn't just let it pass.

'Tom, talk to me.'

He looked up. 'I'm sorry?'

'You can't just disappear into your past.'

He smiled. 'I wasn't. I'm happier than you can imagine, but I can't help thinking of Jim up in Glasgow, not knowing whether Juliet and William are alive or dead. It's difficult to jump for joy at the moment.'

'Of course. That's insensitive of me. I thought you were lost somewhere else.'

'Charlotte? Lydia, she would love you – and be happy for us. I'm as sure of that as I possibly can be.'

For the rest of the meal, they talked about other things. Lydia said she would seek out Miss Hollick and try to persuade her to decipher Dr Charlecote's notes. Wilde told Lydia about his visit to Claire Marfield's home in Histon.

'Would *you* go and see her? She must know Marfield better than anyone. And maybe woman to woman . . . you could discuss the men in your lives?'

Lydia laughed. 'I'll do it – but you're not going to turn me into a bloody wife, Tom!'

*

Wilde took his leave of her and strolled towards the Rudge. It was parked at the kerb, just in front of a black Ford with someone asleep at the wheel. It seemed a strange place to park for a quick morning doze. Wilde tapped on the car window.

Slowly, the man's eyes opened, but even before he saw them Wilde realised it was Lincoln Tripp, Jim Vanderberg's charge at the US Embassy. Of course – Jim had said Tripp would be stopping off in Cambridge on the way back to London from Glasgow.

Tripp yawned and stretched his arms, noticed Wilde and smiled sheepishly. He put up a hand in greeting and wearily wound down the car window.

'Good morning, Mr Tripp.' Wilde leant in and grinned. 'How long have you been here?'

'Hello, Professor, what's the time?'

'Eight.'

'Couple of hours, more like three, I think.'

'You should have knocked.'

'Oh, I really didn't want to wake you up. No, sir.'

'Did you drive all the way down from Scotland in one go?'

'Yes, sir. It's one heck of a drive. I never knew your island was so big.'

'It's not my island – and it's not big. It's just that there are no straight roads. By the look of you, you need coffee. Perhaps a proper bed, too. Won't you come indoors? I want to hear what's going on up there.'

'That's the best offer I've had in a very long time.'

Wilde seated Tripp at his kitchen table and set about brewing a pot of coffee.

'Is there any word yet?'

Tripp shook his head. 'I'm sorry, sir, still no news on Mrs Vanderberg and the boy. But you know the shipping line got in an awful mess with their passenger lists. And with survivors taken in all directions, there's a lot of confusion. Plenty of folks still to arrive in Glasgow over the next day or two, but I really think our best hope is the *City of Flint* bound for Halifax.'

'They must be talking to the captain by radio.'

'Yes, sir, but names get taken down wrong. I tell you this, though: the whole thing has got the wind up the ambassador. We knew he was sending his wife and most of the family home, but Jack was up in Glasgow yesterday and told us the old man is now insisting on sending them in batches. He won't risk the whole bunch in one ship.'

Wilde took the point. With nine children, Joe Kennedy had a lot to lose. He changed the subject. 'Mr Vanderberg says you are interested in meeting people in Cambridge. Was there anyone in particular?'

'Well, sir, I thought you might be able to point me in the right direction. If I'm to make my mark, I need to get acquainted with the great and the good everywhere I go in the world. And in this country, I believe London, Oxford and Cambridge are the places.'

'Among others. But you're right, the university towns are a good starting point. The problem is, though, Cambridge seems to be closing down for the duration.'

'Well perhaps you could at least show me around your college, sir. I believe it's one of the great old ones.'

Wilde handed Tripp his coffee. 'I was just on my way, but I'll wait while you get that down you.' He noted that the young man needed a shave and that his poetic hair could do with a brush or comb. Nor was his costly attire as immaculate as it had been when they met in Chelsea. 'Perhaps you'd like to use my bathroom? I have that rarity in England, a shower.'

'That would be swell, Professor. Sleep can come later.'

'I even have soap and tooth powder.'

Tripp grinned. 'I think I spoke a little undiplomatically in Mr Vanderberg's house, didn't I?'

'Oh, I'm sure you were forgiven.' Wilde smiled. 'And then, when you've freshened up, you can either follow me in your car or hop on the back of my motorbike. Who knows, we might even run into Marcus Marfield.'

'Thank you, sir. I'd sure like to see him again. And hear that voice.'

Wilde smiled again. Yes, Marcus Marfield might indeed count as one of the attractions of Cambridge in young Tripp's eyes. Whether he would actually find him was another matter.

Lydia stood naked in front of the full-length mirror in her bedroom and turned side-on to gauge the progress of her bump. Having told Tom the news, she was beginning to enjoy the thought of her pregnancy, could dream of the human being growing inside her and could think of baby clothes and all that went with it. They had talked of the chances she would be able to train as a doctor. Tom had thought it unlikely, but suggested Rupert might have some idea. He was surely the man to ask.

She dressed, and then phoned Addenbrooke's. Miss Hollick wasn't answering the phone but someone on the switchboard said she was expected later in the day to clear out Dr Charlecote's room and box up his possessions. Lydia thanked the receptionist and decided to try again later after she had gone to Histon.

'Is Professor Cook in college?'

'Who shall I say is calling, sir?'

'Tom Wilde.'

'Just a moment, Mr Wilde.'

While Lincoln Tripp washed away the long night in the shower, Wilde was in the hallway, calling his old friend Noel Cook at Balliol College, Oxford.

The telephonist came back on the line. 'Putting you through, sir.'

'Tom?'

'Hello, Noel.'

'How the devil are you? Still slaving away in the other place?'

'I have been, though not quite sure what I'll be doing now there's a war on. Look, I know we've got a lot to catch up on, but I'm a bit pushed for time right now – just wanted to ask a favour of you.'

'Fire away.'

'Chap called Ptolemy Marfield, I believe he read Greats at Balliol.'

'Indeed, I was his tutor. Just left us with a First. Fine young man when you get to know him.'

'What do you mean "when you get to know him"?'

'Well, he's not very prepossessing. Strong in mind and body, but ungainly and wouldn't win any beauty contests. Mumbles rather. That sounds awful, but I don't know how else to put it.'

'Do you know where he is now?'

'I do, Tom. He's just about to start teaching at a small prep school in Essex. I imagine he's already there, settling in before term starts. One sec, I'll get the address and number for you . . .'

Wilde got through to Ptolemy Marfield without trouble, but he noticed that the young man seemed cautious even as he explained who he was.

'Why exactly are you calling now, professor?' he asked at last.

'You know your father is dead?'

'Of course.'

'And you know that your brother has returned to England?'

'My mother did mention it.'

'Surely it's a big event for your family?'

'In a way, I suppose it is. But I say again, Professor, what has any of this to do with you?'

'Because I brought your brother home – and I'm rather worried about him.'

'I wouldn't worry about Marcus, if I were you – I'd worry about yourself.'

'I'm sorry, I'm not sure I understand.'

A sigh and a long pause drifted down the line from Essex.

'Mr Marfield?'

'Mr Wilde, I'm still not at all sure why you called, but if I may make a suggestion, you would do well to get as far away from my brother as you can. I'd suggest ten thousand miles. A million if it were possible.'

Wilde was taken aback. 'And you?' he said rather weakly.

'I'm already packing. Good day to you, Professor.'

Lydia was about to knock on the front door when she noticed it was slightly ajar. A light breeze caught it and it swung inwards.

She peered into the house and saw a young woman clattering a suitcase down the stairs.

'Mrs Marfield?'

The woman didn't seem to hear above the noise of her own exertions. It was only when she reached the foot of the staircase and stopped to catch her breath that she spotted the newcomer at the door. She jerked backwards as though she'd been hit.

'I'm sorry,' Lydia said. 'I didn't meant to alarm you. The door was open. I did knock.'

Claire Marfield held her hand to her chest. Her eyes were wide with shock and something else. Fear perhaps? 'Who are you – and why are you in my house?'

'I'm Lydia Morris, Professor Wilde's . . . friend.' Suddenly she didn't quite know how to describe herself. 'He suggested I come to see you.'

Claire went to the door and looked out in all directions, then closed it. To Lydia she had the hunted look of a startled deer.

'I'm sorry if I frightened you.'

'You just appeared out of nowhere. Of course I was scared. Now what's this about? We've got a train to catch.' Claire Marfield's voice sounded tight.

Lydia offered her best smile. 'Have you got five minutes? It's just, well, Tom was worried about you. Asked me if I'd talk to you . . .'

Claire gave in with a shrug. 'Come on, we'll go to the kitchen until my taxi arives. But five minutes and that's my lot.'

Walter eyed the newcomer with interest. He was playing on the kitchen floor with a toy wooden mallet that he used to bash round pegs into round holes and square pegs into square holes.

'Hello,' Lydia said. 'I'm Lydia Morris. What's your name?'

The boy didn't answer.

'He's not talking much, I'm afraid. Actually he hasn't said a word yet. I'm beginning to get a little worried about him.'

'He's only two, isn't he? Plenty of time, I think.' Even as they talked, Lydia was acutely aware that Claire Marfield's eyes were not on her but the window, as though she was afraid someone might suddenly appear.

'I hope so.'

'Were you just off on holiday? I'm sorry to have interrupted.'

Claire Marfield paused, as if weighing something up. 'Let's just say I'm visiting friends,' she said at last. A horn hooted outside. Once again Claire recoiled, rather as if she had heard gunfire instead of a taxi. She jumped to her feet and took her son's hand. 'I'm afraid your time's up, Miss Morris.'

'Could I share with you? I came by taxi myself but I let it go. I need to get back into town. We could talk a little more on the way.'

'If you must. Come on – you can lug the bags while I deal with Walter.'

Lydia and Claire Marfield sat in the back of the cab with Walter perched on his mother's knee. The car stank of stale tobacco smoke. Three pieces of luggage were crammed into the boot.

'You seem in rather a hurry to get away. Has something happened?'

Claire Marfield turned towards the window, but not before Lydia noticed tears welling up in her eyes. Walter seemed to sense that something was wrong, too, for he nestled closer into his mother's bosom.

'Mrs Marfield . . . Claire – please talk to me. We can help, I'm sure of it.'

The other woman shook her head vigorously. Tears fell.

'Come to my house. Whatever it is, Tom and I will look after you.'

By now Claire Marfield was sobbing, trying not to let Walter hear her crying.

Lydia leant forward and spoke to the driver. 'Change of plan. We're not going to the station. Head for Jesus Lane. I'll show you.'

'No, no,' Claire Marfield said. 'The station. My train . . .'

The driver suppressed his irritation. 'Station it is then.'

Lydia thought she heard three words that chilled her, though she had no idea what they meant. Claire spoke so quietly that for a moment Lydia thought she might have misheard.

'I saw something,' she said.

'What? Tell me. Please tell me, Claire.'

'Something terrible. I can't. I'm sorry . . .'

By now they were at the station. Lydia paid off the taxi as mother and child went into the ticket office. For a moment, Lydia considered following them, but she waited on the concourse and watched as Claire carried her child along the platform, looking about her warily all the while. Assisted by a luggage porter, she got into a first-class compartment of the waiting train.

A couple of minutes later, there was a piercing whistle, a rush of steam, and the southbound train pulled away.

CHAPTER 21

'Marfield's father left a suicide note, Tom. His wife verified it. There really isn't much doubt that he took his own life.'

Wilde and Dr Rupert Weir were in the Eagle in Bene't Street, having just ordered lunchtime pints of beer.

'Were there similarities with Charlecote's death?'

'Not really. Colonel Marfield sat on a chair, wedged the butt of his shotgun against the wall, held the barrel in his mouth with one hand, used the other to pull the trigger. I've seen it before.'

'Do we have any idea what the note said?'

'The Ipswich coroner's office read it to me.' Rupert Weir dug his hand into the inside pocket of his tweed jacket and pulled out a crumpled sheet of paper. 'Here, I took it down.' He handed it to Wilde.

The note was addressed to Colonel Marfield's wife, Margaret.

A man can put up with shame. But not this loss of hope. Not the discovery that goodness has fled the world. Margaret, he was my life: our perfect son. The glory of his voice in King's Chapel, those Sundays around the piano . . . they were the finest of days. And now I can hardly bear to say his name. For what he has become, I can never forgive.

Wilde read it again and frowned. 'Rather an abrupt ending, Rupert?'

'In my experience there are two types of suicide: the ones who race home and knot the rope around the banisters at speed and hurl themselves into oblivion without a moment's hesitation, and then there are those who put off the dread moment, all the while summoning up the courage to do the deed. The first never write notes, the latter often do. I think it probably helps concentrate their minds. But then the end, when it comes, can be a sudden picking up of a pistol, the thoughts unfinished, the note half-written. Compared to some of them, this note is reasonably clear and rounded.'

'It's suggesting Marcus changed in some terrible way.'

'Well, he went off to the Spanish war.'

'And was that so terrible? Colonel Marfield had been a fighting man. Why would his son taking up arms affect him so deeply?'

Rupert Weir shrugged. 'Perhaps old man Marfield had a loathing for socialists.'

'Maybe you're right.'

Wilde put down his pint, still almost full. He wanted a clear head, and English beer at lunchtime had a tendency to wipe out afternoons. During the morning, he had visited college in the company of Lincoln Tripp. He left the young American in the old court and called on Marfield's rooms, on the off-chance. He was surprised when Marfield answered the door, unshaven, in his pyjamas.

'I appear to have woken you.'

'I'm sorry, Professor. Still trying to get my bearings.'

'That's fine by me. Sleep as much as you like.' Wilde looked him in the eye and wondered about his brother's portentous words. 'Now tell me, where did you disappear to yesterday? And why?'

'I needed air.'

'You weren't by any chance trying to avoid Mr Eaton and Mr Rowlands were you?'

Marfield grinned. 'Am I that obvious?'

Wilde ignored this attempt at charm. 'They've told me a bit about the work you were doing in Spain. They want to know why you broke off contact with them.'

'That's easy – I lost my nerve.'

'Then why didn't you just tell them that? And why are you avoiding them now?'

'I've had enough, that's why. I know their type – they never let you go.'

Wilde made no comment. He had decided not to tell him that they were still in Cambridge. 'So what now? Even with a dearth of students, I doubt whether the Master and Fellows will be keen to allow you to continue your studies once they hear that you have a wife and child, whom you abandoned.'

'Do they have to hear that?'

'Yes, they do – and you have to face up to your responsibilities. I visited your wife again. At home in Histon. You have a fine boy.'

'Really?'

'You sound rather indifferent.'

'Well, there you go.' Marfield shrugged.

'Interestingly, there was a van parked outside her house. In the driver's seat was the woman I saw with you outside the Vanderbergs' house in London. The woman with the gun. Rosa.'

The blood drained from Marfield's cheeks.

'You seem shocked.'

Marfield was silent, his mouth set hard.

'I approached her,' Wilde continued, 'but she drove off at speed.'

'When was this?'

'Yesterday evening. Correct me if I'm wrong, but it seems your past is catching up with you. Don't you think it might be time to come clean about one or two things?'

Marfield was obviously struggling to compose himself. 'There's a lot to think about. For the moment, though, I just want to sing, Professor. Think things through. Perhaps I will go and see my wife and son. But I need time. Please. Is that so unreasonable after two years or more on the front line?'

'Very well. I'll leave you with your thoughts. In the meantime, I have a visitor for you.' He opened the door and signalled to Tripp, who approached with a broad grin.

'Good Lord,' Marfield said. 'If it isn't Mr Tripp.'

Tripp, newly shaven and back to something like his pristine and rather elegant self, stepped forward and the two young men shook hands like old friends.

'To what do we owe the honour, Tripp?'

'Oh you know, Marfield, just passing through. Couldn't resist calling in on you.'

'Then you'll have breakfast with me?'

Tripp threw Wilde a wry look. 'Of course – every man needs two breakfasts. And then I'll be on my way back to London.'

'Just let me throw a few clothes on. Professor, will you join us?'

'No, Marcus, I have things to do. Enjoy your breakfast with Mr Tripp, but don't avoid the hard questions too long. They won't go away.'

Now, here in the Eagle with Rupert Weir, he was wondering about Marfield and the deaths of two men, one certainly suicide, the other less certain. And why on earth was Ptolemy Marfield so afraid?

*

As the train carrying Claire and Walter pulled out of Cambridge Station, Lydia felt she had failed. Claire said she had seen something, but had given no hint as to what that might be. What could she have seen to make her leave her home in such haste?

Despondent, Lydia walked back into the centre of town. On every corner there was a pile of sand and empty bags waiting to be filled. What a miserable way to treat this most beautiful of towns.

Even the grand facade of Addenbrooke's Hospital was undergoing protective work, and the thought that an enemy might bomb a hospital added to her feeling of despair. However, inside the building, everything was its usual bustle of nurses, patients and doctors.

She found Priscilla Hollick in Dr Charlecote's office, carting a cardboard box of books.

'Miss Hollick, can I have a word?'

'Oh, hello, Miss Morris.' The voice was decidedly frosty.

'Could I take you for coffee? There's something I really think you might be able to help me with.'

'Really? Might that have something to do with Dr Charlecote's notebook? I do believe it has been stolen.'

'Coffee?'

'Very well.'

They walked to Dorothy's and settled for a pot of tea and a plate of sandwiches. Lydia took the notebook from her bag and laid it on the table.

'I thought you might be the thief.'

'Actually, it wasn't me. And I wouldn't call it theft. More a little light borrowing in search of truth. The problem is, we can't read it.'

'Why should I help you?

'Because you think there's something unexplained about Dr Charlecote's death. And because you're probably the only person living who can decipher his scrawl. Can you read that last entry concerning his appointment with Marcus Marfield?'

Priscilla Hollick clutched her small slender hands together on the table, on the verge of tears. She looked up defiantly. 'You have no idea what we've been through all these years. I loved him. His wife's illness and death, his crippling arthritis – it was so difficult keeping it secret, all the time knowing how the world would judge us if they ever found out.'

'I understand, truly I do.' Lydia reached out and covered the woman's hands with her own. 'And I would never judge you. If you must know I'm pregnant and unmarried, so I'm in no position to judge anyone.'

Miss Hollick pulled her hands away and furiously brushed the tears from her eyes. 'So we're both wicked sinners and going to hell . . .'

'I don't believe loving someone is a sin. But murder is – and we are concerned that the man you loved might not have taken his own life. Please, Miss Hollick, please help us.'

Priscilla Hollick shook her dark hair and dabbed again at her eyes. 'Give me the book.'

Lydia slid the black-bound notebook across the table. Priscilla Hollick turned it around, then flicked through the pages until she came to the last entry. She sniffed and pulled a handkerchief from her sleeve to blow her nose. 'It's all a bit shambolic, isn't it? The funny thing is, he couldn't even read it back himself, relied on me totally.'

'Did he ask you to marry him?'

'We did talk about it, but you know he loved his wife, too. But not in the same way. And when the awful cancer took her, he was beside himself. After she died, well it was all too soon. Perhaps next year, he said. But now of course, I'm just an old maid. No one will ever want me.'

'You're an attractive woman. And young enough.'

She shook her head sadly. 'No, I'm worn out and I look it. I'm used goods – and not even a child to show for it. If you're in the family way, I envy you.' She sighed, and stiffened her shoulders. 'That's enough of that. Let's take a look at what he wrote.'

CHAPTER 22

'He's at college right now if you want him,' Wilde said. 'At least he was ten minutes ago.'

'Mr Wilde,' Rowlands said. 'Did you really think we didn't know that? Did you think we would have left him on the loose, unwatched, all night long?'

'So you've already spoken to him?'

Eaton was sitting in an armchair, his stick at his side, gripped in his right hand. The empty left sleeve of his suit was tucked neatly into his jacket pocket. He shook his head slowly. 'First we want to watch him and listen to him, see where he goes, who he talks to.'

Wilde had never been sure about Eaton, but it was difficult not to feel for the man after the life-altering injuries he had suffered just three months earlier. Eaton retained his urbanity, but it was impossible not to detect the light quavering in his measured tones. This must be draining him. 'Why would you want to watch him?' Wilde demanded. 'Do you suspect he's up to no good?'

'Don't you, Wilde? Isn't that what's been preying on your mind this past week or more?'

Of course it was. 'But you do understand that he already knows you're here?'

'We accepted that you'd probably told him.'

'No, that wasn't the way it happened. You gentlemen carelessly gave your names at the porters' lodge. He checked there.'

'Ah, then as you say, that was a little careless of us.'

'Why don't you just haul him in?'

Eaton looked exasperated. 'Wilde, this is Britain, not Germany. You can't just incarcerate someone because you think they might be up to something. One might apply for an alien to be interned, but not a British-born subject of His Majesty. Not without sound cause.'

'He's a Bolshevik – isn't that enough?'

Eaton raised an eyebrow. 'You sound uncharacteristically cynical, Wilde.'

'That's because I'm sick of the very name of Marcus Marfield. And I'm equally sick of your secret games, Eaton.'

They were in Rowlands's room, which had the whiff of smoke and expensive eau de cologne. Rowlands turned to his senior officer: 'Actually, Philip, I agree with Wilde. We're at war now. The department is stretched to breaking point. We can't both stay in bloody Cambridge indefinitely in case our rogue agent decides to do something deranged. We could bring him in under the Defence of the Realm Act.'

'No, that's not going to happen.' Eaton sounded more robust. 'There are those who want to intern every potential foe, but that's Hitler's damned way and we're not going down that road. We keep to the higher ground or we might as well capitulate right now.'

Rowlands drew deep on his cigarette. 'You see what I'm up against, Wilde?'

'Why don't you just go to his rooms now and see what he has to say for himself? Yesterday you wanted me to bring him to you – and you were furious when he slipped away. What's changed?'

'The fact that he did a runner to start with. It confirmed that we have reason to be suspicious. And so we are adopting another tack – I hope with your assistance.'

Eaton and Rowlands exchanged glances. Eaton nodded.

'All right, here's the deal, Mr Wilde,' Rowlands continued. 'I'm sure you know a tea room called the Samovar, yes?'

The vision of Marcus sitting conversing earnestly with Elina Kossoff at a small round table and then disappearing into some back room for purposes of their own came instantly to mind. 'Yes, everyone knows the Samovar. Been in Cambridge at least as long as I have. What of it?'

'Do you know the people who run the joint?'

'I'm on nodding terms with the parents, but I know the daughter rather better.'

'They're Russian emigrés.'

'And I suppose that makes them people of interest because there's a war on.'

'They were already people of interest.'

'There are many refugees in Britain. But you obviously think there's something different about the Kossoffs. They've always seemed entirely respectable to me.'

Rowlands tipped tobacco ash into an ashtray, and nodded.

'Are you hinting at something suspicious about the family?' Wilde asked.

Eaton dropped his stick and grasped Wilde's arm with his right hand. 'We need your help, old boy. We simply don't have the manpower. I don't suppose you're going to be rushing to join the British Army any time soon, so perhaps you'd like to help us in some small way and fight for democracy against the powers of darkness. I know you're good at this sort of stuff, Wilde.'

'It's true I'm acquainted with Elina – but I don't have the faintest idea how you think she might be involved. What is it you want me to do?'

'Well, solving the murder of Dr Eric Charlecote might be a start . . .'

'*Charlecote?* Good God, Eaton, what do you know about that?'

'The question is, what do *you* know, Wilde? You're the one who's been running around looking into the case. You suspect Marcus Marfield, don't you – so why in God's name haven't you mentioned this to us?'

'Surely you don't suspect the Kossoffs of any involvement?'

Rowlands shrugged non-committally.

'You do suspect them! And now you want *me* to hare off on a wild goose chase so you can toodle off back to London.'

Eaton shrugged. 'I've had my eyes on them for years. But as I said, we're short of manpower, and we can't list it as a priority. It's the sort of thing Five should be doing, but they haven't a single agent left. Guy and I shouldn't even be here. We should be in London, organising our contacts in Europe and further afield. There's a war on, Wilde.' He paused, then tried to lighten things up with a smile. 'How about your little gyp, Billy?'

'Bobby.'

'That's the fellow. Can't be much going on at college and I'm sure he'd like to earn a few shillings. He could help you stake out the Samovar. You've used him before, after all.'

'And he had his head hammered to within an inch of his life,' said Wilde grimly. 'So no, I won't be asking Bobby to watch a tea shop in his spare time. What would he be looking for anyway? Illicit cakes and scones smuggled in from Mother Russia? More to the damned point, what are *you* hoping I could do?' Wilde was weakening. The problem, as always, was that he was interested. He wanted answers to his questions, solutions to problems.

'Find out what's going on,' Eaton said.

'And then we'll fix it.' Rowlands let out a stream of smoke.

'Look – I'll do what I can, but you'd better tell me what you know. Most importantly, why are you suspicious?'

Eaton patted Wilde's arm. 'Good man, Wilde. Now then, as you know the Samovar is run by the Kossoff family. Nikolai and Anna, refugees from the Bolshevik revolution. Our records show that they settled here in England with their daughter Elina in the early twenties, first in London, then moving to Cambridge in 1932, where they took over an established tea shop and changed its name to the Samovar, adding a traditional Russian twist, as you've probably noted if you have been there.'

Wilde nodded. The traditional samovar urns, the photographs of the last Tsar and Tsarina and their family adorning the walls, the double-headed eagle motifs on the counter. One could almost imagine oneself in a pre-revolutionary Moscow salon. A bit too kitsch for his liking, but the coffee was sensational and the Samovar was always well patronised.

'Your pretty friend Elina has been paying visits to Ivan Maisky at 13 Kensington Palace Gardens.'

'The Soviet Embassy? Why would she do that?'

'Why indeed? We always thought the Kossoffs had a deep loathing for the Soviets.'

'Is that all?'

'No, she's been seen at the American embassy, too.'

'Do you know why?'

'We thought she was probably inquiring about travelling to New York. Many people do.'

'But you were already keeping a watch on her?'

Eaton laughed. 'No, we were watching the embassies. Well, our friends in Five were. Standard procedure. Actually, we're pretty sure she wasn't inquiring about a visa: she's been in and out of the place like a cuckoo in a clock. You have a good friend there: perhaps you could inquire for us.'

'Maybe Elina Kossoff just has a penchant for diplomats.' Even as he spoke, he realised his flippancy was misplaced. There *was* something odd about a young tea shop manageress from a provincial university town paying visits to two important embassies in London, particularly in the case of the Soviet embassy. Did she really have access to Ambassador Maisky? 'But – all right,' he said, 'you've got my interest. And if I were to assist you, what would you want me to do?'

'Well, Wilde, I think we can leave it to you to work that one out.'

Anything that helped Rupert Weir and his inquiries into the death of Eric Charlecote seemed like a good idea. But the idea that Elina Kossof might have any bearing on that seemed an awfully long shot.

'Rowlands and I will be returning to London within the hour. You know how to contact me.'

Wilde went to the door, but turned before opening it. 'How's the war going? The newspapers and wireless tell us nothing.'

'That's because there's nothing to tell. The French and Germans are taking the occasional potshot at each other along the Maginot Line, the Germans are crushing the Poles and we've dropped a few desultory bombs on the Kiel Canal – oh, and ten million leaflets to tell the German populace what a beastly fellow Herr Hitler is. As if they hadn't had opportunity to work that one out for themselves by now, had they so desired.'

'And the *Athenia*?'

'Not much to report, I'm afraid,' Rowlands said. 'Though I heard that the South African minister at the Hague, Dr Van Broekhuizen, has been telling everyone who will listen that he has it on good authority from the British government that the *Athenia* hit a British mine and was not torpedoed by the Germans at all. Nonsense, of course, but that's the way this will be played out. Not much in the way of blood-soaked battlefields on the western front yet, but the propaganda war is raging. Perception is everything, you see.'

'Any more word on survivors? Has the *City of Flint* made port yet?'

'No, she'll arrive next Tuesday or Wednesday. Why – do you have a special interest?'

'A friend and her son are missing.'

'Mrs Vanderberg?' Eaton suggested.

'Indeed.'

'God, I'm sorry to hear that. Damned awful. I'll make it my business to find out what I can for you, old boy. Least I can do.'

Priscilla Hollick handed a sheet of paper to Lydia. 'Here you are, this is my translation.'

Lydia smoothed it down on the desk. Four or five hundred words, written in a neat hand. 'The notebook entry looked rather longer,' she said.

'Eric's notes could be a little clumsy, but I always edit them to a professional standard. Nothing is left out, I promise you.'

'Very well.' Lydia began to read.

Subject: *Marcus Marfield, aged 21.*

Occupation: *Cambridge University undergraduate, turned mercenary. Now returned to England under the care of Professor Thomas Wilde.*

Reason for referral: *Evidence of neurasthenia caused by battle fatigue.*

Symptoms: *Nightmares, shakes, quick to anger.*

The subject arrived with a suggestion that he is suffering from neurasthenia, or shell shock. Let us put that to one side for a moment. An initial diagnosis from observation might suggest this man has a severe personality disorder, which may or may not precede his recent war experiences. He is extremely resentful and difficult. He clearly does not want to be here with me. Outwardly, he may appear to some as a charming young man, but he did not act that way with me. Close to the surface is a hair-trigger. He is convinced that he cannot be hypnotised, but in fact it is extremely easy and within two minutes of his entry to my office, I have him under. He talks angrily in general terms about the cold, the lack of food and the discomfort of front-line warfare. Not once does he mention fear, which surprises me. When I ask him about his bullet wound he says it hurt, nothing more. He describes conditions in the camp in France in an offhand manner, as though he were an inspector of prisons rather than an inmate. I question him further but he descends into a long silence. He rises from the couch and paces about, then looks out of the window. He is shaking. He talks of a ravine and blood, then stops and looks at me with an unsettling smile. Or rather his eyes and mouth are formed in the shape of a smile, but his expression is blank. The session has been long, and I have had enough, so I bring him out. He smirks and says, 'I told you I couldn't be hypnotised.' I disabuse him. 'You are wrong, Mr Marfield. You were hypnotised, and very effectively.' He becomes extremely agitated, launches himself at me and pins me to the wall, his hand at my throat. I have never seen colder eyes and I feel real fear – in myself, not him. He demands to know what he has said. 'Very little,' I tell him. He glares at me, then drops me like a stone, turns away and makes for the door. It occurs to me that he believes he has revealed something of himself, something he wished to keep hidden. As for shell shock or battle fatigue, he doesn't have it. Was he playing with me? I am still not certain, but I have no doubt that he is both an actor and a psychopath.

Lydia turned the page, expecting more. But there was nothing. 'Is that it?'

Priscilla Hollick nodded. 'You saw the way they parted. But you should know that while Marcus Marfield might well have been anxious that he had revealed something of himself that he wished to remain hidden, the truth is he would not have done so. Despite what we read in newspapers and pulp fiction, under hypnosis we only say what we wish to say.'

'But he might have believed he had divulged some secret?'

'Yes, that's entirely possible. And one more thing: just as Eric left, he muttered something under his breath.'

'What was it?'

'He said, "One of the best examples of a psychopath I've ever had in my office."'

CHAPTER 23

'Shall we go home, Henry?' Jim Vanderberg asked his son as they drove back into the centre of Glasgow. They had been to Greenock with Jack Kennedy to talk to the officers on the destroyer *Electra*, one of the Royal Navy warships that had assisted with the *Athenia* rescue operation, and the one that had brought Henry to safety.

'We can't without Willie and Ma.'

'I know, son, but, well, I think Ma would want me to take you back home. That's where she'll expect to find you when she turns up.'

When she turns up. What Vanderberg had not told his son was that a lieutenant on the ship had told him that one of the survivors mentioned a woman and a boy to him. 'She said she saw two or three people in a dinghy – much smaller than the lifeboats – but feared it had capsized. There was a lot of confusion.'

'Two or three people?'

'Well, a woman and a child – and perhaps someone else. She wasn't sure.'

'Do you have a name for this informant, lieutenant?'

'I'm afraid I don't, sir. I believe she was Canadian. Not injured as I recall, so probably not in any of the Glasgow hospitals.'

And that was all he could uncover. No one else aboard the *Electra* recalled the woman's testimony, nor could he find any information about a dinghy with two or three people in it. Vanderberg had never felt so low.

*

Back in his Chelsea house, Eaton flopped into his ancient morocco sofa. The scent of the old leather told him he was home. The trip to Cambridge had taken more out of him than he cared to admit, even to himself. This war was going to be the death of him, and that was before the bombs and bullets started.

Apart from the sheer physical exhaustion, there was the mental fatigue involved in enduring the ministrations of Guy Rowlands, however well meaning he might be. It really couldn't go on like this.

He looked around his comfortable sitting room. His father's paintings adorned the walls. Scenes of southern France, a couple of nudes. He loved this room. To hell with bed, he would sleep here, on the sofa. Perhaps tonight he would not wake in panic, facing the van as it drove into him full-on, accelerating as it threw him into the air so that he fell onto the road with shattering force, smashing his left leg and destroying his left arm. There were days when he felt a deep resentment that this had happened to him. The worst days were those when a well-meaning doctor told him he was lucky to be alive. He didn't feel lucky.

Sometimes this summer he had felt half a man, but these past few days, back in some sort of harness, he had begun to feel if not whole, then at least alive. Exhausted, but alive.

The phone started to ring. He tried to ignore it, but eventually he swore and pulled himself up from the sofa.

'Eaton here.'

'Mr Eaton, you're home.'

'I am, Carstairs – and damned pleased about it.'

'I'm sorry to bother you, but everything's escalating. Streams of information from all stations, Moscow to Warsaw and Berlin to Paris and Rome. There are one or two I thought you should hear without delay.'

'First, what's the word on the ship that went down?'

'Our Wilhelmshaven sources identify the U-boat as U-30, commanded by one Fritz-Julius Lemp, but it sounds like an error on his part. His superiors are not at all happy and have opted for the denial option.'

'Nothing from the Canada-bound steamer?'

'*City of Flint*? No, sir.'

Damn it. He'd love to be able to help Jim Vanderberg. Do a favour, and one day you can ask one in return. Cynical, yes, but he'd been in this game far too long. 'Keep me posted on that if you would, Carstairs.'

'Yes, sir.'

'Go on then, tell me what else you've got.'

For the next fifteen minutes, Carstairs reported on the essentials of communiques from all parts of the world. Eaton listened carefully, took notes where necessary. Finally Carstairs came to a halt.

'Is that everything? Can I go to sleep now?'

'Just one other thing, sir. Captain Daru from the *Deuxième Bureau* mentioned something that may be of interest, though its relevance is not immediately obvious.'

'I'll hear it anyway.'

'There was a shooting near Paris last week. An attempt on the life of Mr William Bullitt, the American ambassador.'

'Why has there been no word of this in the press? Damned difficult to keep a thing like that secret.'

'The thing is, no one knew it had happened. The assassin, a fellow named Talleyrand Bois, killed the wrong man and was then shot by a gendarme. This all happened in the grounds of the Chateau de Chantilly. Mr Bullitt's main residence is the Chateau de St Firmin, which is rather smaller, but a couple of hundred yards away. A case of mistaken identity.'

'How can they know that?'

'Bois – who is a Bolshevik of long-standing and well known to the *Deuxième* – has been in a coma for the past week. Yesterday he regained consciousness, convinced he had done his bit for the revolution by doing away with a filthy capitalist Yankee swine.'

'And the actual victim?'

'An Australian tourist, sir. Has something of the look of Mr Bullitt. Very sad.'

'Thank you, Carstairs.' With a war under way it made sense for allies to keep each other informed, particularly when it involved their American friends.

'One more thing, sir.'

'Yes, Carstairs?'

'Bois let slip that he had been recruited by a Comintern agent codenamed Honoré. The DB were wondering if the name meant anything to us – because it doesn't to them.'

As Wilde entered the Samovar, a bell at the top of the door tinkled. It was nine in the morning and the tea shop was almost empty. A waitress in black skirt and white apron approached with a smile and invited him to sit wherever he wished.

He took a seat against the far wall, close to a door to the back of the shop so that he had a clear view of the whole room.

'What would you like, sir?'

'Coffee, please. Java. No milk or sugar. Nice and strong.'

'And something to eat? We have fresh scones or Welsh rarebit.'

'None of that sounds very Russian.'

The waitress laughed. 'Indeed not, sir. You're not the first person to notice.'

'A scone then.'

She turned to walk away, but he put up a hand. 'Tell me, are you alone here?'

'Yes sir, Miss Kossoff is out this morning.'

'Where are her parents these days?'

'Oh, they're away in America, sir. Miss Kossoff is in charge when they're not here.'

'And she's away, too, you say?'

'She did say she'd be in this afternoon. Shall I ask her to call you?'

'No, no. I'll come back.'

'What was your name, sir? I'll tell her you were looking for her.'

'Tom Wilde. Professor Tom Wilde.' He gave her his college phone number. He doubted Elina Kossoff would call, but you never knew.

He had come here this morning after a long conversation with Lydia late into the night. They had discussed Dr Charlecote's notes and his comments on Marcus Marfield. 'I don't suppose I should be that surprised,' Wilde said. 'There must always be an element of violence to anyone who chooses to go off to war.'

'Says the man who loves boxing and goes down to the gym to beat the living daylights out of some poor sparring partner.'

'Vice versa more often than not these days.'

'Well, just don't expect any sympathy when you get a broken nose and lose your front teeth!'

The conversation had moved on to Eaton and Rowlands.

'And you agreed to help, of course?'

'Lydia, darling, I was already working on it anyway. You're not happy about Charlecote's death and nor is Rupert Weir. And Charlecote's notes go a long way to underpin our suspicions that there is something not right about Marfield. He might not even have been allowed back in the country had we not secured a passport for him – and I feel responsible for that. I don't know what he's up to, but I certainly don't like it. Even his brother seems scared of him.'

She threw him a wry look. 'And we've all got to do our bit for the war effort?'

He smiled. 'Eaton did say something like that.'

'Of course he did. It'll be the stock phrase every time someone in authority wants to take advantage of anyone.'

Their talk turned at last to the Samovar. They both agreed it was utterly pointless trying to stake out the place; they wouldn't even know what they were watching for. 'And so I might as well go ahead and talk to them,' said Wilde. 'Play a straight bat, as my housemaster used to say.'

Lydia started laughing.

'What's so funny?'

'The thought of you at Harrow, Professor Wilde . . . I bet you held your cricket bat like a baseball bat.'

'You know me too well, Lydia.'

His visit to the Samovar had indeed yielded nothing but a fine cup of coffee. He left the waitress a good tip and walked out into the fresh, warm air. The town was busy. A small group of children carrying suitcases was being shepherded through the market and Wilde deduced that they must be evacuees from London. It was said that a substantial number of children and mothers would be coming here.

From Petty Cury, he cut westwards across the edge of the market, striding at a brisk pace. Suddenly he stopped. Among the market square crowd he spotted a familiar figure, small, slender, dark-haired and with a bronzed complexion, unusual in this pale eastern England market town. He had seen her in France; he had seen her confront Marcus Marfield outside the Vanderbergs' Chelsea house; and he had seen her speed off when he approached her van in Histon. Rosa.

She was walking fast along the west of the market place, and he followed her. He put a hand to her shoulder. She froze.

'Rosa,' he said. 'You are Rosa, yes?'

Slowly she turned. 'I have nothing to say to you,' she hissed, her English accurate but her accent plainly Spanish.

'You were with Marcus Marfield in Spain. Please, spare me five minutes at least. I'd like to know more about him – and I might be able to help you.'

She pursed her lips and he thought she would spit in his face, but she gave a scornful 'puh' sound.

'I mean you no harm,' said Wilde. 'I promise you.'

'Men and their promises. Why would I talk to you – you are his friend. You are all the same.'

He shook his head. 'No, that's not true. You know nothing about me – but I am willing to answer any questions you have. Won't you come and have a cup of tea with me. Or just sit down by the river? Five minutes, Rosa. I beg you.'

She was wearing a dark ankle-length skirt and a short blue jacket, perhaps a little too warm for the balmy September weather. She slipped her hand in her pocket. Wilde thrust out his hand and gripped her arm.

'No weapons,' he said. 'That really isn't necessary. Look – I am a professor here at the university. That's how I know Marcus Marfield. My name is Thomas Wilde. We were in France on vacation and his plight in the camp was brought to our attention, so we agreed to bring him home. That's all. Please, come and talk to me. I may be able to help you – and you may be able to explain one or two things to me.'

'He is the devil, and you are his friend, that's all I need to know about you.'

She wrenched her hand away from his grip and pulled it from her pocket. There was no gun. Then she turned away from him and continued to walk towards Market Street. At the corner, she stopped and turned back to gaze in his direction. She raised her chin dismissively, as though to say, 'I despise you.' Even at a distance of a hundred yards he could feel her antipathy.

And then, once again, she was gone. Wilde began to run after her. At the corner of Sidney Street, he saw her again, heading north. Just past Sidney Sussex, he caught up with her. She didn't stop, so he walked at her shoulder, firing questions at her. 'Why are you here? Why were you at Histon in that van? Who sent you? Who do you work for? Why do you call Marfield the devil – what did he do to you?'

His questions were met with silence and a mouth set in grim defiance.

Ahead of them, coming in their direction, was a uniformed policeman on his beat. Wilde had seen him around town, often passing a word or two in greeting. 'Rosa – if that really is your name – you should talk to me,' said Wilde. 'If I stop that police officer now and lay a complaint, you will be arrested and taken into custody. You will be either interned or expelled from the country. Do you want that?'

She stopped. Her eyes swivelled from the looming constable to Wilde and then back. 'OK,' she said. 'I'll talk.'

The officer arrived, halted and gave them the once over. He knew every house in the streets on his beat and he seemed to know every face in town. 'Morning, Professor Wilde.'

'Good day to you, Constable Gates.'

'Is everything all right, sir?'

'Yes, thank you. Just giving this young lady directions to Jesus Lane.'

'What is she, new scholar?'

'I believe she's Spanish, staying with friends. Got a little lost.'

'Ah well, sir, I'm afraid we have to take note of foreigners. Orders of the Chief Constable.' He turned his gaze to Rosa. 'Might I have your name, young lady?'

'Cortez. Rosa Cortez. As this kind gentleman said, I am from Spain, staying with friends.'

'I take it you've signed the Aliens' Register, madam?'

'Indeed, yes.'

The policeman hesitated, then tipped his helmet. 'Well, good day to you, I'm sure the professor here will see you right with his directions – and don't let me see either of you out again without your gas mask boxes.'

They watched him depart, walking with firm, unhurried steps on his circular route.

'Well?' Wilde said at last. 'Are we going to talk now? My rooms in college, perhaps.'

'We go to the river. Marfield will be at your college and I don't wish to see him. He is your creature, is he not? It was you who sent him to Spain after all.'

'Is that what he told you? I promise you I did no such thing. I was as surprised as anyone when he left Cambridge.'

The market square was crowded with Saturday morning shoppers. They walked slowly. Rosa spoke softly of her time on the Madrid line with Marfield: the fighting and the fear and the utter lawlessness of the various factions. As she talked, men and women jostled and pushed. Wilde was the best part of a foot taller than this woman and had to bend his head to listen to her as they walked side by side.

'I thought he was perfect,' she said. 'But then . . .'

'Yes?'

'Little things he said, disappearances for days on end, his contempt.'

'You tried to kill him in France. You shot him.'

'Yes, I wanted to kill him. But now I want to shame him – expose him.'

He was just about to ask her why, when a squadron of Spitfires flew overhead, so low he could see the pilots. They tipped their wings to the crowds, who all waved back. He looked back down at Rosa and was surprised to find her on her knees.

'Rosa?'

She fell forward on to the hard paving. Had she tripped? Had a sudden seizure or heart attack? Wilde knelt down beside her. There was blood everywhere, soaking her long dress, pouring out on to the ground, blood on her blue serge jacket, blood on his hands. Dear God, what had just happened?

CHAPTER 24

The door to the interview room opened and Philip Eaton was standing there, leaning heavily on his stick. It was one o'clock in the morning. Wilde had never thought he would be so pleased to see the man.

'Well, well, professor, what have you got yourself into now?'

'I think you know a great deal more than I do, Eaton. Where's Rowlands? Has he let you out on your own? I was beginning to think you were lashed together like mariners at the mast.'

'Otherwise engaged down in London. I had to use a ministry driver. Actually, I feel rather liberated. Now, tell me exactly what happened and then we can get you out of this place and remove ourselves to somewhere that serves Scotch.'

Wilde told him about his fruitless visit to the Samovar, his encounters with Rosa Cortez, and finally her fatal stabbing in broad daylight in the market place in the centre of Cambridge.

'A deep wound under the ribcage, into the heart, I believe?'

'The police haven't given me the details, but that would make sense,' Wilde said.

'Did you see the attacker?'

'No. One moment we were all looking up at a squadron of Spits, the next moment she was crumpled on the ground. For several seconds I didn't even know she had been stabbed. There was a mass of people. I saw nothing suspicious and I saw no weapon.'

'But there was a pistol in her pocket?'

'So I believe. As I told you, she had one in London, so it was probably the same one.'

'This is a can of worms, Wilde.'

He nodded. He had been held here, pending inquiries, all day long. Was he being accused of anything? No, Detective Inspector Tomlinson said, but they would like him to stay all the same. They would rather not invoke defence regulations to keep him there, but well, if that proved necessary, so be it.

Wilde didn't fight his incarceration. Instead he gave the officer Lydia's number and insisted she be called. He learnt later that she had hurried to the police station, but was kept away from him. Finally he demanded they call Philip Eaton.

And now here he was, back in Cambridge, standing with the support of a stick in the doorway to the interview room. He looked at Wilde with something close to amusement. 'Come on, Wilde, let's get out of this place.'

'You mean I can go?'

'I pulled rank.'

'Thank you. A whisky would go down well. Where are you staying?'

'The Bull again. The bar will be closed but we'll force the concierge to find us a bottle. A ten-bob note usually works wonders.'

The ministry driver had made his way to a guest house for a night's sleep, so Eaton and Wilde hitched a lift in a police car through the dark, empty Cambridge streets. At the hotel, the concierge blinked as though he had been asleep and informed them that the bar was closed.

'We know that,' Eaton said. 'But we want a bottle of Scotch whisky and we'll pay good money for it. Cash in hand.'

The concierge did not need further prodding. 'Yes, sir, of course, sir.'

'And I want to use your phone,' Wilde said.

'As you wish, sir.'

Eaton tutted. 'Surely you're not going to call your girl now, Wilde? She'll be asleep.'

'She'll be awake.'

Lydia had spent most of the day worrying about Tom. At first when he didn't contact her, she went to the Samovar and spoke to the waitress, who said that, yes, Professor Wilde had been there. And had she heard news of the awful event in the market? A woman had been stabbed . . .

Later there was a phone call and she went to the police station in St Andrew's Street, but was told that she couldn't see Professor Wilde. It was Rupert Weir's arrival in his role as police surgeon that gave her the first inkling of what was going on.

Lydia was appalled. 'They don't think Tom's in any way involved, do they?'

'Well, he is involved, of course – but no, they don't think he's the killer. They have, however, been asked to keep him in their charge until the identity and intentions of the dead woman are confirmed.'

'Can they do that – keep Tom without charge?'

'As an alien, they can do what they want with him. At the moment, they just want to cover their backs. But they'll let him out soon enough. It might help if they could locate your chum Marcus Marfield, as he's the only other person around here who knew the victim. Seems he's absented himself.' He didn't mention what he had been told by Tomlinson – that Wilde and the woman had been seen by a police constable on his beat shortly before the murder, and that Wilde had lied to the officer. He had told him he was showing the young woman the way to Jesus Lane, but at the time of the incident they were walking in the opposite direction. Nor had he been at all truthful about his relationship with the young woman. The implication had been that they were strangers, but subsequent statements made it clear that they had met, however briefly, on three previous occasions.

There were questions to be answered and Weir suggested to the detective inspector that this was probably a matter for higher authorities. There was a gun involved and police were searching for a missing green van.

'What about the woman?' Lydia had said. 'Have you performed the post-mortem, Rupert?'

He nodded. 'As far as I can tell from my initial examination, it was a single thrust with a long thin blade, beneath the rib cage and a full inch into the heart. She had no chance. I'll do further tests, but I'm not expecting to find much else.'

'What can I do now?'

'Very little except wait. Look after yourself.' He nodded towards her belly. 'Don't do anything to jeopardise our new young friend.'

But of course, she couldn't just take things easy, eat supper, read, go to bed. And so she had stayed up, waiting for news. Now at last the phone was ringing.

'Tom?'

'I'm out – and I'm with Eaton down at the Bull. I'll be home in half an hour.'

'Come to *Cornflowers*, won't you? I'm wide awake.'

'Of course.'

'Everything all right?' Eaton asked as Wilde came back from reception.

'I think so.'

'Then grab the bottle and two glasses. You pour – you've got more arms than me.'

Wilde managed a smile, but he wasn't fooled by Eaton's jest. They made their way through to the lounge where the concierge switched on a dim wall light in a red sconce. The window was blacked out, of course. Wilde poured two whiskies and both men took a minute or two in appreciation.

'God, that's good,' Wilde said.

'A fine way to start Sunday. Now then, I need to know everything you know about Miss Rosa Cortez. Everything she did, every word she spoke. But first, I have a bit of news for you.'

'Go on.'

'You mentioned that in France you were approached by a man who told you that Marfield was incarcerated in Le Vernet and you told me that he called himself Honoré. Someone of that name has just crossed the path of our cousins across the channel. Information from the French security services suggests a man called Honoré is an agent of the Comintern – the Communist International. He ordered the assassination of America's ambassador to France.'

'Are you serious? Why has no one heard of this?'

'Because it failed – and it has only just come to light.'

'Why would the Reds want to kill Bill Bullitt? I always thought he was well-disposed towards the Kremlin.'

'He was, but not in recent years. In fact, during his time there as ambassador, he developed a deep antipathy towards Stalinism. I think he made enemies.'

'Do you think the attack on him has some relevance to what's going on here?'

'The appearance of your chum Honoré must make one wonder. It certainly makes me yet more certain that Marfield and those associated with him are up to no good. We'll get back to that, but first things first – I want to know about Rosa Cortez. Chapter and verse.'

Wilde went through his encounters with the woman, ending with the knife thrust in the market place. 'One moment we were walking side by side, the next she had collapsed. It shocked me to the core, Eaton.'

'Of course it did. But who killed her? Was it Marfield?'

'No, I'm certain not. I would have spotted him, either before or after the event. He's a difficult man to miss, even in a crowd.'

'But he *is* the connection to the woman. We need to talk to him urgently. I want him under lock and key. Guy Rowlands was right – he shouldn't be on the loose.'

'On what charge?'

'To hell with charges. Whatever he's planning, I want to prevent it. We can hold him under Defence Regulations. But where is he?'

'I last saw him on Friday morning just before I came to you. I left him in the company of a rather dandyish young man named Lincoln Tripp – a protégé of Jim Vanderberg.'

'Tripp? New boy at Grosvenor Square?'

'You've heard of him then?'

'Of course. We know everyone in all the embassies. Tripp's lately out of Moscow. Ivy League Yankee, the sort to make your flesh crawl.'

'Actually, he's quite personable.'

Eaton raised his eyebrow, but let it pass. 'Is it just my imagination or are we beginning to see a connection here? A closing of the circle, perhaps?'

Wilde couldn't see any such thing. His initial impression had been that Tripp and Marfield might share a sexual attraction. Nothing more. But perhaps he had missed something. 'What are you suggesting precisely?'

'Moscow. The US embassy there. First Bullitt is targeted under orders of a Comintern agent named Honoré. Now we have another ex-member of America's Moscow diplomatic corps vaguely linked to Honoré through you and Marcus Marfield. In my world, there are no coincidences, Wilde.'

'You're losing me.'

'Sorry, just thinking aloud.'

'You know, I still have no idea how Honoré knew anything about me or where to find me. I'm damned sure Jacques Talbot, my host, didn't tell anyone. So who, Eaton?'

'It's a good question, but let's concentrate on Mr Tripp for a moment.' Eaton held the whisky glass to his nose and inhaled the heady fumes. 'I'll need to check the files, but I do recall that our Moscow station took note of Tripp's extravagant tastes and his somewhat reckless appetite for the pretty boys and loose women the NKVD threw in his path. But that was par for the course for all the younger officers from the western missions. None of it mattered if you were discreet. You could open your fly, but you had to keep your mouth shut, which most diplomatic officers out there did. And Tripp with his promised inheritance and daddy's allowance wasn't going to get himself financially embarrassed.'

Wilde was beginning to wonder whether Eaton had lost his edge. In the past, his instincts had been finely honed, but this version of the character of Lincoln Tripp seemed pretty baseless. Was this anti-American bias?

'So where is Tripp now?' Eaton persisted.

'Well, at a guess I'd say he must be back in London. He'd been up to Glasgow with Jack Kennedy and Jim, helping the American survivors from the *Athenia*. He was only passing through Cambridge on the long drive back to the Smoke.'

'Do you think Marfield might have gone with him?'

'It's possible. Might explain his absence and present whereabouts.'

'I'll put in a call to London. In the meantime, we need to work out why this woman Rosa Cortez was pursuing Marfield.'

'She said she wanted to shame him.'

'Did she explain why, or how?'

Wilde shook his head. 'We hadn't got on to that. By the way, have the police located her van? I described it to them.'

'Yes, they found it a few hours ago, somewhere east of here towards Newmarket.'

'And what was in it? There must have been things in the bloody van.'

'The thing had been stripped. Panels removed, tyres slashed open, seats torn and gutted. Whoever took it was looking for something. Which brings us back to you, Wilde. I want to hear what *you* know – not what the police have discovered.'

Wilde gave Eaton a hard look. The MI6 man was turning things around and, as usual, was not being completely open. He had implied that he had heard of Rosa Cortez, but so far he had revealed nothing. Instead he was fishing for information. 'I know what you're doing, Eaton, because I know the way you work. But at least tell me this: what did you know about her before all this?'

Eaton hesitated.

'Eaton? Come on, I've been open with you.'

'Have you?'

'You know I have.' But he hadn't, had he. Not about everything. He hadn't mentioned the fact that Marfield had a wife, and with good reason. Why should the poor, blameless woman be involved in all this unsavoury business? 'Damn it Eaton, I've had enough. Anyone would think we were on opposing sides. I'm going home – I need my bed.'

CHAPTER 25

It was almost two o'clock in the morning when Wilde crept beneath the sheets beside Lydia. She feigned sleep but he knew she was awake, waiting for him. He curled himself around her and placed his hands on her warm, gently rounded belly. Soon, surely, it would be swelling. She covered his hands with hers and pulled him closer, and they both drifted off to sleep.

Lydia woke him at eight thirty. 'Rupert's on the phone. He's just going out but he wants to talk to you first.'

Wilde struggled to untangle his brain. 'All right, I'll be down in a few moments.'

'Coffee's on.'

In the hall, he picked up the phone. 'Hello, Rupert?'

'Tom, glad you got out of the nick safe and sound. Sorry I couldn't help you there.'

'My own fault. I misled a constable.'

'Anyway, I wanted to catch you before I go out and bring you up to date on a couple of things. What occurred to me was the nature of the fatal wound suffered by Miss Rosa Cortez. I'm not an expert in the ways of assassins, but I would venture that this was a professional killer's strike. Not that I've ever encountered one before, but there was something very clean and decisive about it. One might almost use the word *efficient*.'

'Did you discover anything else about her?'

'She wasn't wearing any rings to say she was married or engaged and we don't think she'd ever been pregnant. I'd guess her age at about twenty to twenty-three. None of that really helps, does it?'

'No, I suppose not.'

'There was something else, probably unrelated, but of interest to you and me. I had another chat with the coroner down in Ipswich. He knew a bit about Ronald Marfield beyond the suicide note. I must say I was rather surprised by what he said. When I think of retired colonels in Suffolk, I tend to think of blimpish moustachioed reactionary Tories. Anyway, in this case I was completely wrong. Turns out Colonel Marfield was a bit of a leftie. Good friend of Mr Attlee, apparently, having served in Gallipoli with him, and of much the same brand of politics. He even stood as a Labour candidate in the 1935 general election, and suffered a sound thrashing. There's not much taste for that sort of thing in rural Suffolk, as you might imagine.'

'Well, well, that is interesting,' said Wilde. 'I would never have picked up on that from talking to the widow.'

'I thought you'd be interested. What are you doing with your Sunday? Relaxing and spending some time with your gorgeous girl, I hope. I'd invite you around for lunch but I'm a bit frantic today. Edie would love to see you both.'

'Soon then.'

'Indeed.'

Wilde dressed quickly, threw the coffee down his throat, kissed Lydia and went next door to collect the Rudge. He was just about to leave when the telephone rang.

'Is that Professor Wilde?'

'Yes it is. Who's this?'

'Percheron, Professor. Gus Percheron. I've just got back from the west country and there was a message asking me to call you. The porter gave me your number, sir.'

'Ah yes, Percheron, good of you to call. Look, I hope I'm not out of order here, but I wanted to talk to you about a rather delicate matter. It's about Marcus Marfield.'

'Ah.' There was a deep intake of breath at the other end of the line.

'I believe you were at school together before you both came up to Cambridge?'

'Well, yes, sir, we were in the same year.'

'Have you heard that he's back in England? Here in Cambridge, in fact.'

'Good Lord, no I hadn't heard that. When did that happen?'

'About a week ago. I was in France and heard that he was languishing in an internment camp with a lot of other International Brigaders. I managed to get him out and brought him home.'

The line wasn't good and there was some crackling, then a pause. 'I'm sorry, Professor, but why are you telling me this?'

'Because I want to know what sort of young man Marcus Marfield really is. War can affect people in different ways, and before he is accepted back into college, we have to be sure that all is well. I couldn't see any problem at first, but now little doubts are creeping in. Then Mr Laker told me you had brought a complaint to him about Marfield.'

'But I spoke to Laker in confidence!'

'Of course you did – and he hasn't betrayed it.'

'Well, sir, it sounds very much as though he has.'

Wilde was becoming exasperated. 'Can we deal with that later? The thing is, Percheron, you were at school with Marcus Marfield so you've known him longer than anyone else in college – and I want your honest opinion of him.'

'Well that's easy, Professor. He is a vicious bastard.'

'That's quite a damning verdict.'

'Well, you asked my opinion. He can sue me for defamation if he likes.'

Wilde liked Gus Percheron. Though he had never taught him, their paths had crossed in the college. Being small and unathletic, he must have been the sort of lad picked on by school bullies. Wilde suggested as much to him now.

'Yes, I was bullied by Marfield. He bullied everyone at school – everyone less strong than him, that is. The teachers thought he was wonderful, the gilded youth with the voice of an angel, but we all knew what he was like.'

'Why did you come to the same college then? You must have known he was coming here.'

'My father's alma mater. Soon, I'll be joining up – and it'll be the old man's regiment, too. I'm not going to go into all the foul things Marfield did at school, because they'll all sound pathetically trivial to you, but when you're a rather timid boy like me, life can be made utterly miserable by someone like him.'

Wilde waited for more. There was a sigh at the other end of the phone.

'Well, if you must know, he tried to force himself on me. I suppose I was his type. In a woman, you'd call it rape.'

'I'm so sorry.'

'Something I'll have to live with, Professor.'

'And he tried it on again here at college?'

'This time I had a knife. Like all bullies, he doesn't like people standing up to him.'

The line was getting worse now. But Wilde just managed to hear Percheron's final words before he was cut off.

'When I was told he had gone off to fight in Spain, and save the world from the fascists, I laughed out loud.'

The streets were empty save for the hasty steps of churchgoers hurrying to morning service. At first Wilde heard nothing but the growl of the Rudge's 500cc motor. But when he stopped outside the Samovar, he noticed the silence. There were no church bells. They were not being rung on a Sunday for the first time in his memory. How, he wondered, had Hitler been granted the power to silence Britain's bells?

The door to the Samovar was locked and a closed sign was in the window. This didn't surprise him. Nothing opened in this town on a Sunday except the churches.

At the side of the tea shop, there was a narrow alleyway that led beneath an arch to the rear of the buildings, perhaps the entrance to a stableyard in former times. The Samovar side was just a blank brick wall, no windows. At the back, a path ran in both directions outside a line of small fenced yards.

Wilde stood outside the gate that gave onto the back of the tea shop's living quarters. If Elina's parents were in America, then the only one likely to be here was Elina herself. The gate was waist high and had no lock, merely a latch that opened with a flick of the fingers. Wilde walked across the stone-flagged yard to the back door. Above him there was a second storey and above that a blacked-out attic window.

He knocked firmly on the door. There was no answer, so he called out to the upstairs windows. 'Hello? Anyone home?'

No reply. He found a few pieces of gravel from a small herb bed at the edge of the yard and tossed them against the windows. Still no response. Wilde hesitated, and then turned the handle of the rear door. It was locked, but the wood was rotten. Turning his left shoulder to the door, he braced for impact then rammed hard against it. There was a sound of splintering and the door moved, but didn't open. He tried again, and this time it flew inwards.

He stepped into the house, closing the door behind him. Standing still for a few moments, he heard only his own accelerated breathing. He was in a kitchen storehouse, full of tins of tea and coffee, flour sacks and other foodstuffs. There was even an icebox; very modern. Two butler's basins sat side by side with racks for plates and cups and teapots.

Not really certain what he was looking for, he ranged through the ground floor at a steady pace, looking in on an office, which was unlocked, and a food-preparation area, then some sort of laundry with aprons, towels, napkins and tablecloths neatly arranged. When he came into the tea shop itself, he realised that he could be seen by anyone walking past the front window. He moved back deeper into the building, and climbed the staircase to the living quarters above.

Eaton had talked to him about the connection between Marcus Marfield and Elina Kossoff. 'But it's pointless now to ask you to pursue that line any further, Wilde. The death of the Spanish woman takes everything on to a new level.'

'Is it really so pointless?' Wilde demanded.

Eaton looked at him suspiciously. 'You do realise there is a limit to how much I can help if you get caught doing anything illegal?'

'I'd better not get caught then.'

Eaton laughed. 'You're a cocky so-and-so for a history professor, aren't you? None of the dons at Trinity were remotely like you.'

Anything illegal. This was breaking and entering. What in God's name was he thinking? He had played his luck thus far, but he would be in a great deal of trouble if someone walked in; trouble that he would not be able to talk or punch his way out of. But, as ever, once the seed of doubt had been sown, he couldn't help himself.

The decoration of the apartments was not to his taste. Imperial Russian, he would call it. Large, gilt-framed portraits of officers in dazzling uniforms, icons, chalices of the orthodox church inlaid with gemstones. The furniture was heavy, dark and did not look comfortable. The Kossoffs really had brought a little bit of Tsarist Russia to England with them. One wall had bookshelves: volumes in Russian, French and English.

There were three bedrooms, a bathroom and a small upstairs kitchen. Everything was neat and in order. There were no revolutionary pamphlets, nothing to suggest any political affiliation, nothing to mark out the Kossoffs as people of concern to the British security services. Perhaps they were almost too clean.

Wilde came to the bedroom that he took to be Elina's. The bed was freshly made, the surfaces dusted and polished. She had a novel on her bedside table. *The Grapes Of Wrath*, the new Steinbeck. Wilde had read it himself; Miss Kossoff clearly shared a taste for good American literature.

There was nothing here. He wasn't sure what he had hoped or expected to find, but he had clearly risked all this for nothing. At the doorway he lowered himself to his hands and knees for a last look around. He was about to get up again when a dull glint caught his eye on the floor at the far side of the single bed. A small object, wedged right against the skirting board. A brooch perhaps?

He eased himself under the bed and picked up the object. It was a bullet.

CHAPTER 26

As Elina Kossoff pulled up outside the Samovar, she had seen a shadow pass the window of the tea shop. She drove further along the road then stopped, killed the Morgan's engine, and waited.

The history professor had emerged ten minutes later. Elina's instinct was to put a bullet in him then and there, but there were too many people around, straggling towards church. Killing the Spanish woman in the centre of Cambridge had been risky enough. Tom Wilde had been there at her side. Now he was breaking into the Samovar – but why? What was he looking for? She relaxed; there was nothing to find. She didn't make mistakes . . . did she?

Marcus was the one who made mistakes. He was the loose cannon. His visit to the Samovar had been reckless.

At first, Cambridge had seemed a good, quiet place to hide in plain sight, but if MI6 was here and Professor Wilde was sniffing about it was no longer safe.

Timothy Laker was emerging from the chapel as Wilde strode along the path towards the old court.

'Laker, a word if I may. Have you seen anything of Marcus Marfield in the last couple of days? He seems to have disappeared from view.'

The Director of Music smiled broadly. 'He was in the chapel only about two and a half hours ago. Already there when I turned up ahead of Matins, waiting for me. Wanted to sing *Ave Maria* again. He seems obsessed with it.'

'Did he give you any indication of what he's up to?'

Laker ran his fingers through his thinning fair hair. 'What do you mean? What's going on, Wilde?'

'I wish I knew. Do you have any idea where he might be now?'

'His rooms?'

It was worth a look. 'If you see him, try to make contact with me without scaring him away. I think he's trying to avoid me.'

Lydia had been having a rest on the sofa when the telephone rang. She picked it up.

'Hello?'

After a short pause a strange metallic voice came through. 'Is that you, Lydia? Is Tom there?'

'Jim? I'm afraid Tom's out.'

'Oh, well, I said I'd call when I had news. It's not looking good. I spoke to the captain of the *City of Flint* by radio-telephone, and Juliet and William are not aboard, and nor is there anyone answering their description. Coastguard cutters have taken off the worst of the injured, and they're not among them. The *Flint* was our last hope.'

'I'm so sorry.'

'It's worse. I've spoken to the Donaldson line again and they tell me that all lifeboats are now accounted for.'

'Oh Jesus, Jim . . .'

'This line is breaking up. Will you tell Tom I'm returning to London with Henry, please? Jack Kennedy's already returned – he has an important family celebration to go to – and I'll be following him down south today, assuming the trains are running.'

Wilde looked for Marfield in his rooms, but there was no sign of him. Back in his own set, he took the bullet, unfired and still encased in its cartridge, from his pocket and placed it, pointing upwards, on the desk. He guessed it was a .45. He was sure that the revolver found beside Eric Charlecote's body up on the Gogs had been that calibre. Rupert Weir would know. Grabbing the bullet, he shoved it deep into his trouser pocket and strode from his rooms and out of the college, taking Trumpington Street southwards at a farmer's pace.

Weir was just emerging from the mortuary when Wilde found him.

'Anything of interest?'

'No one you know. An old fellow put his head in the gas oven. Sad little tragedy, Tom. But why are *you* here?'

'I want you to look at this and tell me if it could have been fired from the Smith and Wesson found up on Little Trees Hill.' He removed the bullet from his pocket, held it between thumb and forefinger, and then dropped it into Weir's palm.

Weir turned it this way and that. 'It's a .45, no doubt about it. I've seen the gun and the bullet my colleague pulled from Eric's head, and it could well be a match. I'll have to see them side by side to give you a firmer opinion, though. Where did you get it?'

'I can't say at the moment – you'll have to trust me. Look, we need to talk with Philip Eaton. He's at the Bull. Until now this has all been speculation and surmise. This is solid evidence.' Unfortunately he had to acknowledge that it was evidence that was unlikely to find its way into a court of law.

Ten minutes later, Wilde was in Eaton's hotel room, revealing his discovery of the bullet. Eaton remained silent for a full minute, and then winced as he eased himself back into the room's solitary armchair.

'You're in pain?' Wilde asked.

'Always, old boy. Where's Dr Weir?'

'Looking for the Charlecote bullet. The hospital has entrusted it to the police, so he's gone around to get it.'

'But he's pretty sure it's a match?'

Wilde nodded.

'And you found this under Elina Kossoff's bed? What on earth did you think you were up to, going in there like that?'

'I thought you wanted me to investigate the Samovar.'

'I don't remember suggesting you break in.' Eaton attempted to smile, but it looked more like a grimace of pain.

As he spoke, the door opened, Weir's large tweedy figure filling the frame. He was holding up a brown manila envelope. 'Good day to you, Mr Eaton.'

'Glad to see you, Dr Weir. Do you have it?'

'Indeed I do. The duty sergeant had to call Inspector Tomlinson at home. He was reluctant to let evidence out of the station, but when I mentioned your name, he weakened.' Weir removed the Charlecote bullet from the envelope and placed it side by side with the Kossoff bullet on the bedside table. 'Well, obviously, one's been fired and damaged by contact with bone and the other is pristine, but I'd say they were from the same batch.'

'That's all I need,' Eaton said. 'I'm not sure what Marfield and Miss Kossoff are up to, but I have no doubt that they are working for our enemies. They must be picked up and either charged or interned.'

'He's not at college. I just checked,' Wilde said.

'Well, I want every officer in the county on his tail. The whole country if necessary. And we'll need photographs distributed. We have surveillance pictures of Miss Kossoff, perhaps you would find one of Marfield, Wilde? I'm sure the college will have one. Pass me the telephone, would you, Dr Weir?'

The only college photograph Wilde could find was a small, grainy one of the choir, Marfield looking away, his head blurred by movement. It wouldn't do.

'Why do you need it, Wilde?' Tim Laker asked.

'I'd rather not say, just for the moment.'

'Well, his mother must have plenty, but from what you say she may not be cooperative.'

The obvious move was to leave it to the police, but when Wilde suggested that to Eaton, the MI6 man wasn't happy with the idea. 'From what you say, the mother is not an easy woman, so I wouldn't want to trust this to a local bobby. Would you mind going down there, Wilde? Damn it, this is not going well.'

'What's the matter, Eaton?'

'Oh, you know, internecine warfare. Strictly speaking, this is Five territory, counter-espionage, backed up by Special Branch. They don't always take kindly to us sticking our noses in. I've tried to explain that my involvement emanates from events abroad, but they're still sniffy. "Do you really think we have the manpower to hunt down a man and a woman with no evidence of wrongdoing?" is the official line from Liddell. "Don't you know there's a war on?" The problem is, Wilde, I can't explain the bullet.'

'Not even off the record?'

'Yes, of course, off the record. But while that works with Liddell and the boys at Five, it won't wash with Special Branch and the local constabularies. I need that picture.'

*

The sixty-mile ride eastwards to Ipswich took two hours. Wilde found the Marfield house with difficulty, on the north side of the town, in open countryside, up a long incline through farmland. He pulled up in front of an old and quite grand Georgian-fronted farmhouse with an overgrown hedgerow and what looked like a disused well at the edge of the forecourt.

It had a neglected air. The gardens to left and right of the house were untended and the gravel driveway was thick with weeds. He noticed a side window covered in boards as though it had been broken. He rang the doorbell and waited.

A woman of middle years answered the door and Wilde knew immediately that she was Marfield's mother. She shared his startling good looks, though her figure was perhaps not what it had once been. She was tall, almost as tall as Wilde himself. Her eyes were dull blue and her fair hair had a little grey in it. Fading beauty.

'Yes?' she said.

'I'm Thomas Wilde. Professor Wilde.'

'Ah, well, good day to you,' she said and began to close the door on him. He thrust his boot forward to pin the door open.

'Just a few words, please. I won't detain you.'

'I have nothing to say to you, Mr Wilde.'

'I understand that, but I have ridden two hours to come here. Marcus is in trouble and it is possible we might be able to prevent him doing anything more foolish than he has already done.'

'I know no one called Marcus.'

'That is simply not true. I realise that things have not gone well between you, but Marcus is your flesh and blood.'

Margaret Marfield glared at Wilde and then, suddenly, her shoulders slumped and she sighed. 'You are very persistent, Professor Wilde. Come indoors and I will listen. That's all.' She looked down at his dusty boots. 'Perhaps you would remove those first?'

He took off his boots and followed her through to the sitting room. The room looked as if it been at the epicentre of an explosion. Like the garden, this room had a neglected feel to it with peeling paintwork and a threadbare carpet, and it was in chaos. Papers had been tipped up across the floor, books scattered everywhere, cushions slashed.

'What on earth has happened here?' Wilde was shocked.

'I was burgled. The whole house was ransacked.'

'I'm so sorry to hear that, Mrs Marfield. Did they get away with much?'

'They? You mean *he*, of course. Marcus or one of his ghastly chums did this. And no, as far as I can see nothing is missing.' She sighed again. 'I suppose you'd better sit down, Mr Wilde. I'd call for the maid to make us a pot of tea, but I dismissed her earlier today. A widow's pension will not keep this house going for long.'

'Have the police been?'

'What for? I know who did it.'

'But the police would be interested. They're already looking for Marcus.'

'Well, that doesn't surprise me. What has he done apart from this?'

Could she take the truth? Wilde wasn't in the mood to dissemble. 'It's feared he may be mixed up in something illegal.

The details are unknown. But if he can be found and caught, he might be prevented from doing himself and others harm. The police need a good photograph of him. That's why I'm here.'

Margaret Marfield and Wilde were still standing. She held up her palm and swivelled slowly round the room. 'See what you can find, professor.'

Wilde rifled through the debris, the broken ornaments and picture frame glass. There were photographs among the assorted papers and other items; of her, of other relatives and of two men he took to be her other son and her late husband. But none of Marcus.

'I burnt them all. You've had a wasted journey.'

Wilde had never met someone as intransigent as this woman. 'Yes,' he said, 'I suppose I have.'

'I'll show you out.'

At the front door, her face was a cold, hostile mask. And yet he turned to her and smiled as he was putting his boots back on. 'Whatever differences you have between you, whatever he has done here, there is also the matter of an innocent child – your grandson. His name is Walter. If you like, I could pass on some message to him and his mother for you. It's not that far from Ipswich to Cambridge, you know.'

She shook her head, but he wondered if she seemed less decisive.

Despite the woman's coldness, he couldn't help but pity her. Was she all alone in the world? 'This is a very difficult time for you, Mrs Marfield. Do you have any help? Your elder son, Ptolemy, isn't far away, is he?'

'Toll? What is he to do with all this?'

What indeed? Wilde wondered. Her sharp reaction to her firstborn's name posed yet more questions in his mind. Precisely what role did Ptolemy Marfield play in this tragic family? He was certainly involved – his reaction on the phone proved that.

She was pushing at the door. 'I do not care to discuss personal matters with you or anyone else, Mr Wilde.'

'Please, one more thing, are you sure it was Marcus who broke into the house?'

'Yes.'

'What makes you so certain?'

'Because he rang me and asked for something. I told him I had no idea what he was talking about. So quite clearly he came to look for it himself.'

'What did he ask for?'

'I don't care to discuss it. And that's my final word. I told him he had driven his father to his grave and I wanted nothing more to do with him. I said that from now on if he wanted anything perhaps he should look to you, Professor. You've taken him under your wing, haven't you? Good luck is all I can say.'

CHAPTER 27

The fog had barely lifted all day. Soon it would be dark again and hope was slipping fast. They had enough food but there was little water left. Juliet Vanderberg held William in her arms and tried to soothe him. He was seven years old, big for his age, a healthy all-American boy. But here, in this small boat in these vast, grey seas, he was in a bad way.

'Ma, I'm thirsty.'

'I know, honey.' She put the flask to his lips. 'Take small sips, baby, we've got to make it last a while longer.' She felt his forehead: he seemed feverish.

'Are we going home?'

'Soon. Very soon.'

Juliet had always thought of herself as a stoical practical woman, but here in the fog-shrouded Atlantic, somewhere west or north of Ireland, she felt utterly helpless. To think that she had embarked on this voyage to protect William and Henry from the bombs that were expected to fall on London. She had had no fear for herself and no wish to be separated from Jim, but she had a strong instinct that she must put her children first. Now William was hot and shivering and she had no idea what had become of his brother. The bitter irony was not lost on her; in the very act of trying to protect her children she had put them in danger.

Even now she could feel the tremendous shudder and explosion as the torpedo hit. She and Willie had just emerged from their cabin on D Deck on their way to one of the dining rooms on

C Deck when they were thrown from their feet and ricocheted off the bulwark. They had not been injured but were left shocked and dazed. They carried on, unsure what had happened, but one of the sailors told her they had been hit by a torpedo or shell and that she must return to her cabin to collect their lifejackets, then go to the assembly point on deck until the extent of the damage could be ascertained.

She understood that they needed their lifejackets, but her immediate concern was for Henry. Where had he got to?

At first everything was orderly. But then, as they hurried through the gangways, came the black smoke, the stench of oil, the flames and the terror as she called and called for Henry. Nor had she seen Mrs Ballantyne, the woman whose cabin she was sharing, or her maid, Emmy. She had to pray the three of them had found their way to a lifeboat.

In the end, in the dark, she had made her way to the muster deck and had taken Willie in her arms and climbed down to the lifeboats. But as the lifeboat was lowered one of the davit ropes snapped or got tangled and the lifeboat turned turtle as it fell into the dark sea. She remembered nothing then, except that somehow she had ended up in this rowing dinghy with Willie and another woman, drifting. Juliet had scrabbled about for oars, but there were none; no way of steering or making headway. They had called out, but a lot of people were calling out, and in the darkness and the chaos they had drifted away.

Their fellow passenger was an elderly woman named Joyce Harman, from upstate New York. She had brought a hamper full of food and two flasks of water. 'Well, dear,' she said. 'I had bought the hamper from Fortnum's for my niece in Manhattan and it occurred to me that my need might now be greater than hers. The water was almost an afterthought.'

Juliet Vanderberg had been grateful for the woman's foresight, but some of the food was a little rich for Willie. He spat out the tinned fois gras and now the water was almost gone. Soon they would have to turn to one of the alcoholic beverages from the hamper. The port maybe. Willie might like its sweetness. Any port in a storm, Joyce had said, and Juliet had laughed, but Joyce was wearing thin. Her constant refrain of 'If only this fog would lift' did not help one bit.

But it was true. The fog that kept coming and going was a curse. There were no flares, no oars, no compass and no radio. No supplies save the Fortnum's hamper. It was impossible to tell if they were drifting back towards land or further out to sea. And who would ever see them in this infernal fog, or at night? At the moment it seemed they were more likely to be mown down by a passing ship than rescued by it.

Gently, Juliet laid William aside, so she could get back to work. She picked up the two tin cups that were all she had, and resumed the task of bailing water from the bottom of the boat. The leak was slow, but she was slower.

It was almost dusk when Wilde arrived back in Cambridge. He wanted to see Lydia and he needed to report to Philip Eaton, but first he wanted to explore another option. Surely Claire would have a picture of her husband? And if Claire was away, what harm could it do to have a quick look around her house. Breaking and entering was becoming a habit.

The light was fading as he arrived in Histon. He took a flashlight from his saddlebag and approached the back of the property. The garden door was unlocked; Claire really had left in a hurry, just as Lydia had said. Not even enough time to bolt a door. Once inside, he went from room to room, downstairs and upstairs, drawing the blackout curtains before switching on his torch.

He found what he was looking for in the sitting room: a picture of Marfield taken by a commercial photographer, well lit, handsome and kitted out in a smart jacket and tie. Wilde slid it from its silver frame and slipped it into his pocket.

Just as he was about to leave, he paused, turned back and went up the stairs. There had been something he had seen in Claire's bedroom that he wanted to look at more closely. A Kodascope 8mm film projector, with a spool of film attached, on a bedside table that had been moved to the middle of the room.

In the beam of his torch Wilde saw that the film was on the receiving spool as though it had just been played, and that the projector was still plugged into the mains socket. It had been wedged on a slim book to adjust the height. It was facing a white wall, in lieu of a screen.

Wilde was familiar with projectors like this from his lectures. Putting down the torch so that its wide beam threw light on his work, he slotted the end of the film from the full bottom spool into the top reel and flicked the rewind switch. It ran smoothly. When the top reel was full, he switched off the machine.

Now he threaded the film through the cogs so that the teeth locked into the sprockets on the edge of the film, then he fed it down in front of the projector's lamp, secured it in place and clicked film sprockets into the lower teeth, mirroring those on top. Finally he slipped the end of the film into the empty reel and wound it tight. It was ready to roll.

The picture on the wall was slow and blurred, but he quickly adjusted it to an even speed and brought it into focus. The image was small, but good quality and sharp, if a little jerky: filmed using a handheld camera, not a tripod.

In the opening frames, all he could see was clouds. Then a plane appeared, a speck in the distance, which fell into a dive: a German Stuka bomber. The only sound was the clatter of the projector, which was a little ancient and had seen better days, but he knew that the Stuka – Junkers 87 – would have been emitting a high-pitched scream as it went into its dive, terrifying those below.

The plane was so far away and the image so small that it was not easy to see what happened next, but it was easy to deduce that it had dropped its bomb, pulled out of the dive and crawled into its ascent. The film shuddered and a plume of smoke filled the central section of the image.

The camera panned back to reveal Marcus Marfield in the foreground, sitting alone on a broad, smooth rock. He had a beret on his head and a scarf around his neck and was laughing. In his left hand he had a burning cigarette, in his right a long-barreled pistol. His index finger was inside the trigger guard and he twirled the weapon like a cowboy, before he held it up and pointed at whoever was behind the camera. His mouth opened and closed as though he had said 'bang'.

Behind Marfield the landscape was barren and dusty. The camera slowly panned left and a low white building came into view. Six figures were ranged alongside it, with their backs against the wall. Two were young men in working men's clothes, one was an older man in peasant garb. Beside him, a woman of a similar age. His wife? And then, at the end of the line, was a young woman holding a baby.

Wilde watched with growing foreboding. The reel was nearly a quarter the way through and he had been watching for half a minute. Marfield was still in camera shot and was now pointing the gun at the people outside the farmhouse, no more than thirty feet from him. He drew on his cigarette, squinted down the gunsight on the pistol and pulled the trigger. The old woman's mouth fell open; her hands went to her belly. Even in monochrome, even in this small format, Wilde could see blood seeping through her fingers as her knees wobbled and she fell forward on to the hard, unforgiving ground.

Marfield smiled, rose from his rock, dropped the cigarette and strolled over. The camera followed him and as it came closer to the wall, Wilde saw that the three men's hands were all bound in front of them. In quick succession, Marfield shot each one of them in the head.

He then turned his attention to the young mother clutching her child. She was shaking, saying something, pleading.

Please God, no, thought Wilde.

Marfield stood in front of her. The camera had moved around now so that their faces were in profile. The woman was dark and small and looked familiar. Her child was no more than three months old. Marfield reached out and touched the woman's face, then stroked the baby's head. She held the child out, as if beseeching him not to harm it.

Smiling, Marfield took the baby and squatted down to put it gently on the ground. He stood up and pointed the gun at the woman's head. She closed her eyes, bracing her muscles for the shock of the bullet and death. Instead he tapped her face with the hot black barrel so that she opened her eyes again.

His gun hand dropped and, with barely a glance, he shot the baby through the top of the head.

The woman's neck arched back and her mouth flew open in an anguished, silent scream.

Marfield thrust the gun barrel into her gaping mouth and pulled the trigger again.

As the woman fell, he stood back. With the side of his dusty boot, he kicked the baby away, turned with a look of exultation, something close to rapture, and the camera panned again to reveal three more men.

They wore black SS uniforms and they were clapping their hands in appreciation. One of them stepped forward and put an arm around Marfield's shoulder, like a cricket captain congratulating his opening batsman.

And then the film ran out and all that was left was the burning light of the projector lamp and the incessant clattering of the turning spool and cogs.

Wilde flipped the switches and the projector ground to a halt. He sat on his haunches beside the machine and took a deep breath. Nothing could have prepared him for the sight that had just assailed his eyes.

The silence was broken by the staged clearing of a throat.

Wilde turned slowly. Marcus Marfield filled the doorway, his left shoulder against the frame, his right hand holding the butt of a pistol loosely at his side.

'Professor Wilde.'

'Is it real? Did this happen?'

'You decide.'

'You bastard, Marfield.' Wilde looked at the beautiful face that had won so many hearts and saw only putrescence and depravity. It was as if the skin had been drawn back and the crawling insects and worms just below the surface were visible.

Marfield stepped into the room and raised the weapon. Wilde knew there was nothing he could do to prevent his own death. All the tricks he had learnt in the boxing ring, all the muscle honed into his arms, none of it would help him now.

'Lie down flat, on your belly, arms above your head.'

'And make it easier for you? Why would I do that?'

'I'm not going to kill you,' Marfield said. 'Not unless you force me to.'

Slowly, Wilde obeyed. He was computing the possibilities. Every second of life might bring an opportunity. An upward kick that dislodged the weapon, a careless moment by Marfield.

From outside there was a screech of tyres, a car pulling to a halt. Marfield tensed.

'The police. I left word that I was coming here,' Wilde lied.

Marfield pulled the reel of film from the projector and thrust it into his jacket pocket. 'Now,' he said. 'You will stand up slowly. No sudden movements.'

Once again, he obeyed, and rose to his feet, his arms still above his head.

Marfield picked up Wilde's flashlight and went to the window, shielding the beam of the torch as he carefully pulled back the blackout curtain an inch, then replaced it almost immediately.

He shone the torch on his captive. 'You were right. There's a police car. I don't know why it's here, but we are going to leave, quickly, by the back door, and you are going to help me. You know the alternative.'

Wilde understood. Marfield didn't want a body found here. Nor did he want to shoot police officers. A murder now would only intensify the hunt for him and compromise his plans, whatever they were. Once they were away from here, of course, it would be another matter altogether.

Lydia had been worried all day. In the evening she called Eaton at the hotel and he told her that he'd asked Wilde to drive to Ipswich to try to get a photograph from Marfield's mother.

'Why not ask Claire?'

'Who is Claire?'

'Claire Marfield. Marcus's wife. But she's away.'

'Ah.'

There was silence.

'Oh – you didn't know about her, did you, Mr Eaton? Tom didn't tell you . . .'

'But *you* will. And the sooner you do, the better. I'll come around.'

CHAPTER 28

From the back door, they crossed the garden and found a gap in the hedge into the orchard. Behind them, they heard the sound of voices in the house. The police would have no evidence that anyone had been there, although at least one of the doors was unlocked. If someone touched the projector, of course, the heat would give the game away, but even then they would find nothing. Wilde wondered about the arrival of the police. Few people knew about the link between Marfield and this place. One of them was Lydia. But why would she send the police here?

Out in the orchard, Marfield pushed him to his knees. Wilde did not resist. He lay flat out on the damp, dewy grass, the muzzle of the pistol, hard and metallic, at the back of his head.

'Not a sound,' Marfield said, his voice neither urgent nor emotional. 'Not a cough or a sigh.'

No one who had seen the film of Marcus Marfield on a rock by a farmhouse somewhere in Spain could ever again doubt his deadly intent. Wilde found himself wondering about Rosa. That was why the woman in the film had seemed familiar: she looked like Rosa. Sisters? Cousins? It would give her a motive for shooting Marfield through the wire at Le Vernet. It would give her a motive for following him to England.

Had she somehow come into possession of the film? If so, had she brought it to show Claire to warn her about the man to whom she was married? Perhaps he, Wilde, had unwittingly led Rosa here. And if Claire had watched the film, she must have been terrified – which was why she had fled.

The minutes dragged on. Wilde tried counting to gauge the time. He heard the sound of car doors opening and closing, of an engine firing up and then the growl of a police car being driven away.

'Get up. We're going for a ride on your motorbike.'

They waited, standing in the trees, for five minutes, then Marfield jabbed his captive in the back with the weapon. 'Move. And take very great care. Your life is hanging by a slender thread, Professor. But you already know that, don't you?'

Yes, he knew that.

'You will also know that I mean it when I say that if you cross me in any way I will make it my business to find Lydia Morris. I'll let you imagine the rest.'

He said it so calmly and coldly that Wilde knew that Dr Charlecote's diagnosis was almost certainly accurate: this man was a psychopath.

They moved from the orchard, Wilde in front, Marfield behind him. At the edge of the road, Marfield grabbed his arm. 'We move at a steady pace, towards your motorbike. You climb on and I will ride pillion. You start the engine and you drive slowly where I direct you. You will do nothing to attract attention.'

Wilde nodded.

'Now go.'

Wilde mounted the Rudge, followed immediately by Marfield on the pillion. There was no prodding of the gun muzzle in his back; there was no need. Wilde knew what would happen. He knew, too, what would happen when they were away from here, somewhere a gunshot to the head would not be heard.

He kicked the engine into life and prepared to go wherever he was ordered. As he did so, the headlights of a car lit up further along the street.

'Who's that?' Marfield demanded.

'I have no idea.'

'You came alone?'

'Yes.'

'No headlights. Move away. Keep to thirty. Turn first right then left.'

Wilde twisted the throttle gently and set off, taking the first right into a street of detached houses, then left, and quickly found himself at the edge of the urban area, heading north into open country. Without lights, he had to strain to see the road markings.

The road lit up. The car was following them.

'Unmarked police car,' Marfield said, his mouth close to Wilde's ear. 'Now, when I indicate, switch on the lights, then full throttle and keep to this road. We'll hit Cottenham, but don't slow down – straight through and keep on until I stop you.' He jabbed Wilde's back. 'Go.'

Wilde clicked the lights, wrenched the accelerator and the Rudge leapt forward like a sprinter from the blocks.

The road was almost straight and empty of traffic. But potholes, mud and farm waste made it treacherous and juddery. Even without bends to negotiate, Wilde had to fight his way out of skids. The police car had accelerated in pursuit, but it couldn't match the Rudge on this road, and by the time they were in Cottenham, less than five minutes later, there was no sign of it.

He instinctively slowed down as he hit the sharp bends of the large village, but Marfield screamed in his ear. 'Faster!'

Wilde pushed his head down and rode through Cottenham like a racer, taking the bends at upwards of sixty miles an hour. It was Sunday evening, so few people were about, but ahead of them a shadow crossed the road from the war memorial. Wilde swerved and only just missed a man walking his dog. On his left a row of thatched cottages, then up ahead loomed the church with its distinctive and strange gothic tower.

'Keep to the left. Then take the right fork.'

Wilde knew this part of Cambridgeshire well. They were heading for the Fens, where he went to birdwatch when he needed a little peace. All the roads and places around here had strange, slightly sinister names. Setchel Drove, Grunty Fen Road, Wicken Fen. They spoke of a time when these vast acres were more sea than land, before the drainages of the seventeenth century and beyond had made the land fit for agriculture.

The bike shuddered and spluttered.

'Keep going.' The sweet voice had turned sharp like bile.

'We're running out of fuel.'

'You had better be lying, because if we stop . . .'

Wilde sighed. 'No option.' The Rudge ground to a halt, the engine dead. He sat there, legs astride, feet on the tarmac road, at the edge of a deep drainage ditch. How bloody convenient. So this was where it ended: Twenty Pence Road. Life was cheap to men like Marfield. Wilde turned around. 'Well, get on with it.'

Marfield dismounted, the pistol in his left hand, loose at his side, glinting a little in the merest sliver of moon. Marfield had brought Wilde's torch and switched it on, sweeping it in a circle to get his bearings. He nodded towards an old farm wagon in the field on the far side of the road.

'Wheel the bike behind the wagon.'

Wilde had expected to be forced to roll it into the eight-foot-deep ditch, but perhaps Marfield had ideas of finding petrol and using it again. He rested it on its stand in the field; he did not expect to see it again.

'Now?'

'Now we walk. You go ahead. If we see car lights, we get off the road.'

They strode northwards at a steady pace. The night was not cold. Wilde was in front, Marfield behind and a little to the side. The torch was off.

'You might at least answer one or two questions, Marfield. It'll pass the minutes.'

Marcus did not reply.

Wilde was under no illusions about his fate. Trying to win sympathy from a man whose blood ran as cold as a viper's was pointless. But he was curious. 'The woman you shot, her face was familiar. Was she Rosa's sister by any chance?'

No reply.

'I went across to Ipswich today and met your mother. Didn't fill up, I'm afraid, which is why I ran out of fuel.'

Again, no response.

'She's burnt all your pictures, you know. Nothing left. She won't acknowledge your existence. The strange thing is she's like you in so many ways. I rather think you have more in common than either of you realise.'

'Stop here.'

'Am I talking too much? You can easily put paid to that.'

'Stop. There's a house over there, across the field. We're going there, in silence. Not a sound. They will have either a vehicle or fuel or both. If there are people there, no harm needs come to them, but that's up to you. Do you understand?'

It was a modest farmworkers' cottage of poor construction, like so many of the isolated properties in this part of England. The blackouts had been badly fixed. Light escaped at all the edges and corners of the downstairs windows. Upstairs, it did not even look as though any attempt had been made to cover the windows, other than with flimsy cotton floral curtains. But then Herr Goering was unlikely to target a solitary house in the Cambridgeshire Fens.

Wilde nodded towards a car on the forecourt. If the car keys weren't in the ignition, it could be hotwired and they'd be gone in a matter of moments. But looking closer, such hopes were dashed. The vehicle was raised on makeshift jacks and had no tyres. The only mode of transport available was a bicycle that had been leant against the wall of the house.

Marfield ignored Wilde and crept to the window. He laughed. 'He's some sort of police officer,' he said quietly, half to himself, half to Wilde. 'I can see his uniform hanging up.'

Wilde pointed to the forecourt again. Perhaps there would be another car. At the very least there must be some petrol they could steal and use in the Rudge. This house was occupied by innocent people. They had no need to be any part of this.

'Down. Flat on your belly. Remember what I said.'

Wilde sank to his knees, then stretched out flat.

'Stay there. Don't speak. Don't move.'

Until now, Wilde had not thought of escape. He was unarmed against a man with a pistol, a man who would undoubtedly think nothing of killing Lydia if crossed. But having survived this long, it was beginning to dawn on Wilde that there was an option: what if he were to take Marfield down?

The thought did not last more than a few moments. His breath was taken away as Marfield's knee cracked down into the small of his back. He heard the jangle of handcuffs, then cold metal snapped around his right wrist. His left leg was tugged back roughly and the other cuff was ratcheted tight around his ankle, so that the sharp steel dug into his flesh. Wilde immediately suffered a spasm of cramp: the pain was excruciating and he had to force himself not to cry out.

Marfield wrenched back Wilde's hair so that his face was lifted from the earth, and then rammed the muzzle of the pistol hard into the centre of his face.

'Be good, Professor. No noise.' Marfield strode off towards the front door of the little house.

Flexing the palm of his left hand into the grass, Wilde pushed himself to one side to take the strain off his cuffed wrist and ankle. The cramp eased slightly, but he would not be able to stay here long. His eardrums were thundering like a rushing waterfall and his breathing was laboured. He stretched his neck to see that the front door of the house was now open and in the light that spilled out he saw Marfield pointing the gun at someone. Then he stepped inside and for a few moments there was nothing to see or hear. The silence did not last long.

A scream, deep like a man's not a woman's, cut short almost instantly. God, what had Marfield done in there? No gunshot – knives? Wilde waited, helpless and impotent, forgetting his own pain in the terror of what might be going on inside the house.

Minutes later Marfield was back at the entrance in the light of the yellow hallway. The gun and torch were no longer in his hands, but the reel of film was, along with a bundle of newspapers and some sticks. Wilde watched as he scrunched the newspaper up into balls, laid the sticks as kindling, then struck a match and lit a fire on the doorstep. As it flared up and blazed he unwound the film and coiled it slowly into the fire, frame by frame, until it was all burned and utterly destroyed.

'What have you done, Marfield?' shouted Wilde in desperation. 'Please God you haven't hurt anyone.'

Their eyes met. Marfield pulled his right index finger across his throat. 'What sort of copper doesn't have a phone, Mr Wilde? Answer me that, if you would.'

CHAPTER 29

In the early hours, Juliet Vanderberg awoke from a fitful sleep and knew she was losing her younger son. He was burning up in her arms.

The dinghy seemed to sink an inch lower in the water with every hour that passed, and must sink soon, for they were no longer able to bail fast enough and by now the sea was lapping about their feet and ankles. The waves were getting up and tossing them about, pushing them with the current towards who knew where. The fog had lifted, but that was no help. If a freighter or a warship ploughed its way through these waves, it would cut them in half without even noticing what it had done. In the vastness of the sea, their three lives were nothing.

'Oh, my God.' Joyce Harman paused her bailing. 'Do you see that, Mrs Vanderberg? Rocks. Right ahead of us.'

Tom Wilde had lost all track of time and direction of travel. Having been freed from the leg cuff, his hands had been locked together and he and Marfield had set off walking across the fields. Wilde wondered if he was being kept alive for some purpose – as a hostage perhaps – but it was hard to imagine circumstances in which Marfield would need one.

He thought they had been walking for two or three hours and had covered five or six miles, perhaps more. Crossing a rail track Wilde felt an insane surge of hope, but instead they pushed on across the flat black earth. They skirted two villages, and found a bridge over a river – the Ouse or the Cam perhaps?

Sometimes they had difficulty traversing ditches and boggy fens. For a while they seemed to be going north, then eastwards, usually without light though every few minutes Marfield switched on the torch to get the lie of the land. At about one in the morning, a few hundred yards from a hamlet of a dozen houses or so, he stopped. What looked like a small windmill loomed out of the dark.

Marfield pushed Wilde inside through the low doorway, and secured him with the cuffs to some rigid part of the winding mechanism. Then he played the torch around the space, turned and left, leaving Wilde alone in the pitch dark.

Wilde had seen mills like this before. They were used as drainage pumps, a familiar part of the flat fenland landscape. This one, like so many of the others, had fallen into disrepair with the collapse of the peat and turf industries. And yet even in their dilapidation, they retained a certain charm in an otherwise bleak terrain. Tonight, it was a prison.

Twenty minutes later, Marcus Marfield returned. He shone the torch into Wilde's eyes.

'What now?' Wilde asked.

'We wait.'

'What for?'

'You'll see. Or perhaps you won't.' Marfield pulled two beer bottles from his pocket and removed the tops. He handed one to Wilde. 'Here, don't say I don't do anything for you.'

'Thank you.' Even handcuffed, Wilde found he was able to drink the beverage. It was cool and welcome to his parched throat. 'That's good. The best beer I've ever tasted.'

'There's a little pub along the way. Dozen or more crates of beers outside. Shame not to take what's offered.'

'I'll go along with that.'

They drank in silence. Then Wilde ventured a question. 'Why haven't you killed me?'

'Guess.'

'Because you have some use for me?'

'Something like that.'

'Or because you are looking for something and you think I might know where it is? But you've already found the film and burnt it.'

'The other film. You know exactly what I mean – and you know where it is. But there is time enough for that. You will give it to me.'

Wilde tipped some more beer down his throat. 'Why is it important to you that no one suspects you are a fascist? Were you worried that you had revealed yourself to Dr Charlecote under hypnosis? Is that why he died? Were you worried about Rosa? Was that why she was killed?'

'I didn't kill her.'

'I know that because I was there. But you know who did it. Someone is assisting you in whatever it is you are up to. Why would someone kill that poor young girl?'

Marfield took another sip of his beer. 'You know, Professor Wilde, I always rather admired you. I thought you had an intellect well above the common herd. Perhaps I was wrong.'

'What happened in Spain? Did you switch sides? Did you become disillusioned with the International Brigades? I know there were mass executions, instant justice, on both sides. I can understand that someone might feel they had chosen the wrong cause.'

'God damn it, Professor – this country!' Marfield almost spat out the words. 'Britain ignored Spain, and then tottered into a war against Germany like – well, like what? A mouse threatening a cat? Hopeless. The real war, the war against Bolshevism, has been going on for years, and Britain has simply stood by and ignored it. Now they're caught up in it, and our country is on the wrong side of history. And if America isn't careful your country will be too. Because we all know what Roosevelt wants, don't we?'

'I had no idea you felt like this. Why didn't you talk to me when you were in college?'

'Really? And say what? Oh, Professor Wilde, won't you come to Spain with me and kill some Commies? How would you have reacted to that?' He spoke contemptuously.

'That wasn't what I was thinking.'

'No, you just wanted to *talk*. Like that trick cyclist at Addenbrooke's. Because it's all so far away and Cambridge is so cosy. Nothing bad can happen there. All the dons in all the colleges – well most of them – have their CPGB cards or they do a little dirty work for the local Comintern agent, all the time believing that Communism is never going to threaten their comfortable little lives here in the heart of good old England. Well, they're wrong.'

Wilde had never expected such a tirade from Marcus Marfield. Misguided, wrong-headed, perhaps, but there could be no denying his passion. Did that make him more dangerous, or less?

'I have seen National Socialism in action, Professor. I spent two summers there with the Hitlerjugend. National Socialism works.'

'But you agreed to spy for *British* intelligence.'

Marfield laughed. 'What was I supposed to say? Ah, I fed them some guff at first, but then I couldn't be bothered.'

'So how did you end up in Le Vernet with the International Brigades? Why weren't you in Madrid toasting victory with Franco and your friends in the Condor Legion?'

Marfield was leaning against the wooden interior frame of the windpump, torch dangling from one hand, bottle in the other. 'You're asking too many questions. Drink your beer and get some sleep. We've got a long day ahead of us.'

'I can't lie down or even sit properly handcuffed to this winding gear,' Wilde said. 'Won't you at least allow me a little comfort?'

Marfield took a long hard look at Wilde. He was in an awkward position with his hands attached to the machinery at head height. Down below there was some sort of hook bolted onto the mechanism. Marfield tested it to satisfy himself that it was secure.

'I'm going to release you briefly and you will immediately lie face down with your arms outstretched right here.' Marfield removed the pistol and the key from his pocket and patted the ground to indicate what he wanted.

'I'm not going to do anything stupid.'

'You know,' he said, 'I *did* join the International Brigades. I was an idealistic young leftie, like Cornford or Bell. And no one will ever know otherwise.'

'You still haven't explained why that is so important to you.'

He released Wilde cautiously, then secured him at a lower position on the winding gear. Marfield smiled enigmatically in the fading light of his torch, then switched it off. Wilde could hear him making himself comfortable on the dusty wooden floor of the mill and listened as his breathing evened out. Wilde gritted his teeth; he would have no sleep this night.

Claire Marfield had seen enough glimpses of the cold depths in her husband to shy away from venturing too close. There were his silences, the way he refused to engage in argument when there was any dispute. When he said he was going away to the war, he hadn't asked her opinion or apologised for deserting her, and she had said nothing to dissuade him. The truth was, she had always been afraid of him.

So why *had* she wanted Marcus? Why had she given herself to him, married him, given birth to his child? The answer was straightforward: because everyone else wanted him. He was beautiful and talented and, at first meeting, utterly charming. No one could take their eyes off him. He was the glittering prize, and she had won.

But the gold veneer on the trophy was leaf thin.

She might sleep tonight, but it would be fitful. Even in her dreams she would be listening, waiting for his footfalls. He would guess that she was here and would come for her. She was in no doubt about that. But where *could* she hide with a small child? Her husband was relentless.

And so she was here in Hertfordshire at her parents' house, close to the school where her father was deputy headmaster. Where else could she go to? She had no friends onto whom she could foist herself and Walter. Not without some very difficult explanations.

It had been hard enough trying to think up some excuse to satisfy her father. Mummy hadn't given her sudden appearance a second thought, merely put on the kettle and fussed over her grandson, but Daddy kept fishing for information. As always, he asked after Marcus; had she heard anything?

For a brief moment, she considered telling them the truth, but she knew what Daddy's reaction would be. He'd call the police immediately, as though this was some minor burglary or ABH they were dealing with. Daddy always believed that there was right and wrong and that the bobby on the beat was there to sort out anyone who stepped out of line.

If only Marcus didn't know about this house.

When the Spanish woman turned up at Histon univited, Claire's instinct had been to turn her away. But Rosa was insistent. She must hear her story, she must watch her film and see the evidence for herself. Claire had so wanted to slam the door in her face, but that would merely have been a matter of denying what she already knew.

Now she knew too much.

Would he kill her if he thought she posed a threat to him? Oh yes. Without a moment's hesitation. But in her heart she had always known it, hadn't she? It was all part of the thrill, like driving a racing car or skiing down a couloir. You did these things knowing that death waited around every corner. Marcus had always been like that.

Her mother had told her it was the curse of some women to fall for dangerous men. Well, no one had fallen harder than Claire.

Somehow he managed to doze on his knees, slumped against the machinery, his hands above him, chained to some sort of shaft. It wasn't a real, restful sleep, because he was aware of the discomfort, the pain of the sharp metal cutting into his wrists, the enveloping dark and the cold that bit into his bones.

The first thing he knew was the key in the lock, the handcuff slipping from his right wrist. He recoiled in shock, falling backwards.

'Keep still.'

But Wilde didn't keep still. He was a fighting man, with all the reflexes and instincts of a boxer. There would be no second chance. He had one hand free, his right hand, and that would have to be enough. He pulled the left hand and the loose cuff free of the winding gear and lashed out in the dark. It didn't connect, swung wildly in the air, but the follow-up punch with his right hand, low, belly-height, did connect. Hard.

He sensed soft flesh against the firmness of his fist, and then a grunt of pain. Marfield was winded. Wilde had no idea whether he had hit him in the stomach or the balls, but he knew he had made contact.

A flash and explosion rent the air as the gun went off. Wilde was already diving for the little doorway, but in the darkness he didn't quite judge it right and slammed his left shoulder against the jamb. The wood was rotten and fell away, and Wilde tumbled out into the darkness. A second gunshot sounded behind him and he heard the thud as the bullet smacked into timber.

He fell down the step from the mill, unsure of exactly where he was. The first vestiges of light had turned the horizon from black to dark grey and he ran straight towards the trees. Behind him there was a third shot. Marfield must be at the mill door. In the gloom, he must be able to see something of his quarry, if only a vague outline. Wilde swerved, zig-zagged, heard a fourth shot, and then the ground gave way beneath him and he was plunging.

He hit a damp, marshy morass, and the impact took his breath away. For a second or two, he lay gasping. But he couldn't wait even two seconds because Marfield would be right behind him, at the edge of the incline, gun in hand, peering down. At least there was cover here – reeds, sedge, mud and, just beyond, the jagged horizon of a half-submerged woodland. Wilde crawled and scrabbled forward as fast and as silently as he could. He wanted to live.

Elina Kossoff had been summoned to the telephone at 1.15 a.m. When she heard Marfield's voice on the line, her body tensed. What in God's name did he think he was doing calling her here?

'It's all right,' he told her. 'I told the flunkey I was your brother and that your mother had been taken ill.'

'Just say what you have to say.' This was bad, very bad. If the servant ever mentioned this telephone call, it would be quickly established that she had no brother and that her mother was in America. Was such a call traceable? Was MI5 listening in?

'The first film . . .' he began.

'You've found it?'

'She took it to Claire.'

'So Claire's seen it? Where is she?'

'The only place she'd go: Longrow Cottage, village called Whipham, Hertfordshire. Her parents' place.'

'Leave it with me. What about the films?'

'One destroyed. One to go.'

'God in heaven, Marcus! What's been going on up there? Where are you now?'

'Don't worry about me.'

'And Wilde, what are you doing about him?'

'It's all being taken care of.'

Elina carefully replaced the receiver, then picked it up again and listened for any signs that the device was tapped.

The serving man was at the door. 'Everything all right, Miss Kossoff.'

'Family crisis. What's the time?'

'One twenty, madam.'

'Well, I have to go. If Mr Kennedy asks where I am, just tell him I will be back later this morning and that all the arrangements are in hand.'

'Of course, Miss Kossoff.'

CHAPTER 30

At five in the morning, Elina Kossoff drew up in the Morgan 4-4, and parked in the centre of a perfect English village, close to the church, away from the cluster of houses that made up the heart of the community. Marfield had told her that if she lined up the village sign on the green with the church spire, then Longrow Cottage would be in the street directly to her right. The whole place was asleep. Just as it should be an hour and a half before dawn on a dark Monday morning.

She didn't like this. It might be quiet here, but the houses were close together. It would be much easier if Longrow Cottage was isolated. She had options, though. The question was which one was best. And then she heard the sound she had hoped for – the clatter of horses' hoofs and the rattle of bottles. The milkman.

Elina sank down in her seat but it was still dark and the milk float passed her by, the horse walking the route it had walked a thousand times before. Like a pit pony, it didn't need light, and nor did the milkman.

Half an hour later, still dark, the sound of the hoofs and the bottles receded and the float finally left the village on its way to the next hamlet or town. People would be getting up soon. There might even be those who woke to the sound of milk bottles arriving on their doorsteps. No time to waste.

Elina was wearing black plimsolls. She wore a long dark overcoat with its collar turned up, and her hair was concealed beneath a man's hat. It wasn't meant as a disguise, more as camouflage.

For a few moments, she stood outside Longrow Cottage. It was lovely if you liked that sort of thing, with its roses around the porch, just like a Victorian watercolour of a perfect English cottage.

Silently, she made her way through the open gate, up the front path to the door. Two pint bottles stood on the doorstep. By perching the flashlight in a nook inside the porch, she had enough light to see what she was doing, and picked up one of the bottles. With a long, sharp fingernail she prised the gold foil top half off, put the bottle down and did the same to the second bottle.

She reached into her pocket and took out a syringe and a small vial – no more than one inch high by one inch diameter – of clear liquid. Removing the vial's lid, she dipped the needle into the poison. Stealthily she drew up the deadly liquid into the syringe, then quickly plunged it into first one, then the other milk bottle. She tried to make it even between the bottles. The needle was long and she deliberately pushed it through the thick cream that topped each pint.

The empty syringe and vial went back into her pocket. Then, unhurriedly, she replaced the gold foil lids on the bottles, smoothing them down carefully.

She smiled to herself. Had the milkman not come, she would have had to find a way into the kitchen and inject the poison into a foodstuff or drinks bottle. Thallium, in the heavy dosage she had administered, should be quick, and certain. With luck, the link to Cambridge would never be made and the deaths would be dismissed as a family tragedy. One of those murder–suicides the newspapers mentioned on the bottom of page two.

Wilde was soaked to the bone, cold and shivering. He had been crawling through mud and water and sedge for over an hour.

Crawling an inch at a time, so slowly he could barely hear the whisper of the reeds as he pushed them aside. Occasionally, he thought he heard Marfield's footfalls or his breathing, and then he stayed still and shrank as deep as he could into the sludge.

He couldn't be more than a couple of hundred yards from the windpump, but perhaps Marfield didn't know that; perhaps he thought Wilde had got clean away. The horizon was lightening by the minute. Soon the sun would rise and then he would be visible. Now had to be the time to make his break. Please God, his pursuer had already gone.

At least there was a little light to guide him. He was in the shelter of a watery wood, criss-crossed by paths. Thus far, he had remained away from the paths, fearing that Marfield would patrol them in his hunt. Now Wilde would make use of them himself.

With an effort, he dragged himself out of the sludge onto the path. His left wrist was still cuffed and he held the open cuff tight in his fist to stop it clanking. He turned right – west, away from the rising sun. It was a gamble. He began to walk slowly, then ran. If he was to be shot in the back, he might as well not make it easy.

The wood wasn't large. Within a few minutes he was out of the trees and onto typical fenland fields. Black fertile clay and drainage ditches, rich with a harvest of full-grown cabbages. The pungent aroma aroused a distant memory of school corridors mid-morning when the vegetables stewing in the kitchens seeped into every corner of the building. He loped through the crop, across the field, then alongside a straight watercourse, known in these parts as a lode.

Ahead of him was a river that had to be crossed if he was going to carry on in this direction. There was no bridge, so he would either have to swim, or change direction and go south. He was more likely to find a proper road if he crossed the river, but intuition told him that was also the way he was most likely to meet Marfield.

To hell with it. He needed to find some semblance of civilisation, and sooner rather than later. He lowered himself down the riverbank and plunged into the water. It was deep enough and wide enough that he had to swim. A couple of minutes later he was lying on the far bank, panting from the exhaustion and the cold.

Crawling up the bank, he stared into the distance. Perhaps a half-mile away he saw something that brought hope to his heart. Some sort of vehicle – he couldn't see whether it was car or truck or wagon – was trundling northwards along what surely must be a regular road. The path to freedom.

Lydia hadn't slept and nor had Eaton. They had waited half the night in her sitting room, listening for the telephone. How long had it been now since the police told them what they had found at Histon, and described their futile chase into the fens? Eight hours? Nine maybe?

Eaton had brought a pistol, concealed beneath his jacket. He had told her the police had found no one at Claire Marfield's house, but that they knew someone had been there because, curiously, a projector was set up on the first floor, and it was burning hot.

The police had searched the house thoroughly, and the garden. No one had noted Mr Wilde's motorbike, which was parked across the road. But they had thought to leave a car parked nearby for a short while, just in case the intruder – or intruders – were to reappear. It had been a good move; but sadly the motorbike was a great deal quicker than the police vehicle.

Not for the first time, Eaton cursed his injuries. All he had been able to do was call Detective Inspector Tomlinson all night and demand that they find Wilde and Marfield at all costs. At first Tomlinson had been polite and accommodating, but by the early hours, his cooperation was wearing thin. 'If you were to at least give me some idea where they might be heading, Mr Eaton, I would be able to look for them. For the moment, though, we have nothing to go on.'

'They can't be far.'

'That's simply not true, sir. They could be a hundred miles away by now – in any direction. They could have found an airfield and flown away or reached King's Lynn and taken to the sea. They could be in London. So where do I look?'

Eaton had no answer.

'I'm sorry, sir,' Tomlinson said with a sigh so heavy it might have been a yawn. 'I'm leaving the station in the hands of my desk sergeant and going home to get a few hours' sleep. Good night to you.'

'Good night, Inspector.' Eaton had put the phone down and looked at his watch. Good morning, in fact.

He returned to the sitting room. Lydia, still dressed, was curled up on the sofa, awake but heavy-lidded. Eaton looked at her for a few moments then went off to see if he could find a blanket to put over her. Of course, he understood Detective Inspector Tomlinson's point of view; the problem was he didn't believe Marfield and Wilde had gone far from Cambridge. Nor did he believe that Wilde would be kept alive long. His big fear was that it was already too late.

Before he could get to the road, Wilde had an eight-foot-deep dyke to traverse. It was too wide to leap across, so he slid down its steep sides, then grasped at weeds, grass and nettles, dragging himself inch by inch upwards. His arms burned with the effort, his feet scrabbled for non-existent footholds, but his strength held and he slumped on the top at the very edge of the road.

He got to his feet and looked both ways. The road was dead straight in both directions and there was no sign of any traffic, not even a farm cart. And then he found himself laughing. Almost opposite him stood a telephone kiosk, bright red in the first glow of day.

He pulled the door shut after him and picked up the handset. Miracle of miracles, a dialling tone. All he needed now were some coins for the slot. He dug his hands into his soaking pockets and his prayers were answered again. Four shillings and eleven pence in loose change. He called the Bull Hotel, but was told there was no answer from Mr Eaton's room. 'I believe he was called out a few hours ago,' the concierge said. 'Can I leave a message, sir?'

Wilde put the phone down and rang Lydia. After a few rings, a familiar voice said, 'Hello.'

'Eaton, is that you?'

'Good God, Wilde, where the devil are you?'

'Somewhere in the middle of the Fens. Did the police tell you what happened?'

'Yes. Are you OK?'

'A bit damp and one of my wrists is shackled, but I got away from the bastard.'

'Do you know exactly where you are? We'll get help to you.'

'I'm in a phone kiosk. There's no address in here, but there's a phone number. You should be able to trace my location through the Post Office.'

'I'll get on to it.'

'I'm worried about Lydia. Marfield has made threats against her. I'll explain all when I see you, but for God's sake don't let her out of your sight. You're armed, I take it?'

'Oh, yes.'

'One more thing. I didn't see it, but I'm as certain as I can be that Marcus Marfield has harmed a police officer out here. He was looking for a phone. Very isolated little house. There was a scream, then nothing . . . I don't know what happened, but I fear the worst.'

'The police will find him. Help will be with *you* very soon. Stay exactly where you are.'

'Dry clothes would be appreciated.'

The NAAFI canteen beckoned. Breakfast of porridge with syrup, plenty of sugary tea and lovely fatty bacon. Standing out here on the parade ground at first light, surrounded by Nissen huts, the squaddies couldn't bear the thought that they weren't going to get anything to eat until they had marched fifteen miles.

Lance Corporal Edwin Elphick felt as bad as the six men in his squad, all raw recruits. He had realised very early on in his army career that he was not cut out to be a soldier. 'Just get on with it, Elphick,' the sergeant had said when he tried to suggested that others might be better suited to promotion. Of course he understood that men were being promoted fast and well beyond their meagre talents. With the army expanding at this rate, it was bound to be so. And having joined up on a whim (in drink, of course) at the time of Munich, Elphick was seen as someone with at least a little bit of experience.

This morning he had to take these six reluctant men across country carrying rifles and full packs, with only an Ordnance Survey map and compass to guide them. 'No breakfast until you get back, so no hanging about, lance corporal.'

'But sir . . .'

'Don't you know there's a bloody war on? Get on with it, Elphick.'

'Yes, sir!'

'At the double. And don't cut any corners. You and your men will be heading to France to give the Hun a good bashing soon, so chin up and shoulders back.'

Now, just two miles out from camp barracks, on a wide road bordered by poplars, the men were already complaining bitterly. 'Couldn't we at least get a cup of tea somewhere, lance corporal? My rifle's ever so heavy.' Elphick, weighed down by his own rifle and 60lb pack, tried to ignore them. He stopped and consulted the map. Where the sodding hell were they? There was supposed to be a footpath to their right, but there wasn't. Not only that, the map said there should be a water tower directly ahead, and that wasn't there either.

Wilde had no intention of staying exactly where he was: he was far too visible and he had no idea where Marfield had got to. He crossed back over the road, slid into the ditch with his elbows on top so that he could peer in both directions for oncoming traffic and instantly disappear if need be.

Twenty minutes later, he heard the sound of an engine to his left. A vehicle was approaching – from the south-west, he assumed, given the rising sun at his back. It must be coming from the Cambridge direction.

The vehicle was slowing down and Wilde let out a sigh of relief. The man at the wheel had the reassuringly urbane face and hat of Guy Rowlands.

Wilde crawled up from the ditch, dusted some of the mud off his damp, filthy clothes and strode across the road. He held up his hand in greeting as the car came to a halt.

Rowlands braked, wrenched up the handbrake, left the engine running and stepped out. He had half a cigarette in the side of his mouth, which was fixed in something akin to a smile.

'Well, well, Professor Wilde, you have got yourself into a pickle.'

'Mr Rowlands, I can't tell you what a pleasure it is to see you.'

'Well, you're in good hands now,' Rowlands said, pulling a revolver from his pocket. 'This will keep us safe.'

CHAPTER 31

The little boy was lying in a heap by the side of the outhouse, shaking and shivering.

Catherine Cullanan had been woken by a whimpering, sobbing sound. Rolling away from her slumbering husband she had headed to the privy, twenty yards to the west of the house, thinking one of her children might have been taken ill. She bent down. This boy wasn't one of hers, nor had she seem him before.

She knelt down beside the child and spoke to him in the soft lilting Gaelic that she always used at home with the family. He didn't respond, didn't even open his eyes. She picked him up in her warm, fleshy arms and he was as light as down. 'Where did you come from?' she said, changing tongues to English. 'What's your name, little man?'

There was no reply. She wasn't sure if the boy was unconscious or asleep, but she did know that he was burning up and needed urgent care. She had lost a child of her own to scarlet fever three years back and knew what overheating and lack of responsiveness meant.

Her husband, Martin, was up when she got back in the house, so she put the little boy in their own bed and fetched water and a flannel to cool him down. Removing his soaking clothes, she discovered that he had no rash, so it wasn't chickenpox or measles or scarlet fever. A mother needed to have a fair knowledge of all the childhood illnesses in such an isolated community.

'Who is he?' Martin asked, standing at her elbow as she tried to bring the boy's temperature down.

'Your guess is as good as mine, Martin Cullanan.'

'I reckon he came off that ship the Germans sank.' He jutted his chin towards the Atlantic.

'Then how did he get here? That ship was sunk at least a week ago now. He couldn't have survived in those seas clinging to a piece of driftwood all that time.'

'You're right,' said Martin. 'I'll get the lads out. There'll be a lifeboat brought to shore somewhere on the island.'

'And we'll need a doctor from the mainland.'

'I'll fix that.' He put a huge hand on her shoulder and lowered his voice. 'Perhaps I should fetch the priest, too, do you think?'

'I don't know, Martin. Look at him, I really don't know.' Catherine stopped flannelling the boy for a few moments and stood back. 'But it wouldn't do any harm to ask the father to say a prayer.'

Wilde looked at the gun. It wasn't there to protect him.

'As I said,' Rowlands continued, removing his cigarette butt and tapping a long tail of ash into the breeze. 'A bit of a pickle. I'm afraid I'm going to have to bind you and put you in the boot. What you Americans call the trunk, I believe. Damned uncomfortable, I realise, but it shouldn't be for long. That will be down to you.'

Wilde felt an almost overpowering desire to punch Guy Rowlands's self-satisfied face.

Rowlands caught the look and sucked his teeth. 'You know, Wilde, if you cooperate, you can still get out of this intact.'

Wilde didn't believe him for a moment. Once they realised he couldn't help them, he would be dead. In the meantime, he must stay alive. 'The boot it is, then.'

*

Charlie Farrow couldn't run fast these days. Couldn't run at all, truth be told. But then who could at seventy-eight years of age? 'Bother,' he said as they watched the bus disappear into the distance. 'That's a whole hour we've got to wait for the next one.'

'We could go home and have another cuppa,' suggested his wife.

It was a twelve-minute walk from home to the bus stop, which would mean another twenty-four minutes walking altogether. 'No,' he said, 'let's just stay here in the shelter. Nice enough day.'

Agatha patted his hand. 'The sun always shines on our anniversary, Charlie. For me it does anyway.'

'You're as daft as a brush, Mrs Farrow. Always were.'

'But you do love me, don't you, Charlie?'

'Of course I do. From the first moment I laid eyes on you.' He looked at her frail, lined face and saw the girl of seventeen that he had married. In his eyes, she was as beautiful today as she always had been.

'Then let's just sit here holding hands like Darby and Joan.'

As they sat there, smiling at each other, a silver car with an open top pulled to a halt in front of the bus shelter. A handsome young man leant out. 'Have you two missed your bus?'

'I'm afraid we have. But we're fine sitting here.'

'I could give you a lift into town if you don't mind squashing in – I'm heading in that direction.'

Charlie looked at Agatha. They had never been in a car before. 'Be a bit of a treat for our anniversary, wouldn't it?' he said.

'Hop in then.' The young man leant across to open the passenger door. 'I'll take you for a spin!'

Eaton knew that Lydia Morris was not one to panic, even at the worst of times. But when she went next door to get a dry set of clothes for Tom and returned, her face drained, to tell Eaton that the house had been ransacked, drawers turned out and possessions scattered across the floor, it was clear to Eaton that she was close to the edge.

'Look,' said Eaton, doing his best to comfort her. 'We know he'll be back soon. The worst is over . . .'

His driver arrived. Eaton handed Lydia his pistol, patted her awkwardly on the arm and manoeuvered himself into the front passenger seat. As they drove off, he turned to see her in the rear windscreen, his gun dangling from her right hand. She looked defeated.

It took them fifteen minutes to drive out into the Fens north of Cambridge. Along the way, three police cars overtook them at high speed; they didn't stop. When Eaton and his driver reached the remote telephone kiosk from which Wilde had called, he wasn't there.

Perhaps the police in one of the three cars had picked him up. Using the telephone in the kiosk, Eaton put a call through to the headquarters in St Andrew's Street, but they had no knowledge of Mr Wilde's whereabouts. They were, however, investigating a suspicious death in the area, which was why he had seen the police cars.

With a heavy heart, Eaton called Lydia.

Wilde still had the cuff attached to one wrist, but he was now also bound hand and foot with cord and his mouth was gagged. He had been bundled in to the boot of Rowlands' large black car like a sack of turnips. After a few moments, the car had pulled away. Breathing was not easy, and the ride was painfully jarring. Wilde could not judge which direction they were going and he wasn't sure how long he was there, but he imagined it was an hour; time slows to a crawl when you're in pain. The only thing he could be sure of was the deafening roar of the engine, the stink of the oil and fuel, and the poor quality of the roads they traversed.

The last part of the journey was the worst; it seemed to be over a rocky mile-long cart track. At last, the car pulled to a halt, the engine was switched off and he heard a door opening and slamming shut. Then the boot lid was pulled up and daylight flooded in. Wilde kept his eyes tight shut to avoid the glare. Bit by bit he was able to open them.

Rowlands was looking down at him.

'Apologies, Wilde. That can have been no fun at all.'

Gagged, Wilde couldn't respond.

'Now then, the same rule applies. Cooperate with me and you have every chance of surviving this. I have a task to complete. I have no desire for unnecessary bloodshed.'

And there was that other face looking down at him, too. Marfield was idly twiddling his pistol, just as he had done while sitting on a rock in Spain while a cine camera whirred.

Together, the two men hauled him out, ungagged him and removed his leg bindings. His wrists remained tied.

Wilde looked around. They were outside an isolated house in remote farmland. From the position of the sun and his estimate of the time, he tried to work out basic bearings. To the west were hills: they were no longer in the Fens. The only sign of life was another car parked nearby, a silver BMW.

'Where are we?' No harm in asking.

'Somewhere safe,' Rowlands said. 'Scream all you like and no one will hear you. We could fire a howitzer here and no one would know. But we don't really want you to scream. We want you to talk.'

There was no one in evidence in the house. Outside, there was no livestock – no sign of a chicken, duck or pig, and no sheep or cattle in the nearby fields. This was not a working farm.

They sat in the kitchen. Wilde had his bound hands in front of him on the kitchen table. Marfield sat opposite him, still holding the pistol. Rowlands put his homburg on the table, then filled the kettle and put it on the range. The range was alight and there was a bottle of milk: this place couldn't be totally deserted.

Rowlands took a seat at the head of the table. 'The thing is,' he said. 'We know that Rosa Cortez brought over two copies of the film. One is now destroyed, so we need to find the second one. Marfield's mother insists she hasn't seen it – but what if the poor old Colonel did? It wouldn't have been his cup of tea at all. He was a bit of a Trot, your father, wasn't he, Marfield?'

'I wouldn't go that far,' said Marfield carelessly. 'Left of centre . . .'

'But if he had it, what did he do with it?' Rowlands turned to Wilde.

'Perhaps he destroyed it,' Wilde suggested.

'Oh, I don't think so. Marfield?'

'When I confronted my mother, it was clear she hadn't seen the film, but she blamed me for my father's death. There were actually tears – not something that she has been known to shed before.' Marfield laughed lightly. It was an unnerving sound. 'So she must have been upset.'

'Have you harmed her?'

'My own mother? What do you take me for? No, of course I haven't harmed her. In the end though, she did tell me that on the day of the old man's death a woman had called early in the morning. She was carrying a case, and from Mummy's description it sounded like Rosa Cortez. She asked to speak to the old man and they retreated to his study. They were only in there for twenty minutes or so. Mummy said she heard him shouting before the woman left without a word – and without her case.'

'And you think the film was in it?' Wilde asked.

'And a projector. When my mother knocked on the study door, he told her to go away. Apparently he didn't emerge for a couple of hours. Eventually he found her in the kitchen and demanded brown wrapping paper. She provided it, and string, and he went off again to his study.

'At midday she called him for lunch, but he said it would have to wait, and that he was going to the Post Office to send a parcel. When he came back – without the parcel – he shut himself in his study again, wrote a note and killed himself with his shotgun. When she found him, there was a projector in the study she had never seen before – but no film. So the question is, Professor: to whom did he send the film?'

'Your wife?'

'No. Rosa Cortez took that copy to her.'

'A friend, perhaps – or the police?'

'Possible, of course. But here's the interesting part – my mother says he sent the parcel to you. Apparently, my father had often remarked that you were the sort of man he would have liked *me* to become.' Marfield snorted.

'I suppose I should be flattered, but that's no reason to believe he sent the film to me.'

'I agree. But you see, Wilde, she says she saw *your* name and the college address on the parcel as he was carrying it out of the house. So where is it?'

CHAPTER 32

Martin Cullanan walked past the ruins of the belltower down to the harbour. It was a small island, no more than three miles long and perhaps half a mile wide at its narrowest point. Cullanan had lived here all his life, and he knew every foot.

Standing on the quay, he looked towards the south and the grey contours of Donegal on the mainland, and he wondered about the boy. He couldn't have walked far, not in his condition; he must have come by boat, and he could not have navigated a boat alone.

As he turned his gaze to the east, he spotted something, partly hidden by rocks. He jumped down from the quay and followed the shoreline eastwards. A boat, not a proper lifeboat, but a small ship's rowing boat upturned but not smashed, at the edge of the tideline. The tide was out; it must have arrived in the night. On its prow it bore the name of the ship from which it had come: SS *Athenia*.

So this was how the boy had got here to the island. Cullanan was a godly man slow to anger, but he was filled with an unholy fury. What were they thinking, those Germans, to be torpedoing and sinking an unarmed ship full of women and children?

He scouted around, looking for some clues. Above him the seabirds seemed excitable this morning: gulls and kittiwakes, shags and guillemots, all riding on the wind, above the choppy sea. Perhaps a storm was coming, although he had heard no word of it.

And then he saw the woman's broken body. 'Oh Mary, Mother of God,' he said out loud. He turned. Patsy and Eamonn were standing behind him.

'Radio the mainland, Patsy. Tell them to send a launch over sharpish with a doctor.'

'No need of a doctor for her,' Eamonn said.

'But there's a boy came with her, and he's still alive. Catherine's tending to him.'

'I'll do that then,' Patsy said.

'And Eamonn, call the town and Father Michael to join us here. I want that woman's body carried to the church with respect. And we've got to keep looking. There may be more to find, God help us.'

'I wasn't entirely honest with you, Wilde,' Rowlands said. 'When I said you could get out of this alive if you cooperated, that was a something of a white lie.'

'You surprise me.'

'No, I don't. You're a clever man. Your survival is not an option, not now that you've seen the film.'

'Perhaps I haven't seen it.'

Rowlands smiled. He poured three cups of tea. 'Milk, Wilde? Sugar?'

'Neither.'

'You won't *want* to get out alive anyway,' he went on conversationally. 'You'll be begging for death by the time Marcus gets to work on you. His SS friends taught him some marvellous tricks, tricks that our own secret services could only dream of. The pain will go on and on until you tell us the whereabouts of the second film. And when we know that – well – you have guessed the ending.'

'How do you know there are two copies of the film?'

'Because two copies were made, and Rosa Cortez stole them both.'

'So what was between you and Miss Cortez, Marfield? There must have been something. Didn't you say as much? And I knew it in London when I saw you together.' Wilde had to drag this conversation out. Every second, every minute of health and life might bring an opportunity. He'd had one chance – in the windpump – and he'd wasted it. Please God, let there be another.

'Of course. We met in a bar near the Plaza del Progreso in Madrid. A bomb fell in the square, one of many, and we helped the injured. She was UGT – a socialist – and it turned out her job was to liaise with the International Brigades on behalf of the union. We were lovers and fighters.'

'You loved her?'

'Well,' Marfield paused. 'We made love. I enjoyed her company. Is that love?'

'It's not a bad start for most people. But you were also fighting for the other side. I suppose she discovered the truth about you?'

'She became suspicious. I think she became concerned by the pinpoint air-raids and artillery bombardments. And then there were my disappearances – and of course my good fortune never to be present when the mortars rained down on my sector. Also, reports were coming through of the liquidation of guerrilla bands behind the Falange lines.'

'Because you betrayed them.'

'They were criminals and communists. It was my role.'

'Are you saying the people in the film made up a guerrilla band? That old couple? The mother? A baby? Are you saying the baby was a guerrilla?'

Marfield shrugged. 'If you spare a child it will grow into your enemy.'

Wilde felt sick. He thought of the bleak monochrome footage of the mother handing over her child, pleading for its life even though she knew she, herself, was doomed. 'Why did you have to do that? Why make that woman see her child die? Couldn't you have killed the mother first? Why be so cruel?'

Marfield didn't answer.

Wilde tried another tack. 'So Rosa had her suspicions. How did she find out the truth about you?'

Marfield glanced over at Rowlands.

'It's all right,' said Rowlands. 'Tell him. I'm interested myself.' He took a sip of his tea.

'My one mistake. I didn't think for a moment she was so suspicious of me that she would pursue me across the lines, and so I wasn't watching closely enough. She followed me on the day of that raid.'

'Who were those people? That "guerrilla band"?'

'The woman was Carlita Pascual, wife of the leader of a republican death squad. Anarchists or Communists – who knows? They were all the same to us: the enemy. They had been busy for weeks lining up Falangist sympathisers and shooting them. One day a big grave will be found full of their bones.'

'And the woman – Carlita?'

'As handy with a gun as Pascual himself. She knew the risks.'

'Then you already knew her – and she knew you?'

Marfield shrugged, a teasing smirk playing about his lips.

'How did you find her that day?'

'Her husband told me before he died. I can be quite persuasive.'

Wilde closed his eyes, trying to blank out his imagination.

'Have I answered all your questions? This is tedious – and going nowhere.'

'No, you haven't. Why would you make a film of something like that?'

'That was a little present for our friends in Germany. Something of a sideline for the cameraman. He usually shot newsreels for the cinemas, but this was a favour for us. When he returned to Seville to have it processed, he made an extra copy. One for Himmler and Heydrich in Berlin, the other for viewing in the Führer's private cinema in the Berghof. What I didn't know is that Rosa had seen it all. Not good. Somehow she must have traced the cameraman to the studio in Seville and got into the building. It was not a good day for the staff when the theft was discovered.'

'How did you find out it was her?'

'I had my suspicions when I was shot at Le Vernet. They were confirmed when we saw her there at the gate. I suppose it was her who shot me, or one of her friends. Somewhere between France and England she must have changed her mind about killing me and decided to ruin me instead. A wrong decision as it turned out. But we have to live or die by our decisions.'

'What happened in Chelsea that night?'

'She told me what she was going to do. Told me one copy was going to my parents and she was going to use the other to destroy me.'

'You were trying to preserve your reputation as a left-winger fighting against international fascism? That's why you made your way across the Pyrenees and allowed yourself to be interned in Le Vernet instead of travelling to Madrid or Berlin with your real friends.'

'Of course. We have work to do against a great enemy. Now drink your tea, we've wasted enough time already.'

Keep talking. Keep him occupied. Delay. Stall. 'Your father would have been devastated by the film.'

'The old fool. His brain was turned to jelly by the war.'

'He loved you. You were his life.'

'He saw my strength and envied it.'

Wilde turned away to the older man. 'What's this about, Rowlands? I thought you were close to Colonel Marfield?'

'Oh come, come, you know the answer to that! It's about war, Professor – war against Bolshevism.'

'I thought the Bolsheviks were Hitler's friends now? What about the Molotov–Ribbentrop pact? Stalin and Hitler will be going on holiday together next.'

Rowlands barked a dry laugh. 'Don't be naive. You don't believe that. No one with half a brain believes that.'

'Marfield has been your man all along, hasn't he, Rowlands? You never lost him in Spain – you used him to help your friends in the Falange. You ran him as a double agent. How will all this help your war?'

'Because, Wilde, in one fell swoop, we will ensure that Britain and France cannot win, because America will never join them. And without America, the right will win.'

Wilde frowned. 'Really? You can be sure of that, can you? Roosevelt loathes the Germans even more than the British Empire.'

'Roosevelt's hands will be tied. America won't allow him to lift a finger to help Britain. No arms shipments, no food and not a single boot on the ground. Your homeland, Wilde. Home of the brave? Let's see, shall we?'

'You have something against America?'

Rowlands shrugged. 'Not as such.'

'But you do?' He was looking at Marfield.

'Not America, *Americans.*'

'Why?'

'I think we've talked enough.'

After a night with barely any sleep, crawling through mud and sludge, facing death, seeing the horrors of the film, Wilde's brain was not functioning as it should have been. But a thought was forming. Perhaps Rowlands and Marfield were not just talking in general terms. Perhaps it wasn't just an opinion that Roosevelt would not be able to bring America into the war, but their intention to make it impossible that he could do so. Did Rowlands and Marfield believe that they might somehow have the power to direct the course of events on the other side of the Atlantic?

'I think I may be beginning to understand, Rowlands,' Wilde said.

'I doubt it. And even if you did, much good it would do you. Britain and France will reach an understanding with Germany. Hitler is already offering peace and no German wants to fight in the West. They know their true enemy lies in the East. Together, we will be invincible. The Croix de Feu will seize power in France, the BUF here – and then a European war machine will strike eastwards. Stalin and his criminal crew will fall.'

Meanwhile civilians and soldiers alike were being slaughtered in the conquest of Poland. Slowly, Wilde picked up the mug of tea in his bound hands. It was still hot and it would have given him some pleasure to drink it, because he was thirsty. Instead he threw it in Marfield's self-satisfied, beautiful face. It was a gesture of contempt, nothing more. A gesture he knew he would pay for.

Wilde understood pain and how to overcome it. The first time he put on boxing gloves at school he was punched full in the face. The pain had brought hot tears to his eyes – a pain he had not believed he would ever be able to endure again. But he learnt. Pain can be soaked up and overcome.

That was physical pain. Mental torture was something else altogether.

He had expected to be clubbed around the head with Marfield's gun when he threw the scalding tea in his face.

Instead, without a word, Marfield wiped the hot liquid from his eyes and cheeks, rose from his seat, and walked out of the room, leaving Wilde alone with Rowlands. Wilde's feet were not tied and he looked at the MI6 officer and wondered momentarily whether there was anything to be gained from launching himself at him. But Rowlands had his gun in his left hand, trained on his captive. He shook his head.

'For pity's sake, don't do this, Rowlands,' pleaded Wilde. 'You're better than this. I've seen you with Eaton, taking care of him. Marcus Marfield is a psychopath.'

Rowlands pulled a cigarette case from his top pocket, shook out a cigarette and planted it between his lips. 'Why do you think we selected him?' he said, the tobacco still unlit.

'I understand why you have doubts about Bolshevism and the Soviet Union – but how can whatever you're doing help your cause? Whatever you have planned, it's going to look bad. Just like the sinking of that ship. How did anyone in Berlin think drowning American women and children was going to help the German war effort?'

Rowlands said nothing, merely lit his cigarette and waited. A few seconds later the door opened and two people were pushed in, both hooded with their hands bound. Marfield stood behind them. He pushed them again and they both stumbled into the room. One man, one woman. Even with hoods on, Wilde could tell they were elderly. In their seventies, perhaps even eighties, both frail and bewildered. Marfield held his pistol to the temple of the man.

'Well, this is jolly,' Rowlands said. 'Mr Wilde, I'd like you to meet Mr and Mrs Charles Farrow. I believe it's their wedding anniversary today.'

Wilde's eyes widened in horror. Who were these poor people?

'Now then,' Rowlands continued. 'What we need is the location of the film. We really don't have time to beat about the bush, so I suggest you tell us immediately. I'm sure you can imagine the consequences of prevaricating.'

Wilde looked at the hooded man and woman with a sense of utter dread. Did they have any idea what was going on? The man was stooped and shaking and not just with fear. His hands, tied together, fluttered like birds' wings. Parkinson's. Wilde desperately wanted to save these people, but he had no information to give Rowlands and Marfield that might save their lives. *Think*, Tom. Think fast.

'Okay, okay, it's in my rooms at college.'

'You'll have to be more specific,' Marfield said. 'Where in your rooms?'

'On my desk, I think, with all my books and papers. I'm pretty sure that's where I left it.'

'Did you watch the film there, as soon as you opened the parcel?'

'No, I didn't have a projector. I wasn't sure why it had been sent to me. I first saw it at the house in Histon.'

'So the film at Histon wasn't your copy?'

They knew that already. They were trying to catch him out. 'No,' he said. 'That wasn't my copy. I told you, I left my copy on my desk.'

'You're sure about that?'

'Yes, I'm certain.'

'I looked there.'

'You've been in my rooms?'

'It's not on your desk. I've been in your house, too – and it's not there either. So where is it?'

'Wait, now I remember, I needed to make some space in my rooms, so I moved it to one of the bookshelves. I think it's somewhere between Proust and my Shakespeare volumes. You probably wouldn't have looked there.'

Marfield pulled the trigger. The explosion was deafening in the small space and Wilde recoiled in abject horror as the old man buckled and fell heavily to the stone floor. Blood poured through the hole in the hood and swirled in an expanding bright puddle on the stone. He lay on the floor, twitching, dying. The woman collapsed too. An awful sound emanated from beneath the hood over her face. Gasping for breath, moaning. A wailing of utter misery.

Wilde leapt to his feet and lunged forward, but the table was in his way. 'God almighty, what have you done? Who are these people?'

Marfield kicked a chair out of his way and came around the table. He held the pistol square in Wilde's face. 'A sweet old couple from the bus stop. I saw them and stopped and generously offered them a lift. Little bit cramped in a two-seater, but we managed. Sadly there's no such thing as a free ride, as they've now discovered. So the truth, Wilde, the truth. Otherwise the woman is next. And then, if necessary, I will find more. Children, perhaps, or women with babies.'

'Innocent people!'

'Your choice.'

Wilde was lost for words. If he knew where the film was, he would gladly give it up, but how can you tell someone a secret you don't know?

Rowlands lounged against the range, smoking. His mouth was curled down in distaste. Wilde got the distinct impression that for all his nonchalance, Rowlands was disturbed by what he had just witnessed. Perhaps he hadn't understood quite what he was dealing with in Marfield? If either of them was to be worked on, it had to be Rowlands. He tried to meet his eyes. 'Are you going to allow this barbarity to continue, Rowlands?'

'The film,' said Rowlands. 'Try again.'

He had to stop this, find time to delay the inevitable. Where could he say he had left the film? Somewhere plausible, somewhere they would have to go and search, somewhere they would have to take him so he could point out the exact spot. Not his house, nor Lydia's. These people must not go near her. Oh God, at least she had Eaton with her, and he had a gun.

Should he say he handed it in to the police? But if he managed to make them believe him, there would be no more reason to keep him or the old woman alive. At least there would be no more deaths . . . but it wasn't a good enough option. He had to come up with something so that they would go out and look.

The old man was motionless now. The old woman, still hooded, had crawled over his bloody corpse and was holding him, stroking him with her bound hands, weeping. Everything about her spoke of horror, but Wilde was certain her fear had gone. He envied her that.

Marfield held the gun to her head.

'No,' Wilde said. 'Please. I'll tell you everything. Just please, please, let her go. I'll take you there. I knew what had been sent to me and I knew I had to find somewhere safe. I took it to Dr Charlecote's house in Great Shelford and I buried it. It's not easy to find, but I'll show you.'

'I don't believe you,' Marfield said, and shot the woman. 'So now you are going to stay here with Mr Rowlands while I go and fetch someone you *do* care about.'

Wilde glanced at Rowlands. The blood had drained from his face. And then it struck him; it hadn't just been Wilde who was stalling for time. Rowlands really didn't have the stomach for this.

CHAPTER 33

Catherine Mary Cullanan nursed the boy all morning. His temperature peaked and then began to come down a little. Sometimes it seemed to her that she had spent half her life nursing her own seven children through their illnesses. You had to be self-sufficient on a small island.

At times he cried out for his mother. But when his temperature dropped and his shivering ceased, he slept peacefully. At last, in the early afternoon, his eyes opened and he looked up at her as if trying to take in who she might be and where he was.

'Ssh,' she said with a warm, reassuring smile and a voice as soothing as honey and milk. 'You're safe now, little man. You're in a safe place and you'll be fine. I'm Mrs Cullanan, but you can call me Cathy.'

His face crumpled. 'I want Ma.'

'Of course you do. What's your name?'

'Willie. Willie Vanderberg.'

She stroked his face with the lightest of touches. 'Well, it's a fine thing to meet you, Willie. Now tell me, did you come from the ship? The one that sank?'

He nodded. 'But where's Ma? Where's Mrs Harman?'

'How many of you were in the boat? Were there just the three of you?'

He nodded again.

'And was Mrs Harman an older lady?'

'Yes.' He turned his head away. 'Please, I want to see Ma now?'

'She's with the doctor. You'll see her very soon.' Catherine Cullanan tried to smile again, but she wasn't sure her story was very convincing. She had too fine a conscience to be a good liar, but how could she tell the boy the truth? As she moved away from him to rinse the flannel, she crossed herself.

Marcus Marfield found what he wanted within ten minutes. Twenty yards from the road, a tousle-headed boy of nine or ten in short trousers and an open-neck shirt was standing on the riverbank, skimming stones. Marfield pulled in on the grassy shoulder at the side of the road and got out of the car. He had brought Guy Rowlands's BMW again – it was irresistible.

He sauntered over to the boy. 'Hello,' he said. 'I'm looking for the Post Office.'

The boy stopped what he was doing, then pointed westwards. 'Next village but one, mister.'

'I went through there but I didn't see it.'

The boy looked up at the road. 'Is that your car? Never seen a silver car before.'

'It's a sports car, goes like a bullet.'

'Can I have a proper look at it?'

'Why not? Even better, why don't I take you for a spin – you can show me the Post Office.'

He was a healthy, skinny lad, fair-haired with burnished skin from a summer spent out of doors. 'Then will you bring me back here?'

'Easy, I'm coming back this way anyway. What's your name?'

'Peter.' He grinned. 'But my mum calls me pest.'

'No school then, eh?'

'Last day of the holidays, mister. Back tomorrow.'

*

'What if I didn't receive it,' Wilde said, choosing his words with care. 'What if it was delivered to the porters' lodge but wasn't passed on to me? They're not perfect.'

'Lie after lie after lie. Give it a rest, Wilde.'

'But I haven't seen it, Rowlands. If I knew where it was I wouldn't have had to lie. It could be there, at college, waiting for me in the porters' lodge. You could drive me there, gun at my back while I inquire after it. Rowlands, for pity's sake, I don't want anyone else to die at the hands of your murderous psychopathic friend – and I suspect you don't either.'

They were on their own in the kitchen of the remote farmhouse. Wilde's hands were still bound. Before leaving, Marfield had made sure his feet were also bound, to the chair legs, and had fastened cord tight around his chest to the chairback. It seemed he did not trust Rowlands to keep the captive secure.

Every time Rowlands glanced at the two corpses, he shuddered. Finally, gritting his teeth, he dragged them into a pantry, shutting the door on them. All that was left was smeared pools of blood on the stone floor.

'You couldn't bear looking at them, Rowlands.' Wilde wondered about Rowlands's war service. The tie he'd seen him wearing suggested a gunnery regiment. If his experience of war had been confined to several miles behind the front trenches, hurling shells at an unseen enemy, perhaps he hadn't had to face the sheer bloody brutality and mangled limbs of close combat. Perhaps the reality was too much for him.

'If you don't shut your mouth, Wilde, I'll do for you here and now.'

'No, you won't. You think I might have a point about the porters' lodge.'

'Is it true you never received the parcel?'

'Yes it's true. Why else would I have bothered to watch the copy in Claire's house? But is it true about the lodge? Only one way to find out. Come on, Rowlands, you don't want to see Marfield murdering any more poor unfortunates who just happen to be standing at the roadside. I may disagree with your politics, but I suspect you are halfway human. Marfield is insane and he's beyond your control.'

Rowlands looked at his watch. Was he calculating how long Marfield had been gone and when he would return? He must know Marfield would never agree to this course of action.

'You realise that Philip Eaton's either on to you or very close? He has been talking to the Deuxième Bureau. They know about the attempt on the American ambassador's life at Chantilly – and the connection via your man Honoré to Marfield is clear.'

Wilde caught a fleeting expression of alarm cross Rowlands's face. He pressed on.

'What have you got to lose? If I'm wrong – if there's no parcel for me in the porters' lodge, then shoot me and make your getaway. You'll be safe enough – the porters aren't armed. Not that you'll have to resort to gunplay: you can talk your way out of anything – just say you were working undercover.'

The moments passed into seconds and then stretched to a full minute. Wilde could do nothing more than wait. This was up to Rowlands now.

'If I take you there, and if you're wrong, Wilde, I *will* shoot you.'

'I understand that. But it's a risk worth taking for me. It has to be better than the alternative. And if it's not there, well, I'm at a loss anyway. Who knows, the parcel could be just lost in the post. These things happen.'

Rowlands moved towards Wilde and began to untie his feet and remove the cords binding him to the chair, leaving his hands bound. Wilde was able to stand up at last. He groaned as he bent backwards to ease his aching spine. At least his clothes had begun to dry out, but he was exhausted.

There was a noise outside. Rowlands froze.

'That's not him,' Wilde said quickly. 'There was no car.'

'He could have parked it on the drive, away from the courtyard.'

'Then shoot him, Rowlands! Do this one decent thing with your life. Kill him when he walks in the door and put the world out of its misery.'

Rowlands shook his head. There was something about him that spoke of defeat, as though the reality of his actions was suddenly all too much.

There was a knock at the door. Wilde and Rowlands looked at each other.

A harder knock, followed by voices outside.

'You'd better answer it,' Wilde said, deliberately raising his voice. 'Whoever is there will see your car outside. They must have heard us; they'll know someone's here.'

His eyes went to the blood streaking the floor. 'I can't.'

'Just open the door a fraction, and send them on their way. If necessary, you've got your gun.'

Rowlands edged towards the kitchen window. 'Damn,' he said, pulling back as though he'd been bitten. 'They've seen me.'

'They?'

'Soldiers!'

Wilde breathed in sharply. Soldiers had to mean hope, but this time he didn't allow the relief to wash over him. He'd fallen for that once already today when Rowlands's car pulled up at the phone kiosk.

'What do I do?' Rowlands sounded panicked.

Wilde took charge. 'Answer the door with your hands visible. Come clean about Marfield and your plans and I swear I'll put in a word for you. Your testimony will be invaluable to MI5 – they'll spare you from the noose. Come on, Rowlands, you haven't pulled the trigger yourself yet – and you've got no other way out.'

'Haven't I?' Rowlands held his hands up in despair. In the space of two hours he had gone from the confident man who had found Wilde at the side of the road to a shaking hulk.

There was another knock, a little louder.

'Go on,' insisted Wilde. 'Open the door!'

Rowlands shrugged, and then turned the muzzle of the pistol to his chest, carefully positioned in the centre of the heart, and pulled the trigger. The blast was shattering in this small, enclosed space. As he fell, the door opened and two khaki-clad soldiers stood there, blocking out the sun.

'Bloody hell,' Lance Coporal Elphick said, looking at the body quivering just two yards in front of his dusty boots. 'What the fuck just happened?' And then to Wilde, 'And who the fuck are you?'

Wilde held up his bound wrists. 'I'm someone who is very glad to see you, soldier.'

'Jesus, we only wanted directions and a pint of milk!'

Marfield had stopped halfway down the drive. He had seen the squad of soldiers crossing the open field towards the farmhouse. He had encountered enemy soldiers many times in Spain; you had to be fast on your feet if you wanted to survive in war.

'Look, mister, soldiers!' Like all boys, the lad in the passenger seat was intrigued. 'And they got rifles!'

'Let's just wait a few moments.' Marfield put a finger to his lips. 'Better not disturb them, Peter. I think we've come the wrong way.'

'Well, I told you we had, didn't I? This is a farm track, nowhere near the village.'

'Ssh.'

The soldiers had disappeared behind a thicket, but they were clearly going towards the house. How the hell had they found it? Rowlands had been so certain no one knew about this place. It belonged to him and there was no record of the property on his MI6 file.

Marfield calculated his options. He might be able to take out one or two – even three – of the soldiers, but not six or seven. And there could be more, not yet seen. He heard a pistol shot from the house. It was time to disappear.

Unhurriedly, he reversed into a wider space a little way back down the driveway, and then executed a skillful three-point turn. He picked up speed, and joined the open road with only the briefest glances left and right. A few minutes later, he halted by the river and indicated to the boy that he should get out.

The boy pushed open the low-slung passenger door and slid off the black leather seat. He stood beside the car, running his fingers along the sleek contours. 'Wow, mister, that's the best car ever. It's like a silver rocket. This is my lucky day.'

You'll never know, Marfield thought. 'Don't tell anyone, though. I've only borrowed the car, you see – belongs to my boss.'

'Mum's the word. Hey, mister, we never got to the Post Office . . .'

'Don't worry, I'll find it. Village after next.' He waved farewell as he pulled the passenger door shut, then eased away from the kerb under the boy's admiring gaze. The boy had indeed been fortunate. In the next few hours others wouldn't be so lucky.

Elina Kossoff was lying on the bed, up on the fourth floor of the ambassador's residence at 14, Prince's Gate. She had doubts about Marfield, but nothing that couldn't be dealt with. She had always been the problem solver. Working for her parents in the Samovar would have been a trial for anyone, but for Elina it had been an education. Her parents were so used to being waited on in their pre-revolution life back in Russia that she had become their de facto servant, organising the books, dealing with the staff, checking deliveries. And she had learnt to come down hard when any problems arose.

Now, in a short time, she had become indispensable to Ambassador Joseph Kennedy, both in bed and out. She knew there were others, but so what? He liked having her around, and she was efficient. If you want something done, ask Elina. That was the way it had always been with her.

Organisational skill was not the only thing that her childhood had imbued in her. She had also learnt a bitter and visceral hatred of the revolutionaries who had destroyed Russia. Throughout her childhood, she had listened to her father's dinner-table rants, his slamming of his knife on the table as he spat out his loathing of Lenin and Stalin, Trotsky and Kamenev.

There had not been a lot to disagree with. Except for the fact that he never did anything about it.

And then she had met Marcus Marfield and they discovered that not only did their bodies fit well, but their political opinions did, too.

In long conversations, fuelled by love-making and vodka, they had shared a mutual hatred of Bolshevism. And although National Socialism as an ideology did not attract her, she understood its potential to free Russia from the iron grip of Stalin.

Nothing might have happened. They would have made love, drunk more vodka, talked politics endlessly until their affair had run its course. But then Marfield said he wanted to go to Spain, and Guy Rowlands turned up with an idea that could turn their talks and dreams into positive action. Suddenly everything became serious. She and Marfield *could* make a difference.

As she lay back on a bank of pillows, hands behind her head, she wondered what she might have missed. Professor Wilde had been in their house in Cambridge, but she was pretty certain he could have found nothing. All the weapons *had* been there, but by the time Wilde arrived, everything had been packed up and removed. Diligence had always been her watchword.

If only she could be so certain about Marcus.

Now the end was in sight. Later today she would travel up to Wall Hall in Hertfordshire to put the final touches to the party. In the meantime, Kennedy wanted her here in London.

The party was to be a family affair with only a few other guests, to celebrate Rosemary Kennedy's twenty-first birthday and to mark the departure of most of the ambassador's family back to the States. All but Kennedy and Rosemary herself; she was doing so well at the Assumption school in Boxmoor that she would be staying in England with her father.

The others would be going home in batches; the sinking of the *Athenia* had made a big impression on Joe Kennedy, so he wasn't willing for them all to make the journey together. His wife would be travelling on Thursday – just three days' time – aboard the *Washington* with three of their offspring, Robert, Eunice and Kathleen.

Kennedy's eldest boy, also called Joe, had recently returned from Berlin, but he would not be staying in England long – he would be leaving on the *Mauretania* a week from today, followed by Jack, recently returned from Glasgow where his efforts helping the survivors of the *Athenia* had made such an impression on the world. Jack would not be going by liner, however, but by air, aboard the smart new Pan Am Clipper flying boat service.

The last of the family to be leaving would be young Edward, Patricia and Jean, with nanny Hennessy. They'd be aboard the liner *Manhattan* on 20 September.

Like everything with this vast, boisterous family, organising their travel arrangements was a major operation. The ships had to be American because Joe was terrified that the U-boats that had sunk the *Athenia* might still be hunting British vessels. And who could say he was wrong?

The party was a major operation, too. Rosemary's birthday would be a cause for celebration, but it would also be a slightly sombre affair. Not only were they uncertain they would all get home safely, but they were all acutely aware that it might be months or even years before the whole family was reunited.

And so there would be a lavish religious element to the celebrations, to praise God and entreat his blessing on their voyages. Rose, the ambassador's devout wife, insisted on it.

Elina looked at her watch. Marfield should be in London by now. He had called with alarming news; things weren't going as smoothly as they might. And all because the fool had allowed himself to be filmed in Spain. And how had he managed to let

Rosa Cortez loose with copies? The film must never see the light of day.

For this to work, the world had to see Marcus Marfield as an idealistic left-winger, the sort of person Middle America already disliked and would most certainly loathe if he were to harm America's favourite family.

The scorn many Americans felt for Britain and her Empire was never far beneath the surface, and it was a sentiment that had been fed by Ambassador Kennedy himself. He had expressed his doubts about Britain often enough. He had even gone so far as to admit admiration for Hitler and his fascist regime.

Joseph Kennedy, the great appeaser.

When the remarkably wealthy Kennedy arrived in Britain as ambassador, he had been fantastically popular with the people and press. Who couldn't adore such handsome children, with their sporty lifestyles and gleaming teeth? The British had taken them to their hearts from the word go.

In recent months, however, many had turned against their father. Too often he had seemed to favour Germany and the Nazis. At times he seemed contemptuous of Britain. Those in the know understood all too well that he was more interested in the narrow commercial interest of his businesses and the effect war might have on his wealth. He wanted to avoid war at all costs and if war came – as it now had – then he wanted it ended with some sort of patched-together treaty, however shabby and however many small countries were sacrificed to Hitler's rapacious ambition.

He had acquired the tenancy of Wall Hall, a house in the country, from his old friend J. P. Morgan, the millionaire financier, so that he didn't have to face the night raids that were surely coming to London. Wall Hall – that's where they would be holding the party for Rosemary.

But Kennedy's timing was off again. Just as the Royal Family were making it clear they wouldn't budge from Buckingham Palace however many bombers Goering dispatched to the skies over London, Joe Kennedy was scooting to safety.

People called him yellow.

But mostly, he was despised in Britain because he was chief of the 'keep the US out' brigade. He was identified with the 'Cliveden set', the clique around Nancy Astor, seen as much too close to Hitler, much too keen on appeasement. Even worse, it was said he had suggested the average American had far more sympathy for Germany than for Britain.

Britain, he insisted, would be 'licked' by Hitler.

Invitations to parties were drying up. Joe Kennedy was becoming an outcast.

His defeatism was too much, even for those who had hitherto given him the benefit of the doubt. Every upstanding, right-thinking, patriotic Englishman had a right to be appalled by Kennedy and to loathe him.

Rowlands had understood how such feelings could be used, both in Britain and France.

A home-grown assassin who would murder Bill Bullitt in France and Joe Kennedy in England, would kill off any idea of American intervention for good.

Imagine the reaction in America, Rowlands had said, spreading his hands wide: one or more isolationist politicians – and there were plenty of those in Washington DC – wouldn't need prompting to blame Britain and France for the murders. There would be loud voices elsewhere. You could almost hear the words they would use, he said. 'Shot by an English guy, goddamn it – simply because he dared speak out against US involvement in their goddamned European wars? Let the British and their disgraceful empire stew.'

Elina's telephone was ringing. She picked it up.

'I don't trust this line,' she said. 'Are we on?'

'One hour.'

Elina slowly replaced the handset, just as the door opened. Joe Kennedy stood there, grinning, his eyes beady behind his round tortoiseshell spectacles. 'I was hoping I'd find you here.'

'Oh, Mr Kennedy, sir, I have to go out in a short while. My mother's been taken sick.'

'Really? I'm sorry to hear that, Elina.'

'Do you mind if I go out for a couple of hours? I'll be back to tend to all your requirements – and I could also drive you up to Wall Hall.'

He smiled at her. 'Did I tell you we were going to have a singer? Young fellow from Cambridge, voice of an angel. Going to sing *Ave Maria* at the end of Mass. Rose will be in heaven.'

'I'm pretty sure you mentioned that, sir.'

He closed the door behind him and loosened his tie. 'Now then, I'm sure a ten-minute wait won't hurt your mother. You're my girl, Elina. Ten minutes, quarter an hour max. Sometimes family isn't enough and I need my girl.'

She was already climbing from the bed, tapping her watch regretfully.

'You know, I've got my eye on a swell new watch for you, Elina. Swiss movement, jewelled, a real beauty like you.'

'You're a sweet talker, Mr Kennedy.'

'That's my girl. We both know what we like.'

CHAPTER 34

They met just outside the underground station at Clapham South. He was standing with his back to a wall of sandbags. A poster just inside the station entrance said, 'Hitler will send no warning, so always carry your gas mask.'

'You're late,' he said abruptly.

'I got delayed.'

He had changed into clean clothes: a billowing white shirt, open at the neck to reveal his bronzed skin. 'Come on,' she said, firmly taking his hand, 'I'll make it up to you.' She pointed vaguely in the direction of Clapham Park Road, on the south side of the common. 'There's a whores' hotel along there.'

As they walked, he told her what had happened that morning.

'So when you saw the soldiers you just left?'

'There was a shot. A pistol shot, not a rifle. Rowlands knew he couldn't get away, so he must have killed Wilde. It was the only thing for him to do. I could have taken on the soldiers, but that would have been suicidal. There were at least seven of them, perhaps many more.'

'So where is Rowlands now?'

'They'll be interrogating him. But he won't say a word. You know he won't. He's as committed to this as we are. More so.'

Of course he was. He had recruited them both, hadn't he? But Marfield's account had left her reeling. Was he really not sought by the police after all that had happened? Was her own part in all this not suspected by anyone? If they were in the clear, it was a miracle. Marfield attracted trouble like jam attracts wasps.

The receptionist looked up from her crossword, bored. 'Pound an hour, darlings, ten shillings an hour after the first.'

'Two hours,' Marfield said.

Elina held out a pound note. 'One,' she said.

The bed hadn't even been made and the sheets were stained. But they didn't get that far. She ripped open his fly and he pulled up her skirt, then took her standing up against the back of the door; she wrapped her legs around his straining thighs and urged him on. He gripped her buttocks with one hand and her hair with the other.

Across the room the window was open and the curtains were flapping in the breeze.

'Does he do this to you? The old man?'

'More, Marcus, more. Harder, damn you, I want you harder. Fuck me to death.'

'I fucked a nun in a Spanish convent.'

She pulled him into her. She screamed, then groaned and shuddered, sliding against the door, fighting him to continue, to do it more. He roared and drove deeper, then his legs went taut and he screamed with her.

They slipped down to the floor together; he was still inside her. She was breathing hard, then pulled him out, and rose on to one knee, adjusting her skirt and suspender belt. She punched his arm. Hard. 'Fuck you, Marcus.'

'What was that for?'

'For fucking everything up.'

'God, you're a difficult bitch.'

'Marcus, everything that's gone wrong has involved *you*. I've done all the dirty work, cleaning up your mess.'

'And I'm the one who'll get topped.'

She sighed and pulled him to her. She held his beautiful face between her soft hands and kissed his lips. 'You're a brave man.'

'And you are a brave woman, Elina. We are in this together.'

'Of course. But this is not about us. This is for the world we want.'

She was on her feet now, smoothing herself down, combing her hair in the mottled mirror hanging askew above the light switch by the door. 'We will rid the world of Stalin's red cancer.' She kicked him. 'Now, get up. We have to think this through. Between the time you lost Wilde at the windmill and Rowlands picked him up on the road, he called Eaton and the woman, yes?'

'Rowlands heard every word. Wire tap to their phones. That's how he found the bastard out in the Fens.'

'Is the tap still there?'

'It must be – but only Rowlands can access it. And we can't access Rowlands.'

'Eaton must know about you.'

'But he won't have a shred of evidence, except the hearsay of a man over the phone. And that man is now dead.'

'There's the second film.'

'Well, Eaton doesn't have it. Nor does he have any witnesses to my time in Spain. You saw to that yourself with the trick cyclist and Claire and Rosa. So we're in the clear: there's no evidence that I'm anything but a shell-shocked refugee from the International Brigades.'

Hugging her arms around her slender body, Elina went to the window and looked out over Clapham Common. Workmen in overalls were busy digging it up; for more air raid shelters, she presumed. She didn't smoke but she wanted a cigarette. World events, she reflected, were shaped by big powerful people. Men in suits and uniforms, in government and the military.

But it was astonishing what small people could do if they had the will. If they were prepared to harden their souls and do unpleasant deeds for the greater good. In 1914 Gavrilo Princip had changed world history with one bullet to the neck of the Archduke Ferdinand in Sarajevo; such was the power of one determined man. She had the will. And so, she believed, did Marcus.

'They must be hunting you,' she said, still unconvinced by his assurances.

He shrugged. 'Maybe, but I don't think so. I haven't seen the papers or heard the wireless. Maybe they'll play it down? They don't want panicky stories about fifth columnists and German spies: people are jittery enough as it is.'

She wasn't convinced. 'What about the Kennedys?'

Marfield shook his head. 'Even if I am in the papers, the Kennedys don't know my name. I'm just a singer from Cambridge. And when it's done, we'll *want* it all over the press and wireless. The government won't be able to hush it up. The American press will be all over it. This will be the biggest story of the war. America will hate us – and anyone over there who suggests lending so much as a cup of sugar to the British will be derided.'

'So it's on?'

'It's on.'

'And you know exactly where to go, and the time?'

He tapped his forehead. 'I've been there before.'

'You must be careful, Marcus,' she urged. 'There will be a bodyguard, almost certainly armed. You must be taken alive so that you can give your testimony in court.'

'Do you doubt me?'

'Of course not.' But she did. 'My only fear is the second film.'

'I've come to the conclusion Wilde really didn't know where it was. Perhaps my mother was wrong; perhaps my father destroyed it. Anyway, if it turns up next month or next year, the world will have moved on. I'll be yesterday's news. They're going to hang me anyway – so what do I have to lose?'

Nothing, of course. But *she* did. Which was why there were still matters to be resolved.

She kissed him again. 'Go, Marcus. Keep your head down.' I'll deal with everything else, she thought. Safer that way; fewer mistakes.

He laughed. 'I should have married you.'

'We'd have killed each other. By the way, did the nun enjoy it?'

He looked at her for a few seconds then shrugged. He put two fingers to his temple and made a popping sound with his beautiful lips. Elina marvelled at the icicle in the heart. Only Marcus Marfield could do this.

The older woman's body had been found on the rocky shore close to the harbour, not far from the boat. The boy must have climbed or crawled up the shallow slope to the Cullanans' modest white-painted house, where he now lay in bed, tended by the doctor from the mainland and nursed by Catherine.

And so that left the boy's mother. If she wasn't on the shore, and she hadn't made it into the little harbour village where most of the inhabitants of this rocky outcrop lived and worked, then where was she?

Martin walked in the direction of the lighthouse. He walked at a steady pace in a series of long turns so that every inch of ground could be seen. Sheep ambled away at his approach and scuttled if they were too slow and he got too close.

He knew this island as well as any man or woman alive. Like his father and many generations of men before that, he had ground a living from the seas surrounding this place and, from the land, had harvested a few vegetables and bred enough livestock for a little meat and milk and eggs. Times were always hard. In a harsh winter of storms, they might be cut off from the mainland for a month or two at a go.

At the lighthouse, black painted from top to toe, he stopped and looked westwards to the vast empty Atlantic. Next stop, the new world. Clambering onto the rocks, he knew he would find no one alive down there amid the swirling white-water waves that crashed here endlessly at the end of their three thousand miles journey. The sun was in the west now, blinding bright when it slipped away from the clouds.

Dermot, the lighthouse keeper, was waving to him from the balcony. 'A cup of tea, Martin?' he called down.

'No, thank you, Dermot.'

'Martin, we'd have found her by now if she was alive.'

He nodded, but he wasn't ready to accept it yet. Somehow the boy had escaped the boat and stumbled up to their house, so why not the missing woman? The other men said she must have been thrown from the boat when it hit the rocks and if the rocks hadn't killed her first, the merciless undertow would have carried her out and the sea would have done for her. But Martin clung to hope; if she had been injured, she could have crawled somewhere and be lying unconscious. Where though? There were few places of concealment on this tiny island, but that didn't mean there weren't any.

'Will you be killing the pig this week, Martin?'

'Aye, and you'll get your share. But not today.'

Dermot touched his cap. 'God go with you, Martin Cullanan.'

It took Wilde many hours to get home. At first the soldiers were deeply suspicious of him, despite his bindings. They trained their weapons on him, nervous as hell – and with good reason. None had seen battle and yet they had somehow chanced upon a scene of carnage in the English countryside.

When it transpired there was a telephone in the house, they summoned the police and waited. Wilde was told they were in the countryside south-east of Royston, perhaps twenty miles south of Cambridge. For the next thirty minutes Wilde answered Lance Corporal Elphick's questions in monosyllables: it was pointless explaining everything in detail to him when he'd only have to go over the same ground again with others.

When the police finally arrived in strength, they refused to take seriously Wilde's request that they call Philip Eaton or, at the very least, Detective Inspector Tomlinson in Cambridge. Nor were they interested when he suggested they put out an alert to stop a German-made silver sports car driven by a man named Marcus Marfield. Instead they seemed to regard Wilde as their prime suspect. His hands might have been bound, but he was the only one alive out of four people in the house.

In the afternoon, he was taken to a local police station and placed in a cell where his bindings were removed and replaced with police issue handcuffs. It felt like a re-run of his arrest after the death of Rosa Cortez in the market square.

Wilde underwent further questioning. A fourth body had been found, a man in his fifties named Keith Caney, who lived alone in the Fens. A farmer and a widower, and well-respected locally, he had been a special constable, helping out on big occasions or when the force was under strength. His full-time colleagues very much wanted to catch the bastard who had slit his throat and it was taking a lot to persuade them that Wilde wasn't the killer.

At last, some time after dusk, the cell door opened and Eaton was standing there, accompanied by a Special Branch chief inspector from London. Wilde's immediate concern was Lydia. Had she been left unprotected? All he wanted was to get home to her, and make sure she was safe.

'She's with the Weirs out at Girton,' said Eaton. 'She'll be all right. Weir keeps guns and knows how to use them. My driver will take us there soon enough – you'll see her within the hour. But first, Wilde, you have to tell me everything that's happened.'

'Do you have any idea what I've been through, Eaton? I can hardly bear to describe the things I've seen.'

'I understand, old boy. Truly I do.'

Wilde sighed. He felt as though the sun had gone out. 'There was a film,' he said. 'And now it's destroyed. But there's another film – and Marcus Marfield is willing to kill as many people as necessary in order to get his hands on it. More than that, all I can tell you is that your good friend Guy Rowlands is – *was* – a fucking traitor and a Nazi. The only decent thing he did was to shoot himself.'

Eaton recoiled. 'Guy Rowlands?'

'You heard he was dead?'

'Yes, but I thought . . .' he clutched his forehead. 'I thought he died saving you.'

'He killed himself to save himself from a charge of murder and treason.'

'Ye Gods – and to think I brought him into your world.'

'At least at the end he had the decency to be disgusted by Marfield. But that's all. Oh, and by the way, unless you told him where I was, he must have had a tap on Lydia's phone.'

'I'm sorry, Wilde. Truly I'm sorry.' Eaton was shaking. He sat down on the wooden chair to catch his breath. 'I suppose this all explains one or two things.'

'You mean the way Honoré found me in France?'

'Yes, of course. Rowlands must have been tracking you through friends in the Deuxième Bureau. You were set up to bring Marfield home from the moment you set sail for France. That way Guy's part would be invisible. Wilde, there are other things – more recent things – that we must talk about.'

Wilde looked blankly at the floor. He was utterly drained. However slowly and with however much sensitivity the questions came, he couldn't find the words to answer. He simply couldn't describe all the horrors he had seen. Not yet. At last he sighed and raised his head to meet Eaton's eyes.

'You can't do this now, can you, Wilde?'

'I'm sorry. I have to see Lydia and I have to sleep. But you know what – *who* – you're looking for. Isn't that enough at the moment?'

'Come on, we'll fetch you home.'

The drive to Girton seemed to take forever. The night was overcast and they were on severely restricted headlights in accordance with blackout regulations. That meant a crawl.

Lydia was shaking as he took her in his arms at the Weirs' large and pleasant house. She seemed frailer and smaller than he remembered.

'Thank God you're alive, Tom. I was terrified.'

'Me, too,' he admitted. 'I've been worried about you.' He wouldn't tell her, yet, what he had endured.

'I've been fine. Edie and Rupert have been fussing over me. Haven't let me lift a finger.'

Rupert Weir strolled in with his doctor's bag. He had dispensed with his tweed jacket, but still wore his waistcoat, complete with fob chain. He afforded them a broad smile. 'Now then, Tom, let's have a look at you.'

Weir gave him a cursory once-over and proclaimed him reasonably fit. 'A few cuts and bruises. Actually, you look as though you've been dragged through brambles, then dunked in a quagmire, Tom. Nothing a bath and a new set of clothes won't put right. Unfortunately mine are rather too large for you. But for your general health I prescribe a couple of drams, then sleep, followed by bacon and eggs in the morning.' He was pouring Wilde a glass even as he spoke.

Wilde downed the whisky in one and gasped.

'You're very welcome to stay here.'

Wilde looked at Lydia. She gave a slight shake of her head. 'I think we'd rather get home if it's all the same to you, Rupert.'

They made their way back to Lydia's house and Wilde climbed upstairs to her room and lay down on the bed. Downstairs, Eaton was checking his gun, making calls to London and elsewhere. He told them the Cambridge police would be opening up the firearms case and sending a couple of officers over with revolvers as added protection. One would take the front of the house, one the back, and they would remain outside.

Lydia came over and lay down beside him. 'You've scarcely slept in the past thirty hours, Tom.'

'I've seen terrible things.'

'I know, darling.' She could see it in his eyes, dark-shadowed and haunted. 'It's unbearable for you.'

'I have always understood these things happen . . . but seeing it in front of me. The sheer pity of that poor elderly couple. The inhumanity. Blood never ran so cold as through the veins of Marcus Marfield. We brought a monster home, Lydia.'

She held him in her arms, certain that he was about to weep. But he didn't. Instead, his arms curled around her back and he held her so tightly that they were almost one, and his hard belly pushed into her soft abdomen. 'You have to dance with me, Lydia. I want to dance, and I want music.'

Lydia got up, and went over to the wireless set she kept on the chest of drawers. She turned the dial until she found some nameless piece of classical music that came and went as the waves strengthened and weakened. She went back to the bed. 'I have a better idea,' she said. 'Horizontal dancing.' She kissed his lips.

'You haven't slept either, have you?'

She shook her head, and joined him on the bed. They were both fully clothed, but they pulled the bedclothes over themselves, kissed like new lovers and fell into sleep.

Martin Cullanan found her a few minutes before midnight. He had been walking most of the day over these familiar rocks, these stretches of sand and water and sheep grass. He had called in home at suppertime, but he had scarcely picked at his food. Catherine understood that he had to get back to his search and even though it was hopeless, she wasn't going to tell him so. When Martin Cullanan set his mind to something, he didn't take kindly to being told he was wrong.

He hadn't been wrong.

She was on the shoreline, not more than a hundred yards east of the rocks where they had discovered the dinghy and the body of the old lady. The rocks here were sharper, higher and more difficult to walk across.

'Ah, Jesus,' Cullanan said out loud. 'Ah, Jesus, look at you, you poor woman.'

He shone the torch on her eyes; there was no response.

He knelt down beside her, brushed soaking strands of hair from her forehead and put the back of his hand to her brow. The skin was cold and discoloured. Cold, but not deathly cold. Dear God, there was some trace of human warmth there.

'Mrs Vanderberg?'

There was no response.

'Mrs Vanderberg, can you hear me?'

She couldn't hear him, but he could hear her faint shallow breathing now. Her upper body was out of the water, trapped by the rocks, so she was in no danger of drowning. In truth the rocks that had concealed her from the searchers had saved her life, for they had prevented her being dragged out to her death with the ebb-tide.

But she was wedged in, her body twisted and almost certainly injured.

'Mrs Vanderberg,' he said, close to her ear. 'Your little boy is safe. Both your sons are safe, for we have heard now from the mainland.'

There was a flicker of her eyes. Cullanan made the sign of the cross over her. Dear God, he thought, bring this woman through and I'll never doubt you again.

CHAPTER 35

Wilde woke. From the very edge of the blackout he could see a hint of light: dawn. He must have slept for five or six hours. Not enough in the circumstances, but he had things to do. Had to crank up his brain and try to make sense of all that had befallen him. Beside him, Lydia nestled into her pillows, her breathing soft and peaceful.

Silently, he got out of bed and went downstairs. Eaton was there in the sitting room, dozing on the sofa.

Wilde shook Eaton by his right shoulder. They had to talk, work out what Marcus Marfield was planning. Wilde wanted shot of this whole affair, but first there were matters and details that needed to be attended to. Things he had been too tired to address last night.

Eaton woke with a start. 'What time is it?'

'Sunrise.'

Fifteen minutes later, with the curtains drawn back and light streaming in, they were sitting at the kitchen table with cups of strong black coffee.

'I just didn't see it,' Eaton said. He still seemed shell-shocked. 'For the life of me, I never suspected Guy.'

'He must have worked hard to conceal his true loyalties.'

'You understand this secrets game, Wilde. You've studied Walsingham. When someone goes undercover, they must adopt a convincing persona. So when Guy Rowlands was involved with the Right Club and with the British Union of Fascists, it was so he could investigate their connections in Italy, Spain and

Germany. Or so I believed. It didn't occur to me or anyone else that he might actually be one of them. Why would it? He was playing a double bluff. Some of the people we deal with and use, you never know whose side they're really on.'

Wilde had never been at all sure whose side Eaton himself was on. But this was no time for such questions. They were certainly on the same side in this affair.

'It's no longer any of my business,' Wilde said. 'But what are you going to do now?'

'No longer your business? Wilde, please, you have to help me on this.'

'No, I don't. I'll let you know everything I can, but I'm a Cambridge University history don and I'm not even British. This is your war; these crimes are yours to deal with. You, MI6, MI5, the Special Branch, the army, the police, the air-raid wardens and the man in the street for all I care. My concern now is Lydia and our unborn child.'

'I understand that, Wilde, and of course you're right. But—'

'There are no buts in this.'

'But I need to talk to you. Did you not pick up some clue? Was there nothing in anything that was said while you were with Marfield and Rowlands that gave you an inkling of what they are up to? You must have learnt something – even if you didn't realise it at the time.'

Wilde thought back. Rowlands and Marcus Marfield had been very careful not to give away anything specific, even though they had no intention of keeping him alive. The big question was why they were prepared to go to such lengths to prevent the world knowing Marcus Marfield's true politics. And why had he not simply stayed in Madrid, or travelled to Berlin? He would surely have been made very welcome in Germany.

Obviously, he had a mission here in England. Wilde groaned and slumped down on a kitchen chair. This was all going in circles. Two people knew what was planned – Marcus and Elina – and no one knew where either of them was. Were there others? And if so, who?

'I understand why you are trying to keep the press muted, Eaton. But really, wouldn't it now be sensible to make something of a story out of it? You've got Marfield's photograph. That way we might get some sightings. What about the silver BMW? That's pretty distinctive.'

'No sign of it. Dumped in a barn or garage, probably. Maybe even ditched in a lake or deep river.'

'Then we need publicity to track them down. You were certainly thinking that way before – which is why you wanted the photograph.'

Eaton shook his head decisively. 'The death of Guy Rowlands changes things. I don't want to give Marfield any information about what happened after his disappearance. And we have to tread lightly. There's too much fear in the air. People see Nazi spies everywhere. There was even an appalling case of poisoned milk down in Hertfordshire and the press are pestering Scotland Yard to say German agents are involved. It's not healthy. Keep calm and carry on is the order of the day.'

'Poisoned milk?'

Eaton brushed the story aside with an expansive wave of his arm. 'Probably some domestic thing involving inheritance powder – arsenic. Anyway, I only mention it to illustrate what we're up against.'

The phone rang. Wilde excused himself and went to the hall.

'Hello? Tom Wilde here.'

'Tom, it's Jim. They've found William.'

'Jim, that's wonderful news. Is he OK? What about Juliet?'

'They're still looking for her, but William's safe. Washed up in a dinghy on a small inhabited island off Donegal. She was definitely with him – but no sign as yet. I've just flown in, making my way to the coast to get across to the island.'

'Jim?'

'I'll call as soon as I know anything.'

Elina Kossoff had barely slept all night at Wall Hall. There was a nagging doubt in her mind. Marcus had said Wilde was dead, but he had not witnessed it. There was no proof; nothing on the wireless.

And still no sign of the second film.

The key must lie in Cambridge. The authorities were keeping radio silence, but if Wilde was dead, there had to be those who knew. She glanced at her watch. Eight o'clock. She could hear the sound of the staff busy making preparations for tonight's banquet. Dressing quickly, she went to the small office that had been allocated to her, a bundle of clothes in her arms. Shutting the door after her, she turned the key in the lock. First she called Wilde's college, where the phone was answered by one of the porters.

'Is Professor Wilde there?'

'Not yet, madam. Bit early in the day for him, to tell the truth. Shall I leave a message in his pigeon hole?'

'When are you expecting him?'

'Couldn't say, I'm afraid. If he's coming in, it's not likely to be before 10 a.m. But he might not turn up at all. Michaelmas term hasn't started and the whole place is in a bit of turmoil. If he comes he'll probably only be roped into air-raid drill by one of the wardens.'

'Was the professor in yesterday afternoon or evening?'

'Hang on, I'll just ask around.' A few seconds later he came back on the line. 'No, no one has seen him for a day or two.'

'Do you have his phone number?'

'Are you a friend?'

'A very old friend, but I've been away and we lost touch.' Her most soothing voice.

It was enough for the porter. 'One mo. I think I can find that for you. Don't let on I told you though, madam. Not supposed to give out personal information.'

'Your secret is safe with me.'

She dialled Wilde's home number. The phone just rang. No answer. So he hadn't been at college and he wasn't at home. This was promising, but it still wasn't proof. And as for the second film, if Wilde had it, he must have had the stomach of an ox not to give away its whereabouts under the duress inflicted by Marcus.

But wasn't that cause for doubt in itself? From the little she knew of Tom Wilde, he seemed like the kind of man who would have sacrificed himself to save others. Marcus had been clear on the point; Wilde had revealed nothing, even when the old man and woman were threatened. Why not?

Because he didn't know where the film was. That had to be the answer. He had seen the film – in Claire Marfield's bedroom – but he didn't know the whereabouts of the other copy.

That had to mean that Marcus's mother had lied in telling her son she had seen the professor's name and address on the package. Sons tended to trust their mothers a little too readily. But why would she lie? To protect herself, of course. Or someone else.

Elina picked up the phone again to call Mrs Marfield, but thought better of it. Marcus's mother didn't sound like the sort of woman who would even listen to a phone call from a stranger, let alone give out any information. She would have to go and introduce herself.

First, though, the weapons needed to be put into place. A 1928 A1 Thompson sub-machine gun, a Smith and Wesson pistol and two hundred rounds of ammunition, all hidden in one of the lower drawers of her large desk. She unhooked the key on the chain around her neck, then unlocked the drawer. Elina pulled out the pile of household accounts she had bundled in there and gazed down on the boxes of bullets, the pistol and the constituent parts of the disassembled Tommy gun – a bundle of recoil springs, firing pin, bolt, hammer, muzzle, stock and two thirty-round stick magazines, all oiled and wrapped in soft cotton cloth. Beautiful devices; dull, black, deadly. Marfield was skilled in both of them. The Spanish war had taught him well.

She removed the weapons from the drawer, wrapped them in the clothes she had brought with her, and packed them snugly into her large leather valise. 'A good touch to use American armaments,' Guy Rowlands had said when he told her how to find them at at the farmhouse. 'It will add a frisson of horror and anger to the average guy in Iowa or Arkansas. And they are the ones we're aiming at.'

There *was* something Wilde needed to tell Eaton. Something he was beginning to understand, something from the house of death.

'It's about America, Eaton. I'm not quite sure . . .' An idea was hovering at the very edge of Wilde's consciousness. 'Look – it was almost as if Rowlands wanted to crow about what they were doing. He was adamant that America would not enter the war or help Britain and France in any way. Then he spoke of doing a deal with Germany and together forming a European fighting force to take on the Soviet Union. Am I gibbering?'

'No, keep going.'

'There was more. It seems Marcus has some visceral loathing for Americans, though he didn't explain why. Something from Spain perhaps. Oh God, Eaton, I'm still tired and confused. Last night my dreams were ghastly, but I'm pretty sure I remember Rowlands talking about Roosevelt ... But then the slaughter began and my thoughts turned to mush.'

'Was Rowlands just saying what he *thought* might happen?' Eaton spoke carefully. 'Or do you think it was more than that?'

'That's it, you see. It seemed to me that he was convinced he had the power to shift America's position, perhaps bolster the non-interventionists.'

'Well, they're on the back foot after the *Athenia*,' said Eaton. 'Goebbels is chasing his tail trying to blame it on Britain, but I doubt many in America believe him. Germany has made itself the enemy of civilised behaviour.'

'Is there anything they could do to change opinion?'

'I suppose if they could prove that the British really were behind the sinking of the *Athenia* and the loss of American lives, that would make it impossible for Roosevelt to intervene or supply us with the weapons and ships we need. Or if we bombed Germany and killed a lot of Yankee tourists – that wouldn't play well, either.'

'I feel we're close to something ... But what do we do?'

'I thought you didn't want to do anything, Wilde. I thought this was nothing to do with you.'

Wilde chuckled. 'You know me too well, Eaton. I can't leave you in the lurch, can I?'

'You could, if you wanted. It's my job, after all.'

Wilde's tangled brain took another leap. 'You told me about the man, Honoré. The "closing of the circle", I think you said. If the American embassy in France was targeted, why not the American embassy here, too?'

'Or indeed the American ambassador to London himself?' Eaton suggested.

'But why would he do that? Honoré is an agent of the Comintern and it looks as though Marcus is a sworn enemy of Communism. So why would he be taking instruction from a Communist like Honoré?'

'Maybe Honoré isn't really a communist. But forget about that for a moment . . .' Eaton seemed to be following a particular train of thought. 'Perhaps the assassins' politics don't matter. What their masters are looking for is a *Frenchman* to kill the US ambassador in Paris and an *Englishman* to kill the US ambassador in London. Now that really would turn American opinion against the Allies.'

Wilde nodded. 'But – and it's a very big but – if America thought for a moment that the killer was a Nazi and that orders came from Berlin, then the US would come down with all its might *against* Germany. That's why the film revealing Marfield as a Nazi has to be destroyed.'

Eaton put down his coffee cup, shifted in his seat, and rubbed the stump of his left arm. 'My God, we're on to something . . . Do we think this attack is imminent, Wilde?'

'We have to assume it is.'

'The attempt on Bill Bullitt happened while he was taking his regular morning walk in Chantilly. Kennedy likes a morning ride in Hyde Park. This is well known. He would be an easy target.'

'We need to find Kennedy and warn him.'

Out in the hall Eaton was about to pick up the phone when it started ringing. The two men looked at each other.

Wilde picked up the receiver. 'Hello, Lydia Morris's residence.'

A distant voice crackled through. 'Tom, it's Jim again.'

CHAPTER 36

'Good day, Mrs Marfield. I'm Eleanor Ruskin, an old friend of your son, Marcus.' Elina held out her hand.

Margaret Marfield stood in the doorway. She looked exhausted. 'Why are you here?' she said.

'Because Marcus is in trouble.'

'Then nothing changes, does it.' The older woman made to close the door. Elina put a hand out to stop her.

'Mrs Marfield, we both know what sort of young man he is. In a word, he is reckless – a danger to himself. He is not like other men. Sometimes he is more like a boy than a man, but a wild, beautiful, uncontrollable boy. And because of this he needs our help.'

'I suppose you'd better come in,' Margaret Marfield said with a resigned air. 'Better than burgling me and turning the house upside down.'

She led Elina into the sitting room. Elina knew Marcus had ransacked it only a few days earlier, but some attempt had been made to tidy it up. There was damage to furnishings, cushions slashed, drawers were still tipped out and papers and books were scattered over a table.

'This is something to do with his father's death, I take it, and the parcel he sent before he shot himself. I'm not sure what was in it, and nor do I want to know. I would do nothing to harm my son, Miss Ruskin, but I want no more to do with him.'

Elina gave the woman a reassuring smile. 'You have not been honest with your son, Mrs Marfield. When you said you saw the parcel and that it was addressed to Professor Wilde, that was not true, was it? His name was merely the first that came into your head.'

'I told the truth.'

'This is getting us nowhere. If you will not be honest with me, how are we to help Marcus?'

'Tell me again, Miss Ruskin, what makes you think I want to help him? He has brought shame and disaster upon this house. Anyway, what exactly is your relationship to him?' Some of Mrs Marfield's steel had returned.

'I knew Marcus at Cambridge before he went away. He contacted me as an old friend when he returned from Spain because he needed help. Like you, I have no idea what is in this parcel he wants, nor its significance, but I do know he is being driven to distraction by its disappearance.'

'Well, I have already told him all I know. Who knows, perhaps his wife has it. Did you know he has a wife, Miss Ruskin?'

Elina looked around the room. There were no pictures of Marcus on display, but one or two other photographs had been rescued from the debris, including one of a young man in cricket whites who bore a passing resemblance to Marcus, a bulkier man with poor skin and none of his beauty or grace. Did Marcus have a brother?

She rose from her chair and picked up the picture. 'Who is this, Mrs Marfield?'

The older woman hesitated. 'That's my nephew,' she said. 'Marcus's cousin . . . Edward.'

'Not his brother then?' Elina knew instantly that she was lying. 'The parcel was sent to him, not Professor Wilde, isn't that the truth?'

Margaret Marfield shook her head a shade too vehemently. 'Marcus doesn't have a brother.'

Elina prised open the silver frame. The glass fell to the floor and shattered, but she ignored it and held up the picture to study the face. Despite the darker hair and the heavier jowls, the likeness was clear. She turned it over: *Ptolemy, Lowestoft, 1934.*

'Ptolemy? What sort of name is that? Doesn't sound at all like Edward.'

'Please, give me that picture. It means a great deal to me.'

'Where is he? Where does he live?'

'None of this is anything to do with you, Miss Ruskin. These are family matters.'

Elina opened her handbag and inserted the photograph.

'Give that back!'

'You're scared of Marcus, aren't you? He terrifies you – that's why you made up the story about Professor Wilde. You feared for your other son. Where can I find him?'

Margaret Marfield lunged for the bag, but Elina sidestepped her and pushed her to the ground. As the older woman scrabbled to try to get to her feet, Elina looked around. On the table with all the papers there was a telephone. Beside it, half-concealed, was a dark blue leather-bound address book. She crossed the room and picked it up.

'That's not yours, Miss Ruskin. Leave it and get out of my house this minute.'

But Elina was already leafing through the book and there, under the letter M, she found it. *Toll Marfield*, with an address in Oxford crossed out and replaced with the name of a school in Essex. A teacher? She looked at her watch. Time was tight, but it had to be done.

'She's been found, Tom, she's alive.'

'Jim, that's wonderful. Is she with you?'

'No, I'm still on the mainland with Henry, waiting for the boat bringing them over from the island. I'm not sure she's even conscious yet . . . and I think she's injured. But she's *alive*, Tom. Juliet is alive. I had almost given up hope.'

Wilde looked at Eaton, who nodded. 'Thank the Lord, Jim.'

The faint sound of laughter came down the line. 'This isn't driving you back to the church, is it, Tom?'

'Who knows? Stranger things have happened. But look, Jim, we have a rather urgent situation over here. I wouldn't get you involved, but as you're on the line I can't think of anyone better. I'm here with Philip Eaton. You remember him?'

'Of course.'

'This probably sounds insane, but we believe we have uncovered a plot to assassinate Joe Kennedy. I'm afraid it involves Marcus Marfield, the young man we brought to your house.'

'Marfield? I guess brutal conflicts like the Spanish war change people.'

'We'll talk about that later. We were just about to call the embassy. Who should we talk to there?'

'Herschel Johnson's the man – Joe's second-in-command. He also happens to be a good chum of your senior MI5 men. He'll know what to do – and he'll take decisive action.'

'Good idea. I've met Herschel. Jim, I can't tell you how happy I am that you've found Juliet. Lydia will be, too.'

'Well, let's not break out the champagne until we know how she is. But to get back to this Kennedy thing . . . I'm kicking my heels while I wait for the boat. I'll call Herschel for you – it'll save time. Meanwhile, you can contact the cops or whatever else you think necessary.'

'Thanks, Jim. And give all our love to Juliet, won't you?'

'Of course I will.'

Wilde replaced the receiver. 'Did you get the gist of that, Eaton?'

'I think so. Let me call Carstairs and he'll get things moving. We need to drive to London sharpish.'

Lydia had appeared, having walked silently down the stairs on slippered feet. She cleared her throat and they turned to her. 'Well if you two are going to London, I'm coming with you. I don't want to be left alone with that bloody maniac still on the loose.'

The drive to Grosvenor Square and the American Embassy in the heart of London was long and tedious, frequently held up by military traffic. As the driver turned off Park Lane, Wilde consulted his watch. Noon. What, he wondered, had happened since they had left Cambridge? He smiled at Lydia. She didn't look well.

'Lydia – what will you do?' Wilde took her hand.

'I'm going to book myself into a hotel. I'm sorry – I'm feeling weak.'

'Claridge's is just around the corner,' Eaton said. 'We'll drop you there. They'll look after you. You get out here, Tom – I'll be at the office in St James's Street. Call me through Carstairs.'

Wilde leant over and kissed Lydia. 'Will you get a room and sleep?'

'I think I have to, darling.'

'I'll scoot around and join you as soon as I have the lie of the land.'

Herschel Johnson wasn't at the embassy. Nor was the ambassador himself. The whole place was chaotic, with hundreds of Americans demanding assistance. After a few minutes Wilde was shown into an expansive office on the first floor, looking out over the leafy square, where he was greeted by one of Johnson's assistants, a woman of about forty.

'We've heard from Mr Vanderberg,' she said, 'but Mr Johnson hasn't been in today. He's up at Wall Hall with the ambassador and his family so I'm afraid I haven't managed to talk to him yet.'

Wilde was alarmed. 'Then Jim hasn't got the message through?'

'Oh, I sure hope so, Professor Wilde. Mr Vanderberg spoke with Mr Lincoln Tripp. I'm sure he's dealt with it properly.'

'Where is Tripp?' Alarm bells jangled.

'He was just about to set off for Wall Hall when the call came through. He'll be there by now and will have given Mr Vanderberg's message to Mr Johnson in person. Mr Tripp is a very reliable young man. I'm sure Mr Vanderberg has faith in him.'

'But this concerns a threat to the ambassador's life.'

The woman smiled with what Wilde considered a hint of condescension. 'We receive death threats all the time, Mr Wilde. It goes with the territory, I'm afraid.'

'Can we call Wall Hall from here?'

'Certainly, sir.'

'Is there any particular reason why they're all out in Hertfordshire on a working day?'

'It's Mr Kennedy's farewell party for his family before they leave for home. And it's Miss Rosemary's twenty-first birthday tomorrow. It's a big celebration. Mr Johnson and Mr Tripp are both family friends, so they have been invited, too.'

The butler at Wall Hall came to the phone. 'Who is this?'

'Professor Thomas Wilde. I'd like to speak to either Herschel Johnson or the ambassador.'

'I'm afraid they've just left, sir.'

'What do you mean? Aren't they having a party there this evening?'

'Indeed so, sir. We are expecting them back late afternoon. The table is all set for a family banquet.'

'Then where are they now?' Wilde was beginning to feel the cold edge of dread. Things were spinning out of control.

'I can't exactly tell you, sir, but I believe it is a church with some special significance. A Mass is to be said, and there is to be singing. I wish I could tell you more.'

'Does anyone else in that house know where they're going?'

'I don't believe so, sir. It is intended as a treat for Mrs Kennedy, who is a most pious Roman Catholic lady.'

'Look – you have to find out! Someone there must know something.'

'All I can tell you is that it's an hour or so from here, sir.' The butler remained unruffled. 'May I inquire as to your interest, sir?'

'The ambassador is in danger. Look, is Tripp there – Lincoln Tripp?'

'The young American gentleman from the embassy? Yes, sir, he arrived – but he too went with the family. They went in five cars, in convoy.' A slight pause. 'What is the nature of the danger, sir?'

Wilde ignored the question and fished in his pocket for the paper with Eaton's details. 'I'll give you a couple of numbers – call if you can find out where they're going.'

Wilde immediately put a call through to Eaton's office. 'I'm going up there,' he said.

'What do you mean? Where?'

'Someone at Wall Hall must know where they've gone. I'm going to find them if it's the last thing I do. You organise things from this end. Call the office of the Catholic Archbishop of Westminster. See if they know anything about this church service. Must be some event, so it might have been organised through them. Get every constabulary in Hertfordshire and Cambridgeshire and adjoining counties looking for a convoy of five official cars.'

'Very well.'

'I'm sorry, Eaton, I don't need to tell you all this. Oh, and I need a car.'

'I'll send the driver to Claridge's. He'll hand over the keys to you.'

'And Eaton, a firearm would be welcome.'

CHAPTER 37

Lydia was sleeping when Wilde arrived at the hotel. He didn't disturb her, just left her a message, and then studied maps supplied by the concierge while waiting for the car and pistol. They arrived ten minutes later.

He drove out of London at speed. He knew where to find Wall Hall, but more importantly he needed to work out where the Kennedy convoy of cars was heading. A place of special significance, the butler had said. Somewhere north of Wall Hall, and about an hour from the estate. That had to mean something between thirty and fifty miles – a huge amount of territory to consider, from Brackley in the west, to Bedford due north or Saffron Walden in the east.

But the Kennedys were renowned for their Catholicism, so it had to be a Catholic church or chapel. How many of those were there in this Protestant country?

Something like the shrine at Walsingham in north Norfolk – too distant for today's journey, but that sort of thing, surely? The Roman Catholic cathedral in Norwich? Again, too far. Perhaps the church of Our Lady and the English Martyrs in south-east Cambridge. Wilde knew it as a nineteenth-century edifice of questionable beauty, but that also, surely, was too far.

Wilde reached Wall Hall within fifty-five minutes. The gun weighed heavy in his jacket pocket as he followed the footman through the halls and corridors of the elegant mansion to the office of the butler, Hobbs.

Wilde tried to speak, but the butler, dressed in formal attire, raised a finger to stop him. 'Professor Wilde, if I may just get a word in edgeways. You haven't told me why you are worried about the ambassador's wellbeing?'

'There's a death threat – a possible assassin. I am working with the British intelligence services. Mr Kennedy needs to be warned – and he needs protection.'

'He does have a security man with him.'

'All to the good, but that may not be enough. Now, what can you tell me?'

'Very little, sir. I have asked about, but no one seems to have details of where he has gone. I think the person best placed to talk to you would be Miss Ulyanova, who has been organising things, but she is not here at the moment.'

'Miss Ulyanova?'

'Indeed, sir. I believe she suggested the destination to Mr Kennedy.'

'Is she with them?'

'She went ahead.'

'This Miss Ulyanova – what is her role here?'

'Ah, now, sir, that is not easy to answer. I would say she is a secretary or personal assistant, but she is quite new so defining her role is not straightforward.'

If the butler was suggesting some impropriety, he concealed his suspicion with great skill.

'Can you describe her?'

'Not tall, fair-haired . . . very pretty, I suppose.'

'And she has her own car?'

'Indeed she does. A rather splendid Morgan two-seater.'

'Not red by any chance?'

'Indeed, it is, sir.'

Red sports car. Elina Kossoff. It had to be. 'And Lincoln Tripp was here, too?'

'Yes, sir. I believe he also has been involved in today's celebrations and I am told he has booked a most remarkable young tenor as the highlight of the religious event. One of England's finest voices, it is said.'

'I need to use your telephone, Mr Hobbs.'

There was something in the back of his mind. Some memory from long ago. But he couldn't place it. The phone was ringing, but no one was picking up. He was about to cut off the call when Carstairs answered.

'Forgive the delay, Professor Wilde. I was away from my desk for a few moments. Let me put you through.'

Eaton was frustrated. He hadn't got anywhere in his efforts to identify the Kennedys' destination. Nor was he hopeful of the police finding the ambassador's convoy of five cars. 'We're talking hundreds of square miles, Wilde. Not quite as bad as needles in haystacks, but far from easy.'

'Lincoln Tripp is with them. He has invited a tenor along.'

'Marcus Marfield?'

'Almost certainly.'

'Dear God. We have to find them!'

'There's more. Kennedy has an employee with an office here who has been involved in organising the event: name of Ulyanova, but I'm sure it's Elina Kossoff. She's not in evidence either.'

'What do we do, Wilde?'

'I was about to ask you that. Eaton, in the far reaches of my mind, there is a memory – something relevant, but I can't nail it down.'

'Well, there are scores of Catholic churches . . .'

'We can't scour them all.'

'We don't have a lot of staff here, but the secretaries are phoning around the priests associated with each church or Catholic establishment. Could it be a Catholic school, do you think?'

Possible. Worth a phone call, certainly.

'Come on, Wilde, you're the history man. You must know all the sites of interest to Catholics. Something to do with the Reformation, for instance? The persecution of the Catholic martyrs . . .'

Wilde's hair prickled. 'Stop there, Eaton. I think I've got it. It's not a Catholic church – at least not any more. It's a small, half-ruined Protestant church. St Peter's on the Gilderstone estate. Look on the Ordnance Survey. I'll explain all later. Send reinforcements. I've got to go. Pray God I'm in time.'

No one could chance upon the church of St Peter. Half-ruined, covered in ivy, it stood in ancient woodland in the very heart of the ten-thousand-acre Gilderstone estate. Elina Kossoff met Marcus Marfield in a small glade, a few hundred yards from the narrow pathway that led through the trees to the church. There was no road access, so cars had to be parked hundreds of yards away.

He had been waiting there for three quarters of an hour for her to arrive with the weapons.

She handed the bag over to him. 'I'm sorry, I had other business.' She didn't bother telling him that she had been over every inch of the weapons to erase her own fingerprints.

'The service will be under way in half an hour. The full Tridentine Mass. I need to conceal the guns.'

'Why not simply walk in there firing?'

'I have to sing first.'

He was a strange one, but then she had always known that. Why did he have to sing for these people before killing them? The answer, of course, was that he wasn't singing for *them* – he was singing for himself. This had always been about Marcus Marfield.

'Well, it's stripped. You have to reassemble it.'

'The work of two minutes.'

She watched as he opened the bag and removed the Thompson sub-machine gun and knelt down, placing the parts on the unwrapped cotton. He examined each constituent element, then began to click them together, his hands moving fast as though he had done this a thousand times before. He probably had.

'You didn't tell me you had a brother,' she said.

'Is it relevant?'

'Yes, I think it is. He teaches at a school in Essex. Did you know that?'

'No. I haven't seen the bastard in nearly three years.'

'I went there this morning, but he wasn't there. That was all the office would give me. I was wondering if you have any clue as to where he might be.'

'Of course not. Anyway, what's this all about?'

'He has the other film. Your father sent it to him, not Wilde.'

Marfield stopped his work on the stripped gun and gave her a hard look. 'I don't believe it. My father never had any time for Toll.'

'It's true.'

'That's not what my mother said.' He held up the reassembled gun, slid the bolt and tested the safety catch and the trigger. 'Smooth as silk,' he said. He picked up one of the two magazines and slotted it into place. 'Ready to fire.' He pointed it at her. 'Now then, what's this about Ptolemy?'

'Your father sent him the film. Your mother knows this, but she lied to you. She's afraid of you, Marcus – she fears what you would do to your brother.'

'And how have you come to this conclusion?'

'I went to visit your mother. I saw Ptolemy's picture – and it all became clear to me. She told you the first thing that came into her head, which was Wilde's name. Wilde has never had the film.'

'But he's seen it.' Marfield shrugged. 'Anyway, he's dead now. And dead men tell no tales, as someone once pointed out.'

'Maybe. But we still need the film. And so I'm going to leave you now and find your brother.'

'Did it occur to you that I might have an objection to you hurting my own flesh and blood?'

'I didn't say I was going to hurt him. But we must have the film.'

'Did you do anything to my mother?'

She sighed. 'No, but would it really matter to you if I had? You loathe each other.' She leant forward and kissed him. 'Good luck, Marcus. Get the Thompson hidden quickly. This is a remarkable thing you're doing. You're a brave man.'

'Oh no,' he said without looking up. 'This is easy. I hate Americans. All Americans.'

That helped, of course. But Elina was still curious. 'Why, Marcus? Why do you hate them?'

He stopped his work and looked at her with an enigmatic smile. 'Do you really want to know?

'Tell me.'

He shrugged. 'OK. I was on a choir trip to Munich with the school. It was 1934. We sang in the Frauenkirche and various concert halls, but after the rest of the choir went home, I stayed on with the family of an old friend of my mother's. They had a boy of my age, Gottfried, and we got on well, really well. We went hiking with his Hitler Youth troop. It was a pure life, a true life. I felt at home.'

She tapped her watch.

'I was made an honorary member and I wanted to stay there, but of course, I had to come back to Suffolk. However, I persuaded my parents to let me go again the next summer, 1935. I didn't tell my father about the Hitler Youth, of course. Not then, at least. He would have been outraged and kept me in England.'

'Something happened?'

'One weekend our troop was hiking and camping in the mountains around Garmisch. It was early evening and we were singing around the campfire: For today Germany is ours! *Denn heute, da gehört uns Deutschland . . .*'

'. . . *und morgen die ganze Welt.* And tomorrow the whole world.'

He nodded. 'A band of American hikers came upon us, all loaded down with rucksacks. No, they descended on us. They were all a couple of years older than us – jeering college idiots.

They insulted our uniforms, insulted the swastika, finally they insulted the Führer. Gottfried had had enough. He launched himself at them with his hiking stick. One of the Yankee oafs, half a foot taller than Gottfried and twice as broad, pushed him hard. Gottie stumbled, fell on to rocks. His head split open and he died instantly.'

'My God.'

'So you see . . . killing Americans is easy.'

They had put mother and child in a small private room of the hospital. Willie was sitting up in bed telling him about Mrs Cullanan and how she had looked after him and how Mr Cullanan had found Ma. In the other bed, Juliet was asleep, heavily sedated and bandaged. There were no broken bones, but she had tendon damage to her right forearm, some deep cuts to her torso and trauma to the spinal column. But the injuries were not life-threatening.

Jim Vanderberg could not wait to talk to her, to hear what exactly had happened. He also had other tasks on his mind; he needed to contact the family of Joyce Harman to break the news to them and give his condolences. Willie had told him how she had kept them fed and how much she had helped in the days adrift in the dinghy.

Most of all, he wanted to take a boat over to the island to give his personal thanks to Cathy and Martin Cullanan, without whom Juliet would certainly not have survived.

He needed to call the embassy, too. With both Herschel Johnson and the ambassador unavailable, he had had to leave a message with young Lincoln Tripp. His first thought was that that would be fine, but since then doubts had crept in.

The line had been bad and somehow Tripp's response had seemed a bit casual. In fact the more he thought about it, the less certain he was that Tripp had understood the urgency of the warning at all.

The Gilderstone estate lay in the vast agricultural folds between Stevenage and Saffron Walden. Wilde had only been there once, to a special event. Four years ago on this very day, 12 September 1935. St Peter's was indeed a Protestant church, but like every English church of four hundred years old or more, it had once been Roman Catholic.

And not all these old churches, though nominally Church of England, had ever truly cast off their Catholic past. St Peter's was one of these. Every year, it remembered a day in 1589 when a martyr of the Church of Rome was captured during Mass in this little hidden place of worship.

It was a church in which names such as Edmund Campion and Robert Southwell, John Gerard and William Weston had sought sanctuary and brought the Mass to their forlorn flock, suffering under the harsh Elizabethan regime. They were all fugitives, all hunted mercilessly.

On the evening Wilde went there, the way was marked by pitch torches, and the interior was lit by dozens of candles. It was both eerie and ethereal. He had known the story of the poet martyr Barnaby Gilderstone well, and had written a sympathetic article about him, which was why he had been invited. It was not exactly a secret ceremony, but it was not publicised, for the parish priest knew that many in his flock disapproved of honouring the saints of Rome. And anyway, they didn't like coming to this ruin of a Saxon church, deep in the woods, preferring the lighter and warmer confines of the fourteenth-century church in the village.

Barnaby Gilderstone was a Jesuit, a son of the family who lived in the hall. He had been tracked remorselessly by agents of the state, and he had finally been betrayed and surrounded here in this tiny church where he had felt safest of all.

Wilde was not the most religious of men, but he had been moved that night by thoughts of the young priest. Even with his faith, he would have known the horrors that awaited him. As an ordained priest – particularly one of the hated Jesuits – coming into England in secret, he was automatically guilty of high treason, and there was but one penalty for treason – hanging, drawing and quartering. Wilde knew all this, for the religious strife of the late-sixteenth century and the machinations of the Elizabethan secret service were his subject.

The little candlelit gathering Wilde attended had been a solemn, spiritual occasion. Christ himself might have approved of the simplicity of the church, for it amounted to little more than a pile of old flints, scarcely held together. The church had fallen into ruin in the nineteenth century, and its tower had collapsed into the nave in the 1890s. With no money to repair it, all that could be done was to make it safe.

As he drove up, Wilde could see five large black cars parked on the gravel outside the long-abandoned Gilderstone Hall. The drivers stood together by the wall of the old building, smoking, staring at him without interest. Fleetingly, Wilde wondered about recruiting them, but they were unarmed, and explanations would merely take up precious minutes.

Climbing from his car, Wilde checked the Walther pistol in his pocket, looked about to get his bearings and saw the path into the trees that he had taken four years earlier.

He ran at a loping pace. The path was overgrown in places, trees had been blown down, brambles ripped at his jacket and trousers and threatened to trip him. He ran as softly as he could; he had to be fast, but he did not want to announce his approach.

His first glimpse of the crumbling flint church made him stop in his tracks. Lincoln Tripp was standing outside the porch beneath the sheltering branches of a yew tree, wearing the same rather foppish suit in which Wilde had first seen him at Chelsea: silk kerchief dangling from his breast pocket, trilby at a rakish angle. At his side was a man Wilde did not recognise. He was broad and strong with an American crew-cut, and held his hand inside his suit jacket. Surely that must be Kennedy's bodyguard.

And then Wilde heard the voice. The voice of the angel.

CHAPTER 38

The Mass had finished. It had been an exquisite service, reminiscent of those that must have been held here by the likes of Gilderstone and Campion and Southwell three hundred and fifty years earlier. No ornamentation, no organ music, no choir. Just a simple telling of the Latin Mass by two priests – in this case, one Roman Catholic, one Anglican.

And then the Kennedys' young friend, Lincoln, son of their friends and neighbours at Hyannis Port, had opened the door for the singer. Marcus Marfield had entered in his choral scholar's ensemble of red cassock and white surplice. Using both hands, he held a small crucifix to his chest, and he started singing as soon as he entered.

The Kennedy family of eleven – nine children and the parents – along with Herschel Johnson from the embassy, the family's nanny, Luella Hennessey, and Rosemary's godfather, Eddie Moore, and his wife, Mary, were ranged on the ancient pews, facing the altar, a simple table which had been draped in pure white linen for the occasion and was decorated with the Mass things. There was no pulpit.

The power in Marcus's voice was instantaneous, as befitted the Schubert masterwork. No quiet build-up to the *Ave Maria*. And yet it was so pure it seemed to soar to the very heavens, and sent a chill down the neck.

Ave Maria, gratia plena. Hail Mary, full of grace.

All eyes turned to the young man who had entered.

Joe Kennedy sat between his wife, Rose, and the birthday girl, Rosemary. He took her small hand and squeezed it and smiled at her through his round tortoiseshell glasses.

She leant into him. 'Oh, Daddy,' she whispered. 'This is so beautiful.'

'I know, honey.' He put a finger to his lips.

Marcus had progressed to the front of the church now, so they were able to watch him without having to crane their necks. He stood tall, his chin slightly elevated, his fair hair, still short but less severe, glowing in the strange light. He might almost have had wings. Behind him was the altar. The space had been filled with candles, which guttered in the breeze that came through the gaps in the walls. Light streamed in through the windows and through a hole in the roof. The old stone font, worn with time, stood ghostly towards the rear of the church. The font in which Barnaby Gilderstone had been baptised almost four hundred years earlier. How many decades had passed since last a child was christened here?

Marcus was singing the second verse.

In hora mortis nostrae. At the hour of our death.

Wilde was thinking fast. Tripp and the guard were obviously on sentry duty, but they had no idea who they were guarding against, otherwise Marfield wouldn't be in the church now. Somehow the message hadn't got through properly to Tripp.

He had to act fast because he knew the song was short and he feared the ending.

No time to think. Wilde put the Walther in his trouser pocket, with the safety off. He thrust both hands in his pockets and stepped forward, whistling as though he had not a care in the world. He was twenty yards from the church porch when Lincoln Tripp looked up and saw him. He raised his hand, and Wilde strode towards him.

The bodyguard opened his jacket to reveal the pistol in his shoulder-holster. 'Hold it right there, mister.'

Wilde stopped, hands in pockets. 'Tell him who I am, Tripp.'

Lincoln Tripp looked bewildered. His glance swerved between Wilde and the bodyguard.

'My name is Wilde. If you're trying to protect Mr Kennedy, you're on the wrong side of the door.'

The bodyguard turned to Tripp. 'You know this man, Mr Tripp?'

'Uh, yes, yes, I know him.'

'Is he dangerous?'

'I . . . I don't think so.'

Wilde stepped forward. There was no more time for explanations. *Ave Maria*'s last notes were melting away. The bodyguard withdrew his pistol, but he was too slow. Wilde's hands were already out of his pockets. He was a boxer and his punch bare-fisted could lay many men low. Now, with the added weight and unforgiving edges of his Walther, the blow to the side of the bodyguard's head knocked him cold.

The bodyguard spun around and his knees gave way. He was falling to the ground, but a weathered sandstone headstone, the name long since worn away, broke his fall. The pistol flew from his hand as his body cracked into the stone memorial, knocking the wind from him. He crumpled to the ground, blood seeping from the head wound into the dry earth.

Tripp moved to stop Wilde, but the Walther was in his face and he backed away. Wilde elbowed him aside, then pulled open the church door and stepped inside.

The last plaintive syllables of *Ave Maria* had slipped effortlessly from Marcus Marfield's vocal chords. He bowed graciously to his audience, then turned and genuflected to the altar. But instead of rising to his feet, he reached down beneath the altar cloth.

A gust of air and the sound of the porch door opening stopped him, and he turned.

His eyes met Wilde's and then flashed back towards the altar as he scrabbled beneath the white linen covering.

Wilde saw the dark metal of the gun and its shape as Marfield pulled it clear: a sub-machine gun, complete with stick magazine. He registered all this in the split second that it took for him to dive across the aisle and throw himself at Marfield.

The force of Wilde's attack pushed the Thompson out of Marfield's grip, and it slid away from him, under the altar, clattering as it hit the stone wall.

The Walther fell from Wilde's grasp. Marfield saw it and tried to reach out for it, but Wilde was on top of him, grappling for control and managed to kick the pistol out of reach. Marfield punched wildly and caught him in the abdomen, taking the wind out of Wilde. He hit back, connecting with Marfield's jaw.

Even with his injured arm, Marfield was strong – much stronger than Wilde had anticipated – and he had the advantage of youth and speed. But Wilde was the more seasoned fighter and as they wrestled and punched, sliding across the worn stone floor, he seemed to be gaining the upper hand. Marfield's elbow smashed into Wilde's face. Then the younger man was up on his knees, scrabbling to get his cassock up. Wilde rode the blow and realised instantly that Marfield must have a pistol under the robe. He brought his knee up into Marfield's balls, but didn't connect cleanly.

'Hold it right there, mister.'

There was a gun at Wilde's head. The bodyguard, blood streaming from a wound to his temple, was standing over him, arms outstretched, pistol gripped in both hands.

The momentary lapse gave Marfield the chance he needed. He slid from Wilde's grasp and stumbled towards the door and disappeared out into the graveyard. Wilde rose to follow him, but the bodyguard pushed him back down.

'Don't move an inch, or I'll blow your brains out.'

'Get him!' Wilde rasped, pointing urgently at the gaping doorway. 'That's the killer – get him.'

For a moment the bodyguard wavered.

'Look,' Wilde said, pointing to the altar. 'There's a Thompson under there – Marfield was about to kill everyone in this church. He may have other weapons outside.'

There were gasps and wails from the banks of worshippers. All were now standing, backing away to the far reaches of the little church. Wilde looked down. He had a scrap of white cotton in his left hand – torn from Marfield's surplice as he had pulled away.

Jack Kennedy moved forward and placed a restraining hand on the bodyguard's gun arm. 'I think this man's telling the truth. I saw the Tommy gun.' He met Wilde's eyes. 'What's this about?'

'Can we talk later? We need to catch that man. He would have killed you all.'

Wilde pushed past the bodyguard and almost fell out of the church door. Twenty yards away, Marfield had hitched up the skirts of his blood-red cassock, and was pulling out a concealed pistol from his belt. Wilde shouted after him. 'No, Marcus! It's finished. OK?'

Marfield fired two shots, but the bullets whistled helplessly past Wilde. Behind him, the bodyguard emerged from the church and fired back. He missed. Marfield laughed, and shook his head at Wilde. 'I should have shot you before,' he called as he disappeared into the dense undergrowth, and was swallowed up by the enveloping forest.

CHAPTER 39

Every day, the unspoken ghost haunted them. Every time Wilde stepped from the house, he scanned the street from end to end. Every time he left Lydia to go to college, he feared something would have happened to her when he returned.

Something. Marcus Marfield.

There had been no sign of him since the events at Gilderstone. But he was out there somewhere, and capable of anything.

Life had to go on, though. The good news was that the Rudge had been returned to him. It was coated in thick dust and mud, of course, but that was easily fixed. Wilde wanted to spend some time with her, to clean her up, bring a shine back to the chrome, give her a workout along the roads he knew so well, preferably in the more undulating pastures and lanes to the south of Cambridge rather than through the Fens. He had had enough of that flat, watery landscape for a while.

The war wasn't even four weeks old and on the western front, not a lot seemed to be happening. Reports from the Maginot/Siegfried line spoke of desultory skirmishes and bombardments, but nothing else. Germany's eastern front was another matter. Warsaw had succumbed to the advancing German armies and the Soviet Union had invaded Poland from the east 'to safeguard the interests of the Russian minority', but the truth was lost in the fog of propaganda. Wilde feared Poland was all but lost.

Joe Kennedy's family had sailed or flown home to America and arrived safely. No more outrages by U-boats on American citizens had been reported.

And upstairs, Lydia lay naked between the sheets of her large bed. They had talked in a roundabout way of marriage. Both were acutely aware that a baby born out of wedlock might be at a disadvantage. 'Perhaps we have to do it for the child's sake,' she said.

'Do what?' Wilde replied, stubbornly refusing to be the one to ask or suggest marriage.

'You know – marry.'

'Are you proposing to me?'

She had jabbed him in the ribs and left it like that. They were progressing at about the same speed as the war. Which was to say not at all.

Now Wilde was supposed to be brewing the morning coffee, but he couldn't resist slipping out for another look at the Rudge. She had been found abandoned behind an old wagon, and the police had kindly returned her to him. He was their friend now they knew for certain that he hadn't been responsible for the death of Special Constable Caney. Marfield's prints had been found all over the windpump and inside Caney's house. They had been found, too, in the isolated farmhouse where he and Rowlands had held Wilde and had killed two defenceless and harmless old people, and on the Thompson sub-machine gun he had intended to use at St Peter's. They would probably find them on the Rudge, too, if they could be bothered to look.

The whole country knew now that it was a young man named Marcus Marfield who was wanted for the murder of Charlie and Agatha Farrow and Keith Caney. What no one knew, however, was where he was. He had vanished, still in his red cassock and white surplice. That had been over two weeks ago and the manhunt had settled down. There were other matters of concern.

'We know where Marfield's *not,*' Eaton said, when pressed by Wilde during their lengthy and intense debriefing session. 'We've had eyes and wire taps on the Samovar, on both Mrs Marfields – and on Lincoln Tripp. We know he's not with any of those people.'

'What about his brother?'

'We're keeping an eye on him. As much for his own safety as anything, because we are pretty sure the Kossoff woman was looking for him for some reason. Ptolemy Marfield is an innocent in all this; I'm certain he's not hiding his brother.'

The whereabouts of Elina Kossoff – known to Joe Kennedy as Elina Ulyanova – were clear. She was at home, here in Cambridge, defying rumours that rationing would soon be imposed and serving good coffee and cakes at the Samovar. She had been interrogated thoroughly by Special Branch officers in the presence of Philip Eaton, and she had answered everything with a smile. What crimes was she supposed to have committed? The shooting dead of Dr Eric Charlecote up on the Gogs? Why would she do that when she didn't even know the man – and, anyway, where was the evidence? The knifing of Rosa Cortez in Cambridge market in broad daylight? No evidence, no witnesses.

Yes, she knew Marcus Marfield, but so did many people. And no, she wasn't going to deny that they had once been lovers, but that wasn't a crime was it?

The bullet found in her room by Wilde could not be mentioned, of course. Eaton had discussed with Wilde the possibility that they could say it was found elsewhere, perhaps in her handbag, but the conversation went nowhere. Eaton thought Wilde was being a little too priggishly correct in his dismissal of the idea, but for Wilde it was a matter of practicalities. Eaton's suggestions would be laughed out of court.

There was, too, the matter of her work for Joe Kennedy. That must surely have given her access to his movements; knowledge with which an assassination could be plotted. Why did she want a job like that when she had a successful business to run in Cambridge? And why had she used an assumed name? They were good questions, but ones Kennedy himself did not want answered. She said nothing on the subject, did not even acknowledge that she had been there or had ever used the name Ulyanova. The whole matter of her employment in Kennedy's office was not to be re-opened at any cost. Nor would the events at St Peter's Church on the Gilderstone estate see the light of day. War regulations were imposed; no mention of it would be made in the press or elsewhere.

'You can't even begin to go there,' Jim Vanderberg said. 'Joe Kennedy's whiter than white, pure as the driven snow. Everyone in the diplomatic service and in Washington DC knows what he's like, but that's not for public consumption. Any suggestion of extramarital affairs would put the mockers on his presidential aspirations, Tom, so forget it.'

'But this is murder – and the attempted murder of Joe Kennedy's entire family!'

Vanderberg shrugged. 'You know that, I know that – but the good folks back home in the States sure as hell won't. Period.'

'Where did Kennedy meet her? Do we at least know that?'

'Well, he's not going to answer questions like that, and nor is she. If you want my best guess, I'd say it was one of those goddamned weekend house parties he enjoys so much. The Cliveden set, that sort. He always manages to find a bedmate among the staff. At a guess, I'd say this one was deliberately placed in his path. We may never know.'

Apart from her visits to the US Embassy, there was, too, the matter of her call on Ivan Maisky, the Soviet ambassador. Wilde pressed Eaton about that, but the MI6 man had no definitive answer. 'Perhaps it was just a bluff. Good tradecraft to muddy the water.'

Equally difficult was the matter of Lincoln Tripp. He was adamant that he had acted correctly in ensuring that the bodyguard was outside the church. No, he had not been aware that Marcus Marfield was the would-be assassin. If Mr Vanderberg had suggested that was the case, the message to him had somehow got lost in transmission. Why had he not insisted the event at the church be cancelled in the light of the threat? He insisted that he had not realised the severity of the danger. And anyway, Joe Kennedy would have overruled him. He apologised profusely if his actions had been inadequate; he had been as shocked and horrified as anyone by the events that unfolded.

Jim Vanderberg was not happy. He wanted Tripp moved from London back to the States at the earliest opportunity. What the Kennedy clan thought was not recorded. They were old friends of the Tripps and had no reason to doubt his story.

Lastly, there was the matter of an attempted poisoning at a house called Longrow Cottage in a pristine village in the county of Hertfordshire, an incident brushed off as a domestic matter by Eaton when he first heard of it. Since discovering that the daughter of the house, Claire, just happened to be the wife of Marcus Marfield, the incident had taken on new significance.

Claire's father, Joel McPhelan, had always been an early riser. The sound of the horse's hoofs on the metalled road and the clinking of the milk bottles marked the start of his morning.

And then he liked to make a cup of tea and plan his school day; perhaps finish off marking if there was any left over from the night before.

On the day of the attempted poisoning some unexplained noise had drawn him to the window and he had pulled back the edge of the blackout to see a dark figure – a woman, he was certain, although she appeared to be wearing men's clothes – approaching his front door.

She bent down, looking round furtively, and seemed to be fiddling with something. He knew the milkman had already been, for he had heard the hoofs clattering on the road, and the clink of empties being taken and today's pints being deposited, so he couldn't for the life of him see what other reason anyone would have had to be on his front doorstep at that time in the morning.

At breakfast, Joel McPhelan had looked on his only daughter with great anxiety. At the best of times, he was fearful for the safety of his family. He was a timid man, but worried for others, never himself.

This morning he was beside himself with terror.

As his wife cooked bacon and eggs and as his little grandson Walter sat in the high chair being spoonfed porridge, he watched with growing apprehension. Even though the two new milk bottles did not look as though they had been tampered with, he had taken them from the doorstep and put them in the back shed, unopened, and told his wife the milkman had somehow missed their house. Later, he would call the police, but in the meantime he did not wish to alarm his wife or daughter.

There was a matter that had to be addressed. Why had Claire descended on them unnannounced? Of course, she and Walter were always welcome, but her arrival had been precipitous and surprising. Something was wrong, he was certain. And the activity on his front doorstep this morning only served to heighten his sense of dread. Sooner or later, he would have to have it out with Claire. He was sure of only one thing: this involved Marcus Marfield.

Eventually, the forensics laboratory found Thallium in the bottles. More than enough to kill a family of four, including a small child. The forensics boys had tried to lift fingerprints from the bottles, but the only ones they found belonged to Joel McPhelan himself. Even the milkman's prints had been wiped.

And when the police organised an identity parade, Mr McPhelan hadn't been able to pick out the woman he had seen.

Elina Kossoff was off the hook. For now. 'She'll make a mistake,' Eaton assured Wilde. 'We'll get her.'

'Can't you use war regulations to have her interned?'

'I may do that, eventually. But for the moment we'd rather keep an eye on her. See where she leads us.'

'You mean to Marfield?'

'Possibly. Or others. We have to wonder whether this was confined to those we already know about. The link to France makes it almost certain that more were involved.'

'German intelligence?'

Eaton shrugged. 'Honoré could be Abwehr or SD.'

'What if she slips the net? Who's to say she and Marcus won't devise another attack?'

Eaton had no answer to that and while Wilde assumed the Kossoff phone was tapped and monitored, he didn't like the thought of Elina Kossoff living in the same town. Wilde spent half his waking hours worrying about Lydia and their unborn child.

As these thoughts flew round his head, Wilde washed the Rudge down with warm water and soap, clearing out mud from all the little nooks beneath the seats, in the suspension springs, around the tank and the engine and the exhausts, like a nurse looking after a delicate invalid. Only when he was certain he had freed her of all the encrusted filth did he begin to check her working parts and then, at last, he polished her to a perfect shine, so that the chrome dazzled. In all it took him half the day. Every now and then Lydia brought him coffee and sandwiches.

'It's good for you,' she said, as she watched him work. 'All academics should have to get their hands dirty and do some real work once in a while.'

'I can't argue with you about that, Lydia Morris.'

'That's good, too. Because if I'm going to ask you to marry me, Tom Wilde, I want to be sure you take a vow of obedience and keep it.'

He ignored her half-hearted proposal and stood back from the Rudge, satisfied at last. 'I'm taking her for a spin.'

'Can I come?'

'Not in your condition.'

'There'll be three of us soon. You'll have to sell it and get a car.'

'A horse and cart might be more useful once petrol rationing kicks in.' He smiled to soften the words.

He filled the empty tank from a jerrycan, mounted the bike and tried to start the engine. The Rudge spluttered a couple of times, but then roared into life. It was late afternoon and the air was freshening. He hadn't wanted to ride out north of Cambridge – too many bad memories – but something drew him in that direction and in a few minutes he found himself in Histon. He stopped at the kerb outside Claire Marfield's house. Had she stayed with her parents or come back here? Surely she could feel nothing but loathing for Marfield now, after watching that brutal film?

Wilde sat astride the motorbike, the 500cc engine purring gently beneath him. The orchard had been harvested, the fruit stripped from the branches for jam-making or market, and autumn beckoned. He was about to ride back towards Cambridge, when he saw three people walking along the pavement in his direction.

Two women and a child. They looked familiar. As they got closer, his eyes widened in astonishment. It was Claire and her mother-in-law, Margaret Marfield, together with little Walter, clutching both their hands.

Wilde pulled up his goggles so they could see his face and waved.

'New motorcycle, Professor?' Claire said, smiling as she came near.

'As good as.' Wilde looked at the elder woman. 'Mrs Marfield?'

'You're surprised to see me here, Mr Wilde.'

'I am.'

She inclined her head. 'I took your advice. I've come to mend fences with my daughter-in-law. I want to get to know my grandson.'

He was astonished. The chilly Margaret Marfield acting like a human being? He supposed that both women had been victims and they had that in common, but it was the last thing he had expected to see.

'Will you come in for a cup of tea, Professor?' Claire said.

'Perhaps another time,' he said. 'I'm expected home.'

'Well, you're always very welcome, as is Lydia.'

Wilde rode to college, feeling slightly ashamed of himself for having neglected the place these past weeks. He was well aware that his absences would simply add to the feeling among the other Fellows that he was a bit of an outsider. They were right, of course.

The Master, however, seemed happy to see him and shook his hand warmly, expressing his concern for the ordeal Wilde had endured.

'Now,' he said briskly, 'to business. We're expecting about half the usual complement of undergraduates to turn up for Michaelmas.' Sir Archibald was standing gazing out of the side window onto the Master's court. Wilde joined him and together they contemplated the ancient Mulberry tree. 'Wonderful crop this year.'

'Mulberries or undergraduates?'

The Master laughed. 'We'll know about the undergraduates in due course.' He breathed in deeply and held up his sherry to the light, examining its golden hue. 'But whatever their intellectual gifts or otherwise, I want college life to proceed as normally as possible. War or no war, the country still requires educated young men. And those that come here deserve the best we can offer, for who knows what their country will demand of them in the months and years ahead?'

Wilde pretended to sip the sherry that had been poured for him, then put down the glass, hoping the Master would not notice. 'Of course, Master.'

'And you, Wilde, have you given any further thought to what you intend to do?'

'I shall be staying here for the present. I am happy to commit myself to this year, at the very least.' After all, he thought, I will have a wife – *a wife?* – and baby to care for.

'Good man. All hands to the pump. Hopefully not literally. We will need to set a good example to the undergraduates: strict blackouts and well-organised rationing when it comes in. You'll be expected to take your turn at fire-watching each week. And your undergraduates will all have to join the Officer Training Corps, because if this show lasts as long as the last one, they will all be called up eventually.'

'Indeed.'

'What about the Home Guard – will you sign up?'

'As an American citizen, I'm not sure they'll have me. But I'll certainly investigate the possibility.'

'Well, that's your business. Anyway, drink up your sherry' – did Wilde detect the shadow of a wink? – 'and then get yourself off to Horace Dill's rooms. He's been asking for you.'

Crossing the old court, Wilde bumped into Tim Laker struggling with a jerrycan. The choirmaster looked exhausted and even more frail than usual. 'To lose a voice like that – Marfield is irreplaceable,' he lamented.

Did the fact that Marfield was a mass murderer really not take precedence over the needs of the choir?

'Don't look at me like that, Wilde. It's a tragedy – an absolute bloody tragedy.'

Wilde glanced at the jerrycan.

Laker shrugged. 'It's just a little petrol for the Austin. Everyone's doing it, aren't they? How much sugar and coffee have *you* got stockpiled at home?'

Wilde left him and climbed the newly painted staircase to Horace's rooms. The Master had told him that the lung cancer had worsened and Horace had returned to his bed. When there was no answer to his knock, Wilde peeked in and saw the shrunken form slowly rising and falling in the tangled folds of his bedclothes. He was just turning to go, when he heard a low wheezing voice.

'So I was right about fucking Marfield!'

'Were you?'

'Said he was a Nazi, didn't I?'

'Did you? All I remember is you saying he wasn't one of yours.'

'Well, it amounts to the same thing.' The effort of talking, even in a rasping whisper, was too much for Dill and he began coughing. Horace was holding a white handkerchief to his mouth and it had become red with coughed-up blood.

'Can I get you anything? Water?'

Dill nodded and allowed Wilde to hold a glass to his lips. When the coughing had eased, Wilde sat at his side and took his hand. 'Better?'

'I haven't forgotten, you know. The claret.' Their wager was recorded in the combination room bets book. A bottle of claret was the prize, and Wilde had won it by staking the bet that the war would start before November.

'I wasn't going to mention it.'

'The butler has it – a case of Pauillac de Latour. I forget the year but I'm told it's good. To be drunk at my wake with the other Fellows, so you won't have to wait long.'

'Don't talk like that, Horace.'

Dill shook his head. 'I'm slipping away, Tom. I've nothing to live for now . . . not since fucking Molotov and Stalin did their deal with the devil. They killed our dreams.'

Wilde squeezed his friend's hand. 'It won't last,' he said. Even Guy Rowlands had realised that Hitler's true enemy was in the East. What a pathetic creature Rowlands had been with his fantasy of a fascist confederacy of Germany, France and Britain bulldozing the Soviet Union out of existence.

'No,' Dill agreed. 'Of course it won't last. But the damage is already done. I'm not the only one to have burnt my party card.'

Wilde spent a few more minutes with Horace, then took his leave, promising to call the next day. As he climbed the staircase to his own rooms, he could hear the phone was ringing. Scobie in the porter's lodge was on the line. 'Call for you, Professor. Mrs Marfield.'

'Put her through, scobie.'

'Good evening, Professor.' It was the elder Mrs Marfield. She was speaking extremely quietly.

'Mrs Marfield, I can hardly hear you.'

'Claire is upstairs putting Walter to bed. I would like a private word with you. She's going out tomorrow morning at nine, leaving me to look after the boy. Would you mind coming by?'

CHAPTER 40

As he rode to Histon just before 9 a.m., Wilde reflected on the wisdom of agreeing to this meeting. He had started to have doubts about it the previous evening.

'What are you worried about?' asked Lydia. They were having a supper of battered cod and peas in newspaper, from the chip shop.

'I'm worried about whose side she's on. Marcus is still out there somewhere. He's the sort of man to hold a grudge, and act on it.'

'I thought Mrs Marfield despised her son,' Lydia said, dowsing her chips with malt vinegar.

'Perhaps.' But he was far from sure.

So now here he was, knocking at the door to Claire's house in Histon again. Mrs Marfield opened the door immediately. She had been waiting for him.

'Mr Wilde, thank you so much for coming. Won't you come in?'

Wilde entered. He couldn't avoid a quick glance to the hallway doors and up the curving staircase.

'Don't worry, the only people here are you, me and Walter.'

He could smell the coffee. That, too, had been waiting for him. They went to the kitchen and she poured him a cup; none for herself.

'I expect you're wondering why I asked you here, Professor. I imagine, too, that you are more than a little surprised that I have been trying to make amends with Claire.'

'I am,' he said.

She bowed her head. 'I want to apologise to you. I put your life in danger. When Marcus saw the projector in my husband's study, I told him I knew nothing about it. If there had been a film, I said, I certainly hadn't watched it, and I didn't want to know what was in it. But he became insistent in the way only he can, and so I told him Ronald had sent a parcel. He demanded to know to whom it had been sent and I couldn't tell him the truth. I'm sorry, Professor Wilde, your name was the first that came to mind.'

'To whom was it sent to then?'

She held up the percolator to pour him more coffee. He shook his head and waited.

Margaret Marfield sighed. 'My husband sent the parcel to our other son, Ptolemy.'

'So you were sacrificing me to protect your other son? You thought Marcus would harm him?'

That would explain Eaton's suggestion that Elina Kossoff might have gone looking for Ptolemy Marfield. It also explained why Ptolemy had warned Wilde to run as far as he could from Marcus. Clearly, Ptolemy had seen the film.

She nodded slowly and bent her head again. 'I have always been scared of Marcus,' she spoke quietly. 'Most people saw him as this angelic creature with a God-given voice; my husband certainly did.' She looked up and her tone hardened. 'I should have smothered him at birth – just as Klara Hitler should have done with her son.'

These were terrible words for any mother to say. 'Did something happen when Marcus was a child?' Wilde kept his voice neutral.

'Well, I didn't catch him torturing mice or birds, if that's what you mean. But I just knew – even before he went to King's as a chorister – and my fears were confirmed by the complaints of bullying at his public school. Ronald wouldn't see it; but I knew it was serious. It's his nature. His soul is as cold as the inner circle of hell.'

'But your husband became disillusioned – was that simply because of Claire and her pregnancy?'

'Good Lord no, Ronald didn't care a jot about him getting a girl pregnant. It was the politics that did for him. That bloody choir trip to Germany, and then the holiday with his Hitler Youth chum the following year. Ronald's world collapsed when Marcus declared himself a Nazi. Their arguments almost came to blows, though I have no idea why my husband was surprised, because I certainly wasn't. Marcus was born a Nazi.'

'And your old friend Guy Rowlands?'

'Well, of course, Ronald told him everything. He was the first person he'd confide in at a time like that. Guy laughed it off – said it was a passing phase; not to worry.'

It all made sense now. In Ronald Marfield's eyes, his angelic son had fallen from his pedestal by espousing the politics of the devil. The film from Spain was the last straw. To Guy Rowlands, however, Marcus's obsession with National Socialism was merely an opportunity to be seized.

'So where is Marcus now – and where is the film?'

'Toll came home with the film when he learnt Marcus was wanted for three murders. He had watched the film by then and was absolutely horrified. He teaches at a school in Essex, you know, and it seems some woman had traced him there. I'm sure it was the same woman who came to my house. I mentioned her to Mr Eaton.'

'What was the woman's name?'

'She called herself Ruskin . . . She didn't find Toll because he was away for a few days – thank God. When Toll came home he insisted I stop hiding my head in the sand – his words – and watch the film with him. I couldn't bear it, but in the end Toll and I watched it together. It was obscene, and it confirmed my worst fears.'

'And where is the film now?'

'We destroyed it. Toll and I took great care to ensure no trace of it will ever be found.'

'And Marcus? He's contacted you, hasn't he?'

A slight pause. 'No,' she said. 'I haven't heard a word from him. Nor do I ever want to. But I *am* still worried. I am worried for Claire and Walter – and I am worried for you. He tried to kill you once. The thing is, Professor, he won't give up.'

Did he really trust this woman? Either Marfield had fled abroad or somebody was now protecting him – and who more likely than his own mother? And this sudden change in Margaret Marfield's persona, her apology to Wilde and interest in Claire and the grandchild, seemed out of character. What was she concealing?

Wilde pushed away his coffee. He had had enough of this.

'I have to go,' he said. 'Thank you for the coffee – and the apology.'

Together they walked to the door. As he turned to shake her hand, she smiled at him.

'When I said that I wish I had smothered Marcus as a child, what did you think, Mr Wilde? If it were possible to see into the future and know with certainty that you had given birth to a monster, should one act? What would *you* do?'

Lydia was in the centre of Cambridge. She had spent the first part of the morning at her first floor room in Bene't Street where she had been trying to work out how to get her poetry publishing business out of the doldrums. She had to face the fact that in the short term, there was no chance of her studying medicine, so it was back to this.

In the past, she had published a volume of poetry from the Great War and it had enjoyed some success. Was it possible there might be poetry from this new war? It was a macabre thought – and she felt a little like a vulture hovering over a wounded animal. She shuddered. The memory of the tragic fate of so many war poets, a mere twenty years ago, was too fresh in the mind.

Now she was out shopping, looking in the sparse windows on King's Parade opposite the Senate House. Jim and Juliet were driving up with the boys later today to stay the weekend and she needed to get some food in. Doris would help with the cooking, which was something, but Lydia still felt inadequate to the task of catering for a whole family for two days and two nights. What did children eat? Good God, what sort of mother was she going to make? She groaned at the thought. Well, she still had a few months to find out these things.

Here on the shopping streets and in the market, everything seemed so normal – if only you could ignore the sandbags around the buildings, and the gas masks. No gas bombs had fallen on the cities yet. No Nazi boots had marched along England's country roads. Was it possible the whole thing could be settled by negotiation?

Just then she saw a face she recognised, and for a moment struggled to place it. A slender woman of thirty or so, rather dowdily dressed, her face cast down, handbag clutched at her side in thin fingers, gas mask box slung across her shoulder: Priscilla Hollick, Dr Charlecote's secretary.

'Miss Hollick!' she called.

The woman hurried on past her. Lydia hastened to catch up and tapped her on the shoulder. She turned as though bitten.

'Miss Hollick. I'm sorry, did I startle you?'

'Hello, Miss Morris.' The voice was flat, no semblance of warmth.

'How are you? Haven't seen you since . . . well, since you assisted me with Dr Charlecote's notes.' Lydia glanced at her watch. 'Would you like a quick cup of tea? Dorothy's perhaps?'

'I've got to go. I'm meeting someone.'

'Another time then?'

'Yes, another time.'

Lydia watched as Miss Hollick set off at a brisk pace, never turning back. What a strange encounter, she thought. No smile, no social niceties. She looked back to their last meeting. She had thought they had got on well enough.

Oh well. She turned her mind back to the weekend shopping. Doris had complained that the shelves were being stripped. 'Couldn't get Persil or baked beans, Miss Morris, Weetabix all gone, too. Won't be the Nazis as causes the shortages – it'll be our own hoarders!'

The Vanderbergs arrived at *Cornflowers* – Lydia's house – at six o'clock. Work at the embassy had eased after the first frantic days of the war and Jim had been given four days' leave to relax with his newly reunited family. Joe Kennedy himself had thanked him for all the work he had done with Jack in Glasgow, and expressed his heartfelt sympathy for all that the Vanderbergs had been through.

Cornflowers was the bigger of the two houses and so Wilde and Lydia had decided the family should stay there. Wilde was at the door to greet the arrivals.

'Come in, come in,' he said, extending his arms in welcome. All geniality, but beneath the surface, he was on edge: the unheralded appearance of Marfield's mother in Cambridge had unnerved him.

'Let me look at you all,' he said, standing back from them, hands on hips. 'Mr and Mrs James Vanderberg and their two sons – the perfect all-American family. Safe at last.'

Juliet was smiling, but he could see that she was in pain. 'Nothing perfect about me, buster.'

'You look perfect to me, Juliet. Anyway, you're safe and among friends. We have fine wine and good food – the pick-me-up of the gods. We'll play jazz records on the gramophone and feel like human beings again for a couple of days. Come on in.'

Over dinner, Henry and William regaled the company with tales of their adventures, and it was a good story, well told. Every now and then Juliet cut in to correct some small factual error. At the end of the meal, when the boys had left them to explore their bedroom, Lydia asked Juliet if she might talk to her alone in the sitting room. Wilde gave her an amused look.

'What?' she said. 'You think we're going to talk about babies!'

'Well, aren't you?'

'Maybe a bit. I need to know these things. But there are other things, too. Politics. Literature. Art. All those things that go way above your head, Thomas Wilde.'

Wilde and Vanderberg stayed at the dining table with a bottle of whisky, and talked of Lincoln Tripp.

'Remind me, Jim, what exactly did you say to Tripp when you called him?'

'I told him pretty much what you told me.'

'Did you mention Marfield?'

Vanderberg looked uncertain. 'Tripp says the line was very bad, that he heard no mention of Marfield. Nor did he understand the severity of the warning. You know, Tom, I'm not sure exactly what I said. It was a pretty confusing day what with the news of Juliet and William, and yes, the line was not good. I did tell him that Joe Kennedy was in danger and that his bodyguard should be on high alert. I knew Kennedy himself wouldn't want to be involved in dealing with a security scare; things like that happen – part of the job. I'm sure I told Tripp to call you for details. I can't imagine I wouldn't have mentioned Marfield, but – hell, Tom, I don't know.'

'How do you feel about Tripp now?'

Jim took a sip of his whisky. 'I have my doubts, you know that, which is why I want him dispatched home soonest. As does JPK. And I feel guilty for ever bringing him to you, but, well, he seemed like a good kid. Came with a recommendation from friends at the Moscow embassy. Funnily enough, Joe Kennedy told me he never liked Lincoln much and he never liked his father, but he helped his career out of respect for the boy's mother. She's the younger sister of an old friend from the Boston Latin School. Things like that matter to Kennedy.'

'What now then, Jim – for *you*, I mean? Is Juliet still set on taking the boys home?'

'We're debating it, but I think they will go. As for me, I've got a tough one – Berlin.'

'Are you serious? I thought Roosevelt had already withdrawn our ambassador.'

'We have a chargé d'affaires there, Alexander Kirk. He needs assistance. The State Department has asked me if I'll go. There's no arm twisting. Entirely my choice.'

'Don't go. It's too dangerous. Anyway, I need you here.'

'We'll see.'

CHAPTER 41

Wilde was jittery and couldn't sleep. He was listening for door handles turning, for windows breaking. At 3 a.m., the phone rang and he slipped from the bed, leaving Lydia gently snoring, and tiptoed past the rooms where his American friends slept.

'Professor Wilde?'

'Yes, who's that?' His voice on the phone a whisper.

'Osgood, sir, night porter.'

Wilde did not recognise the voice. 'I don't think I know you, do I?'

'New here, sir. Sorry to call at such an ungodly hour, but the doctor says Professor Dill is asking for you. Said you might be available on this number if you weren't at home. Mr Dill's very weak and they don't think he's going to last the night, sir.'

Wilde dressed in a hurry without waking Lydia or the rest of the house, and wrote a note which he left on the kitchen table. He put on his jacket and goggles, and opened the front door. He gazed out into the moonlit street, left then right. Was this what they called paranoia? He made his way next door, where he removed the cover from the Rudge, kicked her into life and rode off slowly into the silent streets of Cambridge.

The moon was almost full, so he didn't use his headlights. Arriving at college, he introduced himself properly to the new night porter, a rough-hewn farmhand of a man who did not look at ease in a bowler hat and suit. He asked after Horace Dill.

'Dr Weir is with him, sir, but he wouldn't have a priest. Just you, sir.'

'Thank you.' He made his way through the shadowed confines of the college into the old court. For a few moments he stopped on the grass and looked up at the dark window of Horace Dill's rooms. Was this really the end? So many arguments and so much laughter over the years; the place would never be the same without him.

Horace Dill's rooms were dimly lit and smelt sickly. Rupert Weir was sitting at his bedside.

'I'm glad you're here, Rupert.'

'He asked for me. And he asked for you.'

'Is he still with us?'

'Slipping in and out. The occasional word seems to emerge from his mouth, but no whole sentence. I think he's asking for his mother. Saw it all the time in the last war: dying boys crying out for their mothers. Heartbreaking.'

Wilde nodded. He leant over and put his hand to Horace's brow; it was cold and clammy, then turned to Weir. 'How long, Rupert?'

'Tonight sometime. Can't be more specific, I'm afraid.'

'Does he have any relatives nearby – someone we should call?'

'The porters don't know of anyone; nor do I. Should we wake the Master?'

'Perhaps not. Look – why don't you shoot off home?' Wilde could see Weir was exhausted. 'I'll stay with him. You've done your bit, Rupert. There's no more you can do, surely?'

'Really?'

'Of course.'

'Thanks, Tom. This is my second night on a call and I didn't get any sleep in the day.' Weir stood up, put his hand in the pocket of his tweed jacket and pulled out a small pewter flask.

He handed it to Wilde. 'That should see you through to dawn. Islay single malt.'

After Weir had left, Wilde took his place by Horace's bedside. He kept talking to him in a low, soothing voice, hoping at least some comforting words would get through. He reminded Horace of his achievements in a long life in politics and academia, and assured him his days had been well spent. He spoke, too, about Lydia and their forthcoming child. In the end he realised he was thinking aloud. 'It's something I never really expected, Horace, not after losing Charlotte and the baby. Now I'm . . . well, I was going to say terrified, but apprehensive is probably a better word.'

He was holding Dill's hand and was sure he experienced a little squeeze of the fingers.

'Is there anything you want, Horace?' Wilde released Dill's hand and poured a few drops of water into his own left palm, then dipped his fingers into it and touched Horace's dry, cracked lips.

Dill was a long way away, close to death. His breaths were shallow and infrequent now and it was hard to discern words among the few sounds he was making. Once or twice, Wilde did wonder whether the old man was indeed calling for his mother, but it was too indistinct to be sure.

And then Horace's eyes opened. They were rheumy and fading, but Wilde was certain that they were looking at him, searching for something, some connection. Wilde took his hand again and Dill clutched his fingers like a man on the edge of a precipice.

'It's me, Horace, Tom Wilde. I'm here.'

'Mother . . .'

'Your mother loved you, Horace.'

Horace closed his eyes, took several urgent breaths. He spoke again and this time the word was clearer – not *mother* but *Marfield.*

'Marcus Marfield?'

Another long pause, several seconds, and then that desperate whisper. For a few moments, his voice – though quiet – was clear. 'He loves him, always has . . .'

'Horace, I don't know what you're saying.'

But there was no more. The breath left him in a long sigh.

Wilde sat beside Dill's body for a few minutes, holding his hands, until he was certain that he had gone.

At last he rose and took a large slug of the whisky. Pulling back the blackout an inch, he saw that it was still dark. He hadn't brought his watch, but reckoned it must be about four in the morning. No hurry now. He could sit here a little longer.

He held Dill's hand as it began to cool, then he finished the flask and smoothed the bedclothes so that he looked at peace. At last, he let himself out, went downstairs and walked across the courts towards the porters' lodge. He would leave all the arrangements in their hands.

Why would Horace mention Marcus Marfield in his dying breath? *He loves him, always has.* Who did Marcus love, apart from himself? Horace had never tried to hide his homosexuality, so it was perfectly possible he had desired Marcus Marfield, but why leave it until the end to declare it? Horace Dill was not a man to conceal his passions. If he had loved Marfield, he would have shouted it from the college roofs. But in any case, Dill had made no secret of his contempt for the young man. No – he must mean that someone else loved Marfield. Were Dill's last words a warning of some sort?

Wilde stopped in the darkness. The world around him was absolutely silent. This ancient college had always been a repository of great learning, but this night it seemed to hold dark secrets, too. His gaze drifted around the old court, taking in all the staircase entrances and the black-shrouded windows, before making his way to the porters' lodge.

Osgood, the new night porter, greeted him. 'Any news, Professor?'

'Professor Dill is dead, I'm afraid.'

'I'm sorry to hear that, sir.'

'When you hand over to the day shift, let them know. They'll see to the necessary arrangements. Death certificate and funeral directors, notification of next of kin.'

'Of course, sir.'

'One other thing: do you know if Mr Laker is in his rooms tonight?'

'The Director of Music? Yes, sir, I believe he is. He came in a few hours ago, soon after my shift began. He was with Professor Barnes.'

'Barnes? I thought he had joined up.'

'I believe so, sir. But I think he's on leave because he has been in and out of college this past week or two. Apparently he's been called away to his regiment tonight.'

'Would you put a call for me through to Mr Laker's rooms, please?'

Osgood was doubtful. 'Won't the gentleman be asleep, Professor?'

'Don't worry. I'll take responsibility for it.'

'Very well, sir.'

Osgood dialled Laker's number, but there was no answer. After a minute he handed the phone to Wilde: nothing but a ringing tone.

'Come on, Mr Osgood, bring your keys, I want you to open Mr Laker's rooms.'

The night porter looked very unsure. 'I shouldn't really leave my post. Are you sure, sir?'

'Never been more sure of anything in my life.'

Before opening Laker's door, the porter insisted on pounding it for a full minute, then called at full volume as though his voice would penetrate the solid wood where his fist had failed. Finally, he inserted the key.

The large sitting room had a homely feel. The baby grand dominated one corner, as far away from the hearth as it would go. Sheet music was scattered across a coffee table. The paintings on the wall were discreetly sexual. Wilde was sure he recognised a nude watercolour as the work of Egon Schiele. It was difficult to tell whether the bony, lean-muscled figure was male or female.

'No one here, sir.' The porter had removed his bowler as a mark of respect.

Wilde opened the door to the adjoining bedroom. Where the sitting room was elegant and inviting, this compact room was rank with the stench of stale tobacco smoke, sweat, and some other smell that was so out of place that Wilde didn't quite register it at first: petroleum.

The oversized bed was a tangled mess.

He couldn't comprehend what he was seeing: it looked like a clutter of bedclothes in need of laundering. But then he realised that a man's body was stretched out on the bed, naked except for a rumpled sheet covering his chest and head.

Wilde pulled the sheet away and revealed the face and tormented body of Timothy Laker. His matchstick arms were stretched out behind him, his bony wrists bound tightly to the bedposts. His ankles, too, were tied to the foot of the bed. A gag of cloth bulged from his mouth. An Egon Schiele work brought to life.

Wilde's first instinct was that Laker must be dead, but that impression lasted only a moment: the man's chest was heaving and his eyes were wide open, looking at Wilde in terror.

'Mr Osgood, come through here would you?' Wilde wanted a witness to this scene.

The porter followed him into the room and his ill-shaven jaw dropped in shock. 'Good Lord, Professor!'

'Do you have a knife?'

'There'll be one in the gyp room. I'll look.'

Two minutes later, Timothy Laker had been cut free and was sitting on the edge of his bed, modesty restored by a dressing gown. Wilde dismissed the porter back to the gatehouse.

'I think you need to talk, Laker – and fast.'

'For pity's sake give me a cigarette, Wilde. You'll find a packet on the piano. Please . . .' Laker was in agony, painfully flexing his joints and muscles, trying to get some blood circulating.

Wilde found a packet of Players and a box of matches and handed them to Laker.

'I take it Marcus Marfield did this to you. You've been hiding him here.'

Laker said nothing, drew deeply on his cigarette and looked down at his shaking hands.

'You told the night porter he was Barnes, didn't you? Being new, he wouldn't have known any better. Not difficult to conceal someone's identity if you move them in and out by night. The question is, Laker – where is Marfield?'

Laker turned on Wilde. 'I could have died just now!'

'Are you sure you weren't enjoying it?'

'How dare you talk to me like that!'

'I think, Laker, that you haven't quite come to terms with how much trouble you're in. You have been concealing a man wanted for murder. Aiding and abetting a violent criminal. People have been hanged for less – you could certainly go down for twenty years.'

'He needed sanctuary – what was I supposed to do?'

'You always loved him.'

'Who wouldn't love him?'

'If you loved him, why did you tell me about Gus Percheron's complaint against him?'

He shrugged. 'I hated him, too. Marcus is Marcus. He always spurned me – until these last two weeks when he needed me.'

It was a story as old as mankind; the lover and the loved. And it was always the latter who held the whip hand. Right now, Wilde had other concerns. 'He's a killer and I need to know where he is. If you help me, I might even testify on your behalf. And why do your bloody rooms smell of petrol?'

Laker was sweating, biting at the nicotine-yellow tips of his finger; smoke swirling around him. He turned his head to the wall and shook his head.

Wilde suppressed a desire to hit him. 'OK. Let's get you to the police station. Marfield killed one of their own – they'll have a fine time with you.'

'Damn you, Wilde! I don't know where he's gone. I had no control over him.'

'And the petrol? I saw you with a jerrycan, remember?'

'He's been building something – an incendiary bomb, I don't know. Something he learnt in Spain apparently. I couldn't stop him. Said he was going to burn some Americans.'

Marfield on the loose with an incendiary bomb, in the early hours when households slept. Wilde felt sick.

CHAPTER 42

As her eyes opened in the dark, she was immediately assailed by a smell of smoke and petrol. She took a deep breath. Her nerves were getting worse. She knew she was being watched, of course. How could she not be aware of the click on the phone line, the watchers in the street?

She slumped back into the pillows. The smell was her imagination. There was no sound, nothing. She closed her eyes; she had slept little these past weeks.

'You said we were in this together . . .'

Her eyes widened, first in panic, then hope, peering into the pitch darkness while her hand scrabbled for the bedside lamp, only to send it crashing to the floor. 'Marcus, is that you?'

'Hello, Elina. Have you missed me?'

She was out of bed now, standing up, naked. She always slept naked. 'What are you doing here, Marcus? What's that smell? Please, turn the light on.'

The beam of a torch lit her torso, her eyes and her fair, wavy hair. She couldn't see him, but he could see *her* pale flesh. Then, from out of the light, came a flash of steel. Even as the knife struck she didn't realise she had been stabbed. She gasped as though she had been punched and her hands went to her throat as she fell back onto the bed. Why was her throat wet?

The blade came again, into her arms and face. Again and again. Ferocious in its speed, but not frenzied: a controlled onslaught. She flailed wildly, aware now that she had been stabbed. He held the beam of the torch to his own blood-drenched and expressionless face. His body, naked from the waist up, was streaked with blood. Her blood.

For a few uncomprehending seconds, her eyes met his. And then her eyelids closed, her hands sank away from her throat to the bed, and she died not knowing why.

The house was ablaze from bottom to top. From the end of the street Wilde could see flames licking the sky and black smoke belching from the windows. He twisted the throttle, accelerated two hundred yards, the front wheel of the Rudge rising from the road, then came to a screeching stop outside the burning house.

A small crowd was gathering, all in nightclothes. The fire roared and crackled. Smoke poured from the roof into the night sky.

Wilde ditched the bike on its stand and raced in the direction of the house, then stopped, helpless. It was an impenetrable furnace and there was no way in.

He heard the clanging of a fire engine somewhere in the distance, back in the centre of town. Please God let it be coming here.

'No one's coming out of that alive,' someone at his side said. He turned to face the man: Neville from across the road, who worked as a floor manager in the Pye factory. Neville's eyes met Wilde's and he turned away shame-faced.

'Neville,' Wilde said. 'Where's Lydia?'

Neville shook his head and shuffled away.

'Has anyone seen Lydia?' Wilde was shouting now, the centre of a growing crowd.

The fire engine had turned into the road; the clanging of its bell sounded like the knell of death. What would they be able to do? There was nothing the firemen nor anyone else could do against such a blaze. Anyone or anything inside that house would be cinders and ash.

And then, at the far end of the road, Wilde spotted a face he knew. Marcus Marfield, naked from the waist up, standing there, watching his foul handiwork.

Constable Edgar Gates was among the first at the scene of this devastating house fire. He'd been three streets away when he saw the glow in the sky. By the time he got there, a crowd had gathered to stare at the huge blaze. First things first, get the fire brigade out. He blew his whistle hard to alert other beat bobbies, then collared a woman clutching a baby.

'Got a phone, luv?'

'I've already called the fire brigade, constable.'

'Is there anyone still in there?'

'If they are, they're done for.'

The crowd was building now. Someone raced up on a motorbike – the householder? Gates was just about to go over to speak to him when he spotted the young man with his hands in his pockets and a bare chest that looked as if it was streaked with blood. There was something about him. As he approached, PC Gates's grip tightened on the haft of his truncheon.

The young man's gaze was fixed on the fire. He had fair hair and his face seemed familiar. 'Do you know something about this, son?' Gates demanded, turning on his torch and looking the young man up and down. He was covered in blood. 'Have you injured yourself? We'll have an ambulance along soon enough.'

The young man smiled, took his bloodstained hands out of his pockets and held them out, palms up, then down. 'My name is Marcus Marfield,' he said. 'You had better arrest me. You'll be a hero, constable. I've killed some Americans . . .'

Wilde pushed through the crowd, fists clenched, just as the constable was putting Marfield in handcuffs. A woman appeared at Wilde's side, and grabbed hold of his arm. He tried to nudge her away, and then saw that it was Lydia, her hair sleep-tousled, her feet bare beneath her dressing gown. He stopped. 'Lydia – thank God.' He took her in his arms. 'Where are Jim and Juliet and the boys?'

'Throwing some clothes on. They'll be out in a moment. Tom, your lovely house – how did this happen?'

Wilde nodded towards Marfield.

Lydia's eyes followed his gaze. 'My God, Tom, it's Marcus!'

'I'm going to kill the bastard. He got the wrong house – he thinks he's murdered us.'

Marfield had seen him. A slight twitching of the lips; his expression was hard to read. Was he gloating? Wilde began again to shoulder his way towards him. Lydia pulled him back again.

'No, Tom – let the hangman do it.'

In the morning, as the last few spirals of smoke rose from the dampened ashes and the firemen finally declared the fire was out, they stood there in line and looked on the ruin of Tom Wilde's home: Wilde and Lydia, Jim and Juliet and their children, Doris, who had worked so hard keeping the house pristine over the years, and knots of neighbours.

Wilde put his arm around Lydia's slender shoulders. 'It's all gone,' he said. 'Everything that I don't keep in your house or at college. Papers, books, irreplaceable photographs, years of research . . .'

'But you're alive – and we're all alive.'

'How I wish I'd never heard of Camp du Vernet. How I wish we'd just left the bastard there to rot. All this, and poor Horace gone, too.'

Jim and Juliet moved closer to them and now all four of them stood arm in arm, with the two boys in front of them, straight-backed and silent.

'This is the way it's going to be, buddy,' Jim said. 'Whole cities bombed and burned to extinction.'

'I know,' said Wilde.

Lydia leant into him and put her arms around his waist. 'No alternative now, Professor Wilde,' she said. 'You'll have to move in with me properly, like it or not.'

He snorted. 'This is all part of your master plan, is it?'

She shrugged, and smiled, then he began laughing and she laughed, too. And those around them were confirmed in their long-held suspicions that they must be mad.

NOVEMBER 1939

CHAPTER 43

'How will you face your death, Marcus?'

'With equanimity and a few well-chosen words. I want the world to know what I was trying to do.'

'When I found you in France – at Le Vernet – you had a much-read copy of the Book of Common Prayer. So, in the light of all you have done, are you able to make your peace with God?'

They were in the condemned cell at Pentonville two weeks after the judge had donned the black cap and pronounced the sentence of death in courtroom number one at the Old Bailey. Wilde had been there. He had not been required to testify because Marfield had pleaded guilty to all the charges laid before him – four counts of murder, including that of Elina Kossoff, and arson resulting in the destruction of Wilde's property in Cambridge.

The whole trial had been over in a morning, and Marfield had been escorted down from the dock into the white-tiled holding cells below with the words of the judge ringing in his ears: that he would be taken to a place of execution where he would be hanged by the neck until he was dead – 'and may God have mercy on your soul'.

'My cause was just,' he told Wilde now in the cold confines of his little cell. 'God will understand.'

Wilde handed him a cigarette and lit it for him. He had come here because Marfield had asked for him and because there were questions that he would like answered.

'You denied involvement in the murders of Rosa Cortez and Dr Charlecote, and yet you must have known of them.'

'You would have to talk to Elina and Rowlands about those deaths.'

'As you know, I can't do that.' Wilde had heard the grisly details of Elina's murder in the courtoom. Her body had been mutilated with a hundred knife wounds.

Marfield shrugged and drew deeply on the cigarette.

'And Tripp – Lincoln Tripp – you have said nothing about him.'

Marfield smiled. 'How do you think I knew the Vanderbergs were visiting you in Cambridge?'

Wilde nodded slowly. He had thought as much. 'Would you be willing to testify that he gave you information and assisted you? Write an affidavit, perhaps?'

'Why would I do that?'

'For the sake of your eternal soul, Marcus! Despite your many temporal sins, I know you have a soul. I have heard it in your voice.'

'Perhaps I will, then. We'll see. You know that Lincoln always loathed the Kennedys? He hated their athleticism and their bright broad smiles. Most of all, he despised their arrogance and belief that they had a God-given right to rule the world.'

'So his motive was personal rather than political?'

'Oh, he had come to loathe the Communists during his time in Moscow, but I accept that might not have been his primary motive. Rowlands approached him in Russia after apparently hearing of various conversations in which Lincoln expressed admiration for the Führer. The fact that he despised the Kennedys even more than Stalin only made him more amenable to Rowlands' approaches.'

'What of Tim Laker? He loved you and shielded you.'

'More fool him.'

Laker was pleading not guilty to the charges of aiding and abetting Marfield, claiming he was acting under duress and coercion. His trial was slated for December; in the meantime he was being held in custody near Cambridge.

The prison officer, standing quietly in the corner of the room, tapped his wristwatch. 'Time's up, I'm afraid.'

Wilde rose from the wooden chair and looked on Marcus Marfield for the last time. He slid the remains of the packet of cigarettes across the table to him. 'Would you like anyone else to come and see you? Your mother? Ptolemy? Claire?'

Marfield's eyes were bright. His hair was longer, and he looked again like the charming young man who had turned up at college back in the autumn of 1936. He shook his head firmly. 'No, please don't let them come. But you can tell Claire and my son that I am sorry.'

On the day of the execution, Wilde watched as a demolition squad pulled down the last blackened walls of his house and began to remove the rubble. He was still unsure whether to rebuild the property or cut his losses and combine the land with Lydia's so that they would have one large garden, perhaps with an outhouse or studio where he could work. If they didn't marry, of course, there could be legal difficulties.

'Well, what are we going to do?' he said as Lydia joined him at the border between their properties. She was beginning to swell now; decisions needed to be made.

'Doris was lecturing me this morning.'

'Doris? She's never been at all judgemental. She always knew we were living in sin!'

'But she's less happy about a child being born out of wedlock. "An illegitimate child will always carry a stain," she said.'

'And what do you think?'

'I think she's right, Tom. But I still don't care. I want to live with you for the rest of my life. I want us to share a home and bring up our child together. But I'm not going to get married just because the world says I should.'

He looked at her with love. Tears were streaming down her beautiful face. He took her in his arms and folded her into his body. 'Same old Lydia,' he said. 'I wouldn't have you any other way.'

At five minutes to eight, Marcus Marfield began to sing. Outside the cell door, the executioner Thomas Pierrepoint and his assistant looked at each other with raised eyebrows.

'Takes all sorts,' Pierrepoint said.

'What's that song, Mr Pierrepoint?'

'Couldn't tell you, son.'

On the stroke of eight they entered the cell and with quick and long practised movements, strapped the prisoner's wrists together and hooded him.

'*Lord now lettest Thou thy servant depart in peace . . .*'

Although the words of Stanford's *Nunc Dimittis* were now muffled by the hood, the vocal line rang strong and true. And so Marcus Marfield, sometime choral scholar and undergraduate of Cambridge University, was bundled the last few yards to the death chamber, singing as he went.

ACKNOWLEDGEMENTS

I owe a huge debt of gratitude to two former Cambridge choristers. Ashley Grote, the Master of Music at Norwich Cathedral, was a chorister at King's and, later, an organ scholar. He took great pains to explain the workings and day-to-day life of the Cambridge choirs. He also introduced me to Michael Keall, who arrived as a chorister at King's in 1939 – the year in which *Nemesis* is set – and trained under the organ scholar David Willcocks. Michael ended his time at King's School as senior chorister in 1945 and eventually became headmaster of Westminster Abbey Choir School. He kindly talked me through the life of a wartime Cambridge chorister and showed me his photograph albums.

As always, it is a pleasure to thank my editor and publisher Kate Parkin for her endless patience and brilliant suggestions, and my agent Teresa Chris for her wise and tenacious support. I would also like to express my thanks to everyone at Zaffre. They are all superbly talented and professional. Last but not least, I am immensely grateful to my wife Naomi, along with all the other members of my family and friends.

If you enjoyed *Nemesis* – why not join the Rory Clements Readers' Club by visiting www.bit.ly/RoryClementsClub?

Turn over for a message from Rory Clements . . .

Dear Reader,

The story of my new novel, *Nemesis,* mostly takes place in the last days of peace and the first days of war in August/September 1939. No one knew what sort of war it would be – but they feared that gas bombs would be dropped on cities and they worried that there would be a return to the horrors of trench warfare.

One thing was certain: the role of America would be crucial. Winston Churchill certainly understood this better than most – and very quickly opened a secret correspondence with President Roosevelt, pleading for warships.

Would America join the fight against fascism – or would they stay out? That question is at the heart of my story.

In researching the book, I wanted to know how people felt at the time. So I read many diaries, newspapers, letters and memoirs based on diaries – contemporary accounts of major events and everyday life.

I love these testimonies because – unlike history books – they were written at a time when no one knew what the outcome would be.

Here are some fabulous examples:

Wednesday, August 30th, 1939: 'We passed the night in a deserted hotel in a deserted Nice. Early in the morning I went down to buy *L'Eclaireur du Sud-Est,* and when I had finished reading the editorial (which advocated peace at any price) I ran up the stairs like a madman to break the news to G that there would be no war.' *Arthur Koestler, Scum of the Earth. 'G' was his twenty-one-year-old lover, the sculptor Daphne Hardy.*

Thursday, August 31st, 1939: 'It has been decided to evacuate three million mothers and children tomorrow from the menaced areas. The six o' clock news is very glum. It is odd to feel that the world as I knew it has only a few more hours to run.' *Harold Nicolson, diary.*

Friday, September 1st, 1939: 'Today, early in the morning, Germany attacked Poland without any prior warning. So war has begun and the world has crossed the threshold of a new epoch. It will emerge from it much changed.' *The diary of Ivan Maisky, Soviet ambassador to London.*

Saturday, September 2nd, 1939: 'Awful news: they are planning to close the theatres! I rushed off to the *New* to see John and Edith Evans for the last time doing *The Importance*.' *Diarist Joan Wyndham, Love Lessons.*

Sunday, September 3rd, 1939: 'A strange, prolonged wailing noise (the first siren of the war) broke upon the ear. We went up to the flat top of the house to see what was going on. In the clear, cool September light rose the roofs and spires of London. Above them were already rising thirty or forty cylindrical balloons. We gave the government a good mark for this evident sign of preparation.' *Winston Churchill, The Gathering Storm.*

Monday, September 4th, 1939: 'Be silent, be discreet, enemy ears are listening to you. Now get ahead, do your job and don't worry.' *Daily Mirror editorial.*

Tuesday, September 5th, 1939: 'Hearing the accounts on the wireless of the loss of the *Athenia*, I remembered something, and digging in the writing-table drawer presently found what I was looking for – the *Lusitania* medal, struck by the German government to commemorate the sinking of this vessel on 7th May 1915, with the loss of over one thousand lives. On one side is portrayed a crowd of passengers at a Cunard shipping office taking tickets from the skeleton Death. On the other the liner, carefully modelled, showing a deck cargo of aeroplanes and guns (which she did not carry) is just vanishing below the waves.' *Lilias Rider Haggard, Norfolk Notebook.*

Wednesday, September 6th, 1939: 'I attended my first war wedding yesterday. The bridegroom wore an A.R.P Badge instead of a carnation in his buttonhole, and the bride carried a gas mask.' *Evening Standard, The Londoner's Diary.*

Thursday, September 7th, 1939: 'I long for you to see our house – all sandbagged up and with paper strips across the windows. It looks like a fortress. Bongie does his rounds every night hammering at people's doors if he sees a chink of light.' *Violet Bonham Carter in a letter from Gloucester Square, London, to her son Raymond. 'Bongie' was her husband, Sir Maurice, an air raid warden.*

Friday, September 8th, 1939: 'The first person to be executed under yesterday's decree – Himmler has wasted no time – is one Johann Heinen of Dessau. He was shot, it's announced, "for refusing to take part in defensive work".' *William L. Shirer, Berlin Diary, a day after a decree authorising the death penalty for anyone endangering the defensive power of the German people.*

Saturday, September 9th, 1939: 'I heard today at the Foreign Office that the French fear the war will last at least until the spring of 1941; here we are more optimistic, though the news from Poland continues appalling.' *Sir Henry 'Chips' Channon, diary.*

Sunday, September 10th, 1939: 'When the siren sounded at midnight the first time, a French colonel banged at our door in the Continental Hotel. "Les avions! Les avions!" In the underground hotel kitchen we huddled in our bathrobes. An American waiting for passage home tore his gas mask out of its case and wore it for hours.' *Eric Sevareid, CBS radio reporter in Paris.*

Monday, September 11th, 1939: 'It is small wonder that, in some cases, the hospitable smiles of the first day or two have changed to lamentations and secret tears.' *Unsigned letter in the Manchester Guardian telling of the hardships rural housewives face in trying to feed evacuee children on 'one and twopence half-penny per day'.*

Tuesday, September 12th, 1939: 'It is difficult to know whether this war is being run by Joe Kennedy, the Home Office or the fighting services. Kennedy has been telling Lord Halifax (Britain's Foreign Secretary) exactly what he thought we should do.' *Guy Liddell, MI5 director of counter-espionage, diary.*

Friday, September 22nd, 1939: 'We will carry on the war against England with icy-cold mathematical reasoning . . . I believe the English people have been enervated by too much city living, that they are hardly capable of heroism, and that, with the exception of the old aristocracy, their culture is worthless.' *Anonymous Luftwaffe pilot in letter to Friedrich Reck, Diary Of A Man In Despair.*

Thursday, September 28th, 1939: 'Today planted out sixty spring cabbage. Might also go in for rabbits and bees. Rabbits are not to be rationed. The butcher says that people will not as a rule buy tame rabbits for eating but their ideas change when meat gets short. Titley says he made a lot of money out of rabbits at the end of the last war.' *George Orwell, diary (Titley was his neighbour).*

Friday, September 29th, 1939: 'Our ultimate war aims should be based on the goal of a long-range settlement for Europe which would prevent a recurrence of situations like the present, as well as liquidating the Nazi regime. They must therefore include plans for an incipient federalisation of Western Europe.' *Julian Huxley, letter to The Spectator.*

I hope you agree that these entries are intriguing. I was particularly fascinated by the last one, by Julian Huxley – discussing the possibility of a European Union before the war had even got under way!

As always, I thank you for your interest in Tom Wilde and Lydia Morris and the world of Cambridge and Europe in bygone days. To find out more, please visit my website *www.roryclements.co.uk*. You can also join the Rory Clements Readers' Club at *www.bit.ly/RoryClementsClub*. It only takes a moment, there is no catch and new members will automatically receive exclusive extras. Your data is private and confidential and will never be passed on to a third party, and I promise that I will only be in touch now and then with book news. If you want to unsubscribe, you can do that at any time.

Of course, I would be delighted, too, if you could spread the word about my books. Online reviews are particularly welcome, and I always read them!

I hope my books give you as much pleasure as I take from researching and writing them.

With my best wishes,

Rory

Turn the page to read the opening from Rory's new book

HITLER'S SECRET

Coming January 2020

CHAPTER 1

The telephone had been ringing in Bormann's office all morning. Many prominent names of the greater German Reich wished to speak to the Führer and all calls had to go through Bormann. Hitler was back in Munich from the Wolfsschanze, his eastern headquarters, and it was a rare opportunity for his ministers to secure a private interview with him. The war against the Soviet Union was almost won and there was much to be discussed.

Each time the phone sounded, the efficient Bormann picked up the handset on the second ring. He spoke with exaggerated deference to the caller. *Of course, Herr Reichsmarshall Göring. Indeed, Herr General. I am at your service, Herr Doktor. Heil Hitler!* The only person with whom he was at all familiar was Himmler, the man he cheekily referred to as Uncle Heinrich.

The office stank of sweat, smoke and cologne. On the desk an ashtray overflowed with the detritus of a constant stream of cigarettes. Later, he would kick his secretary's pretty arse and tell her to clean the place up. She liked having her arse kicked. And fondled.

Sometimes he might put a caller or two through to the Führer. But not this morning. Himmler, Rommel, Goebbels, Ley, Rosenberg, Streicher . . . they could all go whistle. It made no difference to Martin Bormann how important they considered themselves; he told them all the same thing: the Führer was engaged with his chiefs of staff and could not be disturbed.

His chiefs of staff! Bormann laughed out loud at the thought, his shiny, round face stretched tight with amusement. Hitler was engaged in the far more important business of playing with the adorable German Shepherd puppy that Bormann had given him. Settling back in his leather chair, Bormann lit another cigarette. But his good humour soon vanished and his brow darkened. He looked at his watch. He had something else on his mind, something that had to be resolved without delay. Smoke drifted from the cigarette dangling from his yellow fingers. The only time he didn't smoke was when he was asleep or in the presence of the Führer.

There was a knock. Heidi's face appeared around the heavy oak door. 'You have a visitor, Herr Bormann.'

'Otto Kalt?'

'Yes, sir.'

'No reply yet from Charlie Jung?'

'His butler told me he was in Switzerland, skiing or mountaineering.'

Charlie Jung. As elusive as smoke in fog. 'Well, find out the name of his hotel and get a message to him. I want him to call me as soon as possible.'

'Yes, sir.'

'And don't take no for an answer.' He lit another cigarette from the butt of the old one. 'Now give me two minutes, then send Kalt in. We are not to be disturbed.'

'Yes, sir. Would you like coffee?'

'No, Heidi. That is all.'

'Heil Hitler, Herr Bormann.'

Bormann opened the desk drawer and pulled out a photographic copy of a clear but slightly faded sheet of paper. It was titled *Taufschein und Geburtszeugnis* – Certificate of Baptism and Birth. He read it through carefully once more, memorising every last detail.

There was a knock at the door again.

'Enter.'

Otto Kalt was a small man with metal-rimmed spectacles and dark hair. He stood to attention, raised himself to his full height – no more than five and a half feet – and clicked his heels.

'Heil Hitler!' He shot his arm out in the Fascist salute.

From behind his desk, Bormann waved at Kalt to approach. Kalt took two steps forward. No one could have looked less like the Nazis' idealised Nordic Aryan than Otto Kalt. Not even Himmler was such a poor specimen.

Bormann was not much taller, but he was broad and powerful, with the build and demeanour of a hog and the cunning of a cur. He ran his hand through his thinning, slicked-back hair and nodded to Kalt.

He had known and used Otto Kalt, who was of a similar age – early forties – half his life. They had been together since the heady days of the early 1920s. Kalt came from a rural peasant family, but he had been a party member since the very beginning and had risen to some wealth. He was useful to Bormann, for he was obedient and had the slyness and callous brutality of his breed; he would shed blood with no more flicker of emotion than if he were killing a pig, as he had shown in the forest outside Parchim when he had slit the throat of the treacherous Walther Kadow on Bormann's orders. Kalt had always submitted to Bormann, obeying every command. Just as Bormann, in his turn, submitted to every desire of *his* master, the Führer.

Some said that Bormann was like a son to Hitler. Perhaps it was true. If so, then it was even more true that he was like a father to Otto Kalt.

Bormann's loyalty to Hitler had been repaid with immense power and he was now Head of the Party Chancellery. Kalt in his turn had been repaid for *his* loyalty – with the means to purchase a large and splendid farm a little way east of Hamburg.

Pausing for effect, Bormann stubbed out his cigarette and pulled yet another from the box on his desk, picked up the gold, swastika-embossed lighter Himmler had given him for his fortieth last year, flicked the wheel and lit it. As an afterthought, he offered Kalt the packet. 'American,' he said.

'Thank you, Herr Reichsleiter,' Kalt said, taking one of the Luckies.

'Otto,' Bormann said, handing him the certificate. 'I have a small task for you. Read that carefully. Note every detail and then return it to me. It is the birth and baptism record of a ten-year-old girl. I want you to find her and dispose of her – and anyone who has ever been associated with her. It is best if the world never knows she existed. Leave no trace.'

'Yes, Herr Reichsleiter.'

'I cannot stress how important this task is. You have done many favours for me over the years and I have rewarded you well. But nothing – *nothing* – has been as crucial as this one thing. Succeed and I will double your land holding.

'I will not fail you, Herr Reichsleiter.' Kalt bowed his head.

'Good.'

Because if you do, thought Bormann, *I am done for*.

In the hour before first light, Father Huber pulled back the duvet and gazed at the woman's sleep-warm body. She was on her back, her hair tangled across the pillow. Her eyes drifted open and she smiled at him hazily, as though not sure whether this was still part of her dream.

'Come back to bed, Peter.' Her voice was husky, soft and full of sleep.

'You know I can't.' He knelt at the side of the bed as though about to pray, but instead he bent forward and kissed her pubic hair lightly, breathing in the intoxicating fumes. She rolled towards him and, as he stood up, she reached out and tried to fumble beneath his priest's robes.

'Let me kiss you there, too.'

'Trudchen, you are bad.'

'But that's why you love me, Peter. And later, I will confess to the priest and will be forgiven my transgressions.'

'I *am* the priest!'

'And will you deal with me very harshly, Father? Will you make me say twelve Hail Marys?'

He laughed. 'I have made you coffee. It's in the kitchen.'

It was still dark and snowing gently when Father Huber opened the door. Trudchen's house was a little way from the village of Braundorf, a fact which made these nightly visits possible. It was a pleasant, modest chalet, high up on the *Alm*, backed by the mountains, and from there he had a pleasant stroll through the meadow back home. In the short nights of summertime, he had to leave her far earlier than this, but with the long nights of late November, they had more time together. A small but welcome blessing.

The snow had come early this year, however, which could sometimes be a problem. His tracks would be all too visible to the village gossips. And so he had to listen to the forecasts carefully. Today, it was said, the snow would fall steadily, all through the night and late into the day, and so it was proving.

That meant his footprints would be erased almost as soon as they appeared.

Unfortunately for him, that also meant that Father Huber did not see two other pairs of footprints in the snow.

The church of St Mary Magdalene was almost four hundred years old. With its onion dome and its ornate, gilt interior, full of statuary and images from the gospels, it was typical of the older churches in this part of Austria, or the province of Ostmark as the country had become designated since the Anschluss three years earlier.

The first thing you came to, by the door, beneath a colourful wooden wall carving of the Virgin, was an old octagonal baptismal font, deep enough to immerse a sizeable child. Then, ranged along the nave, came the rows of wooden pews, until, at last, you approached the high altar. For all its quaint charm, it was a small, simple church, perfectly fitting the needs of this little country community.

Father Huber entered, stamping the snow from his boots and removing his woollen hat, before lighting candles by the door and switching off his flashlight. The church had not yet been electrified so the only light came through windows or from candle-flames. In the soft warm glow, he made his way down the nave and halted before the crucifix, made the sign of the cross and knelt down to say a silent prayer, confessing his sins of the night, though in his heart he could not really believe his liaison with Trudchen was wrong. Yes, the Roman church demanded chastity of its clergy. But that was a law made by men. How could love be a sin in the sight of God?

He heard a cough. His shoulders tensed; surely Frau Giesler the cleaner could not be here so early? He knew from the way she sometimes looked at him that she had her suspicions. He rose to his feet and turned around, his hands clasped to the cross he wore around his neck. No, it wasn't Frau Giesler, but a man – someone he did not recognise. Someone small and – he hated himself for even thinking it – rather insignificant looking. A traveller, perhaps.

'*Grüss Gott.* Can I help you, sir?'

'Father Huber?'

'Yes, that's me.'

'My name is Herr Kalt, sir. Otto Kalt. I am a lawyer. Please forgive the ungodly hour of my arrival – but I have been travelling many hours from Bremen and decided to push on rather than stopping the night at a hotel.'

The priest did not like this one bit. The man might seem to be of no consequence, but appearances could be horribly deceptive. Peter Huber forced himself to adopt a welcoming smile and extended a hand. 'And why, pray, would a lawyer wish to talk to a humble parish priest?'

Kalt took the hand and held it a few seconds without quite shaking it. His fingers were cold and limp. 'Well first of all, I can tell you it involves a great deal of money.' He shivered. 'Is there, perhaps, somewhere a little warmer we could talk?'

'Of course. My house is next door. Let us go and have some coffee.'

'Ah, thank you, Father. A cup of coffee would certainly go down very well.'

Even though Huber had spent the night with Trudchen, his kitchen was still warm from the previous day, for the blue-tiled *kachelöfen* wood-burning stove retained its heat long after the fire had died down. The priest sat in the corner seat and poured the coffee. Were his hands shaking? He was a slender man of average height, but in these parts where the men were strong from mountain herding and harvesting, he had the appearance of a weakling. Too much time with his head in books. 'Now then, Herr Kalt, perhaps you would tell me what this is all about.'

'Real coffee, Father? What luxury. I am honoured.'

'I had it from before the war and keep it for special occasions.'

'A little sugar, too, perhaps?' He laughed although he had said nothing funny. 'If you have such a thing.'

Sugar was not so rare as coffee, but it was still a precious commodity these days. Huber smiled and gave his visitor one spoonful and left the spoon in his cup for stirring.

'Thank you. Now, Father, I am the bearer of great tidings for a young girl named Klara Wolf, who I am certain is known to you. A large bequest is due to her from a man of considerable wealth and importance, who died not long ago in Hamburg. Killed in a British air raid – can you believe that? And to think Reichsmarschall Göring said we could call him Mayer if ever a British airplane intruded on our territory! Anyway, little Klara is now a very rich girl.'

'Klara? Klara Wolf? I am trying hard to think if I know this girl. The name does not seem familiar, Herr Kalt.'

'Surely a good priest never forgets those he has baptised? Anyway, the name will come to you soon enough. The point is, you see, I require her present whereabouts – and you were the obvious man to come to.'

The hairs at the nape of Huber's neck prickled. He shook his head slowly. 'No, I am afraid not. Forgive me, sir, I fear your long journey has been wasted. Perhaps you should have called ahead.'

Kalt narrowed his small, beady eyes and smiled. 'You baptised her here in this very church, ten years ago – 1931. Her mother, Angelica Wolf – a healthy, pretty young girl of peasant stock – was present, but I believe her father was absent on military duty.'

Huber shook his head again, this time more hurriedly, as though he had a nervous tic. 'No, truly, I do not recall the name.' He studied Kalt. This small man did not look like a lawyer, even with his round spectacles. But what exactly did a lawyer look like? Well-to-do, perhaps? Well fed? This man was thin and wiry, but his hands were rough and callused like a son of the land. In Huber's eyes, he looked like a Gestapo officer recruited from an abattoir; not that Huber had ever seen one of that hated breed, to the best of his knowledge.

The visitor said nothing, merely stirred his coffee and kept his eyes fixed on the priest, waiting like a hyena.

'What can I say, sir?' Huber realised he was babbling, but he could not work out whether it was better to be silent or garrulous. 'If there was such a person baptised here, she is not here now. I know every boy and girl in the village, you see. No, no one of that name. Never to my knowledge. Really, your time has been wasted, Herr Kalt.'

'Oh, my time is nothing. I have all the time in the world. My instructions are to find her at all costs, given the importance of my mission. So I will be staying in the village for the foreseeable future, talking to everyone. Perhaps you would continue to rack your brains, Father. I am sure it will all come back to you in due course, for I have seen the baptism certificate and it is clear that you carried out the ceremony.'

Huber could feel his heart pumping, his lungs and throat constricting 'No, I am sure I would remember.'

'Check the registers. You'll see I'm right. Ten years is not so long ago that you can have completely forgotten.' He drank his coffee, rose from the table and held up his hand in farewell. 'My thanks for your hospitality. The coffee was excellent. I will see you again soon, I am sure.' And then he was gone.

For a full minute, Peter Huber was transfixed with terror and indecision. These past ten years he had feared this day would come, and now it had. What to do? Men like Kalt did not simply accept a denial, shrug their shoulders and go away empty-handed.

He could not deal with this alone. His hand trembled as he picked up the telephone and asked the operator for a number in Berlin – a number he had not called in years and had intended never to call again.

The phone seemed to ring for an age. He was about to hang up when it was answered.

'Hello?' A sleepy voice. Not yet dawn.

'Frau Dietrich?'

'Who is this, please? Do you know what time it is?'

'Father Huber. You know, from Braundorf . . . Peter Huber.'

Silence.

'Frau Dietrich, are you there?'

'Peter, did you really give the operator this number?' The woman's voice was wide awake now and incredulous. 'And you just said my name!'

'I didn't know what to do. There is a man here, asking after Klara. He says he is a lawyer with a bequest for her. But I think he is Gestapo. I thought you needed to know.'

'God in heaven, Peter, how could you do such a thing – call me like this?' He heard a deep groan. 'Oh, Peter, it's closing in now. You have to get out of there – fast. Don't call me again.' The line went dead.

Get out fast? How could he get out at all? It would be hard enough to leave the church and the village – but to abandon Trudchen was unthinkable and he could not ask her to go on the run with him; she knew nothing of this.

There was only one thing to be done: he had to pray.

Not even bothering to remove his slippers and put on his snow boots, he ran from his house to the church. As he opened the great doors, he knew he had made a terrible error. Two men were waiting for him, standing by the ancient font. One of the men was Kalt. The other man, a great deal larger and bulkier, also looked like Gestapo; he had the coarseness of a bull and a face that appeared as though it had never once smiled. Even as Huber shrank back into the doorway, his eyes couldn't help straying to the font. Why was it full of water? He hadn't left it like that. There hadn't been a baptism for weeks, not since September when the little Lang boy had been brought here.

'Ah, Father Huber,' Kalt said. 'This is my colleague, Herr Brunner.'

Huber walked towards the font, his hands clasped together and his head bowed, trying to maintain his habitual humility. '*Grüss Gott*, Herr Brunner.'

The new man, Brunner, said nothing. Without a word, he manoeuvred himself behind the priest. Huber's neck swivelled from one man to another. He realised he was shaking uncontrollably.

'Herr Brunner is my assistant.'

'It is a pleasure to meet you both, but as I have already said, I cannot help you gentlemen.'

'We have a question for you,' Kalt continued. 'Could you please tell us the full name and address of the woman you called in Berlin not five minutes ago? We will have her details soon enough, but you could save us precious time.'

'Please, Herr Kalt, I know nothing of the girl you seek. Or any woman in Berlin.'

Hans Brunner grasped him by the nape of the neck and pushed his head down into the font. The water was shockingly cold. Huber's arms flailed helplessly. Kalt grabbed his wrists and restrained them. Huber was struggling to hold in his breath, to keep his lungs from filling with water, but Brunner and Kalt were too strong for him. Together they held him there, mouth and nose submerged, for a full minute, before wrenching him out again, as water sprayed across the ancient stone floor. Huber gasped for air. Brunner turned his nose up and his broad pig's nostrils flared. 'He stinks. I think the holy bastard's shat himself.'

Otto Kalt laughed. 'This is just wasting time. Finish him off. We'll find the woman in Berlin soon enough.'

Just under four minutes later, Father Peter Huber's body slid to the floor. He was dead, drowned in his own font. Brunner looked at the corpse dispassionately. 'Do you think we should search his house, too?'

Kalt looked at his partner with the forebearance of a kind and tolerant parent to an idiot son of whom little was expected. 'Yes, Hans, that would make a lot of sense. And we should search his woman's house, too, I think.'

'And what should we do with the woman?'

'Dispose of her, Hans. Turn her to ash.'